The Tymorean Trust
Book Six

# INVASION

By

# MARGARET GREGORY

TAT Publishing

# Also by Margaret Gregory

TYMOREAN TRUST SERIES:

Book 1 - Power Rising
Book 2 - Great Ones
Book 3 - The Return to Earth
Book 4 – Earth Mission
Book 5 – Alien Contact

ATAPI SORCERESS SERIES:

Book 1- The Wild One
Book 2 – Atapi Sorceress
Korvu – The Beginning

THE THIRD GENERATION SERIES:

Wanda – From Bad to Worse
Wanda – Choosing Crime
Wanda – Risking Life to live



**Cover designed by msgdragon**
Images by:
© Can Stock Photo Inc. / 3000ad

For permission requests, address the request to the author c/o
Permissions,
C/o TAT Publishing
PO Box 150
Glen Waverley, Victoria, 3150

www.tatpublishing.com

# INVASION

## Chapter 1

Tymos Ward, a Tech 1 at the World Scientific Research Authority Lunar 1 base, glanced across the base canteen and saw the Base Commander, Adam Landin weaving a path between the variously sized groups occupying tables or groups of chairs. He placed his drink on the table and took his attention away from a young blonde Tech 3, wearing the black and yellow uniform of engineering, and waited.

Landin sat down opposite Tymos and studied him for a few minutes.

"What have I done wrong this time, Sir?" Tymos challenged him, with a faint grin.

Landin was not wearing his uniform so he was tacitly off duty.

"Is there something?" he replied immediately, responding to the challenge, and briefly wondering if his Tech 1 knew of a problem that he hadn't reported yet.

Tymos smiled faintly. "What can I do for you, Sir?"

"What are my chances of getting you to delay your leave for three weeks?" Landin proposed, approaching his real question from a sideways angle.

"Is this an official request, Sir?" Even though Landin was as off duty, he wanted something.

"Is this my office?"

"Then, no Sir, to the last question and non-existent to the first." Tymos watched Landin's eyes as he answered. Some tenseness in the Commander's face muscles relaxed.

"That is good to hear," Landin said neutrally. "Since you have been working three shifts a rotation. I thought you might have believed the base incapable of operating without you."

Tymos had been part of the team writing and testing the program for the navigation system for the soon to be launched Genesis 1 mission. He hadn't needed to be present when the navigation controls and computer had been installed. His sister, who had been based at Terra 1 for the past three years, had overseen that. She would also see that the system was fully integrated with the propulsion system.

"No, Sir, nothing like that. I know all departments are tweaked to optimum efficiency," Tymos verbally fenced with his Commander. "I was just doing my bit for the historically momentous event."

Landin grinned wryly hearing a quote from one of the recent speeches made by the Ron Basoli, the Commander-in-Chief of the WSRA.

"No presentiments of doom?" Landin seemed to be joking, but he was serious.

Tymos shook his head and Landin relaxed further. He knew things about Tymos Ward that no one else on the base did. He knew for instance that Tymos and his sister, whilst born on Earth, had alien kinfolk. And he knew that both of them had abilities that set them apart from mere humans. He didn't go as far as to think them super human, but he also had to admit he didn't know everything about them. It was enough that they were highly intelligent, superbly able to handle themselves and had access to information that he did not.

"I heard from Commander Haldstadt at Terra 1 that your sister has been working three and a half shifts each rotation – going over the rocket and the deep space module. He even told me that she had fallen asleep in the garden on her way to quarters on two occasions."

Tymos shook his head as if amused, but to Landin he was implying that Kryslie had no sense of disaster either.

"Krys was seeing Gareth Pitt before he went into pre-launch seclusion. If she is worried, it's hormonal."

"So, will you be watching the launch?" Landin changed the direction of his talk.

"Yes, but not from Terra 1 or the surroundings. I will wait for the vid-cast. That way I can turn off the pre-launch speeches. I am to leave on the last shuttle from here. It has to be grounded six hours before Genesis 1 launches."

Landin rose. "Very good. Give my regards to your sister."

"I'll do that, Sir," Tymos agreed.


"You are finished, Kryslie Ward," an accented voice remarked as Kryslie sat back in the command chair of the Genesis 1 control module. She rotated the chair, which was too wide for her, and considered the brilliant scientist, Suliem Rashid.

"All systems check green," Kryslie told him. She had been checking all the computer systems for Suliem, the designer of the rockets. He had created both the first stage that would lift the Genesis 1 off the Earth and into space, as well as the hyperspace rockets.

Other technicians at the WSRA Terra 1 base were being equally painstaking in checking the manoeuvring engines, life support, sensors, shielding – every aspect of the upcoming flight.

Unnoticed, Kryslie had also been testing the shields, since she had helped develop them three years ago when she had been working at Lunar One. She had also helped modify them to have more properties than the stated ones, and she had managed that by saying it was so that the sensors on the hull of Genesis 1 could see through them.

Her current state of 'ease' hid her intense contemplation of whether to include the parameters for an anti-transmission field, which would prevent matter-energy from entering the ship. Such a possibility had not yet occurred to Earth scientists. A shiver of premonition had stayed her hand as she'd begun to do the programming. Now she was considering what her intuition might be warning her of.

To side-track questions from Suliem, she remarked, "Do you realise that even fifty years ago, your hyperspace rocket was only believed possible in science fiction novels?"

"That is true Kryslie Ward. It is where I got idea from," Suliem grinned widely.

He was a small man, no taller than Kryslie herself and in his seventies. Until a year ago, he had been imprisoned by the World Council. His earlier prototype rockets, created on the orders of the former leader of the Imperium or the once unaligned nations, had resulted in much damage to what had once been the United States of America.

The late Abdul bin Halil had tried to conquer America during a merciless war. He had failed then, but not given up. Suliem's first hyperspace rocket had malfunctioned after launch and crashed back to Earth. It had landed in a remote part of the American continent. That area was still a radioactive wasteland, surrounded by the most advanced shielding available. That it also hid the Tymorean Earth base, was known only to Kryslie and her brother and the rest of the Tymorean missionaries.

A later prototype had been used by bin Halil to coerce one of the leaders of a small nation in the Imperium. That purpose achieved, bin Halil had ordered it targeted on Lunar 1 base, which he felt was like a big brother that would detect his plans for conquest.

Fortunately, in the three years since, Abdul bin Halil had been deposed, and replaced with his son, Arthur - the Imperium and the UWN had become the United Earth Nations.

Arthur bin Halil had ordered the release of the 'wildcat' scientists, as Suliem and his colleagues had been called, and they had, with great relief and enthusiasm, embraced the aims and vision of the World Scientific Research Authority. The upcoming launch was a product of the merger.

Kryslie rose from the seat and joined Suliem at the hatch that led out to the scaffolding and the ladder down. Even though her mind was full of possible scenarios of doom for Genesis 1, none had evoked more than minor shivers of premonition and as her brother had remarked, they might result from her 'liking' for Gareth Pitt.

"I guess I am finished," Kryslie decided. "Too late for anything else. They will be moving this wonder machine into launch position tomorrow."

"Nothing will malfunction on this ship of discovery," Suliem assured her. "I feel that in my bones."

"And if it does?" Kryslie suggested.

"It will be the will of the Gods," Suliem accepted.

Kryslie let him have the last word. She still felt unsettled and didn't quite believe it was just her worrying about Gareth. Yes, she liked him a lot – but she had worked to get to know him because of the same feeling.

As she walked back to her quarters with orders to sleep for a full day – she tried to pinpoint her concern. Gareth Pitt was one of the three astronauts picked for this mission. The selection process had begun as soon as the mission brief had received the go-ahead. Over one hundred highly trained, highly experienced air force officers and Earth-moon shuttle pilots had applied for or been invited into the selection program.

Then, over the past two years of extensive emotional, physical, mental and intellectual testing – the numbers had gradually reduced.

Aaron Casey, Domenic Tweed and Gareth Pitt had been selected as the best of the best. Kryslie had met all three of them, and used the encounter to test their minds for weaknesses and found nothing that worried her. The mission should be a success, and lead to Earth being invited to join the Federation of Peace.

She still felt uneasy.

# Chapter 2

The launch was still five days away, but Kryslie was kept too busy to think further. A malfunction in the south polar tracking array meant she had to go with a team of experts down there by sub-orbital shuttle.

Tymos wished he could have exchanged places with her. Well, except for one thing. With his duties for the prelaunch completed, Landin sent him downside a week early to help the PR people deal with the enormous media contingent. It was really more attention than he wanted to have. The only reason that he didn't even think to his sister the idea of changing places, was that she'd had entirely too much attention three years ago.

He was thrown into the fray within minutes of arriving. The Public Relations Coordinator had advised, "Lose the uniform and read the media briefing." The briefing told him what topics to side step and what were 'need to know' and gave an outline of the information to give out.

After two days, he was thoroughly sick of telling people that, "The WSRA scientists were on the verge of proving that manned faster than light travel was possible" and toning down the wilder theories of where hyperspace could let you travel and what aliens might be encountered by humans.

He seemed to be a magnet for those wanting to know what hyperspace was and how Genesis 1 differed from the spaceflights of the twentieth Century – such as the Apollo Series.

The people seemed to sense he was not just a PR mouthpiece, but really understood what he was talking about.

"The Genesis deep space module is radically different to those primitive ships that first carried man to the moon," Tymos would explain, endlessly it seemed. "Its design gives the astronauts more room to move around and has capability for point two gravity. Nothing like it has ever launched from Terra 1, even when it was known as Cape Canaveral or Cape Kennedy."

Tymos even began to relish the frequent updates presented by Ron Basoli the C-I-C of the WSRA. When these came over the Terra 1 media-vid, his questioners deserted him in droves. They were too busy scribbling down the new details being passed on by Basoli to notice him slip away. He would vanish to where he could listen to the classified technical details being received from the other WSRA bases and tracking stations.

Then he would go out again to new questions like, "How many bases were there?" and "How many tracking stations?" or even, "Was it true that Genesis 1 was based on an alien ship and were the hyper-drive engines copied from it."

At which time, Tymos wished he could vanish to any of the other six Terran bases; though preferably back to Lunar 1. Even the unmanned Lunar 2 would do.

"No, the rockets were conceived by Suliem Rashid, long before the alien ship was found on the moon. Modifications were made, based on a study of the alien ship. The gravity generator was based on the alien technology."

Tymos was permitted to talk of the wrecked alien ship and its dead pilot, but was to avoid talking of the other alien ships. The visit of those had not been widely publicised, though word had got around.

If directly questioned, Tymos was advised to say only, "There was such a ship, but it did not stay long."

His stock answer for further questions on that subject was, "I am not able to give you any details of that." He would use a trace of mental coercion to discourage further questions.

On the day of the launch, Tymos handed in his PR tab and ID and was thanked effusively by the PR coordinator. He grinned back at the man and strolled out into the main concourse of the Terra 1 space centre. With less than eight hours to lift off, it was comparatively deserted, because everyone was vying for a vantage point to watch the launch.

He wandered into the side section that serviced the arriving and departing shuttles and waited for the sub-orbital shuttle bringing Kryslie back from the south polar station. He only half listened to the speech being made by Ron Basoli.

"...This project is undoubtedly the greatest project on which the world's scientists have collaborated."

Basoli's screen image was more impressive than his personal image.

"The craft designated Genesis 1 was designed by..." he quoted a long list of names, "some of whom have only been working for the WSRA for two years."

"Tactful," Tymos commented to the empty lounge. "Not to mention that the rocket was contrived by wildcat scientists and the early prototypes were lost – or crashed."

The warning chimes for an incoming shuttle distracted him and he stood up to approach the door. Basoli droned on in the background.

Kryslie looked tired when she emerged carrying her flight bag. The other arrivals looked no better.

"Fix it?" Tymos asked.

"Yes, it had iced up. It's working, but Tris Hanna and Carey Wills are staying down there for the fortnight."

Kryslie stopped and dropped her bag and began to delve into it as a reason to let the others move past and leave the lounge.

"I have reports to give Commander Haldstadt," Kryslie went on. "Then I will be free to leave. What say you take my bag out to the car – I will meet you there later."

In her mind, 'car' was actually the base of the Tymorean Missionaries. She was suggesting that Tymos return there, by transmitter and she would follow.

"Have you seen the roads around here?" Tymos said as the shuttle pilot walked through the lounge.

"Yeah," Captain Allen remarked, "You'd be faster walking." He grinned at Tymos, mock saluted Kryslie, and kept walking. He knew them both from Lunar 1.

"Good thing we have a better idea," Kryslie murmured.

"And I am sure about a million people would like one in about seven hours' time," Tymos agreed.

"But matter transmitters are still hypothetical, and our personal transmitters could never be operated by non-Tymoreans," Kryslie made her tone resemble a pedantic teacher.

"Don't be long," Tymos told her, as he hefted her bag. She pulled a face at him and walked off with the report padd.

Haldstadt only asked for important details and then gave the report padd to his operations assistant to put on his personal data padd. He dismissed her after asking for her pager, knowing she was going on leave. Kryslie knew it was so she wouldn't be recalled during her leave and that suited her very well.

Within minutes of leaving Haldstadt's office, she had used her transmitter and was half a continent away.


Daniel Ward greeted her warmly when she appeared in the excavated cavern that housed the space monitoring instrumentation.

"Everything ready?" Kryslie asked, going at once to the console that was receiving direct feeds from all the WSRA tracking arrays. She didn't realise that her focussed concentration might have seemed to be rude.

"Yes, Great One," Daniel assured her. "There are still five hours to launch and plenty of time for a bath, a meal and an hour's meditation in the garden."

Glancing at the information coming in, and seeing that everything looked optimal, she agreed. The south polar tracking station had only had rudimentary hygiene facilities, and now that her father mentioned a bath, she felt her skin prickling.

"I'll go with that," Kryslie agreed.

After a thorough cleaning in the shower rather than a bath, Kryslie decided she felt normal again. The meal she had asked for was ready as she reappeared and she took it on a try to the garden to eat. Tymos was there already.

"What kept you?"

"Finding the Commander and getting to him," Kryslie said. She put her food tray down and removed her shoes and socks. The feel of the Earth aura flowing into her from the ground, felt good.

"What was the weather looking like from up there," Tymos asked.

"Clear. Nothing that should move in before Friday," Kryslie said. "Everything seems perfect."

"Too perfect?"

Kryslie shook her head. "Well planned, well prepared," she said. "The uneasiness is still there and before you say anything, I have been too busy to even miss Gareth since he went into seclusion."

"So?" Tymos prompted.

"Suliem made a comment last week. He feels that nothing will malfunction on the ship of discovery and if something does it is the will of the gods."

Tymos did, then, feel a faint shiver. "This is a pivotal point in Earth's history," he thought aloud. "The Elders back home have foreseen that."

"But only that," Kryslie commented. "That could mean that nothing will go wrong or that something must happen, so Earth will join the Federation of Peace."

"Why do I suddenly have a feeling of unease?"

Kryslie flashed him a look. "Hormones?" She eased the seriousness of the moment. "I don't think it was sudden. You were the one to request a long range scout ship be sent here."

Tymos considered that decision. "Yes, I did, and I think I want to check a few things before the launch. I will see you later."


Lexina moved aside to let Tymos use her console. She, Jonko and two other Tymorean missionaries were monitoring the feeds from the WSRA bases and from the Tymorean observers who were further along the trajectory.

Tymos minimised the various inputs and began a series of calculations based on the proposed route of Genesis 1.

The initial trajectory was out between Epsilon Eridani and Tau Ceti, but once out beyond the latter, approximately 12 light years from Earth, data from the sensors on Genesis 1, would feed into the nav computer which would update the course. Earth's spacecraft would be directed on a course through relatively empty space – kept away from the thousands of suns and planets or any other unexpected hazard.

Over the years, especially since Lunar 1 had been operational, knowledge of space around Earth had been extended. Genesis 1 would not be entering truly unexplored space unless it went out beyond Kepler 452b – some 1400 light years from Earth – a mere 8.2 trillion miles.

However, Genesis 1 was not going to concentrate its periods of 'normal space time' exploring within the galactic disc. The scientists hoped that Genesis 1 might travel up through the galactic disc, to see the Milky Way from above.

The capability of the new space drives was unknown and would remain so until they were tested in three days' time. However, Tymos did not expect the spacecraft to travel that far in its 20 days of hyperspeed flight. The missile that was a precursor to the hyperdrives, had not travelled fast enough.

On the screen, Tymos created a schematic, of the sun and planets of Earth's system, and the more distant ones that were also in Rho sector – the 10 degree segment of the Milky Way where Earth existed. He used the copy of the navigation program aboard Genesis 1 to create a representation of the spacecraft's course.

There was no truly 'empty' areas of space around Earth, for even between the bright spiral arms of the galaxy, were thousands of suns and planets. A zig-zagging course, moving up at right angles to the galactic disc appeared on the screen.

Tymos studied the representation, and despite knowing that none of the nearest planets were inhabited, vegetated or rich in minerals, or suited to exploitation or colonisation, he drummed his fingers on the bench beneath the screen.  He still felt uneasy. He added a fringe area, to allow for the slight inaccuracy of the navigation program, and muttered, "Nothing should bother them."

He sensed Kryslie coming up behind him and studying the screen in turn, and heard her propose, "Unless some ship from somewhere will be passing through."

"It is well away from the commercial traffic lanes. Rho sector is isolated from them," Tymos countered.

"Or explorers decide to head this way," Kryslie brought out another of her potential doom scenarios.

"Our observers will tell us."

"Pirates – waiting in ambush?"

"Out there? There is nothing worth their fuel."

Lexina added another. "Aerdna is in Tau sector."

Tymos spun his chair around and stared at her. "Why did no one tell us that?"

"When did you find out?" Kryslie spoke almost at the same time.

Jonko, who had been sitting beside Tymos, concentrating on the data coming in, answered. "Only a few days ago. When our observation ships were getting into position, they detected the planet moving at an oblique angle to the galactic drift. Obs 1 went off station to check. They only reported with confirmation an hour ago."

Tymos ordered, "Send the information to this terminal," as he added two more sectors and highlighted Tau sector - two away from Rho sector. "No, they shouldn't get anywhere near there."

"Did they get close to the planet? Did they detect life?" Kryslie asked with intense interest.

Images from Obs 1's long distance sensors appeared on a separate screen, and Tymos zoomed in on the images, as he recalled everything he had learnt about Aerdna, and the images of the planet from space, that had been in the memory banks of the Aeronite ships that had once invaded Tymorea.

He was aware of Kryslie's eyes focussing on a section of the planet's surface where vast underground vaults were located.

"No, Great One" Lexina told her. "President Reslic only wanted confirmation.  He ordered Obs 1 back on station. However, there is also a new sun forming in Tau sector."

Kryslie gripped Tymos's shoulder, sharing her elation. "The prophecy. It's happening. Right now!"

"Did you doubt it, Great One?" Jonko grinned as he provoked his friends.

Kryslie leant over and punched his shoulder. "Where is your sense of wonder, and awe at the greatness of the creator?"

"Overseeing Earth's greatest creation," Jonko said promptly. He was quoting another of Basoli's phrases.

"Well then, any other scenarios of doom, Krys?" Tymos asked.

"More of the same, and nothing that is really likely." She mentally listed them and Tymos had to agree.

But something was going to happen. His premonition of trouble was getting stronger, but no clearer.

"Well, we watch and wait. If something happens, we have the scout ship, and the relay ships for the long range beam are on standby."

# Chapter 3

As the countdown to the launch continued, the duty controllers in the Tymorean Earth base were also monitoring the human stations and media networks. The biggest of the five screens was displaying the real time media feed going out all over Earth.

Tymos had relinquished his seat back to Lexina, the senior controller, and was giving a running commentary, in Tymorean, that was being transmitted to the three Tymorean Observation ships that were in place along Genesis 1's projected route. He was also the focus of attention of the unusually large number of Tymorean missionaries who were visiting for the occasion.

When the countdown reached zero, and the ignition command was given, everyone in the cavern seemed to hold their breath, until the huge rocket began lifting – slowly at first, and then with noticeably increasing speed.

Tymos dragged his eyes from the visuals, and studied the scrolling figures on two of the smaller screens, aware that Kryslie was doing the same for the other two screens. These were real time status reports that would also be being received by all the WSRA bases. On the audio frequency, Mission Leader Casey was giving a voice over of the status as seen on Genesis 1's instruments. His voice was odd, since he was resisting the enormous 'g' forces as the spacecraft blasted up towards the edge of Earth's atmosphere.

In just over an hour, the three stages of the launch and lift were completed. Dan Ward shook himself and took his mind away from the telecast of the historical moment. He glanced at his children, who were still intently focussed on the figures on the screen – he had the oddest feeling that they were calculating and comparing their results with those on the screen.

For a moment, he seemed to experience the same awe that every other Tymorean felt for them, but then they relaxed, and the notion vanished. They were his children. He recalled them as babies and toddlers, who grew into abominable teenagers until Vincent had diagnosed their rising Tymorean power. They were so different now – mature adults, confident and competent…that was all.

They had been fostered by the Tymorean High King Governor, but even as Tymoros's adopted heirs, they did not flaunt their importance, or glow like saints were purported to do. Rather they needed to be reminded that they didn't have to be serious and busy all the time...

He had heard what they had done on Tymorea, but he found it impossible to believe. It was so incredibly fantastic. How could any human have that kind of power, let alone his children? Surely it was an exaggeration.

For an instant, Daniel's memory of his children as they had been before first going to Tymorea, merged with one of the mighty creatures the Tymoreans considered them. He shivered violently – that was a nightmarish image indeed.

A nudge on his arm distracted him and he turned to see Morin. He was glad to refill his mind with the minutiae of his job as Earthbase controller.

"What is it now? More guests?"

"No, Boss, just Keleb wanting the long range beam set so that he can bring the truck in with the supplies."

"Boss indeed! You impertinent snip," Daniel growled. "Who is free to operate the mass transporter?"

Morin paused to think. "Ah, Jacellan was the last to arrive. She didn't get hooked on the launch. She's in the kitchen with her mother."

"Then ask her to assist you. You know how to set the beam and where Keleb is," Daniel told him. "When he gets back, you can see to storing the supplies. Don't forget to put the perishables in the freezer."

Morin grinned despite the reminder of a past disaster, and trotted off.

Daniel smiled when his assistant was out of sight and he was walking to his office space. It was a small cavern off the main arrival vault. He turned his mind to the tasks that had been neglected in the lead up to the launch. He had a stack of reports from various missionaries to read through, none had been urgent, and now he had a period of peace to tackle them. Morin, a telepathic Tymorean commoner, was a refreshingly normal presence.

For three days, the controllers on duty at Earthbase monitored the progress of Genesis 1 as it travelled out of the Terran solar system. Tymos appeared at intervals during that time to compare their figures with those coming in from the WSRA bases, particularly Lunar 1, and then vanished again. Kryslie had gone off after the launch, without saying where she was going.

Shortly before the scheduled hyper-drive engine test, they both returned within moments of each other and took over the monitoring. A digital display, counted down to the test time. Tymos opened a new screen and was rapidly keying in information. Jonko stared as more than just course information appeared.

"Hyper-drive on line. All systems are green," Tymos reported. "Ignition, Genesis 1 is accelerating to light speed. Light speed. Conversion is successful. Speed is still increasing…stabilising at hyperspeed factor 5."

"All WSRA bases have lost contact with Genesis 1," Kryslie reported. She had an earpiece in her ear.

While the screens displaying data from the WSRA bases went blank, the new screen Tymos had opened did not. Jonko, studying the scrolling columns and the array of green lights, made a mental guess that was soon confirmed when Tymos said, "I have telemetry from Genesis 1 – life signs still good. The crew have quickly adjusted to hyperspeed. Casey is beginning the first of the experiments. All systems running at optimum."

Kryslie went still as she listened to another report through the earpiece.

"Obs 1 is on station at estimated terminal distance. Obs 2 is at the midway point and Obs 3 is now tailing Genesis 1 – just out of sensor range. All report clear space and no other vessels near the track."

Jonko gave his friends an enthralled headshake, "How did you two manage to rig up such a comprehensive monitoring system? Is there any part of that spaceship you can't monitor?"

Kryslie turned and grinned at him. "I had reason to crawl over every inch of the control module and the engines. I just put our sensors next to the WSRA ones. Tymos linked them to the telemetry feed. There is also a passive receiver, recording all the ships functions, independent of the active system, but which continuously downloads data as a microburst every minute. The frequency is not one that is known here on Earth."

Morin, who had crept in to watch the historic moment when the Earth ship had gone to hyperspeed, wasn't interested in the technical number crunching. He turned his attention to the screen still receiving the Terran media broadcast of the events. It amused him to listen to the feigned positive note of the announcer. "In just under a month we will see the results of this historic moment."

"And I'll bet you're thinking that they won't come back," Morin thought to himself. "Well you'll see indeed."

Commander Landin, standing in main mission, watched the telemetry figures from Genesis 1 blink down to zero on the main screen.

Chief Controller Stanley reported formally, "Signal lost."

"Did we get anything, after the hyper-drive engine started," Landin queried.

Stanley gave instructions for a slowed replay of the telemetry signal. "No more than a few seconds, Sir. But the speed went off the scale. Genesis 1 must have travelled so fast as to have got out of range in that time."

Landin hoped that was so. The range of the base sensors had been increased a thousand fold since the program began. That hadn't been enough. "Anything from the Mars array?" he asked.

"Not yet, Sir. There is a twelve hour time lag. I hope that will confirm that conversion was successful."

"Keep everyone alert," Landin directed. "I want to know when the Mars figures come in. In the meantime, analyse those few seconds and bring the results to me. We should have got more than the Terra bases. Monitor all transmission frequencies – the astronauts will be testing the communicators."

Now it was a waiting game, Landin mused as he retreated to his office off main mission. He prepared himself a drink, water flavoured with brandy essence. He didn't want his mind muddled, but he did feel like he needed a drink. Four days of waiting until Genesis 1 dropped out of hyperspace for the first time. Two days of making recordings of the starfield wherever they were, trying communications and doing a number of psychological tests. If a message could be sent, and received, they could get an idea of how fast Genesis 1 had been travelling. One joker in the media had predicted that Genesis 1 would get back before any message did.

Suliem Rashid had made an estimate of how fast the engines might propel the spacecraft, but that had been exceeded. There hadn't been more than a few seconds between stop and full speed. It was no wonder that Rashid insisted on the nav computer controlling the trajectory and course changes.

Landin tried to imagine how far the astronauts were away from Earth now, and how far they would go. They would have a second four day stretch in hyperspace on the way out, with a two day break in normal space before the third hyperspace period when the ship would come around onto its homeward course – this return trajectory would take them through a different sector of space. Twenty-eight days of waiting, unless they received a communication via one of the standard or experimental channels, before Genesis 1 was due back at the edge of

Earth's solar system and in direct contact. Only then would they be sure that the mission was a success. The final test, of the transformation controls, would come three days later when, all going well, Genesis 1 would touch down at Terra 1 space centre. The backup plan was the old method of splash down.


Vincent, Daniel's second in charge, arrived back at Earthbase when Genesis 1 was eight hours into hyper-speed. It would be another eighty-eight hours before the ship dropped back into normal space for the first time. Within moments, he was hearing of Daniel's concerns, that the Great Ones were focussed on the telemetry from Genesis 1 and ignoring everything else.

"I will talk to them," he assured the worried base coordinator. "They will not ignore me."

Daniel gave a terse nod, and followed Vincent as he strode into the monitoring cavern and announced in a normal voice, "Governor Xyron sends his regards, Great Ones. I have a report he has prepared from Tau sector."

Xyron was Vincent's brother and one of the three Tymorean Governors. His role was to oversee all aspects of science and technology on Tymorea.

Kryslie turned away from the screens and reached for the data plaque. Vincent didn't immediately hand it over.

"If you have torn your mind from the screen, Great One, you might as well go and eat. Lusanne has prepared an excellent roast," Daniel said pointedly and loudly.

With a wry smile, for she was now aware of the empty rumble in her stomach, Kryslie stood up and nudged her brother.

"Have a seat doctor," Kryslie invited with a faint bow and a flourish of her hand. "As far as I can tell, the three astronauts are fine, but you are the medical expert."

"Certainly, Great One." Vincent agreed, as he passed over the data plaque.

Tymos stood and stretched. "Let us know if anything changes." He walked over to his twin and they went towards the eating cavern.

"What will happen is that, should you not hurry, Morin will have eaten your food for you, as he did at breakfast, and at lunch. Lately he has been eating as if he thinks the food will disappear."

"Can't have that," Tymos chuckled.


Once they had eaten, Tymos and Kryslie went to sit in the garden before looking at the report about Tau sector.

"For a quick peek, Obs 1 certainly collected a lot of data," was Kryslie's comment as she opened the outer shell-file. The plaque was a self-powered data padd that could project graphs and charts as holograms. "They must have done an orbit of the planet as well."

"That sun is new, but it has been forming for a long time. Aeons before Aerdna transcended."

"And the planet won't be close enough to fall into its gravity effect for years yet," Kryslie spoke absently for she was enlarging images of the surface of the planet and bringing them up as holograms in front of her. "We still don't know what happened to the planet. Its original sun is still in phi sector, but look here – the surface looks melted, fused like glass and pitted with meteoroid craters."

Tymos looked where his twin was pointing. "We know that its orbit was changing, so perhaps it got too close to the sun."

"That doesn't explain how it received enough force to travel to tau sector. There would have had to have been some massive explosions."

Tymos flicked to another section of the report. "There is mention of massive volcanic action." He paused before adding, "You know…this is a bit like the far side of the moon, near where Lunar 2 is."

"Are you saying that Aerdna was hit by some sort of small moon?" Kryslie considered the idea with brows raised.

Tymos shrugged. "I don't know how such a thing could be managed, but I wouldn't say it is impossible. Just that I have never heard of it before. Where are the vaults located on that scan?"

Kryslie brought up the hologram of the full, distorted planet, and gestured to move their point of view. The vaults were on the opposite side, where there was no indication of intense heat. Tymos took the data padd and read the report on that part of the planet's surface. His mind was filled with awe as he told his sister, "The atmosphere didn't boil away. It was frozen. The Guardians are surely looking after that world."

"After the Genesis mission is over, we must visit the vaults," Kryslie thought at her brother, and sensed his agreement in return.

During the following day, Earthbase lost direct contact with Genesis 1 and now had to receive communications and data relayed from the Observation ships. Everything was still proceeding perfectly, exactly as Tymos and Kryslie had worked long hours to ensure. Yet they were restless, and spent so much time pacing the communications room that Vincent was compelled to comment.

"Great Ones, you should either go to the garden and reduce your excess energy, or find something physical to do."

Neither Tymos nor Kryslie responded to the suggestion immediately. Both understood Vincent's reason for speaking to them, but felt his suggestion was for useless action.

Finally, Kryslie announced, "Fine! I'll find something to do." She transmitted out of sight without saying where she was going.

Tymos merely stared back at Vincent and repeated his sister's action. However, he only went into the long range scout ship and began to inventory supplies. He knew his sister had chosen to transmit back to Terra 1 by the long range beam. She was in her quarters, focussing on something, but not sharing her thoughts with him. And that was as well, for he was feeling jittery enough without getting feedback from her.

They both reappeared when Genesis 1 dropped back into normal space and later when they began the second leg at hyperspeed. For a time, the transmitted data kept them interested, but by the end of the second period in normal space they were both as tense as coiled springs. However, this time they didn't wait to be told to reduce their excess power, but went to the garden to meditate. They wished for some hint of the future from the Guardians of Peace, but they received no enlightenment. They felt like they were waiting for doom to hit, that something was going to happen. But so far, nothing had.

"We must be missing something," Tymos decided, springing up from one of the rock seats, and pacing the garden. "The Guardians won't hand feed us information we can get ourselves."

Without needing to verbally agree, Kryslie stood to return to the monitoring cavern with him.

Tymos connected up a spare screen and terminal and began going over the calculations of the course and intended trajectory of Genesis 1. They now knew the speed of the ship in hyperspace, and using that, the result was still the same. He had accurately predicted the exact position where Genesis 1 first dropped from hyperspace. Then using the data from the passive tracer device on Genesis 1's hull, they knew the position of their next entry to hyperspace, and had accurately predicted the second drop out point which was out beyond Tau Ceti, only about 15 light years from Earth. There should be nothing out there to endanger Genesis 1, for all suns, planets and solid objects would be steered around. This third period of hyperspace travel was to bring the ship around onto an Earthward heading.

Kryslie had the data padd with her with the information from Tau sector. She was seated near her brother, aware of his mental activity, but recalling and concentrating on the plans and details of the vaults under the surface of Aerdna. She had already created a schematic of the vaults to overlay the surface scan made by Obs 1. And idly, her finger was tapping one of the sealed off entrances – for she was wondering if she and Tymos had overlooked any vital detail, and also about how the population had adapted to subterranean life.

<h1 style="text-align:center">Chapter 4</h1>

A faint 'ping' caused Kryslie to look over at the screen where Genesis 1's trajectory was showing. Even from where she sat, she could see and interpret the scrolling data. All figures were within the range that had become normal over the past 14 days. Yet she was aware that Tymos was rapidly keying in a complex algorithm. His mind was full of the figures for the course he had helped to program into the Genesis's nav computer.

After a moment, he read the result and thumped the table in frustration.

"We don't know everything about that sector," Kryslie murmured softly. "Let's wait and see."

"They are starting to go off course!" Tymos spoke in a low intense voice to emphasise his next point. "Yet the telemetry being relayed from Genesis 1, is saying that they are adhering to it."

"It still might be something in that sector that is affecting it…"

Tymos snarled, betraying his concern. "If they go too far off track, they will start to get low on fuel."

"When they next drop out into normal space, the nav computer will correct their position and course…"

"And if it doesn't?"

"The Observation ships are still following them…"

"Yes!" Tymos turned back to his screen and set up a second window, and then had a message sent through to the Observation ship that was travelling on a parallel course to Genesis 1.

In spite of the great distance, the message burst travelled from Earthbase to Obs 2, in minutes, not hours or days. The signal went through the Tymorean message relay system, which boosted the signal strength and accelerated it.

Data began appearing on the prepared second screen, updated every minute as a microburst data packet was received. After several minutes, Tymos said, more to himself, "That tells me nothing, just that they are adjusting their course to that of Genesis 1 as they have done all along."

Kryslie glanced at the corner of the screen to confirm which of the ships was sending. It was Obs 2, or Kantai as it was normally known. "Can you tell Konn Reslic to send you his raw sensor data?"

"I'm waiting for it. Konn has as good as told me that I am imagining things, that there is nothing out there that could be forcing Genesis 1 off course and so the ship must be following the programmed course."

"Well, the medical telemetry is normal," Kryslie reported. "So nothing has alarmed the crew."

"They have no reason to be. Since, as I said, their screens are telling them that all is going as planned."

That was true enough, and now Kryslie wondered how they would react when they dropped back into normal space and the nav system reset to what it was seeing directly.


Tymos stayed at his terminal all during the Earthbase night shift, and by morning, he had a series of white position dots, created each time they received a relayed data packet from the tracer Kryslie had attached to Genesis 1. Already the dots were noticeably on a different track to the predicted one.

The two morning shift controllers arrived, followed by Daniel. Kryslie quickly gave up her seat to Anndra, moving to nudge her brother so that Michel could take over. Before he moved, Tymos pointed out the anomaly.

"I've got the raw data from Obs 2 coming in. See if you can find a reason for the deviation. Konn Reslic swears there is nothing out there, but there has to be!"

"Maybe fresh eyes are needed," Daniel suggested when Tymos still hadn't moved. "Lusanne has a hot breakfast ready for you."

Tymos pushed his chair back and rose, still keeping his attention on the screens. He finally turned when Kryslie nudged his mind, "Come on."


Lusanne served them breakfast in the eating cavern, chattering at them to eat up, there was plenty more, and then switching to gossip about what she had seen when she went to visit some of the other missionaries and saw more of Earth. After five minutes, she realised that the Great Ones were oblivious to her words – even though they were eating steadily. She sighed and went back to her kitchen.


"It will take two days to get to Genesis 1's position," Kryslie mused aloud. "And that is using the long range beam relay for part of the way."

Tymos stopped staring at the pale yellow paint of the cavern wall, and gave his sister a wry grin. Their thoughts had been so close that it might have been one mind thinking them. He had been thinking that they should go out there – just in case – and then arguing that they had no proof of anything dangerous going on. They couldn't interfere. The humans had to make this trip to prove that they had the technology to hold their own in space. Only if another race interfered with them, could they justify interfering.

"We can't prove that it isn't a problem with Genesis 1," Tymos stated the point that was forefront in his mind. "We checked everything, but electronics can fail."

"And tired minds can miss vital, obvious or important points," Vincent remarked, having approached without either Great One being aware of him.

"We're fine," Kryslie assured him automatically.

"Did you sense me coming?" He saw Kryslie's expression changes to one of sheepish awareness as Tymos slumped back in his chair.

"Rest for a few hours. You will be told immediately if anything changes."

"More than it is already," Tymos growled.

Vincent merely inclined his head sideways for a moment. That he stayed beside the table, told both Great Ones that he was invoking his authority as 'medical officer' and he would stay there until they decided to obey his suggestion.

Kryslie rose first, having no inclination to overrule Vincent, when he was most probably right. Periods of intense mental concentration could be as tiring as physical activity. "Come on, bro, just for a couple of hours…"


On the third day of Genesis 1's third period of hyperspace, Jonko trotted into the garden where Tymos and Kryslie had been 'banished' as a result of Daniel's pointed comments that their fidgeting was distracting the workers.

"Tym, Krys, we've just lost the signal from Genesis 1."

"What? Do you mean the relay from the Obs ships?"

"No, I mean they have lost the signal," Jonko corrected his report.

He was almost bowled over by Tymos as he took off at a run towards the monitoring cavern.


The schematic on the screen showed the planned route of Genesis 1 in yellow, and the white dots of the actual track being taken. Genesis 1 was now in sigma sector, still getting further and further off course. Tymos slipped into the seat that Jonko had vacated and changed the parameters of the screen so that a greater volume of space was included. The pinpoints of light representing celestial bodies multiplied, and one that was down in the lower right hand corner was labelled 'Aerdna'. The new sun that was forming in Tau sector was also visible, but offset from the planet.

Tymos's eyes moved from the last received position of Genesis 1, following the projected and actual course, and stopped at the forming sun. He heard Kryslie murmuring, "They should not be going anywhere near tau sector, and I don't believe that their course change is due to that sun that is forming. If it was, the Obs ships would have been aware of it."

The figures scrolling on the screen became the focus of Tymos's attention for a moment, then he asked, "Why weren't we told that Genesis 1's speed has been increasing?"

Lexina, sitting quietly in the other controller's seat, answered, "It is still within your predicted normal speed range for the ship."

"It has been doing a steady equivalent to our warp 5, and now it is nearly at our warp 6," Tymos noted, as if considering possible reasons. "How long before they are due to drop back into normal space?"

"Another 18 hours," Lexina answered immediately.

"Calculate their course assuming current speed and trajectory until the time they are due to drop into normal space."

A green line came up on the screen, aimed directly between Aerdna and the new sun.

"Adjust that to allow for the same rate of increase in speed."

Tymos stared at the screen, mentally adjusting the line by changing variables. Genesis 1 could conceivably go dangerously close to the new sun.

Silently, Kryslie remarked, "The nav program should detect that and steer them away."

In the same manner, Tymos reminded her of her earlier statement, "The nav program shouldn't have sent them anywhere near tau sector."

Kryslie asked aloud, "Assuming that they keep going in that direction, how far will they be from that sun at the point of nearest approach?"

Lexina made the calculation and told her.

"Estimate the radiation intensity at that point."

On hearing the figures, Kryslie mused, "Close. That is about 90% of the shield tolerance of the ship. The nav program should make them drop out of warp if it detects an unexpected hazard."

"Timewise," Lexina added, "The ship shouldn't get that far."

Tymos had begun to tap his fingers on the bench top, as he studied the screen, hoping to see another position blip appear. "It's moot, since we have no idea if they are actually keeping to the track we have seen."

His eyes were flicking between that last position and the sun and marked planet in tau sector.

Kryslie pulled up a chair and sat next to Lexina. She let her eyes scan the entire screen, while Lexina handled the occasional communication that came in from Homebase and the regular reports from the Obs ships who were also trying to find Genesis 1.

Five hours later, Kryslie suddenly leant forward, pointing to the screen. "Give me more detail of that section."

Tymos reacted quickly, sharing her memory of a pinpoint flicker. He stared at the screen, mentally counting from the moment his sister reacted.

"Yes!" Tymos hissed, exultantly. He was counting again, and after exactly the same time interval, another pinpoint of light blinked on and off a short distance away. "That has to be Genesis 1!"

"It can't be!" Lexina blurted. "It has to be a sensor ghost."

"Ask Obs 2 if they saw that," Tymos directed. Lexina complied, and waited for the reply.

"Negative, Great One. Konn says it has to be a sensor glitch."

Kryslie murmured, "The frequency that data came in on is the same as that used by our communications network. It could have been picked up by the nearest relay buoy."

"Then why didn't we get a signal sooner?" Jonko asked.

"It might have just come on range," Tymos suggested. "But I doubt it. It had to have been blocked or the Obs ships wouldn't have lost the signal."

"A cloaked ship?" Kryslie voiced the thoughts flowing between her mind and her twin's. "Its proximity could have nudged Genesis off course."

"That would mean something was keeping pace with it," Lexina deduced. "But how would it get so far away in such a short time? It would have to have been travelling at the maximum speed of a large cruiser…"

"An energy tether," Kryslie said aloud, causing everyone to look at her. Tymos met her eyes and more thoughts and ideas passed between them.

"Let's wait until we can get an accurate course projection," Tymos suggested aloud, still looking at his sister.

Kryslie nodded and asked Lexina to put all the data from the microburst message signal on the screen. She studied the figures, and mentally spoke to her brother. "Medical telemetry is showing a stress reaction."

Tymos nodded slightly, and sent back, "I think they are heading toward Aerdna."

"Are we reading too much into this?" Kryslie asked, in turn, playing devil's advocate.

"Do you want to risk that we are not? When we know who were the allies of the Aeronites in the war, and that they caused the cataclysm that sent Aerdna here?" Tymos switched from silent speech to audible, to direct the duty controllers.

"Tell President Reslic to direct Obs 1 to go to Tau sector. They will need to be cloaked when they arrive via the long range beam. I want them to look out for any signs of a grounded ship or a base on a planet or moon, and for any ships in the area. I don't want them going too close to Aerdna. If they pick up the tracer signal on Genesis 1, I want it relayed to our ship, and if they intercept any communications, I want to know about them too."

Tymos stood abruptly, and with a glance at Kryslie, moved from the bench. They left the cavern together, taking the passage that led to the side cavern where their long-range scout ship was hangered.

Daniel, who had been a silent observer to the recent audible conversation, followed them into the passage and called, "Where are you going?"

"To see what is happening out there," Kryslie told him, calling back over her shoulder. "Genesis 1 is heading for Aerdna."

Tymos added, "Have Vincent direct the long range beam to the first of the relay ships."

Rather than immediately obeying, Daniel increased his pace and said, "Great Ones, may I remind you that our overriding directive is to not interfere in Terran activities, unless they are endangering other races."

"We are over-ruling that order," Kryslie told him abruptly, merely glancing back again, and not slowing.

Daniel slowed, shaking his head, and turned went to the infirmary cavern, to give Vincent the order from Tymos. Maybe his second in command could explain why his children were about to go haring off into space.

Vincent was surprised, but immediately stopped the work he was doing on the computer, rose and trotted out along the passage to the main cavern. He went first to the smaller cavern where the ship was now warming up its on-board systems. They arrived as the ground manoeuvring engines started with a deafening roar.

Tymos emerged from the side entry hatch, now clad in a silver and gold metallic flight suit, snug fitting, and nothing like the cumbersome balloon-like suits of the Genesis astronauts. Vincent strode up to him to ask over the noise, "How far do you intend to go via the relay beam?"

"To the tau-sigma sector border," Tymos said instantly. "When we get there, I will have Obs 2 meet us. I want a closer view of what is happening because I do not like the coincidence of Genesis 1 being forced into tau sector where Aerdna is now."

Vincent stared back at Tymos, feeling a tingle of premonition. "There is no reason to think that Genesis 1 will endanger the planet or the vaults below."

"One possible reason for Genesis being so far off course is that it is being affected by a pirate ship."

Vincent's sharp intake of breath when his mind made the connection that Tymos had implied, was only noticeable in his expression of shock. Immediately, he said, "I will set up the beam and alert the relay ships," as he trotted over to the beam controls.

Daniel seemed rooted to the spot, so Tymos suggested, "I'll be bringing the ship out; you need to move."

He did, but moments later he had to clap his hands over his ears as the pitch of the ships engines increased, and sounded like those of an aeroplane just before take-off. His eyes caught a brief glimpse of Kryslie, also in a flight suit, racing back towards the ship and carrying a shielded crate. She had streaked past him at an incredible speed. Before he lost his lower jaw, he snapped his mouth shut. Moments later, the nose of the scout ship emerged into the big cavern where the glowing mauve oval of the long range beam terminus hung in the air. The ship surged forward, as if it were going to slam into the far rock wall, but instead seemed to be sucked into the oval glow…and was gone.

Morin, who had come running to see what was making the noise, breathed out in the abrupt silence. "Wow! I didn't think a space ship could take off underground! They could've slammed into the wall if the beam failed!"

When he got no reaction from Daniel, he looked at the base coordinator's white face, shocked expression and rigid posture, and ran to find Vincent.

Daniel found it hard to calm his mind. He tried to minimise the shocks of the past minutes by making a mental list of dot points. First, his children had simply looked at the screen and known what to ask. Second, they had snapped out orders like they were generals. Third, they had ordered Vincent around like he was a servant, even gave him orders for the Tymorean Governor's. Fourth, they had blithely disregarded the cardinal rule for Tymorean missionary work. Fifth was the implication of a disaster of a magnitude that he couldn't imagine. Sixth – simply deciding to go millions of light years across space in an instant. And finally, was how fast they had moved.

As Vincent trotted over, followed by a worried Morin, Daniel asked in a strained voice, "Could someone please tell me what is so important about that planet? And if they know what they are doing?"

"Be assured, Daniel, they do know," Vincent said quietly as he put an arm behind Daniel's shoulders and urged him towards the kitchen and lounge. "You cannot think of the Great Ones as children — even if they, are in physical years, much younger than you."

"Do you mean that there is more to the title of Great One than being members of the High King Governor's family?"

"Indeed my friend. I did not realise that you did not understand," Vincent apologised. "You arrived on Tymorea as the missionaries were being recalled and only a short time before we went into sanctuary on Dira. You would have had little time to realise we were at war. Let me tell you what the Elders foresaw..." He led Daniel to a seat.

"But there was no sign of that when we came back to the temple and returned to the palace. No, I remember, some of the buildings were rubble but..."

"Many years passed while we were in Dira," Vincent explained. "The Great Ones protected the forests, the animals, the crops in the ground and the common people. They sent the Aeronites back to their ships and told them to take off. They confronted the Ciriot, who refused to leave — and those died. When the actions of the Ciriot made the surface uninhabitable - they purified land, sea and air. With the Guardians help they also brought life back to the surface."

"I never could believe that. It seems totally inconceivable. I thought it had to be propaganda to reassure everyone..." Daniel sank back into the chair, still cupping a mug of cooling Earth tea that Morin had pressed into his hands.

"They and Llaimos are advocates of the Guardians of Peace," Vincent went on. "Tymos and Kryslie have a mission here. Earth must become part of the Federation of Peace. Beyond that, beyond this moment in history — I don't know, but the Guardians speak to them. By Tymorean definition they are God-touched, and therefore by right and power — Great Ones."

"And that gives them the right to order even the Governors around?" Daniel demanded.

"Yes," Vincent said simply. "The wisdom of the Great Ones comes from the Guardians."

After a while, Daniel nodded. He was beginning to understand the awe betrayed by all of the new missionaries that came to Earth.

"Then what is it about that planet? Is that the main reason they went off or was it Genesis 1?"

"I believe it is both. This is a pivotal point in Earth's history. The Genesis mission must succeed, so that Earth can join the Federation of Peace."

"Would they have gone off if the ship wasn't going towards the planet?"

Vincent shrugged slightly. "Have you heard talk of Aerdna – that it transcended its orbit after a cataclysmic event?"

"Yes, when we were looking into that Aeronite ship three years ago," Daniel recalled. "Many Aeronites fled to the colonies."

"The cowards fled," Vincent corrected. "The stupid died when the atmosphere froze on the ground. Those that believed in the words of Peace Lord Xeric, prepared. Before he left Tymorea, he was given a plaque by the Great Ones. It contained all the information they needed to survive in underground vaults."

"My God!" Daniel said in awe. "And it was all the doing of my children?"

"Not all. They drew together data from our scientists and from those of a thousand other worlds," Vincent explained. "And just as the Great Ones allowed Tymorea to recover, they promised the Aeronites a rebirth when Aerdna came into the influence of a new sun…a prophecy that is even now coming to fruition."

Daniel finally sipped his tea as Vincent added, "So that is why it is better for both Aerdna and Earth that they go out and discover what caused this strange coincidence."

"I see that now, and I must accept that they are capable, but…the way you defer to them…should I?"

A faint chuckle escaped Vincent. He smiled and said, "In Tymorean culture, they outrank the Governors, and they are not constrained by our laws and customs. However, I mean no respect when I say, you should continue to act as you have. Between your rearing and the Governor's training they have not become arrogant like many powerful people. I think even Great Ones need to be reminded of their humanity and that they should relax and have fun on occasions. No one can work full out indefinitely. There will be times when they must, but I do not think even the Guardians expect them to work all the time."

"But they usually defer to you and me," Daniel said.

"They have been well taught to respect their Elders. And they are still growing into their wisdom," Vincent said.

# Chapter 5

At the border of Tau and Sigma sectors, after exiting the long-range beam from the most distant relay point, Tymos allowed their ship to drift whilst Kryslie confirmed their position and listened for any comm signals from Genesis 1, who should have dropped from hyperspace by that time.

"I have their position," she told her twin as she programmed it into the nav computer. "I think that whoever was blocking the signals, no longer thinks it necessary."

"Then they won't be expecting us, if that is the case," Tymos decided. "I have the latest telemetry from Obs 1. We can decode it as we go along. Meanwhile, you take the controls while I stretch my legs and get us some food."

They unstrapped from their current positions, and whilst Tymos went towards the tiny galley, pulling himself quickly along the guide rail to keep from drifting, Kryslie slipped into the main pilot's seat, activated their hyperdrive and gradually increased speed to near hyperspeed factor 8 – staying a hair's breadth below the red zone of the engine's controls.

"Have you got the cloaking shield up," Tymos asked, when he returned with a handful of silver covered packets.

"First thing I did, bro," she confirmed, reaching out for a protein packet, which Tymos opened for her.

He slipped into the co-pilot's seat to eat one himself.

The screen in front of Kryslie was not showing a view of space ahead of them, but was opaque with a simulation of space with the pinpoints of suns. When he had finished eating, Tymos brought up a grid and transferred information from latest status microburst from Genesis 1, which had been relayed by the Tymorean message buoys.

"We should be close enough to get the telemetry direct from Genesis 1," Kryslie suggested.

Tymos gave her a pained look, but took the hint and set their comm set to scan for Genesis 1's frequency, and then had the unit switch between that and the Tymorean frequency. By his calculations, Obs 1 should be near the errant planet already, but as they were proceeding with extreme stealth, they would only be sending microburst signals at intervals to Obs 2 and Obs 3. If anything of importance was reported, the Obs ships would relay them.

As they continued on towards the position of Genesis 1, Kryslie allowed part of her mind to consider what might be occurring on the ship. They'd be in normal space, the nav computer should have updated their position and should have instigated an alarm when was found to be different to that which was programmed. One of the crew would program the data to check the automatic system. They could check that the new course would head them back towards Earth…they would have no choice but to trust it…yet, they had ended up so far off course.

She was confident that the three men would not panic. They had food, water and oxygen supplies to last for a longer period than their planned travel time. They would probably just go ahead with the next set of experiments.

The next microburst transmission came directly from Genesis 1 and confirmed that the ship was drifting, as was expected during a normal space experimental period. The crew's adrenalin levels were elevated, but they were still working purposefully. Their position was within tau sector, approximately four light years from the planet, and about as far from the forming sun as Pluto was from Earth.

The transmissions continued, reassuring the Great Ones, although doing nothing to answer the question of how they had got to be so far from their expected position. When the next expected transmission did not come, it was like a surge of lightning along their nerves.

"Static," Kryslie told her twin, referring to the comm channels. She instinctively checked their own position. They had been travelling in hyperspace for almost a full day cycle. She slowed their ship's speed and headed directly towards Genesis 1's latest position. An hour later, they dropped into normal space, just out of range of Genesis 1's sensors. For the last half hour, they had once again been receiving transmitted positions from the ship, although she had needed to have the attenuation set very high to hear the transmission.

"They are closer to the planet," Tymos noted. "And they have not used manoeuvring thrusters. Any indication of Obs 1?"

Kryslie turned on the active sensors and did an ultrashort, all around sweep – tuned to detect one particular element, which was the signature element of the highly effective Tymorean cloaking screens and the means by which cloaked Tymorean ships could locate each other.

A symbol appeared on the 3D grid overlying the main view screen, it was close to the wandering planet. Tymos labelled it Obs 1. Sometime later, they heard the ping from a similar sensor sweep, and the ID symbol for Obs 2 appeared on the screen.

Tymos opened a short range comm channel and ordered Obs 2 to, "Stop for docking manoeuvres." He began to inch his scoutship towards the larger Observation ship, using short range sensor pulses to line up the docking hatch. The required knowledge to do this was in his mind and his skill was instinctive.

Tymos and Kryslie opened their head pieces as the lock closed behind them. The clear face screen curved out of sight inside the rest of the helmet. They nodded in response to the formal greeting from the two crew who met them, before striding past in the direction of the central monitoring control room. While their scout ship had the latest equipment, it did not have the full range of instruments that were built into the Observation ships, and Tymos hoped to get more information from the Obs 2 sensor array.

On entering the central control room, they were greeted with perfect correctness by Konn Reslic, the Captain of the ship and the fourth son of the Tymorean President. Tymos gave him a brief nod of acknowledgement and immediately demanded, "Bring up the trajectory of Genesis 1."

A 3D holographic sphere flashed into life in the centre of the room, seemingly hanging in the air. Data points appeared but they stopped at the point where Genesis 1 had first disappeared. Kryslie passed a data cube to one of the duty crew, and the details that she and Tymos had collected were added to the hologram. It gave a much clearer idea of the current positions of Genesis 1, the planet Aerdna, the new sun and all other visible objects in the nearby space.

Tymos saw the new sun, still a safe distance away, the wandering planet drawing along a number of small moonlets, and the ship. The latter was at the centre of the hologram, and in that view it looked as if the planet was hurtling towards the ship and the new sun was also moving towards it. Lines for trajectory and predicted course, wove through the display.

"Alter the focus to have the planet at the centre," Tymos ordered.

Kryslie stayed by one of the crew stations and asked for a separate control panel. "We should be able to pick up direct telemetry from Genesis 1."

The fleet officer obeyed immediately, and then reported his success to his captain.

"Medical telemetry please," Kryslie directed.

"All is within human normal, Great One," the officer reported.

Kryslie studied it for herself. "Heat and radiation levels?" she asked, and that data flicked up onto the screen. They were still within safe limits. She felt a nebulous idea, flitting in her mind.

Tymos studied the new view in the holosphere. The changes were slow, but the Genesis 1 was subtly being pulled towards the planet.

"Have you received any notification from the Obs 1?" Tymos asked.

"Not yet, Great One," Konn Reslic reported. "They are in stealth mode and will maintain comm silence unless they find something."

Tymos continued to watch the projection.

Kryslie finally grasped the nebulous idea. "Direct probes to examine between the ship and the planet," she directed, looking at Konn Reslic.

"At once, Great One." He gave the instructions and then asked, "May I ask what you are looking for?"

Kryslie nodded. "Energy, radiation, matter waves, communications frequencies, the full spectrographic range to see if something is being emitted to affect the ship."

The probes were dispatched as soon as they were programmed, but they needed to travel approximately four light years. However, due to their small size, they were able to travel as fast as a cruiser at full speed.

Tymos paced slowly around the holosphere during the half hour that it took the probe to reach its programmed position. Kryslie analysed the direct telemetry readings until the probe data came up in the holosphere. Then she switched to studying the data that came up on the screen at the crew station. There the data was presented at graphs of spectrographic frequencies and wavelengths.

Kryslie saw a sharp peak in one and ten seconds later it was repeated. After a third, she pointed to it and asked, "What is causing that?"

Konn, looking over her shoulder at the data, began a computer analysis of the sensor result. He brought the readings up on the screen.

"Tymos?" Kryslie mentally summoned. "I have seen something like this before."

The information was in her mind, and Tymos picked it out. He continued to study the holosphere, mentally counting. He saw the tiniest of jerks in the course of Genesis 1. His mind went into higher gear, with information flashing through it. What he sought came as a flash of memory of seeing something flashing by...

"Ciriot!"

Tymos's announcement was met with a murmur of indrawn breaths, and Kryslie sensed the officer near her tensing.

Konn Reslic found his voice first. "Great One, the Ciriot have never been known to be active in this sector, and there have been no reports of any of the pirate clans since the Return."

Kryslie snapped, "Irrelevant! Somewhere on that planet, some creature is operating a Ciriot attractor beam. One burst every ten seconds. Warn the scout ship."

The orders given, Konn dared to question her again. "Great One I have never heard of such a device."

"To our knowledge it wasn't used on Tymorea during the war," Tymos told him. "I encountered the information when we downloaded Ciriot ship data to storage. There should be a record of it in the archival storage at the palace on Tymorea."

In fact, Tymos had first encountered the knowledge in the mind of a dying Ciriot. "Perhaps you could notify your commander and request retrieval of that data."

Again, Konn obeyed and instructed one of his crew to do so. The rest returned to their duties, but kept glancing at the Great Ones who were staring intently into the holosphere or the figures on the screen. Konn Reslic hovered near Tymos. He was less in awe of the Great Ones than his crew for he had first known them as mere students.

"Course is changing faster," Tymos said.

Konn glanced at one of his officers who made quick calculations on the computer and announced, "Confirmed, Sir."

"Course telemetry," Kryslie said to the controller beside her. The woman brought it up immediately.

The voices of the Genesis crew were audible on the audio frequency, and Kryslie asked for it to be amplified.

For the benefit of the Tymorean crew, Kryslie translated. "The Genesis crew have realised that their position is not stable, but they believe that it will not matter as the nav computer will compensate prior to returning to hyperspeed."

"Perhaps," Tymos murmured. "There has to be a cloaked ship around here, possibly Ciriot. Genesis cannot have got here so fast on her own." He raised his voice and added, "Where is Obs 1?"

A flickering blue blip appeared in the holosphere, moving towards the planet. Tiny figures beside it gave its trajectory and speed. It was moving at maximum impulse, and approaching the planet from a different vector to Genesis 1. It would be in position to orbit the planet in an hour.

Mentally responding to her brother's comment, Kryslie suggested, "It dropped Genesis 1 here? Do you think it was so that attractor beam could take over?"

"That beam is at extreme range, only just pulling it."

The image of a worm jiggling on a hook passed through Kryslie's mind, making her think that Genesis 1 was bait for something, and an instant later she thought at her twin, "Could Obs 1 have been seen when it came near that planet the first time?"

"Seen and identified?"

"Uh, huh."

"Why didn't they attack? The Ciriot pirates are usually in packs…"

"Used to, bro. We hit them very hard when we destroyed their base and personnel on Tymorea."

"They've had more than a century to recover."

"True, but they have never been out this far. Konn was correct there, but they were the ones to cause the cataclysm that sent Aerdna out here – some of them may have been tracking it."

"Do you think they had a base on the planet from before the trancession? That they know of the vaults?"

Kryslie shrugged slightly when Tymos glanced her way. "We will need to find out. But assume they have a base there. They'd need to be supplied periodically. I doubt that the base would be very big, or Obs 1's scanners would have detected a sign of it."

"It could be under the surface," Tymos considered. "If they do as they did on Tymorea, they'd use a tribe ship as a base. They could have as many as twelve smaller ships within it. More than enough to take out one ship."

"Not if they weren't sure if Obs 1 was alone, bro."

"Okay, so they decided to pull into their hole…" Tymos allowed a lot of ideas to flit through his mind, and because Kryslie was sharing those thoughts and adding ideas, he finally concluded, "One of those pirates spotted Genesis, and must have seen the three escorts – and would have identified them as Tymorean."

"The static was so that they would lose the trail when they pinched Genesis from under their noses."

"So if they think they succeeded, why this cat and mouse game?"

"They can't know if we left a hidden ship around here. They wouldn't want to reveal their base if we were watching."

"I want to know where that Ciriot ship is. Can you do a short range scan for strontium and manganese?"

Kryslie nudged the duty officer aside and programmed the scanners. The two elements were signature elements of the Ciriot physiology. She also set the computer to analyse the spectrographic data for those elements.

Tymos began his pacing again, waiting for any report from Obs 1 that would indicate an anomaly under the surface of the planet. Kryslie watched the probe data on the screen and listened to the astronauts on

Genesis 1, proceeding with their schedule. They still had over 36 hours before they were due to begin their homeward course.

A tonal sequence announced the change of watch, twelve fresh crew arrived and each went to their assigned station. Those they were to replace did a hand over. The presence of the Great Ones was mentioned, and surprised glances went to where Tymos and Kryslie were standing. The ensign who was to replace the crew near Kryslie was almost rigid with awe as he stuttered the ritual greeting. She spared a moment to put him at ease before returning her concentration to the screen.

Konn Reslic remained after his duty period had officially finished. He acknowledged the change of watch, and then strolled over to the currently vacant engineering station. A slight scowl formed on his face as he watched the Great Ones directing his crew at the various stations. He couldn't object for when Great Ones were around, they were in command and these two would continue to be for as long as their ship remained docked with his.

There was no indication in their manner or expression to indicate that they were worried by the prospect of a cloaked Ciriot ship prowling around in near space. Yet his ship, was a stationary target – if their phantom ship did exist, it could accidentally run into them.

When Tymos suddenly stiffened and began to turn around, he felt himself reacting to the sense of alarm.

"Cut all sensors!"

"What?" Konn caught himself before demanding an explanation. He had no right to question a Great One, but didn't the young know-it-all realise that they were blind without sensors?

He twisted to look at Great One Kryslie, when she announced into the suddenly quiet chamber, "Sensor sweep."

Before his own mind finished belittling the statement, the screens at every duty station pixelated, or had lines of static scrolling up them. The screens automatically reset in the next moment, but Great One Tymos directed, "Passive sensors only."

The next moment, a chime sounded. A glance around the stations, told him that it was the station that was set up to detect the Ciriot signature elements.

Fesnel, the second in charge of the crew of Obs 2, came over to his senior officer. He arrived as Konn gave a quiet snort, and in turn tacitly begged an explanation.

"I have never observed that phenomenon when we were the subject of a sensor sweep," Fesnel commented.

"Nor I," Konn admitted, "The Great Ones would have us believe they felt it coming. And it may well be true, but I would rather be out hunting those Ciriot beasts than sitting here as a tempting target."

Rather than responding to that comment, Fesnel glanced around at the duty stations, to be sure everyone was concentrating on their assigned tasks. His eyes then followed the two Great Ones, who were once more calm and seemingly relaxed. He was unsettled by his Captain's attitude, which bordered on disrespect for the Great Ones. While his own feeling was one of awe.

When the sensor sweep swept past Genesis 1, moments before it reached Obs 2, Kryslie heard the reaction from Astronaut Tweed over the voice channel, picked up by the duty station next to her. Simultaneously, Tymos recognised the cause, and called the warning to cut sensors. The highly trained crew obeyed instantly, and so when the sensors passed by Obs 2, there was no feedback to betray their position.

All screens blacked out, and when he called for passive sensors, about half the screens came live again. Everyone waited tensely to see if the sweep would be repeated, and those manning the passive sensors were ready to analyse anything they received.

Tymos moved over to his sister, to find out if she had heard anything further from the Genesis astronauts. At times such as this, their minds were like one, unless they each needed to concentrate on different things. So he was not surprised when she immediately told him what he had wanted to know.

"All instruments on the ship reset. They are just coming back on line. Casey went to check the electronics on one of the experiments, thinking that the reset might have been due to that."

Tymos stayed and listened to Tweed reporting verbally for the cabin recorder, as each instrument returned to operational. Pitt commented that the 'glitch' was like the one that had dropped them from hyperspace 13 hours early.

"That would explain the elevated adrenalin levels," Tymos murmured, just as a warning chime sounded over the comm from Genesis 1, and Tweed called for Pitt after expressing an unprofessional curse, ending with, "…and how the hell did we get there!"

"I would have expected them to have discovered the error in their position when they first dropped back into normal space. The astrogation program should have updated the nav program at that time."

"Yes, it should have, but I suspect that phantom ship managed to get partial control, for the status reports the duty helmsman added to the verbal log were from the predicted course, not the actual data."

Kryslie felt herself shudder. "I don't like the idea that the Ciriot might have got into the nav system and found the coordinates for Earth. Even if they do not know how to translate Earth language to their own."

"Yet!" Tymos warned. "That means the sooner Genesis 1 gets away from here the better, ideally without the phantom ship following."

"Before they do, I want to do a quick remote system check and send a code to the computer."

"Wait for the next sensor sweep. If they are hunting for our ships, they will keep it up. Meanwhile, I will go back to the holoscreen and see if I can see where that phantom ship is."

When the second sensor sweep went past, close to 200 seconds after the first, Kryslie brushed the hands of the young ensign beside her, and the woman quickly withdrew them and then watched in amazement at the speed with which he Great One entered a subroutine.

Kryslie then spoke to the woman, "I want one quick sensor probe, aimed directly at the human ship – on my mark."

Tymos was watching the 3D holoscreen and the seemingly random dots that represented the cloaked Ciriot ship. When the dots moved behind Genesis one, he told Kryslie, "Mark!" and she echoed it.

When the data, sent as a microburst from Genesis 1, scrolled onto the screen, Kryslie studied it, mentally commenting to her brother, "They don't have the scrambler field on, but all the others have reset."

"I didn't make that one a default setting," Tymos told her.

"I can send a signal to activate it," Kryslie offered.

"Do it, and make it default. It should stop the Ciriot ship from being able to remote access their systems and it should also interfere if they try to use an energy tether again."

In the next interval between sweeps, Kryslie sent the relevant code, and confirmed that it worked after the following sweep. She then went back to leaning against the console to listen to the audio feed from Genesis 1.

Each time their systems had reset, Tweed's curses had grown more inventive. Now she heard Pitt, "We need to find out what is causing these blackouts if we ever want to leave here. If we can even find our way back at all."

"The diagnostic on the nav system showed green, so it is working fine," Casey's voice was calm.

"Then it must be the astrogation system that is glitching," Pitt insisted,

"Then we will put the experiments on hold and run checks on all systems," Casey proposed.

"You do that, Cap. They're a dead loss anyway. I've decided that I am going to check our position the old fashioned way – assuming that I can find any stars that I recognise. If the nav system is right, I should still be able to recognise some from our last stop."

The audio channel fell silent after Casey agreed to Pitt's idea.

However, moments later, the Obs 2 Comm officer reported, "Obs 1 has located the outer edge of the vaults, Great Ones."

# Chapter 6

Aboard Genesis 1, Pitt opened up the direct viewport and saw the unfamiliar field of stars. He set the computer to recording the vista. It had just confirmed the save, when the computer reset yet again. Only this time, it had been just the computer; the lighting in the cockpit had only dulled, not gone black. He realised that the timing of the glitches was eerily regular, and it had to be some function of the ship…maybe the power generator. That might also explain that odd sensation, before they had dropped back into normal space, when the computer had showed that they were going at twice their theoretical maximum speed in hyperspace. He and the others had all felt nauseous for hours, but the initial periods of hyperspace had not adversely affected any of them.

Pitt forced his mind back onto what he was doing, and activated the astrogation program, in test mode. He would check every subroutine – starting with the calculation of brightness and distance away of all the stars in the saved scan. The screen became white as numbers designating celestial bodies began to overlap each other. Expecting another power glitch, he saved the progress, just in time.

During the next three minute period, he spoke over the ships internal comm system. "Cap, did you or Tweed change anything about five minutes ago?"

"Negative. Why?" Casey responded.

Tweed added, "Not me…everything is checking in the green."

"Did you notice that the power only dipped last time?" Pitt's voice sounded matter of fact, but his stomach was queasy.

"Sure, maybe it's sorting itself out. Found where we are yet?" Tweed asked.

"No, still working. The computer is still dropping out."

"Keep at it," Casey encouraged. "We will re-check the power generator."

The computer finally finished gathering data on all the celestial objects within the range he had specified. Then he cleared the congestion on the screen by keeping only the one hundred nearest or brightest objects. That should be enough data points to give him a match with the stars at the last stop. He opened the file from the last stop and had the astrogation program do a comparison.

The computer reset again, mid calculation, and he had to start again, but it had only achieved, at best, a 30% probability of a match. The next time the program finished and saved, and looking at the very low probabilities, Pitt cursed, borrowing some of Tweed's favourite expletives. "It's got to be this damn program," he finished, as he thumped the terminal. Well, in the microgravity conditions, he only made himself float away from it.

Casey returned, having heard the curses, and pushed Pitt back. "Well?"

"Inconclusive, Cap. Which means, we are further from our last stop that we expected to be…if the program isn't corrupted."

"Assume it isn't," Casey proposed.

"Freaking gremlins! Okay, Cap, you're right. We had the computer telling us that our speed had increased for a time, which may be because that area of space had less cosmic dust. However, we dropped out very early."

"So, what can you do?"

"Well, we have the data from all the old NASA and WRSA probes and missions stored on the backup computer. I'll run a comparison against them."

"Did your red headed tech tell you about that?" Casey's voice was teasing now.

"Yeah. I thought she was making out that we were incompetent, but she said it didn't hurt to have it there. Seems she was right. I'll keep at this…"

To speed up the process, Pitt settled on using the data from the twelve nearest objects. He set the computer searching for a match, after building into the program regular save times and a command to continue from the last save when the computer reset.

Casey watched for a while, as keen as Pitt was to find out their exact position.

"These glitches are too regular to be natural. If you can't find a problem on this ship – what the hell can be causing them?"

"There will be a logical explanation. It only started after we dropped back into normal space this time."

"But not right away, Cap."

"No, but let us continue here." Casey brought up on the 3D grid, their course so far. The last point was what the computer had calculated based on the intended course during the last period in hyperspace. He studied it while the other screen scrolled through stored starfield data.

A ping made his eyes go to the now static screen as Pitt exclaimed, "That's impossible!"

Casey added the calculated coordinates of their position based on the stored data to the 3D grid and had to agree, but only said, "Keep going through the stored data. There may be a fit that is closer than 83%."

He wondered at that value, as the comparison continued.

Tweed joined them and waited. A second ping announced another match. The coordinates were virtually the same.

"The same location from a separate data set," Casey commented. "I would have to accept that as our position. Why don't you bring up that old data and see what doesn't match what is here?"

Tweed volunteered to do that, and he began that comparison in a new window on the screen.

"That planetary sized body," Pitt saw at once. "It must be a wanderer. It wasn't in this area when the NASA probe went through. What is the other one that was number ten on my list?"

"It's a lot smaller and it must be very dense. It may be a stray asteroid. I'll open up the assay data…mmm…iron, tungsten, manganese, strontium. Too bad we can't grab it and take it back with us."

"Save what we found and do a back-up," Casey directed. "Let's look at that wanderer planet. The science bods back on Earth will be interested. How far off it are we now?"

"About four light years," Tweed read from the screen.

Pitt zoomed in on it, but even at full magnification, it was only the size of a marble.

"Well, we have a location, save it to the nav computer. Pitt, your sleep period starts soon, but I want to try setting up the experiments again – linking in the back-up generator. Let's get back to business."

Pitt told Casey, "Give me a few minutes here and then I will join you." He set the computer to record more of the starfield, for Genesis 1 was slowly rotating. He would pick another section to analyse later.

Casey went with Tweed, back to the large hold where they were doing experiments related to man travelling faster than light.

When he had finished in the experiment hold, Pitt should have gone for his sleep period, but he had gone back to check on his program. In the hour that he had been away, the ship had rotated several full revolutions. He picked a dozen sections of the star field – using the wanderer planet as a marker, and set the computer to repeat its calculations using each set. This time though, he omitted the planet's data point, and the too small to be seen asteroid. One calculation after the other returned the same position based on data recorded by the WSRA Farsight mission in 2107. He had to accept that they were indeed way off their expected position.

Yet the actual coordinates of Genesis's position were changing by a small amount with each subsequent calculation. He played around with the calculations, adding in the wanderer planet, and finding that the distance between Genesis 1 and that planet was decreasing at an alarming rate.

He calculated how close they would come by the time they were due to return to hyperspace. With relief, he decided that they would be long gone before the movement became a problem…whatever was causing it.

He made other calculations, calculating the distance and direction of the mysterious asteroid away from them. He had the computer locate it in each section of the scan that it appeared. The first thing he realised was that it wasn't always in the same place, with respect to a direction and distance from the planet. Then he noted that the sequential calculations of direction and distance off from Genesis 1 might well have been random, although he triple checked that he had considered them in time order.

He muttered to himself, "It has to be the damn program!" He decided that he did need to sleep and rest his mind before trying to re do the calculations.

He left the computer recording, walk headed for his bunk. Sleep didn't come, for he was aware of his accelerated heart rate and the roiling in his stomach. He tried to figure out where in the program the bug was, but an insidious fear kept intruding…that some unseen presence was nearby – stalking them.

# Chapter 7

The Tymorean Earth base had settled down after the departure of the Great Ones in long range shuttle. Daniel noticed Bynan sitting by herself in the communal eating room when he went in to have his lunch. Seeing how she was hunched over the table, hands cupping a cooling mug of some beverage, caused him to take the seat across the table from her. He knew she was personal assistant to Ron Basoli of the WRSA, a particularly important role at this time, but one that the young woman managed with quiet confidence.

"You haven't visited for a while," Dan remarked. "We don't see enough of you."

Bynan looked up and forced a smile. "It has been hectic. The boss told me to take two days off."

"So what is the problem?" Daniel asked.

"Basoli is the problem," she admitted. "Or rather, I think he has a problem – but he won't talk about it. That makes me assume it is personal."

"Tell me from the beginning," Daniel invited. He needed to know if the problem would affect Basoli's handling of the deep space project.

"I'm not sure when it started," she admitted. "It may have been after a visit from his brother."

"Brother? Oh yes, Reginald Basoli – CEO of World Trade and Investment Corporation," Daniel recalled.

Bynan nodded. "I wasn't told anything about the meeting."

"When was this?"

"Maybe a month ago – well before the lead up to the launch."

"How did he seem after the meeting?" Daniel asked.

"Thoughtful, worried, troubled," Bynan recalled.

"There was more?" Daniel prompted.

"Yes, today, after the media conference. Two official types arrived and wouldn't tell me anything. They just sat and waited for the boss. All I heard was they were from some Government agency."

"Can't be WSRA related. The Government doesn't have any jurisdiction over it," Daniel mused.

"They were in there several hours. When they left, the boss was looking awful. I mean, most people wouldn't have noticed, since he has still got pinkish sunburn from being down near Terra 1. I thought he looked sick, but he sent me off."

"Do you think the cause will affect his ability at work?" Daniel asked.

"I don't know, but when I left, there was this really odd little man hanging out with the media group. He followed me out, asking questions about the boss's private life. He was a right nuisance, but security shooed him off. They said he was from a gossip newspaper."

Daniel didn't call his aide Morin, he simply thought of his need – since the telepathic commoner would probably sense it. "Have Vincent join us, please, Morin."

Moments later, the Tymorean doctor and psychologist, walked into the eating room. He was currently on-base keeping track of Genesis 1 through the reports relayed through Homebase.

He listened to Bynan's concerns and decided, "I will go and speak to him – ostensibly a follow up to the launch, and to plan the debrief for the return. I will see what else I can learn."

Vincent had met Basoli some years ago, and had since insinuated himself as a consultant psychologist and psychiatrist to the WSRA.

Vincent reported to Daniel privately.

"Basoli is a very private person," Vincent admitted. "I know what the immediate concern is – but I sense that there is a lot more than that causing him stress. More that is, than the Genesis mission."

"Is it something we need to concern ourselves with?" Daniel asked bluntly. "Our mandate does not allow us to take sides in purely human affairs, if it doesn't have world reaching effects."

Vincent smiled at Daniel who was a very conscientious man. "What was that Earth tale you told me about – the one where lacking a nail lost a kingdom."

"Is that the case here?" Daniel challenged.

Vincent considered. "I think we should follow this up for now. The immediate concerns in themselves are not our affair. It is the deeper concerns that are more important. Ron Basoli is the best man for his position, and now is not the time to have doubt cast on his honesty and integrity – or his leadership of the WSRA. It is too important – for the future safety of Earth – that they join the Federation of Peace. Nothing must prevent that happening."

Daniel saw that he was right. Basoli knew aliens existed, both benign and not. The future deep space missions were to go out and meet races from other worlds.

"I will suggest to Jonko to go and offer his investigative services to him," Daniel decided. "Being on the Investigative Committee is a recommendation of integrity and confidentiality."

"Their mandate runs parallel with that of the WSRA – with a reverence for truth. And they can act as unbiased investigators when approached. Somebody of Basoli's status would not be refused and requesting help will be a formidable statement of his integrity and openness," Vincent confirmed.

"What else can you tell me?" Daniel asked. "What decided you?"

"The investigators were looking into claims of fraud relating to purchases of shares in his brother's company," Vincent summarised. "I am sure Basoli has not deliberately acted wrongly. He is willingly cooperating with the investigators. He told me, that as far as he knows, his brother is honest. That even though they are not really close, his brother has always backed him and vice-versa."

"I can't see the importance," Daniel commented.

"In itself, it isn't. But I feel that the timing of this is...planned. And then there are the gossip writers sniffing around – as if they think they smell corruption," Vincent explained.

"Is that a premonition?" Daniel asked. "Not that I am likely to ever get a divine vision from the Guardians."

"It is too tenuous for that," Vincent admitted. "But don't sell yourself short, Daniel. You remind the rest of us what it means to be human, or in our case normal Tymoreans. And I rely on your understanding of the human culture."

"Hmpfh!" Daniel snorted. "You have that well figured already. What if I send Keleb and my rascal aide to sniff around the brother and his wife?"

Vincent smiled, not convinced that Daniel was not prescient. "Excellent suggestion."


"But Boss, I'm not a missionary," Morin said startled and excited when the request was put to him. He did not leave the base often.

"No, but you have been studying humans via their vid-casts for long enough to be able to speak to them," Daniel remarked, pointedly. "I am sure the woman won't be able to resist you."

"But Boss, the woman is old! You would manage better."

Daniel smiled. "Well, I am really too old, and a stuffy old stick at that. And, thinking on it, all the other men I could ask are too intense and focussed on cosmic crises. So, I think, a cheeky, fun loving, self-confident young man would interest her much more."

Morin blushed furiously at having all of his disrespectful comments coming back at him.

"Besides, my boy, you can hear thoughts," Daniel pointed out. "No, don't try to quote ethics. I did not say pry – just listen to what she blurts out to herself."

"If you say so, boss," Morin agreed. "What exactly are we after?"

"Just see what you can learn about her and her husband. I doubt that she knows details of her husband's business. You don't need to ask questions unless the chance is natural," Daniel told him.

Morin's avid look caused Daniel to caution him. "Keleb will be going with you. He is to sniff around Reginald Basoli who is a shark who won't think twice of swallowing a tiny fish like you."

"What's a shark?" Morin asked impishly.

Daniel pictured one in his mind – mouth open, teeth showing, that snapped his aide's head off.

Morin sobered. "I'll do good, boss."

# Chapter 8

After several hours, the sensor sweep had taken on a familiar regularity. When it stopped, the tension in the Obs 2 duty officers increased abruptly. No one thought it was coincidence  that it happened just after the a microburst message from Obs 1, reporting the presence of a possible Ciriot ship buried next to the far edge of the vaults.

"Captain, tell Obs 1 to withdraw!" Tymos ordered.

Almost immediately, a crewman said, "Six ships have just appeared above the planet."

The main screen was focussed on the planet, and the ships - a motley collection of styles — were forming into an attack formation. Instants later, Obs 1 became visible and was being fired on.

Konn Reslic dragged his eyes from the scene and looked to the Great Ones. Kryslie was trotting from near the consoles towards the holosphere where Tymos was staring intently. They didn't seem to be talking and their expressions were grave.

Damn them, he thought. This was their fault! He turned back to the screen as he heard, "Obs 1 has destroyed two of the attackers." He smothered a hiss of satisfaction as the cloud of glowing atoms dispersed.

Tymos was studying the spherical holographic display intently, and thinking at his sister, "Where is it?" The passive sensors were no longer picking up the elements of the Ciriot ship. Aloud, he demanded, "Passive sensors at maximum, and remote program the probe sensors to the same elements. I want data from both to be updating this display!"

He did not expect the Ciriot phantom ship to stay watching as Obs 1 picked off the launched defenders. Finally, the trail of the phantom ship came up again in the holospheric display.

"Krys, Genesis 1 needs to leave now, when that cloaked ship is distracted. Can you get through to them?"

After finally falling asleep, Pitt only stayed that way for an hour for the intra comm blared a request for Casey and himself to come to the cockpit. It woke him from a nightmare.

He didn't change from his sleeping suit, just dragged himself from his couch and pulled himself along the passage. He rubbed his eyes when he reached the cockpit. The first thing he took in was the wanderer planet on the screen. It was now the size of a watch glass. However, that was not what Tweed was pointing to for Casey and himself to look at. Flashing streaks of light were going back and forth across the face of the planet, like a battle in a tri-vid game. Then a cloud of glowing particles expanded and dispersed.

"That is the fourth cloud like that that I have seen." Tweed's voice was pitched higher than normal. "It cannot be a natural phenomenon. It has to be proof that other races exist."

"Are you recording?" Casey demanded.

"Too right, Captain! This is an electronic goldmine."

"It might well be, but we don't want to end up in the middle of it. Are we still drifting that way?"

"Hardly drifting, Cap. Our speed was…" Pitt paused, pushing Tweed aside to access his earlier calculations. However, seeing again the size of the planet, he rechecked his calculations. "Cap, our speed is accelerating. Do you think we are experiencing a gravity effect from that planet?"

"How far away are we?"

"Just over three light years, Cap. We were nearly four when I last checked."

"I wouldn't have thought so. Tweed, fire up the manoeuvring engines and give us two seconds of reverse thrust."

Tweed slipped into the pilot's couch and complied. Casey looked to Pitt when the burn finished.

Pitt shook his head. "We are still accelerating." After redoing his speed calculation, he felt the blood drain from his face. The nightmare he had woken from had been of the ship crashing into the planet.

Into the silence, whilst Casey thought through their situation, the proximity alarm began to wail. Tweed silenced it and tried to discover what had set it off. A second alarm sounded, this time an impact alarm.

"Damage diagnostic," Casey ordered.

Tweed opened up a different screen and watched as a white line moved along a 3D grid outline of the ship, turning the gridlines from white to green. No area showed red.

For several minutes, none of the astronauts spoke. Casey had gone to a small terminal and brought up the mission folio, and scrolled through the text. He stopped it at a particular section and read it. When he turned, his expression was serious.

"I am proposing that we abort the mission and proceed directly back to Earth," he said to his fellow crew members.

"Why? There's no damage, and think of the kudos for this recording…"was Tweeds immediate rebuttal.

"And we are being dragged into a fight, when we do not know who is fighting who, and why. We weren't able to overcome the pull towards the planet and we only have meteorite lasers as weapons. Pitt?"

Pitt stared back at Casey, part of him reluctant to agree, even though the odd events of the past few days were on the verge of freaking him out. "I know we checked the nav program Cap, but I still don't trust it. We still don't know why we ended up so far off course and if it will take us where we want it to."

Casey considered that point. "We've identified our position here, and we know Earth's position. Put them into the nav computer. You can manually check the course if you must, or we can drop back into normal space every so often to recheck the position. When you have done that, start the check list. Tweed, you and I will secure the ship for hyperspace."

Tymos nudged his sister to get her attention. He needed to know of her progress. She had been concentrating so fiercely, she had not been aware of anything else. She jerked back to awareness, then shook her head, but continued to listen to the audio feed.

Her mind told her brother, "Pitt was sleeping, but I was able to plant images in his mind, based on the sort of things he was thinking before he went to bed. They are aware that they are hurtling towards the planet. Casey is proposing that they abort the mission."

She asked the Obs 2 crew to turn up the volume of the audio feed, so that her brother could hear it. They both relaxed, marginally, when the agreement to leave was reached.

"Tell your boy to hurry it up," Tymos urged. "They only have this one short chance to lose that ship."

Abruptly, an emergency signal rose in intensity, and competing with the Genesis audio. Tymos turned from the holosphere as the alarm was muted to enable the comm officer to make his report.

"Captain, I am receiving an emergency call from the Jokus 2."

That was the official designation of Obs 1. Konn Reslic ordered, "Put it on the screen."

"It's audio only, Sir."

Konn ordered the Genesis audio muted, so that he could hear the emergency message.

Tymos thought at his twin, "We need to get closer to Genesis 1. Go get our ship ready, and keep working on your boy!"

Kryslie ignored her twin's misplaced teasing about her affair with Pitt, and moved quickly from Obs 2's monitoring room.

"…our hull has been breached, engines are out. We are working to bring up emergency power before life support becomes critical. All but six of the crew are in emergency pods, ejecting now…"

"Helm! Full impulse to Obs 1's position," Konn began.

Tymos over ruled him. "Stand down, Captain! Request Obs 3 to assist. Instruct them to go to full stealth mode and approach from the direction of upsilon sector."

Both helmsman and comm officer obeyed Tymos without question, and as they did, a dark red flush suffused Konn Reslic's face. On seeing it, Tymos told him, "Obs 1 was seen, identified, and deliberately hunted down. That spider down there, in that hidden base, didn't want them coming any closer or reporting their presence. Fortunately, we were warned."

"My brother…" Konn tried again, not giving Tymos the respect due to his rank of Great One.

"Captain," Tymos warned. "There are other matters of importance to consider."

"As you wish, Great One," Konn agreed stiffly. He turned away from Tymos and instructed, "Use the passive sensors to locate and count the escape pods. Identify them if possible."

He remained facing away from Tymos until he had his anger and frustration under control. Finally, he turned back. "Great One, am I permitted to ask a question?"

When Tymos nodded, he went on, "If that is a Ciriot ship down there, are we not obliged to confirm and report it?" His mind was saying, "Go down there and destroy it before it kills the humans, and the rest of us."

"By all means, Captain. You should inform the President of the situation here. However, this is not the time for us to risk the rest of our ships in trying to destroy it."

Konn's flush deepened further, but he did not try to argue further.

"That Ciriot base can be dealt with later. Genesis 1 is our current priority."

Konn was still standing rigidly. His mind recalling that the voice in the emergency message was that of his elder brother Jonnsen, and that he might be killed, even as the humans were in danger.

Tymos revealed that he had picked up on the unvoiced thoughts when he went on, "It is the Guardians' will that Genesis 1 returns safely to Earth. Even so, we are constrained by them to allow the humans to learn that space has its dangers, and to allow the humans to use their ingenuity to survive any trouble. We cannot wrap them in protective shields like a mother protecting a baby."

"Will you let them be killed?" Konn demanded, once again omitting Tymos's honorific title.

"We will act, only if the humans have tried everything possible to escape the trouble."

Although Konn's mind oozed resentment, more for being unable to help his brother than for concern about the humans, he forced himself to say, "As you wish, Great One."

Tymos met Konn's resentful stare, and it was the ship's captain who looked away first.

In his mind, Kryslie asked, "Ship's ready. Are you coming?"

"Yes. Have you their course?" Tymos sent back, just as the repeating voice loop from Obs 1 ceased and was replaced by a three tone signal. He, like the rest of the crew, knew immediately what that meant.

"Recall Obs 3. Have them get Genesis 1's course from Kryslie and then take up station with the ship."

Without turning to face Tymos, Konn gestured to the comms officer.

"Captain!"

Now Konn turned. "Great One, am I to follow the human ship as well?"

"Yes, but I want you to watch for the cloaked ship and warn us if it follows Genesis 1."

"And the escape pods from Obs 1, are we to let them be picked off one by one by those creatures on the planet?"

"You have notified homebase?"

"Yes."

"Then let those that respond see to the pods. They each have power to move, and enough air and supplies to last for several weeks. You are not to approach the planet or the last position of Obs 1. Keep all systems at minimum. If it was aware that three ships were shadowing the human ship before, that cloaked ship will be hunting the others."

Although his fists were clenching at his sides, Konn drew himself up – stiffly straight – and gave a curt nod. He turned to give his crew instructions; when he glanced back, Tymos was gone.

Moments later, the landing deck officer reported that the Great Ones' ship had undocked.

Konn announced to the air, not looking at anyone, including his second in command, "I will be in the command ready room."

His face was still red, and he felt as if he had been slapped in the face. The Great Ones had not done him the courtesy of requesting clearance to separate their ship from his.

Alone, he fumed in silence, torn between wishing the wet eared Great Ones into the clutches of their invisible enemy, and shame for his disrespect of them. He cursed, telling himself that they had no experience in space, and didn't know everything. Did they even care that the Tymorean President's heir designate might be dead? Weren't they just as vulnerable to the weapons of that cloaked ship?

When Tymos began to separate their ship from Obs 1, he demanded, "What's holding them up?"

"They are strapped in and are powering up the hyperdrive," Kryslie reported. "I doubt that they are wasting any time – they saw the explosive cloud as Obs 1 was destroyed. That removed any lingering reluctance on any of the astronauts' part. We have a small margin still. That ship is near the planet, playing with the pods by targeting the engines and making them plummet to the planet surface."

Tymos powered their ship towards Genesis 1, which was in turn still accelerating towards the planet. He turned on the passive sensors to locate Obs 3, looking for the particular unique chemical element. Having located them, in spite of the cloaking shield, he took up a position on the other side of Genesis 1, and matched the speed of the human ship. He could travel faster than the Obs ships, before the engine flare betrayed their position. Obs 3 had taken up a stationary watching position.

Knowing that Kryslie needed to concentrate to maintain her mind link with Pitt, Tymos flew the ship and watched the sensor screen for signs of the Ciriot ship. He did not know if Obs 1 had destroyed all the ships launched from the hidden base, or the cloaked ship. Some may have stayed cloaked, in reserve, and might now be hunting other cloaked ships. The change in the signals emanating from the escape pods was telling evidence that something was targeting them. He did not allow the thought of Tymoreans dying to distract him. He had to stay with Genesis 1.

As a wailing tone impinged on his attention, Kryslie told him, "The hyper-drive engines on Genesis 1 are redlining, and about to shut down. That beam from the planet has it in too strong a grip."

With a flick of one hand, Tymos increased the strength of their own shields and added a final shielding layer – one that scrambled all forms of energy that impinged on it, and converted for their own use. Then he increased his speed so that he would slowly draw even with the human ship.

The stealth approach was so that the human astronauts and the instruments of Genesis 1 would not detect them. He was broadcasting a signal that would mute the proximity alarm. The rest of the manoeuvre was not one for a novice pilot – but Tymos had the knowledge of what must be done, and was, despite Konn's belief, a skilled pilot.

First he had to get a short distance in front of the human ship, then match its speed exactly, before slowly edging between it and the source of the attractor beam.

The creatures controlling the beam, would still receive signals that a ship was approaching, but it would not be able to grip them, and it would lose its grip on Genesis 1. The ship would stop accelerating towards the planet.

Tymos glanced at Kryslie once he was in position, but saw her tense posture and sensed her mind was closed to him. He didn't interrupt her, but waited with increasing concern for the crew to try to go to hyper speed again.

He saw Obs 2, on the sensor screen. It was slowly drifting closer to Genesis 1, which might have been coincidence but Tymos doubted it. Konn Reslic was too good a captain to be unaware of the movement. Yet it was too slow for Tymos to feel justified in making an issue of it. Konn was already resenting that he'd had his command temporarily usurped by someone he could still only see as an ignorant student. He gave Konn's disrespect no more thought. If he betrayed his resentments when reporting to his Supreme Commander (and father) they would be dealt with.

Those resentments would no doubt be stronger if he became aware of what Tymos had done. He would deem them disobeying their own injunction against interfering, when they had ordered him not to help the Tymoreans in the escape pods. Yet he could rail all he wanted to. No one on Tymorea, and that included the three co-ruling Governors, would gainsay their actions. In any case, the human astronauts would not be aware of this benign 'stroke of luck'.

None of the three astronauts looked at the others when the overload alarm sounded and the computer shut down the hyper drive engines.

Pitt was holding off panic by a narrow margin as Casey began a diagnostic. It was a useless gesture that probably would not help. His own mind was filling with images dredged from all the fantastic fictional dilemmas that his science fiction heroes had faced. The dreadful weapons, the killing ships and ravaged planets.

"Pitt!"

Casey's voice distracted him. "Bring up the engine manual. See if there is a reset mechanism for the control computer."

"Why the computer?" Pitt found himself asking. "Why not one on the engines?"

Tweed was busily engaged in trying to restart the engines.

"See if you find a mention of that as well," Casey said, distracted by his own task.

Pitt was already bringing the manual up, and he flashed through the screens, starting at the section on the engines and scanning only the headings. His mind was tired, and the situation they were in seemed to be a continuation of his nightmare, with the ship hurtling towards that errant planet. He forced himself to concentrate, as it was awkward using fingers encased on space suits to scroll down likely pages. Casey had insisted that they suit up for hyperspace, although except for the first time, they hadn't.

He became aware of the change in the ship's motion when Tweed, exclaimed, "We've stopped accelerating! Captain, did you do anything? Pitt?"

"I am redirecting power to the engines," Casey admitted. "I don't think that caused it though."

Pitt felt his inner panic rising again, with the blood pounding in his ears like the herald of doom. Above that, he heard, "PITT!" and he was about to reply through the suit comm when he realised that Casey was doing a verbal run through of the systems he was powering down, recording it in case they ever did return to Earth. Tweed wasn't looking his way either. His jerky actions betrayed his frustration with the engines.

"Pitt!" The voice in his head came again, but this time, distracted from his incipient panic, he heard it more clearly; it sounded distinctly feminine, somewhat like the voice of the red-headed tech he was seeing, and bedding, before the mission. She had always called him Gareth, though...

He heard his name again, and this time he recalled when Krys Ward had shown him over the control module and the power module – before the ship had been assembled. She'd been telling him all sorts of tech stuff – showing off he'd thought. This had been before the final crew selections had been announced.

She had said something about manual resets…Pitt unbuckled his harness and floated from the seat. "I'm going aft, Cap."

Not far away in space, Tymos spoke over the suit comm, "They need to hurry it up."

Kryslie raised one hand to let him know she had heard. She had to concentrate, for she was lightly linked to Pitt's eyesight – to direct him to the engine reset. He could have found the information in the manual, eventually. If she could take him to the place, it would be quicker.

Once Pitt reached the engine monitoring panel, he scanned the dials, reading the labels. He didn't see a reset. Looking over again, Krys nudged his mind before his eyes slid over a blank section again.

"That?" Pitt thought to himself. "It's blank."

Immediately, he seemed to hear, "That panel moves."

He pressed on it, but nothing happened until he released the pressure – then the panel slid smoothly aside and out of sight. "This? I press it?"

"Yes! Now!"

"What's the rush?" Pitt grinned faintly, his mind was playing games with him. "Never mind. I want away from here."

The lights on the main panel flicked off, and then returned to green. Pitt spoke over the suit comm, "I've used the engine manual reset. Tweed, try starting it again."

Moments later, Casey's voice said, "That's done it! Pitt, get back here and strap in."

Kryslie withdrew a bit from Pitt's mind, and stirred. "The engines are back on line," she warned her twin.

"So your boy came through," Tymos confirmed, but before his sister could retort, went on. "We had a data burst from the Jacen Tyr. Llaimos is on board and he says that he must speak to us."

"What is their ETA?"

"About an hour."

"Good. That means we can follow Genesis 1 for a while, and check for followers. Any sign of hidden ships?"

"The one we know about is still near the planet. If there are others they haven't come into sensor range. I have sent a warning to the Jacen Tyr."

"I'll tell them what we are doing, and that we will be back to meet them when they arrive."

# Chapter 9

Keleb and Morin returned from Washington late the next day, the latter looking pleased with himself. Keleb just grinned at his enthusiasm as they went in search of Daniel.

"I hope you didn't start something," Daniel remarked and was rewarded by seeing his aide blush.

"No..." Morin admitted. "She tried though."

"So what did you find out, since you seem so pleased?" Daniel returned to business.

"She drinks too much," Morin said with disgust. "And most of what she said was outright lies. She'd say one thing and her mind was contradicting it. So I let her gabble on and kept buying her drinks."

"Get to the point, Morin," Keleb prompted.

"Well she and her husband haven't had anything between them for years. They coexist, that's all, but she won't leave him. If you ask me, she would if something better came along..."

"Morin..." Keleb drawled warningly.

"She thinks that if she divorced him, she'd get nothing. She reckons her husband's company is in trouble and if she tried to get a settlement, everyone will know it."

"That's interesting," Daniel agreed. "Was there more?"

"In between thoughts of wanting to tumble me and how unfortunate it was that I wasn't rich – I caught bits of regret that she hadn't stayed engaged to our Ronald."

Daniel's eyebrows lifted.

"Of course, I ran him down as a stuffy do-gooder who'd never be rich," Morin reported. "She was well oiled by then. She said she had been engaged to Ron B, but had dumped him after an argument. Her mind said he had dumped her and that had caused the argument."

"Was there anything else?" Daniel asked patiently.

"Yeah, Boss. She thought she could have killed our Ron for dumping her. She seemed quite pleased that someone had mugged our Ron that night. Seems she had hit on Reggie for consolation."

"I don't know if that is relevant," Daniel considered. "That was all you got?"

"Hey – I only had a few hours," Morin protested. "I was going to suggest a movie and a meal when she spotted someone she knew. She stalked off in a really spiteful mood."

Daniel considered that what he had heard sounded more like gossip but said, "Very well done. It has given me a few ideas. How about you go and delve into the media archives for items about Ron, Reginald and your woman friend? Go back, oh, twenty to twenty five years. And don't go off on side tracks."

"Sure boss," the irrepressible Morin agreed with a grin. He trotted off.

Daniel glanced at Keleb who was lounging in a chair. "Have you anything to add?"

"I managed to get close to Reginald Basoli," Keleb said, shuddering at the memory.

"I take it you don't like him," Daniel deduced.

"Imagine how you would feel if a cobra reared up at you suddenly – an inch away from your face," Keleb described. "That is what he feels like to me. And he is a pathological liar too. He is spreading a believable line about why the company ceased trading. He is implying a hostile takeover in progress."

"Really?" Daniel commented. "Did you look into that?"

Keleb nodded. "I am not sure about a hostile takeover, but Ron B has been buying up shares in the company. He doesn't yet have a controlling interest. I think it is making Reg B hostile. I checked the stock exchange web site for the history of the company. There was a bit about how Reg bought out Ron's share of the company for a very big sum, but a pittance compared to the projected worth of the company. I checked the company performance. It didn't live up to that projection. I think it was Basoli's father who was the financial wizard. Oh, the company has made good profits but not huge ones."

"So what do you think about that?" Daniel asked.

The younger man thought about it. "Reg wanted the whole of the perceived profit and was eager to get Ron out."

"Yes, that occurred to me," Daniel agreed. "I wonder how he convinced Ron to sell up. Is there a public record of the sale agreement?"

"I can look," Keleb offered.

"Do," Daniel directed. "I don't think Reg would be too pleased at his brother buying up shares. And keep an eye on that scamp. I should be going back to the reports from our more important work."

"Want what I got, Boss?" Morin asked late in the evening after an afternoon on the computer, linked into the Earth computer web.

"Just the facts," Daniel sighed.

"Ok – twenty three years back, Ron broke his engagement to Francine Hunter, an heiress. It made the second page of the Washington Post. Personal reasons, our Ron said," Morin recited from memory. "Our Ron couldn't be found for comment for a day or two – then he turned up looking as if he had been mugged, but had been cleaned up a bit. Couple of days after that, Basoli senior dropped dead – heart attack. Two months later, Reg buys Ron out and proposes to Francine Hunter. Wedding was all over the papers. Ron was best man."

Daniel waited for Morin to go on. He was relishing something.

"After that, our Ron dropped out of sight until he was head-hunted for the WSRA and nothing on Reggie for a bit. Later that year, nine months after he dumped Francine – the scandal rags claim our Ron is married, with a child – maybe that is why he broke the engagement?"

"I hadn't heard anything about Ron Basoli being married and having a child," Daniel remarked.

"Well, he isn't – hasn't," Morin corrected. "Married I mean – anymore. The supposed wife died six months later – in a fire. He was being looked at for doing her in. That wasn't in the major papers though."

"What happened to the child?" Daniel asked pointedly.

"Don't know, Boss. Died too I suppose."

"See if you can find out, Morin, without using the scandal sheets. Try the law enforcement archives for a start and try to track down the wedding, birth and death certificates."

"Gotcha, Boss."

Keleb's follow up was brief. "The sale agreement is in the public domain. There is no 'hands off' period given – nothing to stop Ron buying up shares."

"So...that matter should be easily settled. Could you send the voice record of Morin's report, and yours to Jonko? Add anything else Morin finds and get him to check also for official reports on the fire he mentioned. I want facts – in case the scandal sheets try to twist the truth to destroy Basoli."

Keleb nodded and went to get to work.


Daniel watched the younger men go off with seemingly undiminished energy, and merely shook his head. Let them stay up all night if they wished. He was for his bed.

As was his habit, he went via the communications chamber to glance at the activity logs, and check for recent reports from the missionaries scattered around the world. There was nothing from the Great Ones, not that he expected any. They had been gone three days, though, and he hoped that they had found Genesis 1 and it was safe.

Across the chamber, Vincent was sitting back in a comfortable chair, reading a data pad, but he was also frowning.

"Is there a problem?" The question caused Vincent to glance at Daniel, who continued with the question most on his mind. "Is it Genesis 1?"

"The human spaceship is fine," was the immediate reassurance. "The Great Ones found it and stayed close by until it went to hyperspace again. They believe that some ship – cloaked so as to be unseen – had been affecting it. They are certain though that no unknown craft followed it when it left."

"That's reassuring. What haven't you told me that is causing you concern?"

"It is almost certain that the cloaked ship was a pirate craft, intending to overcome the crew and steal the technology. Obs 1 found a Ciriot ship almost buried under the surface of Aerdna."

"Ciriot? Like those who attacked Tymorea?"

"The same. And smaller ships launched from that ship took out Obs 1."

"Casualties?" Daniel asked, understanding Vincent's concern.

"Unknown, but all of the escape pods were ejected. However, something was firing at them."

"Have Tymos and Kryslie followed Genesis 1?"

"This message says that they will follow for a short while, but they must return. Llaimos is coming out on the Jacen Tyr and needs to talk to them."

"The Jacen Tyr, what is that?"

"It is the President's ship – the flagship of the Tymorean Peace Fleet."

"Well then, they will soon have everything under control. And there is little that we can do from here," Daniel said logically.

"Yes, that is true. Yet there is another point. The Genesis crew have aborted the mission and plan to return directly to Earth, without any more stops in normal space for experiments. Tymos estimates that they might get back as many as four days early."

"Well, while that might surprise the Earth Controllers, but we will pick them up before them – so you will be able to go ahead and be at Terra 1 when they get the news," Daniel said, setting that problem aside.

Vincent rose saying, "I should indeed trust the Great Ones to see they arrive back safely."


The following morning, Daniel was awake well before his aide, who he suspected had stayed up most of the night surfing through multitudinous websites – and probably most were unrelated to the task he had been given.

When he heard the sound of his aide begging a late breakfast from Lusanne, he decided to head that way.

"Morin!" Daniel thought with a stern tone to his mind. Thinking at his aide was more discreet than yelling.

"Boss?" Morin greeted cautiously when he found Daniel in entering the dining cavern.

"You haven't mentioned your research to anyone have you?" Daniel asked quietly.

He received an indignant, "Of course not! I have been very careful accessing the data and who would I speak to? Why Boss?"

"Bynan went to work today and has already fended off two scandal writers and several other calls from people asking personal things about Ron Basoli," Daniel said. "She thinks some calls have got through or emails – because he has virtually locked himself in his office."

"It wasn't me!" Morin stated. He was absolutely serious for once.

"I really didn't think it was," Daniel apologised. "I just wanted confirmation. Did you find out anything else last evening?"

Morin nodded. "Ron B does have a child – a girl. She would be about 23 now. From the birth certificate, her name is Jean. The mother was Olynda de Yves and I found her death certificate. Way I calculate it; she was only 17 when the baby got started. Ron B would have been thirty something. Bit shady of him."

Daniel ignored the commentary and considered the facts. "Did she die in a fire?"

"Yeah, like I told you – at her house. Place was in her name. Baby was rescued by a passer-by – some old gypsy woman. It was put in foster care until they tracked Ron B down. Police thought it was suspicious – couldn't prove it. They think a candle fell on the floor – on purpose. Ron B had just gone off on a trip. Actually, he had a flight booked and he cancelled it and took a later one."

"He was questioned?" Daniel prompted.

"Made a statement saying he had delayed his flight because his wife didn't look well, but she convinced him to go," Morin reported.

"What about a medical report on the wife?" Daniel requested.

"Smoke in lungs but not a lot. Autopsy also showed signs of radiation induced mutations. They think she died or collapsed, knocking or dropping a candle – and died before the smoke really got to her," Morin told him.

"Who uses candles these days?" Daniel asked rhetorically.

"Witches, priests, gypsies, dropouts..." Morin obligingly suggested. Then he realised that Daniel wasn't hearing him.

"Run some of the dates by me," Daniel directed. Morin watched his boss's face as he recited from memory.

Daniel had never had a premonition before, but now he did. It was the mention of 'old gypsy' and 'radiation mutations'.

The wife might have been a gypsy, might have been related to the tribe that died not far from the Tymorean base. From the dates, Olynda must have been born three years before the rocket crashed, and poisoned the land. She must have been far enough away not to have been killed by it.

"Add what you just told me to Keleb's report so that it gets to Jonko."

"At once, Boss!" Morin trotted off.


Daniel turned around and saw Keleb waiting for him.

"You look like you just had a revelation," Keleb remarked. "I have seen both Tymos and Kryslie with that look."

"Maybe I have," Daniel admitted. "But if I have – I don't have a clue what it means. Do you know anything about the tribe that died above?"

Keleb shook his head. "Not a lot. I remember Kryslie mentioning them. There might be something in the old records Tymos brought here from Rhyn's place. From during the long gap before we got here. But from what I know of nuclear blasts – there wouldn't be much left and gypsies don't keep a lot of records anyway."

"True. I wonder if any of them were away from the tribe when the rocket hit – and survived," Daniel mused.

"They would have needed to be at least twenty miles away," Keleb noted. "Kryslie said the radiation levels were instantly lethal to a radius of ten miles. Is it important?"

Daniel shrugged. "How much of Morin's last report did you overhear?"

"Most of it," Keleb admitted.

"Kryslie told me that Tamir Grainger lived with gypsies years ago. It might just be an interesting coincidence." Daniel shrugged again.

Keleb murmured, "Perhaps I will check into those old records for a bit and then do a perimeter check. I might even visit the blast site. Maybe an idea will occur to me."

# Chapter 10

Moments after Genesis 1 went to hyper speed, Obs 3 and the Great Ones' ship followed. Tymos switched to active sensors, and searched for any other ships. The absence of results reassured him. After a while he asked, "How's your boy?"

Giving her brother a look of disgust, that was hidden by the suit hood, she told him, "He's glad to be gone, and I think the same is true for Tweed, and Casey too. Their stress levels are decreasing, and they are about to start the next set of experiments. Has Obs 3 seen anything?"

"No…I'm decreasing speed."

Kryslie moved from the co-pilots seat and headed for the galley. They had a short while before they needed to return, and could use the time to eat and drink, and do other personal things. She returned with two heated drinks, with steam escaping from the sipper lids.

"I don't like the idea of that Ciriot ship being on Aerdna. They are right on the edge of the vaults, and probably have made an access for themselves to get to the people," Kryslie aired her concern.

Tymos twisted the seat around and took his drink. "It would not surprise me if that is why President Reslic is coming out on the Jacen Tyr, or maybe it is related to what Llaimos wants to talk to us about."

"If Llaimos is here, we might be able to get him to go down there and see what the Ciriot have been doing," Kryslie suggested.

"It's an idea. Someone needs to and we can't. Once we are free here, we need to catch up with Genesis 1. Anyway, where's Obs 2 – surely they should be here by now?"

No tickle of premonition ruffled their minds, so they did not leave to return to near the wandering planet, Aerdna, until the time they had to go to meet the flagship of Tymorean fleet.

On their return into normal space, the cacophony of sound on the Tymorean comm frequency came as a shock. Kryslie interpreted the incoming messages and cursed. "That stupid lack wit! Didn't you tell him not to put Obs 2 in danger?"

"Not in those exact words. I assumed, that like the President's other sons, Konn had sense."

"Except when it is shadowed by an overblown sense of his own importance, and he is trying to prove himself smarter than we are," Kryslie continued. She would have gone on but Tymos cut her off.

"Let his father deal with him. He is not our concern."

"No, but the Jacen Tyr will have to respond and retrieve those escape pods as well as those from Obs 1."

"True, but they will need to stay here a while anyway. So one of us can transmit over and see what Llaimos wants, and the other can stay here and monitor things. Genesis 1 will be well enough for now. It won't take us long to catch up to them, our speed is greater."

"You go," Kryslie decided after a brief pause. "If I get near President Reslic, I am likely to tell him exactly what I think of his son. Besides, while I can still vaguely sense 'my boy', it will be better if I am not distracted."

Tymos grinned faintly, not because the current situation was a cause for levity, but because of the colourful description of Konn Reslic that Kryslie was inventing in her mind.

He quickly sent a microburst message, coded to the Jacen Tyr, providing the coordinates for a long range beam. He was ready, mere minutes later, for the appearance of the glowing oval beam terminus in the open area at the rear of the cockpit. He wasted no time transmitting along it.

Kryslie slipped into the pilot's couch and took over monitoring the sensor readings, and paying attention to the sense of Gareth Pitt, still faintly in her mind.

The probe was still sending data, but the first thing that she realised was that the attractor beam had stopped, or at least was no longer directed towards the direction where Genesis 1 had been. The planet bound Ciriot had lost that prey. On her screen was the drifting hulk of Obs 2 – a huge hole blasted in the port side. The disintegrating weapon that had caused the hole, had not penetrated right through. A brief active scan told her all she needed. Life support, engines, in fact all systems – were dead. Most of the escape pods had been jettisoned, judging from the smaller holes in the hull where they had been. She counted three that were still in position near the bridge of the ship.

The hulk slowly rotated, revealing a crude boarding hatch attached to the forward section of the hull. Dark streaks around it, revealed that entry had been achieved by burning through the hull. The entities that had forced their way in were gone. Had the bridge crew managed to escape, or had they been captured or killed? Nothing alive remained on the ship. President Reslic would handle that situation, but she hoped all the crew had escaped. She knew the depraved tortures that the Ciriot like to inflict on strong willed victims. Even Konn Reslic did not deserve that.

What had Konn been thinking? That the cloaked Ciriot ship would have followed Genesis 1? He had been meant to watch out for that and report, and then follow Genesis 1. Now he couldn't. But what had betrayed Obs 2's position? And what kind of weapon had disabled the shields to allow the destructive beam to hit the hull?

Kryslie searched for the communications channel being used by the Ciriot – not that she would be able to understand their clicking speech without a translator unit – but the tone might tell her something.

She was assuming that the base below was in contact with the cloaked ship, and knowing that its prey had escaped, would want it found again.

Alarms began and Kryslie checked other sensors. Visuals showed that the Jacen Tyr had de-cloaked – a huge statement of implied might. A flight of Tymorean interceptors launched to go after a flight of Ciriot scouts that had launched from the hidden base. However, neither event was the cause of the alarms her sensors were giving her. One was the proximity alarm from something that had passed very close to her. Three others were from the elemental sensors. She sent her brother a mental warning.

"The visible scouts from the base are decoys. There are others around. Three just passed close to me."

She received back, "I will warn Reslic. Have you a location on the original ship?"

"No. Just the fast moving bogeys. I have all our shields up at full strength, so warn me when you are about to return."

# Chapter 11

Tymos was met by his brother, Llaimos, and they hugged briefly before he pulled away to nod acknowledgement to Jono Reslic, who was the President Governor of Tymorea and the Commander in Chief of the Tymorean Fleet. Reslic, bowed to Tymos and greeted him with the formal words, "We are honoured by your presence, Great One."

Tymos glanced at his brother, for if he were to hold to protocol, then Llaimos's reason for being on the Jacen Tyr had precedence over any other request, yet he knew that Reslic wanted to talk to him as well. Llaimos sent mentally, "Later, my purpose can wait."

"Sir, you need to speak with me?"

Although he out-ranked the Tymorean Governor, Tymos did not feel comfortable neglecting the indication of respect.

"I would welcome your knowledge of the current situation, Great One."

"Yes," Tymos agreed, gesturing to the hatchway that led to the strategy centre.

When Reslic moved, Tymos caught sight of another figure that was standing back out of the way. He recognised Stenn, his friend, and another of Reslic's sons. He was not wearing a fleet uniform, which suggested that his presence was in a civilian capacity. The figure followed Reslic, keeping his attention on his father, and not even glancing Tymos's way.

Four of the Jacen Tyr's senior crew were waiting for them in the strategy room. After receiving the deferent greetings of the four men, Tymos began his report.

He summarised all that he knew that was relevant to the Genesis mission and what he knew of the possible Ciriot outpost on the surface of the planet. He included the actions originating on the planet and his deductions relating to the attack on Obs 1. When he got to mentioning Obs 2, he chose his words carefully – intending his criticism of Konn to be perfectly factual and fair. After all, he had not been present when Obs 2 had been attacked. He only knew that Konn had been highly concerned about his brother.

Tymos had no doubt that Reslic would thoroughly investigate the matter, and merely nodded slightly when Reslic said, "With your leave, Great One," and turned to lead his officers towards the bridge.

Stenn remained with Llaimos but was now looking at his feet. Tymos went over to his friend and gave him a friendly thump on the back. "You look well," he greeted.

"I am well enough, Great One," Stenn said formally, looking up because protocol did not let him ignore those of higher rank. "I have been assigned as an aide to my father since I recovered. Now I am to assist Great One Llaimos."

Tymos gave him a second, gentler thump as the intracomm was activating a squadron to overfly the planetary coordinates of the surface base that Tymos had supplied, to try to locate a way in from the surface.

"Stenn, you don't need to be formal with me. We're friends."

"You are most kind, Great One. It is just…"

Tymos knew what he didn't say. Stenn was recalling the time, three years before, when his power had been usurped by an evil entity and he had been rogue.

Llaimos rescued him by suggesting that they move into Reslic's private cabin to talk. Tymos agreed, turning his mind to wondering what it was that Llaimos had come to say, and walked in unison with his brother, letting Stenn follow – as the well trained assistant.

Their talk had to wait for more announcements. The salvage team was to assemble in the shuttlebay for a briefing. They were to recover the escape pods from the surface and land an infiltration team. Llaimos had been given the Commander's stateroom for his use. Now he gestured to Tymos to sit in one of the armchairs. Stenn moved to stand behind Llaimos.

When the intracomm fell silent, Llaimos began, "The Elder, Jak, has spoken of a seeing that I believe is relevant to the situation here. The details are not clear – but he spoke of hearing an old man's voice, a man addressed as Exlan. He had the sense of being enclosed by rock and having a group of people around him, listening to the voice as if it were important."

Tymos felt the same sense of premonition that must have alerted his brother.

"Yes," he said thoughtfully. "I felt disquiet by having Ciriot on the surface of Aerdna. We are all part of the life below. We pledged them a rebirth."

"But not into slavery," Llaimos added with passion. "We need to know if the minds of those below have been interfered with – and we need to know the words of Exlan."

Stenn watched as the two Great Ones pondered for some moments. He felt insignificant and unworthy to be hearing of a prophecy. The Guardians of Peace blessed the Elders with their visions, not people like him. Even though Great One Kryslie had healed him three years ago, people still looked at him with suspicion. He couldn't blame them. He had been rogue, his power being used by an evil entity. Many thought that being made aide to his father, the President Governor, was so he could be watched.

"There was more?" Tymos stated. Llaimos nodded.

"He also saw, in a subsequent vision, an old woman walking out of a blackened wasteland. It was like he spoke to her and asked her name. It was Nala, and she told him – 'I am old and I have things that must be said. Of all my kin, only one is left. I go to her – my great grandchild.' Does this mean anything to you?"

Into Tymos's mind came a vision, as had been passed from Jak to Llaimos. Jak had said, "Perhaps. Great One, this will mean something to you."

Tymos studied the face of the old woman – brown and weathered and with a fine bone structure. Her demeanour was proud and her clothing oddly familiar. He let his mind flick through memories.

"A gypsy," he breathed. At that moment, he knew her words would be important.

He sensed Llaimos did not understand the reference.

"On Earth, there is an ethnic group, originally Romany, but over time becoming a mixture of ethnics. They were called gypsies, because they were always travelling from place to place. Many Tymorean missionaries have moved with them. This, I think, I need to act on, and soon."

Yet he couldn't do anything immediately – Genesis 1 was his priority, but when the human astronauts were safely back, then he would seek Nala. A prickle run up and down his spine. The gypsy's prophecy would be important. For Earth.

Suddenly he was impatient to leave, but he needed to know all that had happened to the Obs ships and on the planet. He stood abruptly, no longer able to sit still. Llaimos copied him, and they returned to the strategy room.

Reslic, overseeing the activities of various teams, was instantly aware of the return of the two Great Ones.

"Great One, your deduction was correct. The outpost is indeed Ciriot. It is a ship buried under the remains of a town. However, a part of the hull is still visible above the ground. The infiltration team has landed, and are looking for a way in. The salvage team report that all the pods are empty."

Llaimos and Tymos maintained neutral expressions, not betraying their concern that the Tymoreans must have been captured by the Ciriot. A sharp intake of breath betrayed Stenn's realisation of the same fact. He must know that two of his brothers were missing. Yet he said nothing.

"What of the ships that launched from the planet? And those that Krys mentioned?" Tymos asked.

"Two immediately went to hyper speed, in two different directions, each emitting multi directional, multi frequency signals. They are being pursued."

"Calling for help," Tymos mused. "But that other ship was still around. It did not follow Genesis 1 when it left."

Reslic reported. "However, the other four ships engaged our flight, and were destroyed. We haven't sensed the others."

"That unsettles me," Tymos admitted. "They have not shown themselves, so we cannot know the capabilities of those ships or the phantom ship. I was surprised that Krys and I, as well as Obs 3, detected no pursuers going after Genesis 1."

"Particularly when they were so intent in drawing the human ship to the planet," Llaimos murmured.

"I am certain that they saw and identified our observation ships as being Tymorean," Tymos stated. "I think the phantom ship did not want to face three to one odds. They maintained their advantage, by staying cloaked when we were not expecting them, nor any other race."

"Why did the Obs ships not sense the proximity of the phantom?" Llaimos asked.

"That is an excellent question. The proximity alarm on Genesis 1 did not activate either. Yet I believe that their proximity was the initial reason that the human ship deviated from the planned course."

Stenn coughed self-consciously, almost flinching when both Great Ones looked at him.

"Great Ones, since the return, Governor Xyron has been examining the ships left by the Ciriot. Some of the ships come from places that we have been unable to identify. No two ships were completely alike."

Tymos's mind immediately went back to the war, when he was sabotaging ships of the Ciriot. "Yes, as pirates, the steal what they need to survive. The question remains, do they know how to replicate the technology they acquire?"

"Are you asking whether they stole some of our ships?" Llaimos asked. "If they discovered weaknesses?"

He looked thoughtfully at Stenn, who had gone very pale and swallowed convulsively. When he began to speak, his voice was unsteady. "They hate us. And if they did discover a weapon that worked against us…they would find someone who could duplicate it."

"You?" Tymos asked gently and with sympathy.

The laugh sounded like some strange bird call. "No, I was never interested in science. Though my ship was taken from me."

"Then it may be possible that they have discovered ways to get control of our ships," Llaimos proposed.

"Not control…just to get past some of our protections. They blew Obs 1 into atoms, and Obs 2 has an enormous hole in its side."

"Great One, you must be most careful," Stenn pleaded.

The sentiment behind the warning was plain to Tymos who move to give his friend a brief embrace.

"We will be, and will make them regret taking on your brothers."

Stenn stood straighter, taking that as a promise.

"I don't suppose you learnt anything about their weapons?" Tymos asked with a wistful lift of his brow. A shake of his head and a faint wry grin was Stenn's only answer.

"Oh well, never mind. Perhaps you would go and tell the transportation officer to program the long-range beam to my ship. I might want to leave fast."

Stenn trotted off, his posture straight and purposeful.


Tymos turned to his brother. "We need to know how much the Ciriot have interfered with the population in the vaults. I sure that they must have. The temptation would have been irresistible. You might have to go there without Krys and myself."

"That I will do," Llaimos agreed. "I can call on as many experienced missionaries as I need. Do you want to be advised of what we find there?"

"Yes, even though Genesis 1 and Earth are my current priority. The report from the infiltration team will tell us a great deal."

"Will you stay for that?"

"I feel that I must."


Even though Tymos calculated how long it would take the shuttle to land the team, how long it might take to find the ground entrance to the hidden base, and to overcome the inhabitants – time passed slowly, seeming to be a day cycle instead of mere hours.  He spent most of the waiting time pacing the strategy room, or staring at the globe that showed the position of his ship and the flitting Tymorean interceptor ships. He also watched, hawklike, for the position of the phantom ship. There had been no sign of it since the Jacen Tyr had arrived and uncloaked.

The Ciriot pirate clans were cowards, attacking only when they were sure they had the upper hand. One look at the Tymorean flagship should have sent them fleeing…

Yet the Ciriot were vengeful creatures…

# Chapter 12

Stenn Reslic approached, distracting Tymos from his thoughts.

"Great One, The infiltration team has returned from the planet. The Commander in Chief asks if you wish to attend the debrief in his private meeting room."

"Yes."

Tymos turned his pacing into a purposeful stride, feeling the need for some activity after the long wait. When he entered the meeting room, followed by Llaimos and Stenn, Reslic was alone.

"Great One, you will be relieved that the two Ciriot ships that went to hyper speed have been neutralised. "

Tymos nodded. That was one less concern.

"The buried ship is now deserted. Do you wish it destroyed?"

"Have we copied any data from within?"

"Data transfer is underway."

"I think…leave it intact, but sealed so that no one can enter or leave through it. If we destroy it, it may damage the integrity of the vaults. Do you know if the Ciriot penetrated the vaults?"

"Commander Wexen will have the details when he arrives," Reslic told him.

The Commander announced himself moments later, and entered accompanied by Jonnsen, Reslic's eldest son, who was the Captain of Obs 1. Both men, on seeing Tymos and Llaimos, immediately bowed and spoke the traditional greeting, "Your presence honours us, Great Ones."

They straightened, both still dressed in armour with only the headpiece removed. Jonnsen's was blackened and scraped.

Reslic gestured for the Great Ones to sit, before seating himself. Then, looking at the newcomers, said, "Report."

"My team had very little to do, Commander," Wexen began. "When we arrived, Captain Reslic and the others from the grounded pods had the six Ciriot cornered and were in the process of freeing the six captured crew from Obs 2."

Reslic turned his attention to his son, who took that as a directive to speak.

"I had directed the pods to power towards the planet, Sir. When the Ciriot began firing on us, they targeted the engines, so we fell uncontrolled to the surface. The landing was hard, and we were all thoroughly shaken when our pods finished bouncing and rolling, but we were all basically unharmed. Since we were armoured, and armed, we decided to find the base. We found the entrance when two Ciriot came out – probably intending to make us prisoners…"

Tymos ignored the report of the fight, but became more intent with the mention of two Ciriot prisoners."

"You will need to keep them within a security field. I have no wish for any of our people to be infected if they succeed in suiciding."

He would like to question the creatures himself, but he doubted that they would reveal information easily, and they would need a voice translator. To get anything helpful from them would take more time than he had.

Captain Wexen spoke again. "A download of the ships computer banks is underway. We have completed a thorough search of the ship and a series of interconnected rock caverns. The Ciriot have been infiltrating the vaults – their traces have been found going in about 10 miles. There are Aeronite remains in one of the furthest caverns, as well as a cache of local goods."

Tymos met his brother's look. Llaimos merely nodded and confirmed in mind speech, "I will go there."

"What do you wish us to do with the ships computer and internal systems, Commander?"

Reslic deferred to Tymos, who directed, "I have instructed the Commander to leave the ship intact, and to seal the ship both from the vaults and from the surface. Can you lock all the ship's systems and the computer so that we are the only ones who can access them?"

"Yes, Sir, but what if more of the Ciriot come and can break such locks? Wouldn't it be better to destroy or remove the computer?"

The question triggered a rapid series of images to flick through Tymos's mind. He paused to recall them, and finally said, "No. Our lock out techniques should suffice. The data on that computer might one day be needed there."

Wexen seemed sceptical, but he merely said, "As you wish, Great One."

Reslic noticed the look and said, "We will maintain a watch – in case more Ciriot ships come to this place. How are the captives you rescued?"

"They are all with the medics, Sir. Captain Konn Reslic will come here as soon as the medics release him."

"Go and bring him here as soon as they do." Reslic again glanced at Tymos, who guessed his implied question.

"I will leave the debriefing to you, Commander."

Reslic gestured a dismissal and Wexen and Jonnsen left the room.

Llaimos had been silent during the report, now glanced at Stenn who was carefully edging his way behind the chairs. He made no comment, simply turned to face his brother and asked mentally, "What can Konn Reslic tell you that is important?"

"He can tell how it was that the phantom ship found his ship and damn near destroyed it," Tymos thought fiercely.

"Did you not say that the ship forced Genesis 1 from hyperspeed?" Llaimos provoked silently.

"Genesis 1 was not cloaked, nor does it have as many shields and protections as Obs 2!"

"The ship located Obs 1…"

"I must check, but I believe Obs 1 was not cloaked when it first went to check on the planet," Tymos mentioned his theory. "So they were recognised and then, the Ciriot base was actively searching for them. They should not have known of our other two ships."

A loud indrawn breath caused Tymos to look around at Stenn, and see him intently studying his feet. Then he looked away and saw Wexen leading Konn Reslic into the room.

In that look, he took in the torn uniform, currently pulled into a semblance of 'on'. It was not only shredded, but liberally discoloured by patches of blood. Konn's face, and likely his whole body was now coated with the spray on wound sealant, which did nothing to hide the grazes, cuts and bruises.

The unfocussed look on Konn's face drew Tymos from his seat. "A moment, Sir," he requested of Reslic, as he crossed the distance. He placed a hand over Konn's eyes and sent healing energy into him, to heal the concussion and to sense what else the Ciriot had done to him. He reached the conclusion that those who had questioned him, had been in a hurry.

"It appears, Sir, that whatever the Ciriot wanted to know, they did not find out from Captain Reslic. And since he proved so…resistant…they did not have time to interrogate the other prisoners; nor it seems could they implant an energy mote into him. No doubt all the space was occupied."

"Thick," Stenn muttered very faintly to himself.

Konn's face flushed red and then paled again in remembered humiliation and guilt. He had disobeyed the intent of Great One's command.

"Thank you, Great One," Konn said stiffly, as his enormous headache eased.

"Report, Captain." Reslic insisted as Tymos moved away, and Llaimos directed Stenn from the room before him.

Tymos returned to his seat, rested his elbows on the arm supports and steepled his fingers in front of his mouth. Reslic was also seated, but Konn was not offered that respite. He stood at attention, his uniform – what was left of it – falling open.

If his Commander was driving home a lesson, Konn kept his face impassive. Only the alternate reddening and paling betrayed his humiliation as he recited facts without attempting to justify himself.

Even knowing that the Ciriot phantom ship would be looking for him, he had switched to active sensors, and gone to rescue the pods from Obs 1. The mind images that accompanied the recitation, were clear in Tymos's mind, for he had made the mind link when he had healed the discommoded Captain.

Konn had directed his ship to approach the nearest escape pod, moving with all stealth, then put a tractor beam, on it to bring it into the flight deck. The instant that it had come within the ship's shields, all systems on Obs 2 had gone dead. His ship had become an uncloaked, defenceless, stationary target.

Only the superb training of all Tymorean fleet members had prevented mass deaths. In the instant that all systems went dead, they had sealed their armour and switched to emergency oxygen. Mere seconds later, all heard a loud explosion that was the outer shell of three sections explosively decompressing.

Emergency power came up, and all crew were ordered to escape pods. The six bridge crew, including Konn, had been trapped by the decompression seals slamming shut. Too late, they had realised that the Ciriot pirates were cutting into the hull on the other side.

Reslic questioned Konn without pity, ensuring that he learned every relevant detail. Even when the recitation told of how the six on the bridge were caught up in some kind of tangling net, he demanded details.

What the Ciriot Leader had done to Konn in an effort to make him talk was horrendous, but it was not the worst type of torture that Tymos knew the Ciriot were capable of.

The captors, using mechanical translators to convert the clicking Ciriot speech to Tymorean – had demanded to know about Genesis 1. Konn had not told them anything, even though he really knew very little about it.

Seeing the image of the Ciriot face in Konn's mind, Tymos memorised it. For it seemed that in their own places, the Ciriot did not go cowled or armoured.

Reslic finished his questions, and turned to Tymos. "Have you anything to add, Great One?" Reslic asked. Tymos shook his head. In Konn's mind was the justification that he had gone to find his brother. Only his brother had ended up rescuing him.

While Reslic mercilessly recited the outcome of his defiance of orders, Tymos checked in with his sister. He heard in his mind, "Two of the bogeys just flew past, very close, and went to hyperspeed. Nothing on the big phantom."

"Anything from your boy?"

"The link is fading, but so far, all I have sensed is normal."

"Obs 3?"

"Their microbursts are all negative – no sign of pursuers."

A third mind voice entered the conversation, that of Llaimos. "Tymos, the ensign who is going through the recorded logs from Genesis 1's audio have heard an odd noise. A kind of 'clang'. It was followed by the activated proximity alarm. The humans were agitated for a time, then after checking all systems, disregarded it."

Alarm surged through Tymos as the part of Konn's report about the power loss when the pod came into Obs 2's flight deck – within the shields. Could they have sent in a bomb of some kind? Perhaps, but Obs 1 had not done anything like that. The important question seemed to be that of how the Ciriot had deactivated the shields on Obs 1.

An electromagnetic pulse could have blacked out all systems, but the Obs ships had shields to transmute such a pulse. Obs 2 could have unknowingly brought a pulse generator within – what if the Ciriot had put something on Genesis 1's hull? Inside their shields…

Reslic's voice, as he iterated the point that with Obs 1 out of commission, the other two ships were needed to provide protection for the human ship, brought another idea into Tymos's mind.

Firstly of the vengeful nature of the Ciriot, deadly enemies of the Tymoreans, who had stolen Genesis 1 from within the protection of the Obs ships. Now, two of those three ships were destroyed or badly damaged. Obs 3 was well away, but his and Krys's ship wasn't. The Ciriot could be looking to destroy the third ship before leaving the area, and they thought they were safe and unsuspected.

Tymos stiffened and strode from the room. "Krys!" he mind sent as he headed for the beam terminus on the flight deck. "Get ready to leave. We have to catch up to Obs 3. Don't drop any shields until I say so."

He sent a quick mental farewell to Llaimos, as he stepped into the long-range beam and warned his sister.

"Great One, the beam is becoming unstable," the operator warned.

A surge of power reached him through the mind link with his sister. He reached for her mind and got no answer.

He transmitted.

# Chapter 13

Tymos seemed to fall to the floor of the ship. The terminus blinked out of existence, leaving him in darkness and silence.

In microseconds he knew he was not in vacuum, as there was still air. Seconds later dim red lights came on and he saw Kryslie lying on the floor.

Caustic language, unbecoming of a Great One, seared his mind as Kryslie pushed herself up. She had sensed his "What happened?"

"Just as you contacted me, I noticed that the shield power was falling. Something slammed into them so hard that the ship began to roll. When I dropped the anti-transmission field for you, something hit the ship and everything went dark."

The answer came to Tymos in a flash. "It must be some kind of matter energy weapon, and the anti-transmission field blocked it. Obs 1 and Obs 2 probably did not have that kind of shield up. There must have been an electromagnetic pulse generator with it."

"Figure the whys later, bro. Have you got your armour sealed?"

"How long to the restart?"

"Two minutes and sixteen seconds." Kryslie was mentally counting down. She heard her brother sealing his armour. "Why haven't they taken another go at us?"

They both heard, "My guess is that they are saving their skins," from Llaimos. "Reslic sent interceptors off – the engineers identified the frequency signature of the phantom ship's engines."

In their darkened ship, without the air cyclers operating, the silence was not absolute. Tymos's suit comm picked up ominous creaks and groans from the hull plates. Aware of his recognition of the sounds, Kryslie admitted, "My ears are still ringing." Then she added, "We did not need this!"

"They thought we were Obs 3. My guess is that if they think they have disabled us, they have now gone after Genesis 1. I think they have tagged their hull. Can you still sense Pitt?"

"No, and I won't be able to find him again at this distance."

The restart sequence flashed up on the main screen, the air cyclers started up, the light brightened and the bridge systems began to activate in sequence. Normal bridge sounds returned.

Tymos and Kryslie stood and moved to the computers, restarting the most vital subsystems. Damage control was first. Kryslie read the damage reports, checked the affected systems, whilst Tymos began a visual check, section by section. They worked seamlessly, their minds linked like they were part of one body.

"Hull integrity compromised, tail section," Kryslie warned, knowing her brother as almost there. "Manoeuvring engines powering up in the green."

It did not take Tymos long to find the problem – a metre wide hole where the hull had been disintegrated. The atmosphere here was thinner, but the emergency force-weld was holding. He set to work, first wresting up a floor plate and carrying it to line up with the hole. Then he pushed with all his strength to get the panel through the force interface. With a clang, the panel was sucked through and forced into the conformation of the wall. He finished the repairs by squirting permaseal around the edge of the panel. The gel hardened quickly under the pressure of the force weld. Under foot, he felt the engines coming up to idle.

Even though they both worked quickly, repairing overloaded circuits and damaged sensors, it took far too long to get the ship ready for hyperspace. Time neither felt they could afford.

Tymos endured his sister's mental mutterings about Konn Reslic and what he deserved until she repeated the lengthy list for the third time.

"If he survives his Commander's dressing down, on top of the Ciriot attempt to break him – I thought of asking to have him assigned to us," Tymos commented.

"He won't survive me!" Kryslie threatened, but she wasn't that angry anymore. "I get what you mean. Creatures like that energy mote three years ago won't be able to affect him."

"Exactly! He might be useful."

"We are all green," Kryslie said. "Strap in."

She took them to hyperspeed, along the course of Genesis 1 that she had programmed from memory, since their nav computer memory had been wiped and it would have taken too long to reload from the back-up. Tymos, reset all the sensors from default settings to maximum sensitivity, and added subprograms to detect the phantom ships engine signature as well as the elemental signature of the Ciriot. Then he extrapolated the course of Genesis 1 to estimate an intercept position.

The Earth ship had left almost ten hours before them but could not travel as fast as their ship, which was exponentially faster. They should catch up to Genesis 1 within three hours. However, when they did reach the interception point there was no sign of the ship, not even the traces of their exhaust trail.

Tymos continued flying along the expected course of Genesis 1 for a further half an hour and then dropped back into normal space.

"When did we last get a signal from Obs 3?" he asked.

"Just before we left. All was well then, according to Captain Ostin. I'll ask for an update."

Kryslie sent the high-power microburst to Obs 3, with the urgent coding, and waited for a reply. When ten minutes had elapsed and no reply had been received, she looked at the signal properties or earlier messages.

"Damn, Tym, all the messages relayed to us for the six hours before we left, are identical. Even down to the time signature."

"Obs 3 should be around here. If something is blocking our transmissions, it has to be that phantom ship. Put full power through the comm set on the highest frequency and see if you can punch it through. If not, try the low frequency band."

Even as Kryslie was doing that, she was thinking at her twin, "Those creatures must also be near, and probably have Genesis in their sights."

"I hope they have not got closer than that," Tymos fervently wished. He was busy bringing up a schematic of Genesis 1's intended course, their own course, and was considering what might have happened, as well as when and where.

The most likely, and worst scenario was that the phantom ship had caught up to Genesis 1. Which could have occurred up to six hours before their own ship had been space worthy again. So what might that phantom ship do once it found its prey?

They would be wary, Tymos decided. They would want to be sure that there were no other ships shadowing the juicy target. So they would probably shadow Genesis 1 for a while.

Had they noticed Obs 3 and disabled or destroyed the ship? If they had sent out a signal dampening field, any mayday would not be heard.

If Obs 3 was out of action, or the phantom ship thought it was alone…what then? They would no longer be able to use the energy tether on Genesis 1, not since Krys had programmed the extra shield as a default. And the other shields on the ship were as strong as those on Tymorean ships.

"Krys? Anything?"

"Not yet, bro. No, wait a minute…Obs 3 are okay. They lost the trail of Genesis 1 about six hours ago. They are doing a hop search around that position. I am sending their current coordinates and their search pattern through to the nav computer."

The data was incorporated into Tymos's schematic.

"That damn phantom must be blocking signals from Genesis 1," Tymos allowed his irritation to show in his voice. "They could have been re-broadcasting Genesis 1's signals at a time delay, so Obs 3 is searching in the wrong area. Like they were doing with those messages from Obs 3 itself."

"Their hop search might turn up something," Kryslie proposed, but privately she doubted it. Hopping in and out of hyperspace in accordance with a particular search pattern, might allow them to cover a wider area, but they could just as easily miss their target. "I think we would be better off searching back along Genesis 1's track. They obviously didn't get this far."

"I have been working on that idea. I estimate that the phantom ship could have caught up with them any time after four hours into the flight." Tymos indicated that point on the schematic. "They probably did as they had before – forced it off course. I'm going to head back, sensors at max to pick up the Ciriot trace elements and the phantom ship's exhaust trail."

"Then I will pull up the nav charts for this region and see if I can find somewhere they can duck into and hide. They won't have an easy time breaking those shields I put on Genesis 1."

Confident of their abilities and those of their ship, they began their search.

# Chapter 14

**Prophesy of Exlan**

Five generations had passed since the sun had shone on Aerdna's frozen surface. Exlan had never seen the sun, but he described a beautiful place, so clearly that the respectful crowd around him could almost feel the warmth, imagine the light and the smells of fresh air, plants and flowers.

The vision, preserved from long ago, gave people hope. It was the promise of the Great Ones who had given the people the means to survive.

Llaimos and Stenn transmitted into an unused section of the tunnels. They moved carefully into the occupied areas, speaking respectfully and asking the way to Exlan, the Wise One. News of his death had spread, and the strangers were told, regretfully, that this was so.

As they moved, Llaimos tested the minds of people at random. He found the hope of a new sun was still strong in many minds. In some he sensed a shadow – like something ominous – waiting and brooding.

As they moved from the underground city to the less populated fringes of the vaults, the people grew more savage. The man with an inner peace stood out, to his mind, like a beacon. Llaimos went to him and found a very old man tending the injury of one of the people. He looked up with glazed eyes, milky in the artificial light. His mind touched that of Llaimos.

"Great One," he voiced. "You do me honour."

He would have prostrated himself had not Llaimos gently lifted him to his feet. His patient, now bandaged, scuttled off.

"Wise One, what is your name?" Llaimos asked.

"I am Julinir. My Grandfather was Xan and my grandson is Axir, now leader of the convocation."

"We seek one who has heard the prophecy of Exlan. I am Llaimos."

"Come, Great One, and I will tell it to you," Julinir promised. "Your friend is welcome too."

They followed the man to a plain little dwelling, in an area where the cavern roof arched into a dome high overhead. Stenn, looking around, preferred that to the warrens of the underground city.

Inside the little dwelling, Julinir offered them water and a place to sit. He stood, respectfully, and introduced his topic. "Listen to the prophecy of Exlan, son of Mogath, grandson of Xezir, Peace Lord and Saviour."

After a pause, he continued in a strong voice.

"Our world is about to be reborn. Soon we will be able to live like our ancestors – on the surface – in warmth, light, and fresh air. Then, the frozen seeds will germinate and grow. Yet there are also seeds that are dormant and are weeds. These are waiting to grow and overcome us, to draw evil here. These seeds give rise to hatred and jealousy and are nurtured by evil forces – alien forces.

"Our world, newly lightened, but covered with a dark cloud, smothering all that is good in us, smothering hope. We have the power within us to fight it, but it is dormant. Without it we cannot root out the evil and destroy it. Without it, the aliens can move amongst us, within our defences. The weeds will grow unsuspected. When the time comes they will attract the evil ones, drawing them here to enslave us."

The old man fell silent, giving reverence to the prophecy.

"Wise One, how do you interpret these words?" Llaimos asked.

The old man spoke quietly. "I am an old man. Once I could teach the children and imbue them with the vision of paradise. That power has weakened. I can no longer give the children the will to see Aerdna regain its rightful place. Instead of working towards that, the new generation wants an easy life and to pleasure themselves and they no longer listen to me. The population is growing, when for generations we have kept it steady. Fewer of the young ones want to work the hydroponic farms that we all depend on. My wisdom is no longer heeded because they listen to the insidious whispers of evil. They cannot see they are weakening us all."

Julinir looked pleadingly at Llaimos. "Great One, can you teach them – help them? Exlan had such a power of personality that everyone listened to him and believed. I cannot do that, so the children who should be our saviours are becoming our downfall."

Llaimos sensed the desperation in the plea. "Yes," he promised. "I have seen the need." After a thoughtful pause, he asked, "Have you noticed people suddenly changing their manner?"

Julinir nodded. "Not in large numbers – one here, one there. But it is increasing."

"Wise One, we promised the people of Aerdna our protection. You shall have it." Llaimos fell silent as a vision of the future of Aerdna – as the aliens wanted it – filled his mind. The aliens – the Ciriot – had turned on their former allies, in remembered hatred. The Aeronites had failed to subdue Tymorea for them and Ciriot had died in large numbers there without gaining any of the treasures of Tymorea. Their antipathy burned fiercely. They would enslave those who had failed them.

"Wise One, I thank you for your wisdom. I must return to my ship for a time, to bring your words to my brother and sister. They fight the Ciriot in a distant place. I will return after that. You have my word as a Great One."

Stenn had said little, the whole time he had followed Llaimos. Once they were alone again, he ventured his thoughts.

"Is it Earth that your siblings must protect?"

"Yes."

"Have you considered that on such a world, more strongly protected; it will be harder for them to work by stealth to weaken the people?" Stenn asked.

"I have. And something is nudging my mind – something I learnt, I think, from the mind of a Ciriot." Llaimos tried to grasp the fleeting thought.

Stenn noted, "Here the people are simple, unsophisticated – closer to primal. Earth humans are more educated, more aware... they will notice abhorrent behaviour and act."

Llaimos spoke thoughtfully, "Seeds waiting to grow, to draw evil – how?"

"They would have to come in ships," Stenn proposed. "If they intend conquest, they would have to learn strategic targets – have a beacon to aim for. How could a person become that?"

"How indeed," Llaimos wondered. "Perhaps the prophecy of Nala will tell us more. When we return to the ship I will organise what I will need when I return here. I want you to tell this prophecy to my brother and sister. Perhaps it is to them that the answer will be revealed."

But even as Stenn gave the expected agreement, "Your will, Great One," his mind froze and his body felt ill and sweaty.

He knew how it might be done. It had been done to him. When he tried to speak of it, he could not. And now, he feared that the evil entity that had possessed him three years ago, still held his mind.

# Chapter 15

Vincent left off waiting for contact with the returning Genesis 1 when Daniel relayed a message from Bynan.

"Basoli is acting really strange."

"I will transmit by long range beam to Washington and talk to him," Vincent decided.

Daniel gestured to one of the loitering missionaries to direct the beam to the safe location in Washington. To Vincent he added, "Maydean is watching the WSRA HQ building. I will let him know you are coming."

Vincent nodded and prepared his appearance, taking up the ubiquitous laptop case. When he arrived in the vacant and 'forgotten' office in the Washington Hospital, it was still late morning. He left the building and took a taxi to WSRA headquarters.

There was a great deal of activity around the building, with people watching re-plays of the launch and progress reports on screens facing the street and in the lobby. In addition to that, there were camera teams standing by – even though Genesis 1 was not expected back on the tracking screens for six more days.

A man detached himself from the group of loitering reporters and began to walk across the lobby without seeming to be interested in anyone. He matched paces with Vincent and paused as Vincent spoke to the security desk and quoted a meeting with Basoli.

Vincent turned to Maydean as if the man had been with him all the time.

"The group upstairs have special passes," Maydean murmured. "Issued by the WSRA board. None of them intend to leave. They sleep up there and have food sent up."

"Is there a list of names of those who were to be there?" Vincent asked.

"No, the passes were sent to important scientific journals and major media networks. They are sticking to Basoli like leeches."

"They can't be expecting anything yet," Vincent murmured. "Or are they? Stay available. I will talk to security about letting you up if I need you."

Vincent knew the way to Basoli's top floor office, and had to pass another security check before being allowed on the floor. He immediately noticed the signs of the long term occupation in the open foyer and wrinkled his nose. The guard noticed his glance but betrayed nothing.

Every one of the twelve lounging men, who had usurped chairs from somewhere, eyed Vincent with intense scrutiny. He appeared to ignore them. When he spoke to Bynan he pitched his voice so that the nearest reporter heard only, "...collect psych profiles if they are ready."

Bynan paged Basoli and passed on the message. She directed Vincent to enter.

Once in Basoli's office, he knew Bynan's observations were correct.

"I don't know about psych profiles," Basoli apologised, as he half stood to greet the one he knew of as a doctor.

Vincent sat and waved that aside. "That was for the vagrants outside," he explained. "I thought you might appreciate a non-critical chat. Why don't you get security to remove them?"

"The Board..."Basoli began.

Vincent interrupted. "Should be invited to visit you. They will, I think, be unimpressed by the mess out there. I am sure you find it unpleasant and their hovering distracting."

Basoli leant back in his chair and relaxed slightly. "Some of them represent important media networks. WSRA needs their good will."

"If that is so, I think it might prove interesting to get from those media networks, the name of the contacts who gave out the passes. Then find out who they gave the passes to and what media section they represent."

Basoli considered that. "They are like vultures. I cannot go anywhere without them following to see if I make a mistake. Are you saying that some of them are not what they purport to be?"

"I can almost guarantee that," Vincent stated. "If they are truly interested in the Deep Space Project – they will not learn much here. You are an administrator, even if you are to fly out to Terra 1 before Genesis is due back. The most up to date news will be at the bases, not here."

"That is what Bynan keeps telling them," Basoli growled. "I don't know what I would do without her. I am trying to figure a way to get those vultures out there, interested in the Deep Space Display at the University."

Vincent smiled. "Get them free passes. I suspect that might interest them. Then have security stop them returning."

Basoli relaxed enough to smile. "Let me see if I can organise that." He turned his attention to his computer.

Vincent watched him and saw a fleeting look of anger cross his face. His face was hard as he typed instructions. He finished with a grunt of satisfaction.

"The Chancellor will send the invitations; Bynan will check names and media affiliations so the invitations can be personally inscribed. Apparently Arthur bin Halil will be there this afternoon, so the invites will double as security passes. I have requested the two most influential board members to visit later today and they can see the mess for themselves."

Vincent nodded with a smile. "So with that problem being dealt with, how is the other problem – with your brother?"

He deliberately mentioned Reg Basoli even though Ron had not blamed anything on him.

Basoli sighed, admitting that Vincent had guessed right and not fighting it.

"That young man you recommended is a credit to his profession," Basoli remarked, relaxing further. "The federal investigators have assured me that I have done nothing wrong buying up shares in the company."

"But?" Vincent prompted when Basoli fell silent.

"But my brother has been involved in a number of highly questionable deals over the past few years. Not illegal – just skirting the edge of legal. This time I think he slipped up and has been caught lying to the securities commission."

"Will that affect you?" Vincent asked.

"Not directly," Basoli revealed. "I have an accountant who looks after the shares and acts as my proxy. He has records of all instructions I give him and all actions he has taken as my proxy. He is very astute and won't back anything that doesn't feel right."

"Your brother seems to be a charming and persuasive man," Vincent suggested.

"He is," Basoli said flatly.

"I sense you have reservations," Vincent suggested. He gently encouraged Basoli to talk about his brother and prepared him to learn that his brother had lied about many things including his staunch support for his younger sibling.

Vincent wanted to introduce the topic of his daughter but Basoli had not given him an opening.

Nor had he referred to whatever had made him angry when he had looked at his computer. Next time, Vincent hoped, as he took his leave.

# Chapter 16

**From the journal of Jody Basoli**

The whole Washington Campus is as tense as a bow string waiting for Genesis 1 to reappear on the scanners. It's still days away from when it is due to return but no one can talk about anything else. I'm sick of it. I went off campus to my apartment. Maisie who is flat sitting – keeps the spare room ready for me.

I had not been there long when my land lady came up and knocked. She said there had been some official types asking for me. I thanked her and didn't care. She must have rung them, for they arrived an hour later.

They had questions about Uncle Reginald. Did I work for him? (No.) Did I have shares in the company? (Yes, the hundred he had given me for my 18th birthday.) What did I know about the company? (Only the hype.) There was more of the same. I couldn't help feeling they thought Uncle Reg had been doing illegal things.

Then they switched to my eminently respectable (big laugh) father. They didn't know what to say when I said I hadn't spoken to him for five years. I was glad to see them go. The interview left me with a very uncomfortable feeling.

I didn't want to think ill of Uncle Reg. He had been more of a father to me than my own. He had always been there for me. He covered for and apologized for the times when my father had work functions that were more important than my milestones. He always said that my father loved me and was proud of me – but always with a hint of disproval aimed at my father.

The interview though, made me recall the old gypsy woman I had met three years ago – just before I started at the Uni. She had said to me, "Don't believe everything you are told."

She told me also, that kin ties were important – the ties of mother and father. I didn't believe her.

Now, recalling that wisdom, I began to wonder if I really knew anything about Uncle Reg.

I knew enough about my father to call him a hypocrite – even though Uncle Reg had tried to keep things from me. Father could blithely lecture about the importance of truth and integrity when he was living a lie.

I may not have spoken to him for ages, but I have seen him on campus several times and his face is on all the campus view screens these days.

I needed a total change of scene, so I went to the mall. It was three years since I had done anything so frivolous. I bought a milkshake and sat and watched the people around me.

My eyes strayed to a pale haired young man with a really cheeky laugh. He was flirting with a woman nearly twice his age. It amused me until I identified the woman as my aunt Francine. Unfortunately, she saw me and recognised me. It didn't occur to me to try to avoid her until it was too late.

She was drunk and in a vile and spiteful mood.

I refuse to record the spiteful things she said to me – they began with 'ungrateful brat' and went from there. All that made sense was that Uncle Reg's company was in trouble and somehow it was my fault.

When I finally could, I fled back to the Uni and decided that I was going to apply for a leave of absence from my studies.

I needed to think on things – find out things.


I went back to my apartment and threw things into a backpack – ordinary clothes, this journal and stuff. I had the idea of cornering my father and asking questions.

What I wrote in the letter I left Maisie was that I was going to Terra 1 for Uni.

When I went out into the street, I stopped in a moment of complete dislocation. I felt like I had an urgent job to do – and no idea what it was.

Then I spotted a stooped figure in my side vision. I swear – it was the same old gypsy woman I had spoken to years ago. It seemed suddenly important that I speak to her. So I went towards her, lost sight of her, and finally spotted her so far down the street that I wondered how she had got there so fast. I was intrigued enough to follow...and follow...and follow.

I lost her completely, and then realised I was heading out towards the land I had inherited from my mother and I decided to go there.

Before I got there, Maisie rang my phone. Someone had trashed the apartment – and I shivered. She was okay and I told her who to contact to get things fixed.

I could not stop the unworthy thought that Uncle Reg or Aunt Francine was behind the vandalism. And I had the feeling that the vandals had been looking for me. I must have only just missed them.

My land was like a park amidst the new houses. It sloped down to the river. My mother's house, burned as it was, had been razed long ago.

I found the old woman sitting there on a bench seat. I went to sit beside her.

"Who are you?" I asked. "I seem to have been seeing you out of the corner of my eye."

She seemed to tense a moment, but then relaxed. "I am just an old, tired woman," she said in English and then repeated it in some foreign language.

After a while, when I didn't know what to say, she drew out an old printed and laminated photo and pressed it into my hand. She then covered my hand with her old, wrinkled, brown spotted one.

"That's for you. I no longer need it." She seemed to be looking into me.

I glanced at the photo – a man and woman and I guessed it was their wedding.

"I don't understand," I said.

"Look," she said tapping the photo.

It took me a long time before I really saw the details. I had thought the man had looked like Uncle Reg, but the woman wasn't Aunt Francine. There seemed to be a visible sense of 'loving' in the photo – something I had never sensed between my aunt and uncle.

The old woman spoke in that foreign tongue again. Then I knew! The people were my mother and father. I looked into the eyes of the old woman.

"Yes," she said and then fell silent. I sensed there was more for me to learn.

There was. The dress looked like the one my father had sent me for my 18th birthday. The one I had hated because it was old and dowdy. At the time I had preferred Uncle Reg's gift of shares in his company – because back then I had wanted to be in business.

Still the old woman was silent.

"Why give me the photo?" I asked.

"My granddaughter is long dead. I have no further need for it. It is all I have to give you."

"You are my great-grandmother? Why did you not tell me?"

"Child, there was no place for me in your life. You were cared for."

"Why tell me now?"

The woman seemed to shrug. "I am old, child, and I think you are ready to listen."

I didn't notice the old woman leaving. She had given me a completely different interpretation of the facts that I had learnt about my father.

Truth wasn't absolute. There were shades of truth. Perhaps saying nothing was not the same thing as lying. Perhaps my trusted Uncle had been lying to me all the time.

Did my uncle really hate my father and want to take everything away from him?

Did my father really care for me or not?

Some facts seemed not to have changed. Father had rarely been around, was always distant, impersonal...or had that been a reflection of my attitude to him? I needed to know.


I dragged my pack around and dug through the odd stuff I had packed. My little netbook computer was there – a habit.  I sent my father an email through the Uni internal mail system. I asked him for a meeting, and to be fair – I made it for two days after the Genesis ship should have returned.

And then, I didn't know what to do. I sat until a patrolling policeman suggested I move on.

# Chapter 17

Genesis 1 was a very small speck in the vastness of space. Without any signal from the tracker device Kryslie had built into Genesis 1, Tymos and Kryslie were effectively searching blind. However, they knew giving up was not an option, as they persisted in their search. They alternated flying the ship and watching the sensors, begrudging even the time needed to eat, drink and take short power naps when they were too tired to focus.

When Tymorean fleet interceptors joined the search, Tymos sent them to trace the boundaries of the interference. The Jacen Tyr arrived after retrieving the remaining escape pods from Obs 1 and Obs 2, as well as salvaging those from the planet and bringing the wreck of Obs 2 into the flight deck. The flagship took over control of the search pattern.

Late on the third day cycle of the so far fruitless search, Tymos abruptly slowed the ship and concentrated fully on the search grid that he had on the screen. He was not startled when his sister came up behind him with a hot drink, for he sensed she had woken from her two hour power nap. He welcomed the coffee, since he was finding it hard to consider the vague feeling that had made him slow down. One mouthful of the drink however, jolted him upright in the pilot's couch.

"Coffee laced with the restorative powder," Kryslie told him. "I decided that we both needed it."

"I won't argue that I did. But since you've been snoring for the past two hours – you look at that screen and tell we were we should try next."

Kryslie held her drink carefully whilst she looked over her brother's shoulder.

"Your method isn't exactly scientific."

"Scientific isn't working. I will leave that to Reslic. I have decided to try intuition."

Moving to the co-pilots couch, Kryslie asked, "Where are the rest of our ships?"

Tymos fingered the control pad and glowing blue dots came up – representing the Tymorean ships. Kryslie sipped coffee and studied the display. They were well away from the other ships.

"So, what idea made you come out this way?"

"Working on your idea of where they could hide while they tried to break the shields. The nebula where that sun is forming is out this way. It occurred to me that if Genesis 1's shields were near maximum tolerance – breaking them would be easier."

"That makes horrible sense. Okay, say they do that. They would not want to stay too close to that new sun either. If the shields were down, they could tow it anywhere."

"Hmmm," Tymos agreed, "They could."

Kryslie stopped to think. Her sleep had not been restful, it had been full of nightmares. "That nebula would interfere with the comm signals – is it part of the interference zone?"

"Yes, and it is making it hard to calculate the centre of the interference."

"Well, let's try…there!" Kryslie pointed to a slight bulge at the edge of the mapped zone. It was part way back towards where the other Tymorean ships were searching.

"You take the helm Krys. I'm going for a power nap. Wake me when we are nearly there."


It had been thoughts of the Genesis crew being tortured by the Ciriot that had disturbed her sleep. She had seen the results during the war on Tymorea. Too much. She had tried to clear her mind, using every technique she had been taught, but the images persisted. It might have been a result of her fears for Pitt, or a premonition – but she prayed to the Guardians to help them, even though she knew that she and Tymos were meant to be that help.

After she had turned the ship, and set the automatic helm to travel at the speed that maximised the sensitivity of the sensors, she went to the galley for a snack, and then to the head to give her face a spray wash. She had woken with a headache and hoped to ease it. For good measure, she gave herself an analgesic hypospray, and then returned to the helm.


The slowing of the ship an hour later, roused Tymos from sleep. "Krys? Why have we stopped?" he thought at her.

"Come and see what I have found," was her tantalising response.

Since she wasn't letting him see what she could see on the viewscreen, he redressed in his ship suit and returned to the bridge.

He had to expel a long low whistle at the sight. A ship hung in space, an ugly amalgam of three or four disparate styles. He had to wonder how it even managed to travel in space. Yet, one look at the sensor readouts told him that this was the phantom ship that had been coveting Genesis 1.

"Have you any idea of how many creatures are on board?" Tymos asked.

Kryslie shook her head, and grimaced. "No, and I don't know why they are just sitting there either, or if they will suddenly go to hyperspeed. I cannot send a signal to the Jacen Tyr, and I don't want it to get away again. There must be a way to disable it completely…"

The same idea suddenly came to each of them, the question spurring their minds to recall information from when they shared the memories of the three Tymorean Governors.

"I'll get the powdered hull sealant and some solvent," Tymos said, his smile slightly malicious.

"I'll calculate the coordinates," Kryslie spoke at the same time.

Ten minutes later, after transmitting first the sealant powder, and then the solvent into the hyperspace engines and the sub-light engines using the bulk matter transmitter, Kryslie slowly moved away. She smiled at the thought of the furore that she hoped would erupt on the Ciriot ship.

Tymos chose not to return to sleep. He sat in the co-pilot's seat and began scanning all comm frequencies in the hope he would pick up either Genesis 1 or the Ciriot ships. He had earmuffs on so as not to distract his sister.

After another hour, Kryslie prodded him and asked, "Bro, can you do something about a headache?"

He removed the earmuffs, stood and stretched, thinking he needed a break. He walked to Kryslie and began to massage her temples.

"Too much concentration," he proposed as he gently kneaded the face muscles with his thumbs. "Helping?" he asked.

"No. Not one little bit."

"Hmm," Tymos hummed, thinking. He decided to use a little of his healing energy. "I can't see any problem."

"Headaches don't always have a discernible cause," Kryslie reminded him. "But that is helping now."

Tymos kept at it until Kryslie pushed his hands away. "That will do thanks. I will get us some food and drinks – we might be getting depleted."

Kryslie did feel better after eating, but when she returned to monitoring the sensors, the headache returned full force – causing her to gasp.

Tymos sensed the cause. "Krys – we don't get headaches. When did this start?"

"When I woke up. I didn't sleep well. Since then it has been getting worse."

"I don't think the headache is coming from you," Tymos considered. "Could you be picking it up from your boy?"

Tymos sent healing energy into her mind and then they linked minds. Kryslie was able to analyse what she was receiving as an observer. After another searing jab of agony, she sensed the mind – it felt insane, but in it was a picture of herself.

"Yes, it's from Gareth," Kryslie confirmed, but Tymos had seen the image too.

"They have to be close," Tymos said. "And the Ciriot have them. They will be cloaked, and they probably have Genesis 1 cloaked. You put all the power that you can into a signal to the Jacen Tyr and I will go and tweak the mass sensors and the scrambler field."

"And strengthen all the other shields, I do not want experience another attack like the last – or worse. That ship didn't have any of the scouts docked to it. There could be a pack of those pirate wolves."

"Yes," Tymos agreed.

# Chapter 18

**From the journal of Jody Basoli**

I found myself following the dirt track along the river. It was peaceful there – totally unlike the hectic high pressure life at Uni. After half an hour, I came to a campsite where there was an old, red painted wooden caravan propped on wood log supports. Two lovely old Clydesdale horses were tethered nearby, cropping grass and low tree branches.

I stood uncertainly for a time, and then seemed to feel a pull towards the van. I went up the wooden steps at the back and into the dim interior. It smelt of lavender and cedar and what I could see was neat and sparse. Along one side was a bed and the old woman lay there as if asleep. I could hear faint breathing. When I touched her hand, she woke, saw me and smiled.

"It is near my time, child," she told me.

"I wish...I had known you better. Is there anything I can do for you?"

She didn't speak for a long time.

"What I would like, you cannot do," she sighed.

"Tell me – it might be possible," I told her.

"Take me back home."

"Home?"

"Sliding Springs," she whispered. "Take my ashes to join those of my family – my husband Pietr, my son, Domenic."

I promised her I would find a way, and then she seemed to doze for a while. I sat on the edge of her bed, holding her hand. I felt that I did not want her to die alone.

After a while she began speaking in whatever language was native to her. It almost felt as if I should understand it. The intonation of her words seemed important. Then she stopped, opened her eyes and said "All that is mine is yours. What is in the drawer, take it."

I said I would and in that moment I felt a jolt, like of electricity and the woman's eyes stilled and her hand relaxed. I felt for a pulse, but she was gone.

That was my first close encounter with death and at first I didn't know what to do.

Call the police, I remembered. Or an ambulance. No hurry, I knew, and the old woman's face was peaceful.

"Nala – be at peace," I said.

Finally I remembered my promise to her and I looked for the drawer she mentioned. There were many drawers for all her meagre possessions were stowed for travelling. I felt a floor board creak and checked there. The board lifted easily to reveal a hidden drawer. In it was a small box secured with a combination lock. Now was not the time to solve it so I put it in my pack.

It was time to see to Nala's other request – to go home. I went out of the van and called up an ambulance. The police came too, and they had their suspicious questions.

I couldn't tell them much, just that she had come by and told me she was my great grandmother and I showed them the picture of those that linked us. I had come to see her here and I had been with her when she died. I told them her name, Nala de Yves. And mine I said was Jean Olynda de Yves. I left off Basoli. My father didn't need to be involved in this and the name I had given was the one I was using at Uni.

They took her to the police morgue and I waited nearby while they did an autopsy and decided there was no foul play. They allowed me to take charge of the body. Since Nala had no living family, but me, I decided there was no need for a memorial service – not there. My memorial to her was to take her home. Now I have to wait until the cremation process is over. Two more days. There is no rush.

I stayed in Nala's caravan and decided to either donate it to a museum or create one near where Nala called home – as a tribute to those who died.

# Chapter 19

Aboard Genesis 1, once they had again successfully achieved hyperspeed, the three human astronauts had fallen back into the routine of offset shifts and sleep periods. Those awake, usually two at any time, continued with the experiments prepared for hyperspace. These were well behind schedule due to the inexplicable glitches.

Those odd events had unsettled them all, but everything now seemed normal.

Casey, before he went off for his sleep period, decided that they would drop out of hyperspace after a day cycle and recheck their position. They were all in agreement about heading directly back to Earth without any more two day breaks. If they arrived back early, it might just mean that they would need to go into orbit until a suitable re-entry window was calculated.

When Casey returned, Pitt went off for sleep. He hoped that his sleep would not include re-runs of the odd happenings. However, those events had drained him and he was asleep soon after lying in his bunk. He was roused from the sound sleep, when the proximity alarm shrilled through all the ship's speakers. He began to get up as the noise dimmed while Tweed called for Casey over the intra-comm.

"Captain, the proximity sensor is telling me that we are too close to something – but all the other sensors are at baseline."

"Override the program and instigate a sequence of 2 second course deviations. See if we can fool that sensor into stopping."

After the second course change, the alarm stopped, only to start again once they had changed to a different heading that was at a tangent to the first. The urgency of the alarm increased in pitch and the ship's computer disengaged the hyperdrive and the ship dropped back into normal space.

Different alarms began them, a cacophony that accompanied the sudden hyperactivity of all their sensors.

Tweed swore, in the instant before the forward viewscreen blanked out.

"Tweed! What's going on?"

"Captain – we were heading into some damn sun, yet the sensors had all been on zero. Now they are maxed out. We need to get the hell out of here."

Pitt was dressed in his armour and heading for the bridge. He slipped into the third couch and joined his crewmates in trying to determine what had caused them to head into the direction of such danger."

"Hull integrity and life support are still fine," Casey reported, just as the ship shuddered as if it had been hit by a giant fist.

"Resetting sensors," Tweed called.

"Shield two down to 60%," Pitt called. "Rerouting power." His mind was trying to focus on his tasks, but memories of all the sci-fi vids he had seen kept intruding – cloaked ships, pirates, powerful weapons that could blow ships into atoms…

Then he recalled things that his red-headed tech girlfriend had told him. There had been an alien ship at Lunar 1, and others had come. The latter had been invisible until a scrambler field had been included with the base shields. He accessed the shield generator program, realised that one shield was off, and turned it back on.

"One of the shields was off, Cap. I have it back on. Our shields are the same as those on Lunar 1, my tech friend said that shield interfered with those about the ships they hadn't been able to see."

"Are you talking invisibility?" Tweed scoffed. "No one has…Oh, shit!"

The unprofessional oath caused Pitt and Casey to look up at the viewscreen. Visible as hazy outlines were five ships forming a tetrahedron around them. The shield matrix was flaring at intervals, betraying the attack on them. Genesis 1 was virtually unarmed. They had laser weapons for disintegrating meteorites, and personal weapons – still locked in a bulkhead. He didn't even know why they had them – it wasn't as if they planned to land on a hostile planet. Now Pitt suggested them to Casey, and the mission leader did not argue.

"I doubt they will do much," Casey warned as he passed weapons and ammunition to the other two. "But those ships out there are not acting friendly, and these might be needed. I am reluctant to start firing first, but if they have a way to force their way in – we will defend ourselves."

"Captain, we dropped out of hyperspace due to the proximity alarm. We did those course deviations and so should have been well out of the way. But as soon as we went straight, they were back. I don't think they are friendly," Tweed stated.

"I agree with that point," Pitt agreed. "They are still firing at us and we have made no hostile move."

New alarms blared and all three knew what they meant and they instantly sealed their suits. The hull had been breached.

Tweed went to his console. "Airlock," he said over the suit comms. "Shields are overloading – failure imminent."

"Send out a mayday call, and fire off one of the distress beacons with our situation. Hopefully it will get back to Earth, eventually," Casey directed.

All knew that there would be no help from Earth.

Casey and Pitt went through to the airlock. Even before they got there, they felt the air rushing to where a palm sized orange glow was evident on the airlock door.

This was not a situation they had expected to meet, but both had been highly trained fighters before they became astronauts. They told Tweed what was happening and he sealed the bulkhead to the bridge.

Resist as they did, it was to no avail. The intruders were armoured, and they overpowered their victims. The suits of the astronauts were cumbersome, and within minutes they were down, with legs and arms tangled in some kind of mesh.

Tweed, knew when his fellows were taken, and worked rapidly to put a lock on the ships computer, renewed the distress call, but the crackle of static suggested it wasn't getting through. He tried to think of a way to destroy the intruders, but by then it was too late. The emergency bulkhead was blasted open and the door flew at him, knocking him back and trapping him long enough for the aliens to approach. As he tried to rise, an evil looking weapon was touched to the face plate of his suit.

The intention of the intruders was obvious as they searched every part of the ship. Their prisoners were tied up and unable to talk to each other. That had been their first task, yanking the comm. wires out of the suits.

When the search was over, the leader came back. It was the one wearing purple armour not black like the others. He fired at the helmet clamps and yanked the head coverings off his victim's heads. He did not remove his own. There was still air to breathe, so the intruders had sealed their entry point.

A gauntleted hand gripped each face and examined it – comparing each victim. Casey spat at the armoured figure, getting spittle on the face plate. The armoured hand hit him.

Casey merely glared at the armoured figure. He wondered if the clicks and guttural sounds he was hearing was their language, since the rhythm and variations in tone suggested speech. If they were asking questions – he couldn't tell. Then the sound of the 'speech' changed to high pitched squees and squeals. When he betrayed no reaction, the sounds changed again. He guessed, when the sounds stopped, that they had run out of language variations. Not surprising if they hadn't encountered humans before.

That was when they selected him for examination and took out a wicked looking long knife and began to peel his suit off. They picked at the fabric of the flight suit beneath it and pulled out the tubes that were to deal with waste products. The flight suit was slit and removed, and they began to examine him with ruthless thoroughness.

Pitt and Tweed struggled uselessly, trying to get free to help Casey, but they only succeeded in being subdued. They were treated with a weapon that caused extreme pain, and then paralysis and unconsciousness.

By the time they were finished with him, Casey was screaming with pain caused by physical blows, laser like shocks, heat weapons and extensive range of torture devices. When he blacked out, they turned their attention back to the ship.

The invaders knew that they had found a new species and avidly wanted to learn the location of their home world. They tried to operate the ship's computer, but found they were locked out.

They searched further and found laminates of star charts and Earth's solar system. They examined everything and found little of overt value, but much of interest in determining information about the species.

Nor did they rush – they and their victims were cloaked. No one was around in this sector of space. They knew in which direction the ship and its weakling crew had been travelling and they would head that way next. But first, they would learn all they could from the grubs that flew the ship.

The leader straightened from trying to force speech from the grub form that had head fibres the colour of the polluted sands of his home world. These grubs were weak. If he hadn't reduced the vigour of his blows, he would have killed them before learning anything. The creatures had screamed in a sensually satisfying way, but they lost consciousness too quickly. He hadn't finished with them yet, but he would leave them for now, and have them taken to his tribe ship. There he had the facilities to see what these grubs were made of.

The tribeship was safely hidden in a swirl of the nebula. The crew of his mobile command ship – which was attached to the prize ship - were powering back there, the four scout ships of his escort were forming a protective tetrahedron.

Leaving the unconscious grubs with a single guard, the Ciriot leader returned to his command ship to examine the booty his crew had removed from the prize ship. The star charts were the greatest treasure –

the patterns were unfamiliar, and that meant that it was a whole new sector of space to loot and plunder, starting with the world the grubs came from.

His pleasurable waking dreams were rudely interrupted by the eruption of alarms. He heard the sudden babble from his crew when they could not determine the cause. He emitted an arrhythmic series of clicks, cursing his over confidence and being caught in his own style of ambush.

Immediately, before the ambusher thought to block transmissions, he slapped the intership communicator, sending out a message to his tribeship containing all the information he had learnt about the new species and calling them to him to help protect the prize. It went out in all directions, on all frequencies.

Then he ordered the four escorts to find the cloaked ship. He saw on his view screen, one of the four ships firing a pattern of shots aimed at trying to cause a shimmer from the enemies' shields.

While the escort ships were seeking the cloaked ship – the Ciriot leader strode back into the prize ship, calling on more of his crew to attend him. He had left the grubs in heaps on the deck, but he wanted them secured, and unable to try to escape. He wanted them to remain unconscious.

While he waited for the restraints, he sent a powerful mental thrust into the minds of each grub. He had acted barely in time for the creatures were just rousing. They relapsed immediately. Their minds were no match for his. None of their kind would be a match for him. He would find their world, find all the treasures, and be a hero whose name would be remembered for ever.

He stood looking down, exultant in his thoughts of vast wealth, until he sensed movement behind him. He moved aside and let his inferiors reapply the tangler restraints, and ordered them to be made tight and secure. Once he was satisfied, he ordered two of his inferiors to stay with the prisoners, and the others to return to their normal duties.

When all of his inferiors suddenly drew weapons which in that instant seemed to be aimed at him. He sensed a presence behind him and spun around, his own weapon drawn.

"Stop!"

He heard the mechanically translated voice and issued orders to his crew via his armour comm unit. More of his inferiors were racing up behind the two intruders. The first to arrive tried to grab them but were repelled by some force, so they completed a circle around the two figures with weapons aimed, ready to fire.

"So, who are you?" the pirate leader demanded, sure of the upper hand even though the intruders were armoured and did not seem afraid of him.

"You dare defy a Ciriot Prince?" one of the black armoured figures demanded.

"Yes, indeed," the taller of the two figures agreed, calmly. He broadcast a powerful thought to "drop weapons" and imbued it with a strong compulsion. The black clad Ciriot obeyed, but immediately tried to grab them up again. The purple leader was not affected.

Kryslie and Tymos drew their own weapons, turned to different sides and fired at the feet of the disarmed figures to drive them into two corners. Then with Tymos watching the leader, Kryslie collected the fallen weapons, and tossed them in a direction away from both groups. Two of the disarmed aliens suddenly leapt towards the pile, snatched theirs back and fired uselessly at the newcomers, only to find their weapon targeted and fused into molten metal.

The leader made no move to use his own weapon. He was amused, rather than angry. He saw the beams fired at the intruders bounce off their silvery armour, or rather be reflected from it at a distance of three inches from the figures. He changed tactics. He approached the intruders, deciding they were weak, as they had not tried to kill any of his inferiors, or himself.

"It seems we are equal. I would be honoured to know with whom I contend," the translation was vocalised from the translator machine.

Neither Tymos nor Kryslie were fooled. They knew too much of the Ciriot.

The leader glanced at their weapons, recognised their deadliness, and then seemed to ignore them.

It suited the Great Ones to make their head pieces clear. The leader did not copy the gesture even as he stared at their faces.

"You are merely interfering children," he said with contempt.

He fired his weapon at them from close range and saw they were unmoved. He sprang at them with power assisted movements and felt himself hit a solid, unmovable object.

The smaller of the two figures grabbed him with ease and threw him to the metal floor and then held him down with one hand as he tried to struggle up. The larger of the figures had his weapon aimed at the lesser Ciriot, calmly shooting at any who began to move forward.

"We are not children, Ciriot!" Kryslie said implacably. "We are Advocates of the Guardians of Peace and the humans you have tried unsuccessfully to subvert are now under our protection."

"You are not so powerful! We disabled your ship," the purple clad prisoner countered, still struggling.

"Who said we only had one ship," Kryslie asked with contempt. "We are not alone."

"Let's talk about this," the Ciriot leader tried. "We'll split the spoils."

"You were not listening," Kryslie reminded him. "I did not say the humans were our prey – you are. The humans will be protected. And I believe your kind say 'talk is for cowards' – or has it changed?"

The prisoner cursed and squirmed. He realised that his captor knew what he was.

"Yes, I do know," Kryslie confirmed and revealed that his thoughts were open to her. His return lance of mental pain did not seem to affect her. "I know your kind, and in the past hundred years or so, the Ciriot have not learnt wisdom nor that piracy is against the agreement created by the Federation of Peace. We have judged you and your crew guilty of piracy and causing great harm to innocent people. By our authority as Advocates, you will be questioned as your prisoners were questioned and you will be executed."

Kryslie felt her prisoner put up a mind shield. Without compunction she tore it down and invaded his mind – no secret remained and when she had finished, he could not even choose to suicide.


Moments later, armoured troops from the Jacen Tyr materialised. The cornered black clad pirates realised they were about to be taken by implacable enemies and panicked. They tried to push past the newcomers using brute force – to no avail.

The leader of the Tymorean force merely watched the unequal fight and oversaw the removal of the prisoners. If the Tymorean President Governor sensed what Kryslie had done to the pirate leader, or her still simmering anger, he made no comment. Nor did Tymos, who knew its cause.

"Prisoners, Your Excellency, as requested," Kryslie said in a controlled voice. "This purple one is the leader. No sign of external control. His mind is strong like some we have encountered before and is as irredeemable. He is guilty of physical and mental torture and what I did to him is less than he has done here. However, he managed to send off messages before we arrived, and all the information he had gathered on the humans and their ship."

Jono Reslic merely inclined his helmeted head and took control of the Ciriot leader. "The Jacen Tyr is at your command, Great One," he offered. "Have you need of it?"

Tymos responded. "This ship cannot fly and the humans need medical treatment. Can you bring the joined ships into your ship dock?"

"Certainly, Great One," Reslic confirmed. "I will have medics standing by. When you have finished here – there is a message from Great One Llaimos needing your attention."

"I will have a more detailed report for you too, Your Excellency," Kryslie told him. "Could you have someone bring our ship into the flagship too?"

Reslic bowed slightly and took his prisoner away. Kryslie fingered a control pad on her sleeve, so their ship would uncloak.

Tymos had gone to examine the human astronauts. Kryslie glanced around at the damage done to the interior of Genesis 1, and then went to the nearest astronaut. It was Casey.

Kryslie's anger simmered, but now Tymos shared it.

"The Ciriot certainly know how to inflict maximum pain and damage and still keep their victims alive," Tymos remarked, keeping control of his anger. His mind told hers the extent of their injuries. "I can help heal them, but will they be sane?"

Kryslie considered the incoherent and faint thoughts she sensed. "It will take time, and if it were not that they were all strong willed and resistant – by now they would have been insane."

They felt the jerk as an attractor beam locked onto the joined ships. During the transfer process, Tymos and Kryslie began to remove the wickedly tight Ciriot tangler restraints, and found blankets to cover the naked and tormented bodies of the three astronauts.

During this process, Pitt was vaguely conscious, though too weak to move much. Four days without food or water, enduring torture and blood loss – had left him with no strength. It took all he had to move one broken boned hand to touch the figure bending over him.

"Who are you?" His voice was no more than a faint whisper.

Kryslie darkened her helmet before turning to face him. She spoke in Tymorean, but sent her meaning mentally. "Friends. We will help you recover."

"Others?" Pitt managed to ask, in as faint a whisper.

"They are alive still, and will be helped too. The evil ones are gone."

That was all Pitt managed, before lapsing into unconsciousness.

Kryslie removed her suit glove and touched Pitt's face, sending energy into him. She could not heal like her brother – but he was so depleted, only now was not the time to start healing his mind.

# Chapter 20

"Kryslie? Are you okay?" Tymos asked as the ships settled into the ship bay of the Tymorean flagship.

"Yes," she decided. "But only just. That Ciriot was vile, and he was as strong as those we met back home. He thought he could weaken me by spewing out all he had done to Casey, Tweed and Pitt. Only, I had the feeling he was holding back on something...."

"He won't be able to hurt anyone else. Reslic will see to that after learning everything it knows."

"It's done enough damage, and it managed to transmit all it learnt about the humans before we jammed all frequencies. And there are still some small ships we haven't accounted for, though he was expecting his tribe ship to come to his aid. At least we don't have to worry about that. But what if he learned Earth's coordinates, and ships from other Ciriot tribes go there...with all of this and that possibility, I feel we have failed."

"We do what we can," Tymos said simply. "We warn Daniel, and have all our people look out for them."

"For their victims you mean. Those ships won't be easy to find – they will be cloaked like they were on Tymorea."

"We know more about them than these lot realise. We know how they think and the sorts of places they are likely to hide. We can get others to keep watch on such places."

"Earth is a big planet!"

"I know, but we still can't do everything ourselves and right now we have to see what we can learn here, help the fleet engineers repair Genesis 1 and help to heal the crew."

"And worry about the fact they will be overdue," Kryslie murmured. "Repairs and healing won't be done in a few days."

"Leave that worry to the humans," Tymos advised. "It is up to us to see they do return – even if late."

Banging began on the hull of Genesis, and Tymos gave his sister a nudge to start making a list of repairs needed as he trotted to open Genesis 1's side hatch. The medical teams were waiting, ready to enter, and Tymos led them to where the injured and unconscious astronauts lay under the silvery thermal blankets.

He waited as the three men were lifted onto floating trolleys, and moved from the ship. Only then did he remove the head piece of his armour. He also forced himself to stay in place, for his mind had sensed how bad the astronauts were, and was urging him to help heal them. He knew though that the Tymorean medics would be able to stabilise them, and tend their injuries. He would only be duplicating their efforts. It was better for him to wait, until the medics had done all they could.

Kryslie re-emerged when the medics had gone, she had removed the head piece of her armour already.

"I think we can be thankful that the Ciriot expected to have plenty of time to strip this ship. Many bits and pieces have been pried out of bulkheads, some completely some still dangling from wires. The engine room is a mess. They were definitely interested in the hyperspace engines, because they had started to disassemble all the connections and had yanked out the bulkheads that were protecting it to get to the connections. They had completely disconnected the in-system engines. "

"At least the engines are not on the way to wherever they retrofit the ships they steal."

"Or that tribeship of theirs," Kryslie smiled maliciously at the idea that the ship they had disabled would soon be a prize of the Tymorean fleet.

"You'll be right to fix them?" Tymos asked with concern. He hadn't had much to do with them. "You know them, don't you?"

"Better than Suliman," Kryslie assured him. "Though every single indicator light is showing red. There's no way of telling which of those faults caused the hyperspace engines to power down. Those Ciriot were lucky they didn't explode. And I will need you to check the programming, before I get to the stage of re-balancing them. Anyway, I'll finish in here, since you have more hands on experience with the motley Ciriot ships."

Tymos headed for the bridge of the Ciriot ship. He passed through the crude boarding hatch – and decided as he passed that it had once been a proper airlock from some unfortunate ship. Once through it, he passed through two separate sections, each from a distinctly different design of ship. The bridge, which had its hatch wide open, was of yet another style, and from just his initial glance around, he decided that the Ciriot leader had been in a hurry when he had returned to his prisoners.

The computer at the command station was still active. The technology was strange to him but with the need to identify it in his mind, deep memories, shared with him by Governor Xyron of Tymorea, began to surface. He moved his hands instinctively, touching parts of the touchpad controls, and soon he had access to the last information that the leader had accessed.

Segments of the code from Genesis 1's computer scrolled on the screen. He recognised it, because he had written large portions of it, and gone over all the rest. He also realised that the segments he was reading where from random parts of many subroutines.

"Krys? I think one of the astronauts managed to lock out the computer, but they have been trying to copy the data anyway. We will need to check that it hasn't been corrupted."

The reply was instantaneous, "That might be difficult, bro." She sent a visual image of a gaping hole in the main bulkhead. "I was going to ask if you had seen it in there."

"No, but I haven't looked everywhere. What about the back up?"

"There are lots and lots of glowing Ciriot smudges on the bulkhead, but they didn't find it."

Tymos chuckled, "I must comment on that when they get back. I had discussions with the computer crew about locating it in a shielded storage area – Landin finally backed my suggestion. Still, it isn't much use without the main unit. I will have to try and interface it to one of ours."

He sensed his sister's amusement, just before she thought at him, "Isn't it fortunate that I brought along a duplicate – pre-programmed exactly as the original was."

She had fetched the spare unit just before leaving Earth, having felt the need for it in a moment of premonition. Then she hissed, "Those bastards miscalculated. Genesis 1 will get back; Earth will be warned and will become part of the Federation of Peace."

They both continued working, Tymos observing all he could in the alien ship, and Kryslie making an extensive mental list of all the things that needed repairing. She also made a list of things that needed to be manually checked, since they did not have the computer able to run diagnostics. At least she knew where the Ciriot had been most interested; she only had to adjust her eyes to see into the UV end of the spectrum. They left behind an oily residue that glowed at those wavelengths.

She did wonder what the Ciriot made of the microwave heater that was used to heat up some types of vacuum sealed rations. The latter they had left in mingled heaps on the galley floor. They had opened some at random and tasted them, but then had spat the half chewed mouthfuls out in globs on the floor.

Tymos returned to Genesis 1 at about the time Kryslie had decided she had finished checking everywhere.

"What did you find?" she asked.

"Enough artefacts to delight a xeno-anthropologist. If they can identify the origin of all mismatched ship parts and looted bits and pieces, we might learn where else these pirates have been. I tried to access other sections of the computer memory, but I think they have added an extra layer of encryption since I last managed to get my hands on a Ciriot ship. Not surprising, I suppose, since that was over a century ago. It might even give us an idea of where their homeworld is, but that isn't a priority. I'll have Reslic get that ship back to Tymorea and Xyron's scientists and techs can see what they can make of everything."

"Do you think they have learnt where Earth is?" Kryslie asked him, sensing that there was something he hadn't purposely not let her see in his mind.

"They'd have one line on a direction from Genesis 1's course," Tymos reminded her, but then he showed her something that made a shiver travel down her spine like lightning.

"They found the back-up star maps! Damn! That was my idea. If I hadn't insisted…"

"No! It was a good idea, Krys. Especially considering what happened. Anyway, they can't be sure which part of it relates to Genesis 1."

"Can't they? They will quickly find out that it is space that their kind has not explored before. And there are not very many likely planets that might be home to a space going race."

Aiming to distract his sister's anger at herself, Tymos announced, "I've seen enough in here. I want to see what damage they did outside Genesis, other than that hole where their boarding hatch is. From what I was hearing about what happened to Obs 1 and 2, I think the Ciriot somehow forced something through the shields, which caused the ship to lose power."

"You do that, bro. I'll prepare a message for Daniel and Vincent. They'll both need to know what has happened here. I will add all that I can think off that will help them locate the Ciriot ships, if they get that far."

Tymos went out, and found that a team of fleet engineers had wheeled in three trolleys of equipment. All the engineers, both men and women, gave him the ritual bow, and the murmured greeting of, "We are at you service, Great One."

Before replying, or giving orders, Tymos first scanned all of Genesis 1's hull that he could see from the ground, and then climbed up to examine the upper section, starting at the place where the ships were joined, and then using the recessed ladder that circled Genesis 1. Blackened scarring marred the hull, damaging some of the external sensor units, but targeting the connection between the hyperspace engines and the hull. A neat bit of targeting, Tymos was annoyed to have to admit. He would remember to mention that to Reslic, as it was a useful way of disabling a ship or forcing the engines to shut down.

He jumped down from the top of the ship, landing as gently as if he had been in the partial grav of his ship, rather than the normal grav of the Jacen Tyr.

While his sister murmured, "Show off" in his mind, for she had been aware of all he found, his manoeuvre was the quickest way down, and only required him to use a little of his personal power.

"Separate the ships," he told the engineering team. "We need to make the hull space worthy, and able to stand atmospheric re-entry. Check all the outer sensors, some are damaged. We can test them once Krys and I connect up the spare computer core and load the back-up memory. Leave the engines and the computers to us."

Krys had emerged and wandered over to the engineering team leader. She asked, before he had a chance to murmur any greeting, "Do you have a spare data pad? I will give you a list of all the damage inside. We may not be able to fix it all, so concentrate on the most vital systems first. I will get it to you when I finish entering the information. Another thing, do you have a spare utility belt – I want to get started fixing the engines right away."

Without a second's delay, the engineer unbuckled his own belt of tools and handed it to her with a bow of respect. He straightened, and his gaze fell on something behind her.

A soft summons caused her to turn, "…Great Ones."

She had recognised the speaker even before starting to turn, for she had heard the full greeting of, "Not so fast, Great Ones."

"Stenn! I thought you went off with Llaimos."

"I did, but he told me to stay here and give you a report and to pass on what he heard from Exlan."

"That can wait until we have the repairs started," Tymos said when he joined his sister.

"The Commander, aka my father, thought you would decide that and also suggested that you tell him what you have found out before you lose yourself in some other task."

"I was just on my way," Kryslie told him, but noticed the glance Stenn gave the utility belt she was buckling on.

"Ah, good. However the Commander also opined that he had information to give both of you."

"I've got to make a list of the things I need the engineers to look at…" Kryslie told her friend.

"I have often been told that one shouldn't keep the Commander waiting. So, you go, and I will find a thought recorder so you can be dredging the depths of you bottomless and well-ordered memory with the stuff for the engineers, while Tymos is listening to whatever is important. Multi-tasking at its finest, since I happen to know that whatever Tymos learns, you know picoseconds later."

# Chapter 21

Daniel was collating reports from his widely scattered missionaries. He wanted to know the general feeling about the deep space mission and Genesis 1.

So far it had been positive. It seemed to have cemented the alliance that Arthur bin Halil had forged between the old Imperium and the former United World Nations.

"Boss!" Morin interrupted urgently. "Coded message from Homebase coming in."

Daniel rose at once. Such messages were rare and usually important. The message relay was in the same area as the scanners. The translation was coming up on screen as he arrived. He quickly scanned the contents and then read it carefully.

"Let me know the instant Genesis 1 appears on our scanners," Daniel said sharply. "Lexina, do we have 24 hour coverage on the return vector through the satellites or do we need to deploy portable units?"

Lexina calculated quickly. "Units at points alpha, delta and phi would give us twenty per cent overlap."

"Organise them, please," Daniel directed. "Genesis 1 should've been just about in our range, but now they are going to be late. The ship was attacked, and the Great Ones need to do repairs before they can get back. But we are to look for cloaked Ciriot ships."

Lexina stopped herself echoing the last two words.

Daniel continued, "Information is coming through, we need to add parameters to the scanners to try to spot them if they come here. It isn't guaranteed to help us since it seems those creatures steal ships from everywhere. What have we got that can send out a disrupting signal?"

"We can program our satellites," Lexina told him. "It still won't give us full coverage as they won't necessarily come in on the vector Genesis 1 will be following."

"It may still help. We have been told to look out for victims, what exactly are we likely to see?"

"I know Ciriot like to torture their victims," Lexina said with a shudder. "Keleb might know more."

Daniel didn't need to tell Morin to find Keleb, the aide hadn't left the room, and was listening uneasily to the conversation.

Keleb came at a run, listened to the question and said immediately, "I'll ask Homebase to check the archives. I know some things, but

Tymos and Krys saw more of it. I know they made detailed reports for the archives. And I will warn all our area coordinators, and have them pass the word to be alert."

"Do that. Morin, get on to Vincent and tell him what has happened. Where's Jonko."

"Ah, Boss…he's off to check up on Basoli. May be he can get our Ron to admit he's a father."

"Go and call Vincent you impertinent imp."


Jonko presented himself to the security desk and asked to speak to Basoli. His ID ensured instant compliance. He was directed to go up to the top floor.

He smiled to himself as he saw the signs of the reporters had been cleaned away. Interesting how some of them had lost interest when they had become the focus of the Investigative Committee. Those ones hadn't stopped to question why he was asking them questions. Unless they assumed that the WSRA had the right to involve him and they had things to hide.

Bynan winked at him as he entered the room but was then instantly all official and business like. She escorted him into her boss and quietly withdrew.


"I don't think you need to worry about the scandal sniffers," Jonko advised Basoli as a greeting. "They seem to have been scared off." He sat himself in the chair in front of Basoli's desk. He explained what he had done and got a faint smile of acknowledgement.

"Now, about your brother," Jonko went on. "There is not much I can do except advise you to get him a lawyer."

"I have arranged that," Basoli admitted. "He tells me he couldn't afford one. He has told me he has tied all of his personal capital up in keeping the company afloat. He says he is an innocent victim."

Since Jonko had already proven certain facts to Basoli, he made no further comment.

Basoli shrugged and relaxed back into his chair. For a time he stared out the window towards the view that included the White House. The building was still used by the democratic leader of the North American continent.

"You have been a great help, Mr Goss," Basoli thanked him. "I suppose I should not monopolise more of your time. I expect you have other duties."

"That is true," Jonko agreed. "I often have more than one investigation going at a time. However, if there is something else I could help you with...?"

Basoli looked uncomfortable and tapped the desk top.

"This is a personal matter," he said, hesitantly.

Jonko waited for him to continue.

"I need to find my daughter," he almost blurted. He sounded as if admitting that was an admission of guilt.

"She's missing?" Jonko queried, hiding his interest.

Basoli nodded. "I think so."

That was interesting phrasing. "You are not sure?" Jonko asked, leaning slightly more forward in his chair.

Basoli shook his head. "I know missing persons are more in the jurisdiction of the FBI and police, but I don't want to go that far."

Jonko suggested, "Why don't you give me a little background detail and an indication of why you need to find her?"

"She may be perfectly fine," Basoli vacillated. "She may resent my prying into her life. But my brother implied he had done something to her – taken her from me. And, even though my daughter and I haven't spoken for years, I do have concern for her."

"Of course," Jonko agreed. "How old is your daughter?"

"Adult. Twenty three. She is enrolled at the Washington Uni under her mother's name – Jean Olynda de Yves. I found out that she applied for leave of absence a few days ago. The next day she sent me something of an ultimatum via email, from who knows where. I tried to reach her, first at the Uni and then at her apartment – she wasn't there. Her flat-sitter said she intended to see me at Terra 1, but her apartment was vandalised just after she left – or supposedly left."

"It does seem more of a police job if you think she has met foul play," Jonko considered.

"I don't think she has," Basoli said. "And they will tell me she is legally adult and doesn't have to see me."

"What is it that you want to know?" Jonko asked.

"That she is well," Basoli said. "I sent back a reply that I'd meet her – but got no acknowledgement of the message."

Jonko was thoughtful. "You mentioned an ultimatum – would you let me read it?"

Basoli tapped at his computer to bring up the message, and turned his monitor around.

Jonko read the message. There was no greeting, just, "An old woman once told me that family was important. Is it? Am I important to you? You gave me a name, paid for my care and my schooling – but never gave anything of yourself. Uncle Reginald always covered for you and it always sounded like he was apologising for you. I don't really know you at all. I have learnt things about you, father, all your nasty little skeletons. I don't understand how you can talk about truth and integrity when your past holds so many secrets. So many things that would shame anyone. I feel like one of those unspeakable secrets.

"The WSRA teaches us to make no claims without proof. I will do that much for you – I promise. You have told me nothing. Uncle Reginald tried to keep the facts from me. I intend to find out the whole truth. When I do – maybe I will walk out of your life forever, but then again – truth is relative. The facts can be viewed in different ways. There can be shades of truth. To be fair, I should at least hear your version. If I can find that knowing old gypsy, I will ask her too. I will be where the old house was – two days after your spaceship is meant to return. If you truly care for me – you will be there. You – no proxy – no apology – no excuses.

"If you don't come – it won't matter. I can live without you, without Uncle Reginald and all his lies, without the Basoli name. I will be out of your life forever."


Jonko sat back. The missive had not been signed. "Angry, confused, yearning, and afraid," he summarised and allowed himself to appear thoughtful. "I will put out feelers," he promised. "If I hear anything to indicate she is okay – I will tell you. If I hear of foul play – I will notify you and the police. I won't necessarily tell you where she is."

"That is all I can justify asking," Basoli said, accepting the limitation.

"I may not be able to find out anything," Jonko warned. "Particularly if she has decided to drop out of sight."

Basoli nodded tersely and Jonko stood up to leave. "I will be in touch. I hope all will go well with the Genesis 1 return."

"As do I," Basoli agreed. "That is where I need to keep my attention. There are still many people who think it is a waste of money and a suicidal mission. I don't believe that. I believe the mission is vital."

Jonko nodded and left. He thought to himself, as he smiled at Bynan, that the man did not need the extra stress.

# Chapter 22

**From the journal of Jody Basoli**

While I waited for the ashes of Nala, I lived in her van and wondered how anyone could tolerate such a life with so little. Yet, I don't think Nala had been unhappy. Her simpler life might be better. She had lived to a great age. Certainly her life was different to the high pressure learning at Washington Uni.

The simple travelling life was nothing like studying astro-science, but I liked my choice – revelled in it.

Uncle had got me interested in business and the mathematical intricacy of high finance – but it hadn't really satisfied my mind. The decision to apply to the WSRA Uni had been sudden – and right. But now I had a simple, limited permutation, combination lock – owned by a gypsy – and it was no easy thing to open. I cannot think how that could be, unless the lock was broken. Still, it occupies my mind – in between keeping up with news on my netbook – which I will need to recharge soon, and writing in this journal.

It was odd, but no one seemed to notice the caravan, the whole time I was in it. Yet, when I had walked back from town after getting money from the bank, and charging my computer at the library, a curious crowd had gathered. So had an official from the local council. The people were told to move off, once I had admitted to being the owner of the van now.

More red tape. I could not leave it there as it was on public land and camping there was not permitted. I could have moved it to my land, but then I would have to explain that I owned it – and prove it. Anyway, I had no experience of horses – so I spent most of the next day finding a garage for the van and a hobby farm to take on the horses.

After that, I had a reluctance to return to my flat. I could not get over the feeling that people were looking for me. I went back to the library and tried to find the place Nala had mentioned.

The name should have been familiar, but the tiny township where the rocket had landed was long eradicated. The area had been renamed, from Sliding Springs to Hope Valley.

Then I looked into how I could get permission and equipment to enter the blast zone. There was a research station 10 miles in – mostly unmanned. That would be as far as I could go. With my Washington Uni ID I could claim I had research to do at the hut.

And then, since I hoped to leave tomorrow, I looked into ways to get there. Planes were booked out with people wanting to go and see Genesis 1 return. Trains didn't go near enough, so that left buses and hiring a car to go the last part of the way. I memorised bus routes and numbers and considered driving. I wasn't used to driving much, and while I could navigate well in three dimensions, I was hopeless at it in two dimensions.

I had a 12 days before I needed to be back to the house block to see if my father cared enough to come.

# Chapter 23

Reslic, in his role as Commander in Chief of the Tymorean Peace Fleet, promptly dismissed the crewman he was talking to as soon as the two Great Ones entered his private briefing room. From behind them, Stenn said, "I'll just get that recorder."

"Great Ones," Reslic greeted with a bow.

Tymos and Kryslie returned a bow of their own, to the same degree, as one did when greeting another of equal rank and importance. Although their rank was higher than that of the Tymorean Governors, they didn't feel right and comfortable making that claim.

It was also protocol for the Great Ones to initiate the meeting, but Reslic came straight to the point, once he had invited them to sit.

"The Ciriot leader chose to suicide. He was placed in a shielded cell until I could question him – a matter of less than ten minutes."

"Huh! He was arrogant enough when we first faced him, even contemptuous of us 'children'." Tymos said.

"All show! It didn't take much to overpower him and then he tried to offer us a share of the spoils. A coward by their own definition," Kryslie continued. "Even so, his mind was still a pit of unrepentant evil."

Reslic moved the direction of his gaze to a point behind the Great Ones. The door of the room had opened quietly and someone had entered.

"Ensign?" Reslic implied the question of the cause of the interruption.

"Sir, I have a recorder requested by Great One Kryslie."

Reslic gestured the speaker forward and Kryslie turned her chair on its swivel base to take the device.

"Thank you and thank Stenn for finding it so quickly."

The ensign was very young, one of Reslic's sons or perhaps a nephew. He blushed at being spoken to by a Great One. He merely bowed and retreated quickly.

Kryslie activated the recorder, she might as well record her report for Reslic, with thought images accompanying he spoken report. Later she could make a new file for the repairs.

"I am not sure if you are aware that the Ciriot that wear purple are sub-leaders and they direct those in black. They are in turn sub-servient to those who wear crimson and the overall leader wears red."

Reslic merely nodded and waited for her to continue.

"The purple ones are hereditary princes, but junior in rank to the ones in crimson. They have mind skills that they use to amass more and more power. That one, coward though he was, enjoyed the opportunities of his rank, including torturing captives."

Kryslie's face took on a slightly blank look as she began to speak of the thoughts, knowledge and memories that she had squeezed from the now dead Ciriot. Many of the memories came with the recollections of the orgiastic pleasure of torturing a long series of victims. From her memory of these she recalled and described the form of different captives – species she had not seen before, that now as she described them she found names coming into her mind.

Pushing the sensations of debauched pleasure aside, she recalled other memories of rituals, of day to day activities, places where he had been, planets he had landed on. However it was clear that the Ciriot was from one of the pirate clans – bred in space. He had never been to the Ciriot home world and had never fared to learn much of it. His goal, like others of his rank was to increase his standing with the superiors of his clan. In finding a ship of a new and unknown race, and maps to their world, he had been sure of his success.

Reslic listened intently to the detailed recall of all Kryslie had stripped from the Ciriot's mind. He was impressed, but kept his face impassive and his thoughts shielded. The Great Ones knew the most about the Ciriot. Indeed, the majority of the data in the archives had come from their efforts. Of the Ciriot culture, most was known about the pirate clans, but nothing at all about the world that spawned them. After that race had failed to win the war they had incited on Tymorea, and all the males on the surface had died, including six of the tribal leaders or Princes – it was assumed that the survivors on the clanships had fled back to the home world. There had been no reports of Ciriot activity from that time until now.  Now – the pirate clans were back.

However the information had been gained, it was needed and the Great Ones were tools of the Guardians of Peace.

When Kryslie finished speaking, he considered all he had heard.

"The details you have reported, might help us identify where the pirate clans fled after their defeat at Tymorea. It might even give us a line on their homeworld. I will send this report to our xeno-biologists. What did you learn of their interest in Genesis 1?"

"They were long distance explorers, the clanship we found belonged to the coward. He had cobbled it together from parts in some floating scrapyard. Succeeding in getting it spaceworthy was some kind of rite of passage. He headed out this way having recalled the tale of their treacherous former allies on Aerdna, and how his forebears had orchestrated that planet's downfall. It was an important point that although he was out here alone, he was still in contact with his paternal clan – one of those that were decimated by us. The ship on Aerdna was from another scion of that same clan, who was stronger than the one we caught.

The dead Ciriot was warned away from Aerdna, but soon after that ship saw Obs 1 and sent out an alert. The dead Ciriot followed Obs 1 back to its position escorting Genesis 1, and realised that he had found a new species. He warned off his kin from the planet, but was in turn ordered by his elders to force the ship there for it to be examined."

Tymos took over the narrative, proposing how he believed that Obs 1 and 2, as well as Genesis 1, had been overcome, adding, "The engineers should find a device like a limpet mine attached to Genesis 1's hull. It had to have been forced through the ship's shields. When on Obs 2, listening to the audio from the human ship, I heard a clang, preceded by the ship's proximity alarm."

He changed the topic and described aspects of the motley scout craft that had attached itself to the human ship.

"Some of the smaller pieces missing from Genesis 1 are in storage boxes in there – as if they were getting ready to transfer them. However, I did not find the computer core from Genesis. I might suggest that after copying the memory from it, it was sent back to the tribe ship."

Reslic help up a hand to pause the conversation, them activated a comm unit from his desk to request a report from the teams sent to salvage the tribe ship disabled by the Great Ones. He listened, and then directed the Tymorean ships to cloak and be on the lookout for a returning Ciriot scout ship.

"The ship you disabled is deserted," Reslic stated.

"Then it is unlikely that any scout ship will go there," Kryslie commented. "I would say that the underlings of the dead Ciriot that are still alive, and the clan kin of those from the planet base, are now under the command of the clan patriarch."

"Could they extract useful information from the human's computer?" Reslic asked.

"What I saw on the computer in that scout ship, tells me that one of the humans managed to lock out the computer and activate the anti-intrusion program. What I saw were fragmented files," Tymos explained, "and the more they try to access it, the worse the code will be scrambled."

"They did find the back-up star maps," Kryslie warned. "Hard copies laminated with tough protective plastic. We have them back, but the Ciriot copied them and transmitted the data to his kin."

"I will activate further units of the fleet and have them on stand-by in case they are needed," Reslic stated, and then he asked, "What are your immediate plans, Great Ones?"

"Fix the ship," Kryslie said immediately. "I know the engines and Tym knows the programming. We can be doing that while the Fleet medics are treating Casey, Tweed and Pitt."

"They will not be well enough to proceed for many days yet."

"When I have connected and tested the spare computer core and tested the programming, so Krys can run diagnostics, I will do what I can to heal the humans faster," Tymos promised.

"By then, and when I finish with the engines, they will be well enough to have the sedation reduced. I will be able to examine their minds," Kryslie said softly. "We will need to be careful to remain unrecognised."

"Is it your wish that we move the flagship nearer to Earth, Great Ones? Then the humans will not have as far to go — nor be as late returning."

Tymos nodded. "Yes. They will be late, whatever we do." He and Krys rose at the same time, Reslic followed suit immediately as protocol demanded. He took the recorder that Kryslie handed him. "There is a file on that for the engineers. I promised them a list of needed repairs."

"I will pass it on," Reslic said, before continuing with, "Are you going to eat before you get started?"

The idea of food had been far from their minds, but the mere mention caused their stomachs to growl.

"Of course," Tymos stated his agreement.

# Chapter 24

**From the journal of Jody Basoli**

When I finished investigating all methods for getting to Hope Valley, I decided that driving myself was going to be the most time efficient option. I would not have to worry about making connections while integrating modes of travel.

I had enough money to buy an old open backed truck with a towbar. It had been for sale at the garage where I had arranged the store the red gipsy wagon. When I asked the owner about hiring a camper trailer, he surprised me. He told me to look under the front of the wagon.

There, very neatly folded away was the hitch for connecting it to a car. Nala, it seemed, had preferred the pace of the Clydesdale pair. When he offered to reconfigure it, I had not hesitated in saying yes. It hadn't even taken an hour. Now only the long poles and harness from the horse hitch would stay in the garage. He also checked the wheels, which were ordinary car tyres, and lowered the chassis to suit the truck.

During that hour, I had walked to collect Nala's ashes, bought some supplies and did some last minute internet searching on Hope Valley. It had been a worthwhile check, for I had been unaware of the protocols for visiting the area. However, as a result I sent off two emails to two of my teachers at Uni. One had agreed to send warning of my intended arrival to the leader of the National Guard unit that was permanently stationed there. The second arranged for the equipment I would need if I were to visit Emmanuel's hut, and the required Uni documentation.

By then, I was itching to be gone.

I was all too aware of my ultimatum to my father, and the need to be back in Washington for the date I had given him. Part of me wanted to see if he would come, and a stronger part was urging me to forget the meeting. It was Nala's words about the importance of family that won out.

I was going to have to drive most of each day to get there, do what I needed to do and return. At least with the van, I could pull over when I got tired and sleep for a bit. When I got to Hope Valley, I was still going to have to wait for the person who would escort me into the hut. I hoped I wouldn't have to wait long.

During my rest breaks, I was never disturbed, but twice, when I had gone to stretch my legs, I had returned to find a small but curious crowd around the wagon. I didn't wonder at it for the gipsy wagon was an anachronism in this day of space flight.

I could not forget that fact, for whenever I was in range of a radio station that was all anyone ever talked about. They were counting down to the expected return in a week's time. All the talk did was make me travel even faster.

# Chapter 25

Stenn Reslic found Kryslie, looking like a mechanic as she lay under one part of the hyperdrive engine with only her feet protruding. He gently nudged her leg to get her attention.

"Great One, my father is muttering about having information for you."

Kryslie stopped working and eased herself out from under the engine.

"Idiot! The President doesn't mutter!" Kryslie said as she propelled a low trolley out so that she could see the speaker, and then rolled over and pushed herself up.

"Maybe not when you are around," Stenn cheerfully agreed. "And I still have that report for you from Great One Llaimos."

"Is that the reason why you interrupted me?" Kryslie demanded.

"Yes, Great One," Stenn said, returning to his formal manner. "That and to remind you that you have missed two meals already and even Great Ones need to eat."

"Damn you, Stenn. You aren't my parent. Have you given the same ultimatum to my brother?"

Stenn's face creased into a wicked smile. "My brother, Konn, was sent to Great One Tymos, since he is not in his Commander's good graces right now."

"I should think not," Kryslie murmured. "How are the crew of Genesis 1?"

"They are all sedated and the healers have stabilised them and set the broken bones in place," Stenn reported. "The ship repairs are progressing non-stop although we cannot match all the materials perfectly."

"I see no harm in having some evidence of our benign intent. It will help convince the people of Earth," Kryslie told him. "However, it is my intent that they will be confident of their engine and computing technology."

"Is that why you are doing this yourself, Great One?" Stenn asked.

"Will you stop Great One-ing me," Kryslie insisted. "At least in private. I am doing it because I helped build the engine and fit it in the first place. I know Tymorean specialists are the best around, but they don't have the time to learn this system. So, show me where the food is and give me your report."

"Yes, Gr...Kryslie," Stenn agreed.

While eating mechanically, Kryslie listened to Stenn talk, aware that Tymos was listening just as intently.

"Will you send all that onto Daniel at Earth base? We don't have time to consider it yet but I agree with Llaimos – it is important. Maybe Daniel can start looking for this Nala. Will Llaimos be staying on Aerdna?" Kryslie asked.

Stenn nodded. "I believe he will return home and bring back missionaries to help him, once he has studied what is needed."

Kryslie stood as soon as she had finished eating. "Where is his Excellency?"

"On the bridge. We are heading towards Earth," Stenn told her. "Even if you fix the engines, the humans are not fit to be in control – and I don't think you want them recognising you."

"You are quite correct," Kryslie agreed. "The Ciriot disconnected the hyperdrive engine. I think they were planning on taking that too. The engine itself was not vandalised. I am almost through with the reconnections."

Tymos added quickly, "I have connected the spare core and checked the programming. It is ready for when you need to do engine diagnostics."

Kryslie waved acknowledgement as she went to speak to Reslic.

"You have information for me?" Kryslie omitted the usual honorific due to one of Tymorea's Governors. She wanted to return to the task she had left, and remained standing.

"Yes, Great One," Reslic confirmed, standing up from where had sat to oversee the search for hidden Ciriot ships. "You will need to be aware that not all possible scout ships from the tribe ship on Aerdna or the one you disabled, have been accounted for. The six that launched against us were destroyed as were the four escorts with the ship you have here."

"I believe Obs 1 took out some before it was disabled and destroyed. The Genesis crew were spooked by the space battle. Four of five were destroyed."

Kryslie knew that tribeships tended to have a complement of twelve scout ships. That left maybe nine still roaming around. Very possibly, one of the ships had another of the purple clad Ciriot in it. There had not been one of them on the planet base.

"I hope they are not hanging around, waiting to follow us to Earth."

Kryslie met Reslic's eyes, she didn't need to tell him to do all he could to find them. Trouble was, they could have preceded the Jacen Tyr. "Have the Ciriot prisoners told you anything?"

"No." Reslic expanded on his terse answer. "Most of them seem to be little more than youths full of bravado. They know only that our kind are to be killed on sight, and claim they will still succeed. I have separated them from the four more stoic ones."

"Then they are of no use to us. Terminate them."

Kryslie had not thought to have the prisoners killed, but when she spoke, she knew that the Guardians of Peace had spoken through her. From Reslic's expression, she knew he was aware of it.

"Keep them isolated, and reduce the air until they are only just alive. If any have those green motes in them, you will begin to see a green nimbus of light and energy which will make for the nearest, strongest energy source. A scrambler field will negate them."

"As you say, Great One. What of the others?"

"If they cannot be made to talk, they too are of no use to us. However, the stoic ones will, most likely, have motes in them. Make sure that they are well dead before destroying the bodies, and check the amount of energy absorbed by the shields."

"We didn't notice any affects when the leader you captured died."

"I doubt that he was much older than those young braggarts you mentioned. I would also believe that he was too cowardly for any mote to choose as a host. Though, when I examined his mind, there was no sign of one."

Reslic nodded, and Kryslie turned to leave.

"Great One, if I might offer you some advice?"

Kryslie turned back, "Of course, Your Excellency," she agreed.

"It would be wise if you did not keep missing meals. I say this because you are not where you can restore your energy levels from a planet's aura. Have you noticed that?"

"Yes, but time is important. We cannot leave here until Genesis 1 is ready to return and it may be that Ciriot ships are already on the way to Earth."

"You cannot help the humans if you have drained yourself. Healing, like physical activity takes energy," Reslic reminded her.

Kryslie nodded, feeling rebuked but appreciating the lesson. "I will keep that in mind."

Reslic allowed a faint smile as Kryslie walked off. In spite of all they had done, the Great Ones were still young, earnest, intense and focussed.

<h1 style="text-align:center">Chapter 26</h1>

Casey was vaguely conscious – sedated enough that his mind was drifting rather than thinking. He had no recollection of events, but seemed to recognise that he was in some kind of medical facility. His attendants did not look odd. They were dressed in white and spoke too softly for him to hear their words. He felt no pain, but sensed his body was immobilised.

He thought then that he was beginning to hallucinate. Two distinctly odd figures were walking towards him. One was tall, blond haired, powerfully built and wearing what might have been a black uniform. Certainly he would be able to fight in it. And was that a sword that he had strapped to his back?

The other was shorter and wearing an over robe of silver and gold, and had his face hidden in the hood of gold fabric.

A gentle hand reached out from the silvery sleeve and touched his forehead.

"Casey, how are you feeling," Tymos asked in English.

"Floating. Is that how it should be?"

"Yes," Tymos agreed. "Casey, I have brought you an important visitor. He is President Governor Jono Reslic, Commander of the Tymorean Peace Fleet. You are on his flagship."

"I am?" Casey said. "Thank you."

Tymos went on speaking, impressing his words in Casey's sluggish mind.

"When you are again well, you will remember what I am saying now. It is very important."

"Yes," Casey agreed, almost vacantly.

Tymos told him in short terse sentences all that had happened to Genesis 1 and by what race.

"You were helped by the Tymorean Peace Fleet. Your ship is within ours, being repaired. When you return to Earth you will take greetings from us and an invitation to join the Federation of Peace."

Interest began to stir in Casey's mind along with a hint of pain.

"What happened?" Casey asked, trying to focus his eyes on the silver and gold clad figure, who still had his hand on his forehead.

"As I mentioned, you were tortured by a group of Ciriot pirates. We are healing your injuries," Tymos repeated quietly. "Proof of what I say will be in your ship's memory. You must ensure that your leaders are alerted to the probability that these pirates have heard of Earth. They are evil, unrepentant."

Casey seemed to shiver as if from a memory.

"Listen now to the words of President Reslic," Tymos directed.

Casey focussed on the taller man, as Reslic explained about the Federation of Peace and its aims and directives.

Tymos spoke again when Reslic had finished.

"We will document this. I am able to translate it into your tongue. We will provide the means for your people to recognise our ships and those of the enemy."

Tymos lifted his hand, and Casey lapsed into sleep. He glanced at Reslic who simply inclined his head and turned to leave the medical section.

Before he left, Tymos checked Casey's condition as shown by the monitoring equipment and his own gift of healing. He had been sending healing energy into Casey during the interview. That was enough for now.

Casey's external injuries had been repaired by the Tymorean medics and the broken bones had been set. The burns, gashes, bruises on the outside had been treated and covered. The energy Tymos had sent had helped the bones to heal and the internal damage to mend.

Tymos followed Reslic's advice and went to the catering section for a meal. The caterers had instructions on what to serve the Great Ones and presented him with a high energy meal.

After eating, he returned to the medical section and went to astronaut Tweed.

Kryslie found him there later. "Engines are back on line and the diagnostics are all green," she said as she sat beside him. "How is he?"

"Improving slowly, but faster than without my help. I am concentrating on knitting the bones and closing the internal damage. They won't be fully healed when they return but they will be able to fly the ship. I can't do much more for Casey except further strengthen the bones."

"Do you think we need to escort them once they enter the sun's system?" Kryslie asked.

"We can shadow them until just before re-entry," Tymos mused. "But they will have to recalculate the re-entry window. We can't take over for them – but landing either by touchdown or splash down will be hard on them."

"I am feeling the need to be in two places at once," Kryslie admitted.

"When I am finished with Tweed and Pitt, I could return to Earth," Tymos considered. "You could borrow an interceptor to follow them inward."

"Yes, I will do that. How was Casey when you spoke to him?"

"Calm, but he was well sedated. When he began to be interested, the pain began to return. He has not yet recalled his trauma," Tymos warned.

Kryslie nodded and went to Casey. She too was dressed as her brother was in the gold and silver over robe, with her features hooded.

In some ways, her task was harder than her brother's. His skill was in purely physical healing. At times it was delicate work, but mostly it wasn't. Kryslie needed to heal Casey's mind without injuring it further, and without changing the essence of the man. To do it, she must take all of the mental trauma into herself – not to remove it, but to help Casey deal with the memory and not be weakened by it.

She set to work, her hands glowing faintly purple, and one was resting lightly on his face, the other holding a bandaged hand. The medics came and went at intervals, checking the monitors and noticing the improvement in the body's chemical balance and the slight improvements in the brain activity. They had not had to renew the strong sedation and the patient was calm.

Kryslie felt faint movement from the hand, seconds before the eyes opened suddenly. There was sense in them now.

"Who are you?" Casey asked.

Kryslie answered in Tymorean, but sent the meaning to his mind.

"I am a healer," Kryslie didn't give her name. "Do you recall what happened to you?"

Casey's whole body tensed, causing pain. "Yes," he hissed.

"Those that hurt you cannot hurt you or anyone again."

Kryslie gently massaged his forehead. Casey hadn't noticed that she had spoken English that time.

"My crew," Casey asked then. "Are they all right? Can I see them?"

"They are recovering too. Like you, they were treated cruelly. You, however, are not yet healed enough to move without re-breaking many bones."

"Why do you keep your face hidden, like the ones who attacked us?" Casey asked.

"It is so I may concentrate on my healing, for which I need to use an inner sight. I do not wish to be distracted by what my outer eyes see."

Casey accepted that and relaxed and let her work as he drifted into an almost trance like state. Kryslie spent more than six hours with him, until

Stenn Reslic – dressed in a low ranking space fleet uniform, arrived and waited to be noticed.

"My minder has arrived," Kryslie finally said to Casey. "I will be available if I am needed."

"Wait! How come you speak English?" Casey asked.

"It is simple. I am a mind healer and I needed to talk to you and be understood."

Kryslie released Casey's hand and advised. "Sleep for a while." She saw Casey's eyes close.

Konn Reslic was hovering by her brother.

"Dinner time," Kryslie guessed, giving Stenn a wry grin. He grinned back for an instant.

She shook her head and commented, "I am an adult. I don't need to be escorted."

"Yes, Great One, but my orders come from the President. So if you disagree, you can tell him where to put his orders!"

# Chapter 27

**From the journal of Jody Basoli**

The National Guard maintained a perimeter 6 miles out from the fence around the blackened area. Alarms, cameras, motion sensors and all the latest devices gave them warning of anyone trying to sneak through. I didn't need to, since all my permissions were in order. I still half expected an interrogation from the duty guards when I arrived towing Nala's gipsy van, but they didn't even mention it.

Perhaps my being a student at America's most prestigious university was a sufficient testament to my character. And perhaps they were used to teams from the Uni coming to study the area.

They did inform me that there were no conveniences inside the buffer zone and if I was to be there for a while, I should park near the outer ring of trees. I didn't need to be told not to enter the zone without a guide.

As soon as the road broke out of the trees, I understood what the guards had only hinted at. There was a quarter mile wide zone where absolutely nothing grew. There was not even a speck of grass. The dust, a fairly thin layer over fused rock, was sterile.

Vehicles did travel along this dead zone, for I could see plenty of overlapping tyre tracks.

I pulled off the road and turned to the west, travelling along to where one of my Uni teachers had told me there was a spring. One that had pure water, which flowed into the forest and away from the ravaged land. I stopped in the shade, for even on this mild day, the sun seemed to be of desert strength. I decided to explore more on foot.

I didn't have to go far to sense the uncanny stillness and silence. It seemed that even birds and insects shunned this area. I soon hurried back to Nala's van to get myself settled and make a cup of herbal tea on the tiny stove.

My own interest in the Genesis mission, caused me to turn on my netbook computer, once I had discovered that my phone had signal, and I could use it as a link to the internet.

Invasion

Genesis 1 should have been back in range of the WSRA base sensors. I felt a stirring of alarm, when the news announcer reported that there was still no sign of it.

# Chapter 28

Vincent departed Earthbase and insinuated himself in Basoli's retinue when he flew out to Terra 1 the day before they expected to see Genesis 1 return. He stayed in the background as the 100 strong media contingent swarmed Basoli as soon as the emerged into the arrival lounge. Commander Haldstadt had two squads of security men ready to escort the WRSA's top executive into a private briefing room.

No one noticed when Vincent disappeared abruptly from the arrival lounge and appeared just as suddenly behind all the dignitaries greeting Basoli.

Refreshments were being passed around while Commander Haldstadt brought his superior up to date, although there was no information yet on Genesis 1. Vincent listened to the various low conversations going on while Haldstadt was talking. He noticed Vice-President Arthur bin Halil was present, with his own body guards, acting on behalf of President Adamson who was tied up on UEN business. It was not surprising, since the Vice-President's interest in science was well known.

Once Basoli had finished taking in Haldstadt's report, and his own glass of iced lemon juice, he pushed himself up from the seat he'd occupied and gestured to his escort detail. He left the room by a different door to that which he entered. It took him via one of the staff only corridors and back to the media room to arrive where a podium had been erected for his benefit.

In the briefing room, a closed circuit video monitor showed Basoli ascending the podium, so he was now speaking from slightly above the heads of all the reporters, and getting their attention by a tap on the microphone.

Heads swivelled and conversations ceased. Most of the reporters had recorders on an upward extending stick, ready to catch every word, although a couple were still using a data tablet and stylus.

"We are all here to await the triumphant return of Genesis 1," Basoli began, going on to say, "Although it is still too early to be able to direct contact with the crew. Our experiments to create a communication system has had no results – so our messages will probably arrive a long time after our astronauts return."

There was a ripple of amusement at that, and Basoli went on, "If all has gone as scheduled, the earliest that we can expect to see Genesis 1 on our screens will be tomorrow morning."

Basoli ignored several sharp questions prompted by that statement. "First word will come from the Lunar 1 array, and that will be as soon as Genesis 1 drops back into normal space, just outside the Sun's heliopause."

"What if they miss the re-entry window?" someone called out.

"We have a series of re-entry windows calculated, to allow for the contingencies that they were either early or late," Basoli went on calmly. "I have been told by my experts that the actual speed that Genesis 1 will travel at, will depend on the amount of matter in the areas it passes through. All that was explained prior to the launch. The possibility of a later return could be a result of various experiments taking longer to complete than expected. The schedule was not timed down to the second."

Vincent was confident that Basoli was handling the media easily, in spite of his load of private issues. Though with the thorough screening every media rep here had undergone, those private issues should not be the subject of questions. With everyone else still watching the monitors, Vincent decided to ease his way towards the Vice President, who was talking to Commander Haldstadt. He was in time to hear the latter say, "Arthur, if everyone who helped with this project wanted to be here, we would need a room five times as big to hold them all. Although, I would much rather be in a room packed with scientists and technicians that that media pack out there."

Arthur laughed, agreeing with that sentiment. His life had been much simpler three years ago, before he had inherited his father's political position, and later the Vice-Presidency of the new UEN council.

"Anyway, Kryslie Ward and that brother of her's are on leave. They should be back tomorrow, although since they had not taken any leave in the past three years, I would be happy for them to extend it."

Vincent glanced back at the monitor showing Basoli, and tuned out the near conversations to concentrate on the questions being asked by the media. They were a way to judge the bias of the reporter. There were the ones who were impatient to have Genesis return so they could find out what new wonders and discoveries had been made, and the diametrically orientated group who were already predicting that the spaceship would not return. The 'it's a big waste of money' group and the xenophobes who espoused staying planet bound 'so no aliens would find Earth'.

"A little late for that," Arthur bin Halil commented so only Vincent heard him.

"So I believe," Vincent replied, turning to the Vice President. "I notice that sentiment was ignored in favour of pointing out the potential manufacturing opportunities that will be a spinoff of the mission."

"There is a precedent for that, looking back at the post-Apollo era in the 20th century," Arthur agreed, but then changed the topic. "Are you to be a part of the medical evaluation team – when the astronauts return?"

"I am glad you are on the side of the positive outcome group," Vincent remarked before answering the question. "Yes, I am on the team. The other medics are on standby to either be flown here for the landing or out to the recovery ship."

"I am hoping that they will touch down here as planned. I have never been on a boat out in the open sea. Would you have a cure if I get sea sick?"

"Few people need to suffer that these days."


When Basoli returned to the room, Haldstadt had some of his staff ready to show the visiting dignitaries to guest accommodation. The media reps would either have to find a room at one of the hotels in the nearby towns, or sleep in the media room on the floor or in chairs. That first night, most chose to go elsewhere for few considered it likely that Genesis would return early.

Vincent accepted a room, and retired promptly – at least that was what the staff acting as hospitality officers believed. In fact, once he had locked his door, he contacted the Earthbase and requested a long range beam, and then transmitted back there.

The emotional atmosphere at Earthbase was distinctly different to that of Terra 1. While the humans were avidly awaiting news and blissfully unaware of the iniquities suffered by the crew of Genesis 1, the Tymoreans knew that the ship would be returning late, and that a deadly enemy might have followed them.


Daniel looked haggard. He had the base screens manned around the clock, having called in extras from Homebase to double the complement of watchers. Even with a scrambler function built into the satellite signals and local detectors, to emit a field to disrupt cloaking fields, he couldn't be sure that they'd see the Ciriot infiltrators. Earth was a big planet and they couldn't observe all of it, all of the time.

He had relocated all of the missionaries that he could, trying to cover likely places where the aliens might land and dig in. Keleb had said - remote, sparsely populated areas. The missionaries knew to look out for odd happenings. However, the blackened lands above the caverns that were Earthbase, might be a very attractive place for the Ciriot to land.

Vincent sent Daniel off to sleep and, once he had gone, sent off messages – one to Commander Haldstadt at Terra 1 and another to Commander Landin of Lunar 1. It was better to have the continuing absence of the Tymos and Kryslie Ward to be officially sanctioned, for neither would return to those workplaces when their true work was unfinished. They would not return until Genesis 1 was safely down.

His third message was to request an update from the Jacen Tyr, and was answered by the Tymorean President and Fleet Commander. Reslic reported, "We need another two days to finish repairs to the human ship. By then the astronauts will be strong enough to withstand re-entry and splash down. The Great Ones have been working ceaselessly, speeding the healing. Probably on the third day they will leave here, but will have to travel two days to get to the heliopause of Earth's sun. We are positioned so that they will be returning along the correct vector."

"And the three astronauts, how will they be after the Ciriot torture?" Vincent asked, knowing that no human doctor could conceive the depth of the alien treatment.

"Great One Kryslie is confident that they will be able to put it behind them. We have kept them sedated, and today we have reduced it. They will be allowed up tomorrow, as they will need time to accept that aliens rescued them, and to check out their ship for themselves."

"So, they will be about four days late," Vincent noted. "Do you know when the Great Ones plan to return?"

"I will ask, but as they have finally agreed to rest and sleep, I will not disturb them. I will ensure that Earthbase is kept up to date. Have you seen any sign of Ciriot infiltrators?"

"No, and I in turn have made Daniel go off to rest. We are all hoping that seeing no signs is a good thing as we cannot be everywhere."

"Nor can the Great Ones," Reslic observed before ending the communication.


Vincent's disquiet increased; what Reslic said was true, but the Great Ones were the tools of the Guardians of Peace, and he would trust that they would deal with whatever eventuated. Yet he too felt the pull of the need to be in the scanner room, adding one more pair of eyes to watching. The screens there showed six different vectors around Earth, each angled towards one of the re-entry vectors.

When Daniel reappeared six hours later, he dragged his eyes from the screen and transmitted via the long range beam, back to Terra 1 for a couple of hours sleep.

At the end of the following day, the Earth media were already muttering uneasily and predicting that Genesis 1 would not return. As a second day without contact passed, they became even more vocal, demanding that Basoli appear, and seeming more like sharks circling, ready to rend him apart.

Vincent, knowing but unable to admit that Genesis 1 would return, advised the WSRA Chief, "Hiding is not the answer. You believe that they will return. Go out there and share that belief. Take control of the press conference they are demanding and keep to your belief."

Dressed impeccably, Basoli appeared once again on the podium. He arrived, without pre-announcing the press conference, and waited to be noticed. When he was, the reporters immediately sent barrage of questions and accusations his way. He silenced them all with calm dignity, ignored all the calls for answers and spoke without referring to notes. This was not a prepared speech.

"This is a worrying time for all people of Earth, not just those of us who worked to make the deep space mission possible. This mission has forged ongoing bonds that has united Earth into a co- operative whole. The hopes of all the Earth's people are riding on this mission."

Basoli had to raise his voice over the renewed questions. "This mission is not purely speculative. It is because we know other races live amongst the stars and we cannot afford to be isolationist."

There was silence for a stunned moment. Many did not know of the alien visit to Lunar 1 three years ago. Then there were demands for an explanation. He briefly outlined the events of the encounter three years ago.

"We made friends – and human skills and ingenuity protected Lunar 1 from the hostile element we encountered."

He did not mention names, but his mind automatically recalled two particular Lunar 1 technicians.

Basoli continued, "So we know there are friendly and hostile species out there. We need to make allies. The Genesis astronauts, Casey, Tweed and Pitt went up knowing the dangers. All are highly trained fighting men, drawn from the armed services. They did not go expecting a fight but they were prepared. We planned for every contingency we could conceive and Genesis 1 was designed with the priority of keeping our astronauts alive.

"Yes, Genesis 1 is overdue – but we should not give up yet. Our deep space pioneers are the best of the best – are courageous and inventive and full of the ingenuity of all the human races. Humanity has had wars –

and endured. Let us not give up on our brave space pioneers, at what seems to be the first setback."

The first question voiced by a reporter was, "Do you truly believe they will return?"

Basoli answered, looking directly at the intent eyes watching his every body movement. "I have every confidence that they will."

The further barrage of questions was silenced with, "Do I have proof? Not yet. The proof will come first from Lunar 1. The media will be advised immediately. Until then, questions are superfluous."

Basoli left the podium spotlight, feeling shaky from the intensity of the emotion emanating from the media. And he did believe that Genesis 1 would return. Dr Vincent had reminded him of the resilience of humanity and all the planning for the mission. It had strengthened his deep belief that the mission would succeed.

"I believe you," Vincent said softly as he joined Basoli. "I believe they will return."

"I think we are the only two," Basoli admitted, glad for the moral support. Yet his mind was reminded of another that he wished would return. "I wish I could be as sure about my daughter. I don't know if I will be able to leave here to meet her as I promised."

Basoli had finally spoken of his daughter to Vincent. "Have you tried emailing her again?"

"Yes, but she hasn't answered. If I am not there she will probably say that it proves that I don't care."

"Surely she will realise why you cannot come," Vincent proposed.

"I no longer know her or how she thinks," Basoli said. "If I ever did."

"Do you have someone who could meet her for you?" Vincent did not admit that he knew the answer to that. Basoli had only told him a small part of what he had told Jonko.

"She said she would not accept a proxy."

Vincent considered. "I see. How about someone she does not expect to be a proxy? Someone who can approach unexpectedly and gain her rapport? You must have a number of young, highly intelligent, employees. Perhaps one of them with similar interests to your daughter...?"

"I don't want to advertise my problem," Basoli growled. "Too many think I am not fit for my job now, because of all the adverse personal publicity I have had recently, thanks to my brother."

"The WSRA only hires people of the highest integrity," Vincent insinuated. He was leading up to suggesting Tymos and Kryslie Ward.

The Great Ones might not realise it yet, but Vincent himself was positive that the person they needed to talk to was Jean Basoli.

"If it looks like I can't get away – I will consider it. That investigator friend of yours, John Goss, has said he will try to find where she went after taking leave from the University."

Vincent knew Jonko had not found her yet, only that she had taken care of the remains of an old gypsy – Nala de Yves.

# Chapter 29

**From the journal of Jody Basoli**

I drove back to the local town of Hope Springs, needing to get more supplies and to recharge my phone and netbook. The local guy who was supposed to act as my guide and escort me to Emanuel's Hut, had still not contacted me.

While things charged, I had time to catch up on the news. I had expected to hear that Genesis 1 was back and safe, but instead my father's face was on the news and the media reporters were on the attack. Yet somehow, he made them all go quiet, and he was speaking without notes, so I knew that this was not a planned speech.

He spoke from the heart, and I knew that he believed every word he said. He astounded me, since I had become so cynical about his idea of 'truth'. Had I ever allowed myself to get to know him?

Then I recalled how his work had always seemed more important than me. I had thought that once I had decided to attend the WSRA University, and actually achieved the criteria to be accepted at the prestigious Washington campus, that we would have things in common and that he might have…. What?

Commended me? Favoured me? Tried to talk to me?

Would I have listened then? Accepted his advance?

Probably not. But now?

After that speech, I knew he would not come looking for his one errant child. Not with the importance of the Genesis project to all of Earth. I couldn't blame him. The reputation of the WSRA rested on his shoulders. Should he vanish, be unreachable, they would think him just another thief in the night. He had to stay.

Maybe I should make the offer – to delay our meeting? Part of me still thought, "To hell with him," but this period of uncertainty was probably hellish enough.

I think I will wait and see if his belief is proved. Maybe I am wrong, and he is as much of a charlatan as Uncle Reginald.

It may be all moot. I would still have a four day drive back after my business here was complete. If only that damned guide would turn up. This area was beginning to spook me.

Nala could not have known what it was like. If it were my ashes that some future relation was to free on the winds, I would wish it to be in some less desolate place – maybe on a tropical island, or some autumn filled mountaintop. Yet, I had promised her, and I wanted to keep that promise, so that I can have closure.

If I had to, I could still free them here – send the ashes onto still blackened ashy ground.

Nala was dead, her spirit gone to be reunited with her long dead kin. Surely it could no longer matter to her?

No. I would stay and do as she asked. She had wanted that of me – only that. It was the least that I could do as the last of her descendants.

# Chapter 30

"We are within range of Earth's solar system," Jono Reslic advised the Great Ones. As he was thinking that they both looked exhausted, he felt the sword on his back begin to vibrate and heard a faint hum. The Sword of Judgement was an artefact of the Guardians of Peace and at this moment it seemed to be affecting the Great Ones. First Tymos and then Kryslie seemed to recover – like wilting plants, taking in moisture. Or the Guardians infusing them with power and energy. Both had closed their eyes as if listening to something.

Tymos spoke suddenly. "We need to talk to your guests, now that they are properly conscious and functional again. Have you prepared the message capsule?"

"All is as you requested, Great One," Reslic assured them.

"Where are the humans?"

"We have allowed them to return to their ship and they have freedom to move about the maintenance bay, Great One."

"Then I had better re-dress for my part," Tymos commented. "As the nameless faceless and mysterious alien."

In his mind, Kryslie teased, "With a big head."

He replied in kind, "You have one the same size!"

Casey was nudged by Pitt as the tall blond haired, male alien and the anonymous silver and gold clad figure entered their space. Each of the humans found the arrivals vaguely familiar, but none recalled from where. All three were annoyed at being treated like prisoners, even though they were being treated well. They were wary of these aliens, who had no place in their memories.

Reslic gave a faint bow of greeting to the three humans, when he was at a polite speaking distance away. He spoke in Tymorean, but a mechanical device translated his speech. "Greetings once again. You may not recall that I am Jono Reslic, Commander of the Tymorean Flagship, Jacen Tyr, aboard which you are currently guests. There is much I need to speak to you about. Would you prefer to be seated?"

"We'd rather stand!" Pitt answered, straightening and betraying by his new stance a touch of belligerent defiance. Casey and Tweed both subtly copied his attitude.

Reslic noted that they had found and were now wearing their side-holstered weapons, but made no comment.

"I will abide your choice," Reslic agreed, and made no move to be closer. He understood their caution.

"You will, no doubt, have many questions," Reslic proposed. "You are welcome to ask what you will."

"What the hell happened to us?" Pitt demanded immediately. "We look and feel like we were put through a meat grinder."

"And our ship was damaged," Casey added, in a calmer tone.

Tymos nodded to Pitt and spoke softly. "That is quite an accurate analogy. Your ship was attacked and boarded by Ciriot pirates. They attached a portable airlock and blew a hole in your hull."

He sensed, by the tensing of muscles suggesting residual pain, that their memory of the events was returning - all of the memories, but they stayed reasonably calm — a result of Kryslie's mental healing. The memory was not so immediate now.

Tymos gave a terse account of events that had befallen Genesis 1.

"Your distress message was heard," Reslic explained. "We were able to come to help you."

"What about the pirates?" Tweed challenged.

"Those that attacked you are in our custody for questioning. Their ship is being studied," Reslic informed him.

"We would like to see the ship, and your prisoners," Casey stated. He was testing the good will of the aliens speaking to them.

Reslic nodded. "The prisoners are intractable and if released would be extremely dangerous. I will permit you to observe them, but not closely."

He did not miss the involuntary start of a movement of hands reaching to side weapons.

"You have the right to hate them. Our people have been preyed upon by their kind. Our planet took many decades to recover from their attack on it."

Casey quietened another outburst from Pitt and asked, "Our ship has been repaired. Is that your doing?"

Reslic was able to tell him everything relevant and ending with, "We did a hull integrity test before bringing you here. You are free to leave when you wish, though we have a request to ask of you."

"What's that?" Pitt demanded.

Reslic spoke again about the aims and purpose of the Federation of Peace. Casey nodded as if he now remembered hearing it before.

"We wish you to take with you, an invitation to the people of Earth — to join us. Contained in this capsule is all the information you will need to know to explain our purpose and recognise our ships and to contact us, if we are invited to talk to your leaders."

The three humans exchanged glances and Casey finally nodded and said, "Ok."

Reslic then asked, "Has your ship passed all your diagnostics satisfactorily?"

Casey nodded cautiously. "How can you prove what you have told us?"

Tymos spoke again, "We did not touch your ship's back up memory. If you had interior monitors to store images, you might have a record. We only connected your spare memory core."

"Spare?" Tweed said in surprise.

Neither Reslic, nor Tymos spoke. Let them assume it was on their ship. No need to create questions.

"Who fixed us up then?" Pitt demanded.

"The healers here on the Jacen Tyr are excellent," Tymos told him.

Reslic added, "And the Great One helped to speed the healing."

With a lightning move, Pitt drew a sharp knife and slashed his wrist. "Prove it!" he stared at Tymos.

Tymos paused to say, "That is an extremely foolish action." But he moved forward with a soft rustling of cloth and placed his hand on the bleeding wound. Aware though, that Pitt wanted to see his face, he gripped Pitt's other arm and said quietly. "Please – you need to stay still."

"Pitt!" Casey warned. "We should respect their customs." He too had guessed Pitt's intention.

Gareth Pitt was sufficiently awed by the wound that was healing before his eyes that he subsided. He stared at the hands that were glowing faintly purple.

"Who are you then," Pitt asked, less belligerently.

Tymos answered. "I am an advocate of the Guardians of Peace. I work with the Tymoreans and the Federation of Peace. The crew of Genesis 1 was deemed worthy of our help." He lifted his head far enough for Pitt to see his piercingly bright, blue-green eyes.

Casey also caught glimpse of the eyes and was relieved. Those that had hurt him had eyes as black as evil. "We appreciate your help," Casey ventured. "Though, where are we? Can you help us get back?"

Reslic smiled. "Of course. We are outside the limit of your sun's planetary system. We are about where you would have needed to drop out of hyperspace. You will see that for yourself once you leave our dock."

"Can the trackers on Earth see you?" Tweed asked.

"I don't believe so," Reslic considered. He knew they were too far away to be seen, except by the Tymorean base on Earth. "Until you deliver our invitation to meet, and we are invited, I think it might be preferred that we do not venture closer."

"I'll say," Pitt agreed. "All this..." he gestured around him, "Is a bit more than most humans would be comfortable with. Can you land this ship?"

Reslic shook his head, and smiled again. "No – it was built in space and is docked in space. Perhaps you would like a tour en-route to observing our unpleasant guests."

All three astronauts were eager to accept and did not think it strange that Reslic escorted them or notice when Tymos slipped away.

Kryslie had been checking over their ship and directing the re-provisioning. They had already checked the supplies on Genesis 1 – which had still been adequate.

"We are ready to leave," Kryslie told him. "I would prefer to leave before Genesis 1 and be out there cloaked and ready to follow them for a bit."

"I would have thought that any Ciriot would have the sense to stay clear of the Jacen Tyr," Tymos commented.

"Perhaps, but I am uneasy about having Ciriot this close to Earth," Kryslie admitted. "And cloaked – they will be hard to spot."

"So will we," Tymos almost grinned, but he did not argue with his sister's caution.

They were in the lee of the larger ship when a repulsor beam moved Genesis 1 out of Jacen Tyr's dock. They used the relay from the flagship's sensors to watch as the humans fired up the sub light drives. Once the Earth ship was under way, they moved to a direct line of sight view and adjusted their speed and direction to it. Jacen Tyr accelerated until they were just out of sensing range of Genesis 1, but still close enough to watch for Ciriot activity. The interceptor fleet was launched and deployed in a watching pattern.

The Genesis crew quickly worked out their position and corrected their course to one close to the planned re-entry route.

Kryslie was watching her screens intently as Tymos piloted. The voice comm. from Genesis 1 was audible in the cockpit. After an initial cheer from ground control, as radio contact was finally made with the returning ship, the astronauts were sticking to the proper protocol. They did not answer any questions on their lateness, knowing that such knowledge was not for public broadcast.

"Five shadows, position ... bearing..." Kryslie said quickly after seeing a faint cloud on her screen. "Tymos, right one degree, down point three, increase speed by point seven."

Tymos complied and saw a shadow on his screen. It had the blurred outline of a Ciriot Intruder.

Kryslie sent a microburst to the Jacen Tyr and they confirmed it was not one of the Tymorean ships.

That was enough for Tymos; he fired a high powered energy beam at the shadow. It flickered into visibility as the cloaking field failed. A second burst accurately targeted the hyperspace engine and a third the inertia drive. The Ciriot ship had not had time to target its weapons array on the attacker. It was now a black ship drifting in the blackness of space, but not for long. A Tymorean Interceptor de-cloaked and attached an attractor beam, and accelerated away with the Ciriot ship in tow.

"Four more," Kryslie muttered. She guessed that the others had moved well away. She sent a microburst message to Earthbase to warn them. Tymos tweaked his sensors and moved to a new position, ahead of Genesis 1. If those ships turned to ambush the returning ship – they would be watching.

# Chapter 31

Daniel straightened when he heard Kryslie's voice on the communicator. He hid his feeling of relief that she and Tymos were back from wherever in space they had been.  It meant that Genesis 1 was almost safely home. Then he took in the sense of what she was saying.

"...four unknowns, possibly Ciriot, have entered Earth's atmosphere. We took one out that was retreating out system. Imperative you find if and where the others land. The Jacen Tyr is standing by and Tymorean interceptors are patrolling. The unknowns are cloaked and only vulnerable in close proximity to the scrambler field. Based on previous known behaviour, the ships, if they land, will pick empty, unpopulated areas and dig in. Again, they will be shielded."

"Noted, Great One," Lexina replied. "Are you returning?"

"Will advise, Earthbase," Kryslie responded. "Out!"

Lexina glanced up and saw Daniel staring at the monitor screen. Without the need for direction, she sent a message to all the Tymorean missionaries, to pass on the new information and spur them to greater vigilance. Anndra, brought up a screen with the view from the local sensors.


"Looks like our Ron is a regular hero," Morin remarked, wandering into the cavern after watching the latest vid-cast from Terra 1, where it had been announced that Genesis 1 was on the scanners.

"You are a bit too young to be so cynical, Morin," Daniel rebuked him, not quite absently, although most of his mind was on the information Kryslie had sent. "That speech he made two days ago will surely be listed amongst the most inspiring speeches in human history."

"But our Ron looks like a nobody," Morin commented.

Daniel gave him a quelling look. "Which gave it all the more power. He does look like an ordinary person and he has his share of personal problems too, but he still had faith, still believed in the indomitability of mankind."

"Yeah, well..." Morin squirmed.

"So," Daniel went on. "Did you have something relevant to say?"

"Yes, boss. There is a red mobile structure and an old truck on our perimeter. Want me to check it out."

Daniel went to the perimeter security monitors to look for himself. "How long has it been there?"

"Saw it there the other night, and the next day," Morin told him. "I thought it had gone then, because I didn't see it for the past two days. It must have come back last night because it is there again. Didn't see who was driving it. Must have come and gone by the road in as it didn't set off any alarms. Didn't see it actually coming or going either."

"Have Keleb check with the guard unit, and see if Halran knows anything about it. He is the local rep for the Uni field research group. If he doesn't, tell Keleb to get the people to move on," Daniel directed, shooing Morin out.

"Halran's been off the other side of the zone, boss. Where those crazies tried to enter."

"Well, Keleb can find out about whoever it is, and get rid of them. They cannot stay there."


Keleb gave in to Morin's pleading to go out with him. His recent outing to Washington had sparked his interest in seeing more of Earth.

"Get the jeep into the arrival cavern and program the bulk transporter beam to take us to point alpha," Keleb said. "That should be far enough away that we will be unnoticed when we arrive."

"What if one of the Nat guards do a patrol?"

"I assume you will check before we go," Keleb grinned. "You know the procedure, Morin."

"What are you doing? Getting guns?"

"We won't need weapons. If whoever arrived in that van were dangerous, they would not have chosen that rig to get here. That truck must be fifty years old and on its last legs."

"There have been some right crazies before…"

"I can deal with crazies," Keleb assured him. "I am just going to change into my WSRA grunt outfit. If I don't look too officious, even the crazies will listen to me. So, go get the jeep ready."


Keleb started the jeep once the mass transporter beam had deposited them on the dirt road outside the shield impregnated fence. He glanced at Morin who was looking even paler than usual.

"What's your problem? The transporter beam? You had no problem when you went to Washington."

"That was different. I hadn't just eaten then and anyway - I thought we'd be going that way again – not however we just did."

"It's much the same principal…"

"Doc Vincent said not," Morin argued. "Transmitting is people like you uppity royals moving themselves. This is something scrambling our atoms like we were inanimate objects like the jeep."

"Ok, take some deep breaths and concentrate on breathing in and out."

Keleb didn't tease the younger man, for as an empath, he could feel Morin's nausea.

"Next time get Vincent…"

"Won't be a next time!"

"We have to go back in."

"Can't you transmit me and then bring the jeep in?"

Keleb sighed. "Perhaps. Now let's go see this wagon and truck of yours."

"If it is still there! I reckon it keeps appearing and disappearing."

"Or they have been exploring the area and come back?" Keleb proposed a more likely scenario.

"Yeah, maybe," Morin agreed.

Keleb began driving along the track along the fenced perimeter of the blacklands, going at an easy pace until Morin got over his nausea. It usually didn't take long. He was too interested in everything human, that he would soon be distracted.

"There it is!" Morin pointed, after they had come around a slight bend. When they were closer, he spotted the figure walking towards it, back towards them.

The figure turned, as they drew closer, having heard the jeep's engine, but then continued walking to the wagon to wait.

"I know her!" Morin muttered in surprise. "Seen her somewhere."

"You have only been to Washington and to the towns near here," Keleb pointed out.

"That's it! She's the person Reg B's wife went off after."

"Interesting," Keleb agreed, drawling the word. He knew that Jonko was looking for Ron Basoli's daughter – could this be her? "Is she likely to recognise you?"

"Doubt it!"

"Well, just in case, keep quiet and let me talk."

Once he had pulled up next to the van, he killed the jeep's engine and greeted the young woman using the accent of his youth, from before he had first gone to Tymorea.

"Howdy. I'm Keith Rasmussen, and who might you be?"

"Jody"

"You have some ID?" Keleb wasn't being authoritative, just friendly. "This is a restricted area."

"I know that! I have all the proper authorisations to be here. I have organised to go in to Emmanuel's Hut. Give me a moment, my papers are inside."

While Jody climbed into the red wagon, Morin muttered, "She's a right one. Watch out for a gun."

"You have been watching too much tri-vid. She is on the defensive for some reason, but is not out to con us."

Keleb alighted from the jeep and went to examine the wagon. It was strongly built, but he would wager it was older than the truck. He turned to Jody when she re-emerged with her papers of authority and ID folder. Knowing the routine, he compared the person with the ID, and then checked the papers. According to them, her name was Jean Olynda De Yves….not Basoli.

"So, where is the rest of your team?"

"The team is me. This is personal."

"That's highly irregular. Any investigation requiring access into the restricted zone must have…"

"Another person with them! Yes, I know. I simply want to go in, empty an urn of ashes, and come out. Then I will be gone from this godforsaken place."

"Why here? Some old ashes to ashes reason? Wouldn't it be better to take them to one of those garden cemetery places? It is so dreary here." Keleb was now thoroughly intrigued by this woman. She didn't seem to be one of the religiously zealous types, but he could sense that she was determined.

"It is what my great grandmother wanted me to do," Jody sighed. "And it is the least I can do since I only met her properly half a day before she died." She glanced away, saw Morin watching her from the jeep and turned back.

Keleb suddenly made the connection. "Your great grand ma – she was a gypsy then? Related to those that died here?"

Jody nodded. "Her name was Nala de Yves."

"Mam, take my advice and spread the ashes in the forest yonder. It will benefit you more to think of her there, and not in that blackened hell. She won't mind – she's dead. You are the one who must live on."

As Jody thought on that, Keleb watched her face.

"No. I made a promise. I will have to live with my conscience if I break my word. If Halran is busy, are you able to escort me in?"

"Tom's out the far side, dealing with an issue. May not be back for days. We will need him to get a spare suit for you."

"I have everything I need. I borrowed a suit from the Uni as well as the shielded pack of safety gear."

"Show me," Keleb directed, wondering how he could convince Jody to leave and go and stay in the town. He could take her in, he had gone in several times with Tom Halran, but he would swear that he sensed the ghosts of the dead gypsies in there.

Jody returned again from inside the van, this time with the silvery radiation suit and the pack. She put them on the bonnet of the jeep for him to examine. Stepping back, she watched to see if the seeming low level Uni staff person knew what he was about.

Keleb did, and looked first at the tab on the back that recorded the service check dates, and the date of manufacture. He shook his head.

"This is overdue for a service check. It is over three years old and should be being checked every six months. More if it is used a lot."

"It's one of the highest rated types," Jody protested.

"Yes, it is," Keleb agreed. He recognised it as the type Kryslie had helped to create during her time as a student at the Uni. The ones the Tymoreans used on the rare occasions that they needed to service the sensor ring inside the zone – provided even more protection from the intense radiation.

"Emanuel's Hut is right on the limit of the instantly lethal radiation. It was built there deliberately, but even there you can't stay longer than two hours, or the suit will be at its limit before you get back to the gate out. We do have better suits, since we sometimes have to be in there hours at a time…"

"I won't need two hours," Jody insisted, but it seemed more like a plea.

Keleb resisted the urge to drum his fingers on his thigh. He needed to tell Jonko of this girl. Maybe, since he was a member of the World Council Investigative Committee, she'd listen to him."

"Will you be here tomorrow?" Keleb finally asked.

"I am staying here," Jody stated, then added, "I might have to drive into town to charge my phone though, but I will be back."

"You'd be better off staying in the town. I can meet you there tomorrow," Keleb kept trying.

"With one of the better suits for me?" Jody persisted.

Keleb nodded, thinking she would agree, but was wrong.

"I'll be here. What time?"

"Can't be sure. Can I get your phone's number?"

Jody gave it, noticing that the odd, pale haired young man still sitting in the jeep, wrote it down.

"It might be flat."

That gave Keleb one last shot. "Then you would be better off in town. We do get people sneaking in here, and they are generally not the sort of people you'd like to meet." There was no way to mention the creatures he truly feared might find her.

"I can handle that sort!" Jody claimed. "And the van is sturdy."

Keleb gave in. "Very well. Someone will be here tomorrow, unless more trouble erupts."

As soon as he was back in the arrival cavern, having forgotten his half promise to Morin and used the mass transporter to return, he told Morin to keep an eye on the truck and wagon. He didn't garage the jeep in its usual niche, for he was likely to need it again soon. Instead, he went to the communicator and used it to put a call trough to Jonko's phone.

He smothered a curse when it went through to Jon's message service. All he said was, "Jon, it's Kel. I have seen the girl. Call me. Urgent."

Morin met him on the way to the security monitor. "She's taken off again. No sign of truck or wagon!"

"Have you checked all around the perimeter? She can't have got far."

"Did that. She didn't go out on the road, either! Checked the gate monitor too – just in case she was crazy enough to go in by herself."

"Damn! What the hell is she up to?" His phone suddenly rang. It was linked into the base communications array to get signal. "Kel!" he said sharply. "Oh, Jon. Good. That girl you were after – Jean Basoli? She's here, or rather she's camping on the perimeter track, only the little fool has pulled out of sight. Can you get back here?"

He ended the call and trotted to set up the long range beam to Washington, where Jonko was currently. Moments later, Jonko materialised.

"Are you sure it's Jean Basoli?" was Jon's first question.

"Her ID says Jean Olynda de Yves. Her great grandmother just died – a gypsy - and she was here to spread her ashes. It has to be her."

"No, you are right. She is not using Basoli at the Uni either, rather just her mother's name. What is this about disappearing?"

Keleb explained how in the time it had taken to drive half a mile and transport into the cavern, the girl and her transport had vanished. "She may have gone into town to charge her phone. I promised someone would see her tomorrow, and she insisted she would be here. But if she did, she didn't go by the road, or set off any other alarms."

"Okay, I will go and check in town. Is Tom there?"

Keleb shook his head. "I'll keep watching here, and call you if I see her. Krys sent word that some Ciriot intruder ships are headed towards Earth. I don't like the idea of her on her own in that empty area."

Jonko cursed under his breath.

# Chapter 32

**From the journal of Jody Basoli**

The jeep drove up from behind me. It must have been patrolling the perimeter, but if it came in via the road, surely I would have seen or heard it before this. Unless they had a camp of their own further around and come in before I arrived or when I went into town.

The guy who was driving, the one who got out to talk to me, was friendly enough. Had an accent – Australian I think. Anyway, he had on the same sort of overalls that the Uni technicians wear, including the Uni pocket patch and his name embroidered above it.

I had half expected him to be the officious type, but he wasn't – even if he did keep insisting that I should stay in town. I wasn't having that.

This Keith Rasmussen guy wasn't one I'd heard of, but he must work for Halden out here. Certainly he seemed to know what he was about, when he looked to see if my suit had been checked. He had his regs right. I didn't try to say that the suit was my teacher's personal one – hardly used.

At least I had finally convinced him to bring one of the fancier suits here, for me to use.

I am having second thoughts about going into the town to charge my phone – that guy might report me, and get someone to detain me there.

And there was that other guy. The one who had stayed in the jeep. I know I have seen him somewhere before. That really pale blond hair was particularly noticeable. Maybe I had seen him on campus sometime – since he was with the technician guy.

When they drove off, I expected them to drive out along the road, past the National Guard post, but they didn't. They went back the way they had come from. Odd that, but it's none of my business.

I might still go into town after dark. Meanwhile, I intend to stay curled up in the wagon, have a drink and a snack. I prefer not to go outside more often than to get water, stretch my legs or attend a call of nature. I don't like the desolation here, and I had felt a twinge of regret when Keith and that other guy had driven off.

# Chapter 33

Vice President Arthur bin Halil approached Basoli and asked if it were possible to speak to Kryslie Ward, adding, "I hoped to have her understanding of some technical aspects of this mission. She was heavily involved in the project, I believe."

"Yes, working with your countryman, Rashid, Mr Vice President," Basoli agreed. "I insisted that Commander Haldstadt send her on leave for four weeks. She should be back…Bynan…" He summoned his personal assistant. "Get Haldstadt to send Kryslie Ward here."

They were in one of the conference rooms at Terra 1, waiting for the decision of the Genesis 1 crew as to whether they could get the transformation system working. If they could not, it meant that the Genesis 1 module would not be able to land at Terra 1, and would have to splashdown like the spacecraft of old.

Bynan knew that Krys Ward was not at Terra 1, although she walked towards the base intracomm unit. On her way, she caught Vincent's attention. He gestured for her to do as Basoli requested, but he moved closer to the WSRA Chief.

Bynan returned nodded to the Vice President, saying, "Kryslie Ward is not on base. Commander Haldstadt explained that she asked for and was granted an extension of her leave."

Basoli only caught the, "not on base", and quickly calculated that she should have been back. He turned to his assistant. "I assume her brother is with her, find out where they are, if you can. I want a word with one of them."

Bynan gave Vincent a pleading look. He gestured that he would handle it, and for her to pretend to use the phone. They both went over to the array of telephones which connected to off-base lines.

Vincent took out his Tymorean communicator, embodied in the casing of one of the latest generation of cellular phone. He spoke to Daniel at Earthbase and passed on Basoli's message. After a pause he continued, "Yes, I am aware of that, but I know he needs someone to talk to his daughter, and they need to talk to her and get Nala's prophecy from her. Tell them that."

Once again, Vincent listened, and this time he frowned. "You need to find her again. Make sure that she s watched and kept safe. Have Keleb camp next to her if need be. Just have Tymos or Kryslie call Basoli – or can I give him a number to text them on? Right, I'll tell him."

Vincent ended his call and then wrote down a number on a slip of paper from a pad left near the phone.

To Bynan, he said, "Tell Basoli that you spoke to their father. When they next call in he will pass on the message, or he can try texting them on this number. Imply that they took themselves off into the wilderness somewhere."

A faint smile betrayed Bynan's amusement at the understatement. She nodded slightly and returned to her boss.


Within moments of Kryslie's report of the Earthbound Ciriot intruders, Jono Reslic contacted them and suggested that Konn should join them, on the basis that he was an excellent marksman on all weapons.

Kryslie looked at her brother without speaking. Her first thought was that they didn't need him, but when he spoke and said, "An extra pair of eyes would be helpful," she didn't disagree. She simply gestured for Tymos to slow their speed so that the long range beam could lock onto their position.

Tymos sent the confirmation message, "Beam locked on," and within moments, Konn Reslic materialised within the oval terminus. He was back to being his uniform-perfect self, and the signs of his ordeal had faded.

The long range scout ship being used by the Great Ones had space for four crew, so Kryslie told Konn to dump his carry-on bag in one of the two empty cabins, and then take the navigator's control station. His body language around her was nearly as cockily arrogant as normal, although he gave Tymos a more cautious glance.

"We are just escorting Genesis 1 until the uppermost reaches of Earth's atmosphere," Kryslie told Konn. "But we need to look out for those four intruders. We don't know what they plan to do, so we have plotted out a search grid with Genesis 1 as the central point. Earthbase is also on the lookout, but they are concentrating on the six possible re-entry vectors."

"I know the procedure, Great One," Konn said quickly, but Kryslie also sensed his unspoked addition, "Better than you."

"Good," was Kryslie's neutral reply, before she added, "You will also answer any calls. We want to know the instant any of the intruders are spotted."


After a day in their company, Konn was feeling totally superfluous, and he began to wonder if that was deliberate. He couldn't find anything to indicate that they resented or disliked his presence. They were polite, took turns with preparing food or bringing drinks – even though Konn had volunteered to do that for them.

Slowly he came to realise that the two Great Ones worked like mirror images of each other – or like one mind controlled both bodies. They didn't even have to speak to each other. Sometimes it seemed that they completely forgot about him and all he was doing was sending course changes to the helm, and taking and sending messages as if he were there greenest of fleet cadets. At the moment, his baby brother Ennis – acting as their father's aide – had more responsibility.

He would have liked to have ignored the latest message, except that it originated from Vincent, the brother of Governor Xyron. If it had been directed at himself, he would have done nothing about it. Commoners had no right to demand Tymorean royals to do anything, yet some human, who might have had a Tymorean ancestor somewhere, had the presumption to order a Great One to contact him.

Yet, he passed the message stick to Kryslie, as dutifully as any mindless cadet, and listened as she read the message from the small data screen. He heard Tymos's exclamation of surprise.

"Basoli's daughter?"

"Daniel believes that she was the last person to talk to Nala," Kryslie summarised. "And Keleb confirmed that she was camped on the perimeter of the blast zone."

"I think you would be the best to go," Tymos said aloud, knowing that Kryslie sensed his reasons. "Konn and I can handle the search and escort, and I am sure that you can handle Basoli and his request."

"Okay. Request the long range beam from Earthbase. I just need to grab a few things."

She felt Tymos slowing, and heard him report that the beam was activated. She trotted back to the rear of the control cabin, still in her silvery gold ship suit.


Kryslie transmitted to Earthbase and found Daniel, Jonko and Keleb waiting for her in the arrival cavern.

"It is Basoli's daughter on the perimeter?" she asked before either spoke.

"She said she was Jean de Yves, but prefers to be called Jody. And yes, she is the great-grandchild of Nala de Yves," Keleb confirmed. "We did not ask about a relationship to Basoli, since Vincent says she is estranged from him. But it is her. She is a student at Washington Uni, enrolled under her mother's name."

"She came here. How could she have known that we needed to talk to her? That we even exist here?"

"She said that it was Nala's dying wish," Keleb added. He saw understanding enlighten Kryslie's face.

"We never met Nala, but she must have known of us, and that we were here and that she needed to speak to us of her premonition. She would have known she was dying…" Kryslie stopped talking, to think.

"But the girl could only be half Tymorean, or less," Keleb pointed out.

Kryslie ignored that comment, asking instead, "Daniel, can I bring her here? I don't like the idea of her being out there on her own, and frankly, I don't have time to deal with her just now."

As Daniel nodded, refraining from saying that they were not meant to bring non-Tymoreans into the base, and went to speak to Lusanne about preparing sleeping niche for a visitor.

Kryslie's mind was busy with other things. "What did you say to her, Kel?"

"Just that someone would be around to see her today, with an ultra-protective radiation suit. I was about to go out when Basoli's request came in."

"It's afternoon now?"

Keleb nodded.

Turning her attention to the third of her greeting committee, Kryslie asked, "Jon, what was it that she said in that message to her father?"

"It was an all or nothing ultimatum – meet me on such and such a day, or I am gone for good."

"Kel, has Basoli called here?"

"No, Bynan sent the message."

"Well, I suppose he has been busy. What has been decided about Genesis? Land or splashdown?"

"Splashdown. The crew were unable to fix the transformation controls. According to Morin, who has been glued to the Earth news feed every spare minute, the select group who are to welcome the astronauts back, are flying out to the recovery ships about now."

"Did Bynan give Basoli my Earth cell number?"

Daniel had returned and he answered. "Yesterday, she did that."

Kryslie unzipped one of the utility pouches in her ship suit and retrieved her communicator from it. Although the hand sized unit was Tymorean made, it resembled the latest Earth made communication devices and also linked into the Earth communication network. She turned it on to check for messages. It pinged three times, now that it was back in range of the network.

The first message was a polite, "Please call Ron Basoli as soon as you can. A call number followed." That had come from Bynan.

The second message was a sharp, "Technician Ward, where are you? You were due back a week ago."

The third was Basoli again, a message sent several hours after the first. He began quoting some WSRA regulations at her. She ended that message abruptly, well before it was finished.

"Have there been any indications of cloaked ships? Ciriot activity? UFOs? Meteorites burning up?"

"No Great One," Daniel told her.

"Show me that wagon and truck," Kryslie directed. Keleb gestured her to go to where the security monitors were scrolling through the feeds from all cameras. Once there he stopped the scrolling when it showed the gypsy van. He gave an inaudible sigh of relief when he saw that the wagon and truck had not disappeared again.

The stillness that seemed to wrap around Kryslie spread to Keleb and stopped his thoughts about the wagon. He stared at her, but was unaware of her thoughts.

Kryslie saw a memory from over half a century before superimpose itself over the view of the wagon. In it she and Tymos were visiting a very old man in a wagon that might have been the very one on the perimeter now. The man had been Tymorean – Tamir Janzoet, father of Tamir Grainger who had founded the WSRA. That wagons were often passed down in families suggested that Nala was related to Grainger.

"I had better see what Basoli wants," Kryslie said, turning from the screen and activating her communicator. She tapped in the call number that she had been given.

While the dialling tone continued, she took a deep breath and took her mind back into her WRSA technician persona.

When she heard Basoli answer with a gruff, "Basoli," she said, "Sir, this is Kryslie Ward. You wanted to talk to me?"

"Where are you? It took you long enough to get my message."

She ignored both his attitude and his question, having no intention of lying to him, or telling the truth. "What can I do for you, Sir?"

"I have an appointment tomorrow in Washington that I can't keep. I believe you could handle it for me? Can you be there tomorrow?"

Kryslie considered asking bluntly for details, but forced a more respectful tone and wished he would get to the point. "I believe so, Sir."

She was hearing a noise through the connection – a huffing noise as if Basoli was walking somewhere at a quick pace. Then there was a sound of a door sliding shut.

Finally, Basoli stopped side-stepping a straight answer and explained the situation, adding, "I require your absolute discretion and confidentiality."

"You have that, without question, Sir," Kryslie assured him immediately. "I will report any results to you as soon as I have any."

Basoli ended the call.

Kryslie took a deep breath and did not snarl at the mental image she had of Basoli. He wanted her to mend twenty three years of neglect of his daughter in one short meeting? And that was more important than finding four Ciriot intruder ships and their torturing crews?


"Great One."

Kryslie spun around and saw Vincent.

"I thought you were out on the recovery ship with Basoli!"

"I will be returning shortly, Great One, but there are some items of confidential information that you should be aware of. May I suggest we talk in the garden?"

Kryslie strode that way, impatient to be finished. When she arrived, she sat on an ornamental rock ledge beside the small fountain. It was her favourite place at the base.

"May I suggest, Great One, that while we sit here, you ground out your excess power? You are almost glowing."

Kryslie glanced at her hands, saw the purple glow and followed the suggestion. It was as well that no one had touched her as they might have been zapped and sent flying.

"Thank you," Kryslie told Vincent. She was no longer feeling edgy and angry. "What did you need to tell me?"

"A few things about the current relationship between Basoli and his daughter."

Kryslie listened, nodded and agreed that the information was important. Then Vincent asked her about the Genesis astronauts.

"Nothing has been transmitted to ground control," Vincent confirmed. "And I know they were tortured by the Ciriot. How are they?"

"Physically they are on the mend. Tymos speed healed many broken bones. By the time they splash down, they won't be fully healed, but will be functional. I am concerned that the splash down may jolt them and exacerbate some injuries. They won't be able to land, because the transformation capability is compromised."

Vincent waited while Kryslie paused to consider further.

"Mentally," Kryslie went on. "I succeeded in putting the memories of torture at one remove. They remember it all, but are calm about it."

"Have you concerns there? I intend to be part of the medical evaluation team."

"Good," Kryslie said. "I think Casey and Tweed are going to be mentally and emotionally back to normal once the post-mission check and debrief are over."

"Pitt?" Vincent queried.

"I am not so sure about Gareth. It is nothing I can describe and act on. He seems as confident as before – but he fought me when I was trying to help him. It was like he did not want to be healed. Since then – he has been different. I knew him really well, and he is a nice polite man – or was. Now he is arrogant and annoying and somewhat belligerent."

"Did he recognise you?" Vincent asked.

"No, we stayed hooded and robed. I would have sensed if he had even suspected."

"Thank you. I will know what to look for when they are down," Vincent said.


A discreet signal chime became audible in the garden.

"Great One, please come to the scanner room." Daniel's voice summoned on the base intercom system.

Kryslie stood and strode off quickly, leaving Vincent to follow if he wished.

"I am here," Kryslie announced quietly when she was in sight of the screens.

"Great One, something just flew low over this area," Daniel announced. "Anian, replay the scanner record on your screen."

Kryslie saw the faint cloudy shadow. It was fast, and had to have been low for the scrambler field to enable that much of a picture. "Ciriot infiltrator," she confirmed. Then a sudden thought caused her to ask, "Where is that girl in the van?"

Keleb told her, "It will be very close to that ship's flight path."

"Bring me two radiation suits and an extra personal force field generator," Kryslie directed and Anian scuttled off to obey.

"Do you want the jeep?" Keleb asked.

"No, I will transmit out there. I will let you know if I want back up. If I do, bring weapons. If the Ciriot realise what this area is, and it is likely to be deserted, it would be just a place they might choose to dig in."

Kryslie quickly switched from her ship suit to the radiation suit, one of the 'ultra' kind that Keleb had mentioned to the woman at the perimeter. She, of all those currently at the base, could survive without it, but she had no wish to reveal the fact. Then she added weapons to the holders on the suit.

The second suit was bundled into a backpack and a force screen generator into one of her suit pouches.

Without further word, she strode to one of the smaller exits from the underground cavern system. She cycled out through the airlock entrance and walked to a position just short of where she would be visible from above. The colour stripes on the sleeves of her suit cycled through to black – lethal level of radiation.

From there, she transmitted line of sight to a ridge of a hill range. She would be highly visible there in a silvery gold suit on a blackened landscape – but she did not stay long. A quick look around through eyes adjusted to see into the UV end of the spectrum – showed no Ciriot traces. Wherever they went there were trails visible in that light. She could see none from there to the horizon.

This was only a small section of the extensive banned zone, but it was the part nearest the wagon and truck. She transmitted from the ridge to a point closer to the van and outside the fence so she could oversee the open area. The woman wasn't visible and was probably in the wagon. More importantly, there were no Ciriot trails around it or near it.

As she waited for her suit to transmute the radiation and the stripes to return to the white of safe ambient radiation, she used a communicator to talk to base.

"Keleb, has there been any movement near that van since I came out?"

"No, Great One," Keleb confirmed. "I have been watching. And I checked the recording. Earlier, before you arrived, she walked off to the little spring, and came back. There has been no movement since. She should still be there."

Kryslie acknowledged and planned her approach to the van. She transmitted to a clump of trees some distance from the van and strode openly from there. Every detail her eyes saw was noted and considered.

"Ahoy the van," she called as she drew near it. "Anyone within?"

No answer, no cautious movement, no sound to suggest a presence within. Kryslie concentrated on seeing/sensing within the van. This odd skill of hers took effort.

Empty! Kryslie did not call Keleb to ask 'are you sure', she knew he was efficient.

Instead, she studied the ground. Jeep tracks and two sets of footprints – one set was from Keleb. The smaller shoe prints leading off to the stream and also going up and down the road must be the woman's. More of those prints led in both directions along the barrier, and at places into the trees.

Kryslie quickly climbed the van's wooden steps and looked within, and confirming what her senses had 'seen'. Descending, she glanced in both directions before taking off at a trot in the direction away from that which she had arrived. The prints in the dust over lapped, but the freshest headed towards an area of clumpy vegetation on the rise of a hill. From her memory, she thought there were some small caves there too.

Kryslie did not sense anyone around and so did not moderate her 'trot' which was faster than most people could run. She was feeling a sense of urgency related to finding the woman.

The area had been explored by the wearer of the shoes, the prints going into and out of the caves. The caves looked to be empty and there was no one up in the trees and no sign of the woman.

Kryslie returned to explore back along the way she had arrived, not moderating her fast trot. When that direction led no further than the trees, she returned to the van once more, had a better look inside it and the truck before transmitting back to the ridge.

From there she considered whether the woman might have penetrated into the blackened land. There had been no sign of the radiation suit she had shown Keleb. People could go through the gate, but there was no sign of that being forced open. A Tymorean could transmit through it, or if they had a personal force shield on – force their way through it. Assuming that was, they could ignore the increasing mental pressure to get back from it. Humans would have to be impossibly dense (as some previous intruders had been) or incredibly motivated and fool hardy.

From Keleb's description, the woman was not a fool, was determined to head into Emmanuel's Hut, and had made surprisingly useful preparations. Now Kryslie did call Keleb again.

"Kel, no sign of her here or in either direction. Can you check for intruders inside the boundary? And maintain a watch on the wagon – call me at once if you see her."

"Confirmed, Great One," Keleb replied.

Kryslie transmitted away, arriving at the nearest of the sensor nodes she and Tymos had positioned years ago when they were preparing the base. After scanning the area around it, she went to another to repeat the action. At each place she scanned the terrain with her enhanced distance vision. That she saw nothing to alarm her did not make her feel less apprehensive.

# Chapter 34

**From the journal of Jody Basoli**

I heard a noise like a low flying jet plane as I walked along the fence to stretch my legs. I even felt a wash of heat and smelt burnt fuel. I saw nothing. The noise receded in the distance, into the black land. It scared me, first because I thought it was an official jet and they might report my presence and I would be ordered away. As I began to return to the van, I dismissed that idea. That Keith guy knew I was there. Then I thought that who would take a jet that low over contaminated land?

It was then I began feeling like I really should leave, but I hadn't kept my promise to Nala. And I hoped that Keith would soon return with the promised suit.

Instead of going back to the van, I decided to watch from one of the small caves I had found. It was for no logical reason – except fear. Fear of what – I didn't know.

A while after, I saw a silver clad figure, running really fast and following my trail. The figure was humanoid, and was probably wearing a radiation suit. But I did not know who it was - only that no human could normally run that fast. I retreated into the cave, and when the figure came in, I stayed very still and held my breath and pretended to be a rock. The figure went away without finding me in the dark. I crept back to the entrance and saw it running back to my camp and beyond. When it returned again, it looked around my camp – and vanished.

Fear of staying around here and an urge to flee, warred with my curiosity and my promise to Nala.

Fortunately I had grabbed my pack and some food and water. I used the time I stayed cowering in the cave to try and open the locked box.

Kryslie spent the rest of the day transmitting herself in a search pattern amongst the blackened rolling hills. She saw no signs of the Ciriot. In this area, there were pockets where the radiation wasn't as deadly and the edges of the area had lower levels.

The Ciriot could tolerate a degree of radiation, more than humans could, but they would have to shield their ship if they were in here. It would be hard to find unless the Ciriot started moving in and out of the shield. Only then would she see traces of their passing. The afternoon was fruitless and frustrating.

In the evening, she returned to the base, went through the decom procedure, and went to program some different parameters into the shield matrix and the sensor array.

The following morning, after checking on Genesis 1 through her brother – she transmitted via long range beam to Washington. This was in case Basoli's daughter had decided to go, and succeeded in getting to, the meeting she had demanded. For this trip, she had borrowed some of Lexina's going out clothes.

Kryslie went to the address Basoli had given her and found not a house but an empty block that had been made into a kind of park with benches. She sat on one and watched the people coming and going. After a time, a middle aged woman sat beside her. The woman finally decided to speak.

"Great One Kryslie – do you remember me? I am Donna Diese."

Kryslie turned and studied the woman. "Yes...but you were only a child when we last met. Why did you seek me out?"

"Daniel called me and asked if I knew a gypsy woman – Nala. I did."

Now Kryslie listened intently.

"She was one of us. A friend of my father Ramon – or rather, her son Domir de Yves was."

"I felt sure she had to be, but I have not had time to check the records. Go on," Kryslie urged.

"She worked with Grainger, when he was getting the WSRA started."

Kryslie mentally calculated – it must have been after they had left at the end of the war, after the rocket crashed.

"Did she work on his shield theories?" Kryslie asked and Donna nodded.

"How was it that Nala survived?" Kryslie asked.

"Her wagon broke a wheel," Donna said. "It was going to take a day to replace it. She and her family stopped, and the rest of the tribe went on to Sliding Springs. Then the rocket crashed. Nala's husband Pietr and son Domir rode off to check on the tribe and Domir's wife. She had been travelling with her sister who was heavily pregnant. Nala had Olynda, Domir's child. The men didn't come out. When Nala was ready to go on, she was not allowed into the area. The army had blocked it off and were guarding it."

Kryslie had a faraway look on her face as she asked, "It was the Mont de Ray tribe, wasn't it?"

Her mind was picturing how the tribe must have looked before...

"Yes," Donna confirmed. "Domir married Yulita Mont de Ray. It was a miracle that Nala survived."

Kryslie nodded, but she felt that the miracle was a working of the Guardians of Peace – not a coincidence.

"She died here, you know," Donna went on. "About a week ago. In her wagon which was parked along the river a bit."

Kryslie nodded. "Her great grandchild was with her – Olynda's child."

Donna's eyes widened. "I am glad she wasn't alone. But I did not know Nala had a great grandchild."

Kryslie sensed that Donna had nothing else to tell her, so she thanked the older looking woman and considered the ideas her talk had raised. Donna left, claiming work she had to do.

"I never looked for Tymorean shields!" Kryslie berated herself and thought back to her search of the camp near the fence. "I assumed, that if Nala was Tymorean, her grandchild was a half or less and would be unable to operate Tymorean technology – wouldn't have the power."

Now, Kryslie was sure that Jean Basoli was not in Washington and equally sure that she needed to hurry back to Earthbase.


Kryslie took Keleb with her when she returned to Jody Basoli's camp. She drove the jeep at a speed that Keleb had never dared and stopped it back from the camp. She stood up from the seat to look over the area. Keleb saw her eyes change shape and appearance. He had never seen her do that before.

"Keep your weapons handy," Kryslie warned, freeing her own so it was loose in its holster. "The Ciriot have been here."

"How can you tell?" Keleb asked.

Kryslie flicked her eyes back to normal. "Where ever they touch, or walk, they leave a trace of a trail that is visible in UV light. The wagon and the truck practically glow all over. The tracks lead through the barrier, off to the north-west. I am going to check in the wagon. You check the truck but stay alert. The most you will hear is the swishing of their robes and perhaps muted clicks."

She had already determined that Earthbase had not seen Jody return, but her own observations on this arrival indicated that she must have been back. The solar panels had been arrayed and these did not have any glowing marks on them. She went to the rear of the van. The door was hanging open and half off its hinges. She climbed up carefully and adjusted her eyes to see where the Ciriot had touched.

Inside was a mess – it had been searched and things were strewn over the floor. Amongst the clutter were signs of weapons fire. Disintegrator fire had taken chunks out of the wall, cupboards and the bed. Scorch marks showed where a heat weapon had been fired.

There was blood on the bed and some brownish hairs still attached to a piece of skin. The pillow was rent and the fibre filling everywhere. The mattress had also been shredded as if with claws.

Kryslie examined all of the clutter in minute detail, focussing on 'below' it. She moved enough of the mess to extricate a small backpack. It had been shaken out, but it wasn't empty. Kryslie felt inside it and found a palm sized metal box with a built in combination lock. As there was a faint purple glow on it, she pocketed it.

Concentrating further, she sensed a drawer under the floor and shoved mess aside to get to it. Inside, as if pushed in hastily, was a leather bound notebook and pen, as well as a netbook computer. She took out both and shoved them into the front of her radiation suit.

"Kryslie!" Keleb called sharply. He kept a vision in his mind, hoping she would look.

"Don't do anything, Kel," Kryslie thought at him. She was taking her own weapons out and was ready to shoot when a now visible Ciriot climbed into the van. That one fell without a sound, and Kryslie walked over the unconscious body to reach the door. Before the four Ciriot between her and Keleb knew about her, they too fell soundlessly. The two behind Keleb, grabbed him and spoke in clicking tones.

Kryslie was sending a message to Morin, who was still inside the base. Reinforcements would be coming.

Keleb wasn't helpless. Two to one odds were child's play to him. He had excelled at unarmed combat.

Kryslie looked around. If there were more Ciriot, they had cloaked themselves or gone.

"I want prisoners," Kryslie told Keleb. She was fully alert and sensed the sneak attack even before it reached her. The Ciriot might have been invisible, but he was still physically there and did not expect his intended victim to use his attack to toss him to the ground with stunning force.

An armoured Ciriot appeared under her. She spun around, lifting the alien, just as a disintegrator beam was fired at her. The stunned Ciriot woke and squealed in agony.

The arrival of the Tymorean reinforcements sent the remaining Ciriot fleeing. Kryslie watched them go through the force field, and into the blackened lands.

"Clean up here," Kryslie ordered. She took the book and computer from her suit and pushed them at Keleb. "Keep these safe."

No one dared to try to stop her following the Ciriot. They were moving fast, but Kryslie followed the glowing tracks. She heard the rising hum and felt the rush of heat as the Ciriot craft lifted. It wasn't cloaked at first, and it headed north before vanishing.

Those infiltrator craft could hold twelve. She had taken out six. She listened for the sound of the ship to fade in the distance before returning to the scene of the attack.

The unconscious and dead Ciriot had been taken away. The worst of the traces of the fight were being smoothed away. Kryslie went into the van and began putting things away. She directed two of the missionary fighters to take the damaged bedding away and bring replacements. Keleb joined her.

"Kryslie?" Keleb ventured softly. "Do you think you can find her?"

"I will find her," Kryslie assured him emotionlessly. "Take those things I gave you back into the base, will you?"

"Why didn't we see her come back?" Keleb asked.

Kryslie took the box from her pocket and tossed it at him. "It is a field generator. She must have had that on her."

Keleb sensed the power in it.

"How? She is not Tymorean," Keleb objected.

"Nala was," Kryslie told him. "I think her son and his wife were. If so, Jody is half Tymorean. I think Nala tuned it to her – and I never thought to look for anything like that."

"Then – how did they get her?" Keleb asked.

"She must have gone out without it," Kryslie guessed. "Go, will you? I have a bit more scouting to do here."

The Ciriot did not return to the camp as Kryslie half expected them to. She knew that they, as a race, did not like to be forced to retreat. Near evening, Kryslie had Keleb bring out the jeep to tow the wagon to the base. She did not worry about the now unusable truck.

Daniel met Kryslie on her return.

"Sit, eat, drink and tell me what you are planning, Great One."

"Daniel..." she began to object. "Oh, alright. What is happening with Genesis 1?"

"Ground control have calculated a re-entry window, corrected Genesis 1's course. They are due to splash down off the coast from Terra 1, seventeen hundred hours tomorrow. Vincent has been invited onto the recovery ship. Great One Tymos has reported no problems."

They were walking through a passage of natural rock, smoothed, but not finished any more than that. This one led to the base living quarters and the mess cavern.

Lusanne, the Tymorean that acted as cook and domestic manager, pointed to a table already set with cutlery. Kryslie sat and gestured for Daniel to join her.

The lights in this cavern were on around the clock and the power came from the transmutation of the radioactivity outside through one of the inner shields.

A meal was placed in front of Kryslie and Daniel spoke while she ate.

"I have the Ciriot in stasis chambers. You can tell me what you want done with them. They are truly ugly creatures. The wagon is in the outer cavern, with the other vehicles."

"What else?" Kryslie asked between mouthfuls.

"Landin from Lunar 1 is asking when Tymos will be back and Bynan says Basoli is after an answer to your mission today."

"Well, obviously, she didn't show in Washington," Kryslie said between mouthfuls.

"I could wish...Great One...that you would be more forthcoming with your intentions," Daniel commented.

Kryslie stopped eating. "I am not, because I haven't finished thinking things out and the Guardians have not seen the need to comment on what I have been doing. I don't know everything yet."

"Like remembering to eat," Daniel murmured, and Kryslie grinned briefly.

"I can see the subtle hand of the Guardians in certain events," Kryslie did explain. "I met Donna Diese today. She is the daughter of Ramon, who was a friend of Rhyn."

Daniel nodded, recognising the names.

"She told me that Nala was Tymorean. Both her parents were pure bred descendants of the original missionaries. She worked with Grainger for a time — after the rocket blast that killed her husband, son and daughter. She raised her granddaughter — who was in the right place to meet and marry Ron Basoli, and produce a child."

"The Basoli who would lead the WSRA — where you would be," Daniel concluded.

Kryslie nodded. "The other thing is that the prophecies given to the Tymorean Elders are often given to those who are on the world to which they apply. I think Nala might be one of the last full blood expatriate Tymoreans here. She knew her grandchild had been affected by some of the fallout and needed to have her line continue. She probably didn't know why."

"So what will you tell Commander Basoli?" Daniel asked.

"Firstly that she didn't show in Washington. Then...I think I will mention the gypsy...and that I think she is heading here. Of course, I will keep looking for her and I probably know how she thinks."

"What about finding her? How can we help?" Daniel persisted.

"You can help by checking to see if that Ciriot ship is still in this area. Send out a shielded spy drone to search the area, and have it set to scan in the UV range. Ciriot leave a distinct trail behind them."

"And you," Daniel queried.

"I want you to tell Tymos I need him here. The air force will be up to keep the airways clear for the re-entry. That should be enough to deter the Ciriot interest in Genesis 1."

"You still haven't answered my question, Great One." Daniel had a hint of warning in his voice.

"Very well. I intend that the hunters of innocent humans discover they are being stalked by a much nastier predator."

The face she turned up to meet Daniel's gaze was implacable and he had never seen such a look before.

"I will wait for Tymos. I do not intend to do this alone. They will come back. The Ciriot like strong minded victims and they may have realised Tymoreans are here. If they have, I hope they will concentrate on finding us, and ignore the humans of this area. You should have someone watching for Ciriot in the nearby towns. Look for unexplained deaths, disappearances, abnormal behaviour, unexplained wounds...that sort of thing."

"Anything else, Great One?" Daniel asked, rising.

"I'm still thinking," Kryslie claimed, as she turned her attention back to her meal. Daniel was not going to like her idea.

She stayed there and sent Lusanne to find Keleb.

"I cannot open that box," Keleb admitted. "The computer is damaged, and here is the book."

"Thanks," Kryslie reached for the box and the book.

Within a few moments of opening the book, Keleb realised that Kryslie had forgotten him. He slipped away. He had only glanced at the first page that had been inscribed with the name Jean Olynda de Yves Basoli. She had started to read it and was quickly reading and turning pages.

The personal journal of 'Jody' Basoli, told Kryslie a great deal about her. She had started the journal when she had begun questioning what she had always thought of as truth about her father and uncle. She wrote of her intention to confront her father and force answers from him. Later she had seemed less belligerent, more...yearning. Through it all, Kryslie sensed that Jody was being driven.

But it was the later writings that made Kryslie tense with the beginnings of a premonition. She read what Jody had written about seeing her, and deduced that the woman had been frightened – of her.

Then, "Last night I was terrified. I heard noises in the wind, like the clicking of nocturnal beetles. Yet I know this area is devoid of creature life. If I were closer to the trees, I might have thought it was the snapping of dead twigs and the sound of leaves brushing each other. But there are only low bushes and not even insects live on them.

"I forced myself to confront my terrors. I went out with my torch and looked around. It might have been human trouble makers and I could handle them. Yet there was no one. But I seemed to see dark shadows moving in my side vision – like shadows from a flickering fire. But there was no fire, only the moon and no clouds to scud across it either. When I looked at the barrier, I seemed to see odd glowing patches that I had not noticed before.

"Now, in the morning, my fears seem so childish. Even so, part of me still wants to run, far from here – but I promised Nala I would return her to her loved ones. And when I looked, there were no tracks but mine around the van."

That page was still half blank. Kryslie stared at it. If Jody had Nala's ashes, where were they? Her hand idly flicked through the remaining pages as she considered the question. More writing caught her attention.

This writing was harder to read, and not in the neat careful script Jody had used before. It seemed to have been written in haste.

"I am terrified. I am irrational. There is evil about me. I feel it like insects crawling on me. I feel like I am suffocating. I have to get out of here. My mind is running in endless circles, filled with frightening visions. A voice in my head is telling me to write and I am forcing myself.

"Nala told me there was danger. I had to come here and tell them. Them? They will come, she said. They share her blood and mine. Tymorean, she said. Her people were Tymorean. She is dead now. I... the pain...in my head. I have to go out. My mind is going...I can't fight it anymore...help me..."

Kryslie stayed still and tense – seeming to feel what Jody had felt – her terror and her desperation. She was sure that Jody had not been aware of what she was writing on that last page.

The premonition surfaced, bringing together all the clues she had had all along.  Nala had indeed prophesised before she died and Jody had been her witness. Nala had blocked the memory of it – or the girl would have recorded it in her journal. Nala had compelled her to come here to where those who shared the blood of Earth and Tymorea would find her. The ashes were not important – just a reason Jody could comprehend.

Kryslie berated herself for not acting sooner, for not looking for Tymorean shields. She had had all the clues...

A shiver travelled down her spine, like a further premonition.

"I will find her," Kryslie promised. "I will make myself such a target – one they will find irresistible."

They will find Jody a tough one. They will not break Nala's block easily and they won't kill her.

They won't break me either, Kryslie knew. So – they will take me to their tribe ship – or their base. No, the ship – they can't have been here long enough to dig in.

We need to find that ship and the smaller ones. We have to learn their intentions – how they plan to pillage this world.

A fleeting thought that the Guardians were subtly helping her – crossed Kryslie's mind. A more nebulous one followed – that she was being moved into some place for some reason. The shiver was repeated, but Kryslie told herself, "I have to find the tribe ship, and that will be dangerous. It is a warning to be wary."


Kryslie was in the garden 'lounge' where the sense of being outside was cleverly imitated by the high light painted rock ceiling, the bright light shining through a hardy ring of leafy foliage from trees grown hydroponically and a 'breeze' that wafted summer smells.

She looked to be meditating, and so was not disturbed. In fact, she was trying to extend her 'earth sense' beyond the still radioactive land above her.  But all the while, the sense of the Earth's power was refreshing her.

The return of Tymos was like a sense of oneness, but it was Konn Reslic she heard first. His voice was loud, but muffled by the rock walls of the garden. Kryslie had the sense that he was trying to exert his authority.

"He has none," Tymos spoke to her mind. "I will join you shortly. He is trying to stare Daniel down."

Kryslie sent a mental chuckle. "I know who will win. I believe our esteemed Earth father has been taking lessons from his Excellency. Even I know not to argue with Daniel when he is right."

"Hmm, yes," Tymos considered. "I will leave them to it."


True to his word, Tymos walked into the garden area and removed his shoes and socks. He sat opposite her on an outcrop of native rock.

"The Ciriot have Jody Basoli," Kryslie told him at once.

Tymos felt his sister's determination to rescue her. "Tell me all the details."

Kryslie sent her impressions to his mind even as she spoke.

"Your idea should work, but are you the right one to be the bait?" Tymos asked, concerned.

"I have thought it over. I don't like it, and I am risking being controlled – like Stenn was. But, I have had one of their motes in me and I know how it feels. I should be able to block it and I will have my force shield on all the time. Also, if I need to – I can control Jody's mind and body."

Tymos nodded, uncomfortably. "So I watch and follow where they take you. What if they don't go to the tribe ship? Or Jody is not there?"

"I will get free," Kryslie vowed. "But I feel sure they will have taken Jody there. Here, they know they are threatened. They would not want their prize escaping. So be ready to locate a beam on me. Once we are out, we can take out the ship's drive."

"And destroy the infiltrator ships when they come back to defend the tribe ship," Tymos considered. "I will take Konn. He is the fleet champion on weapons. But first, I will put him to checking the ship and restocking it."

Tymos went to find Konn, and was satisfied that the newcomer now had a truce with Daniel, even if it was an uneasy one. Konn had accepted he had to obey Great One Tymos, but had not taken to the idea of a human being in charge of a Tymorean base.

Konn's mouth didn't quite drop when he saw Kryslie decked out as a mechanic. She wore the silvery radiation suit, without the head piece, and had a belt of tools around her waist.

"Stop staring, Konn Reslic," Kryslie told him. "Do you expect me to attract Ciriot by standing out in the open with weapons ready? I intend to stay alive and bring them to me."

"Great One, let me be the target," Konn tried to insist. "Let me risk the danger."

Kryslie shook her head. "I hope you are not implying I am not capable of this. The truth is, you look too capable and too dangerous. I want to get the Ciriot reacting, and believing themselves superior – and keep them that way. I have no intention of being a meek victim, nor of letting the Ciriot know that their 'lamb' is a ravening predator."

Konn backed off a step as Kryslie looked at him.

Evening and dusk were not far off as Kryslie continued to tinker with the engine of the truck and pretend to try to fix it. She had already realised that the Ciriot vandals had made fixing it impractical. She expected them to return after dark to study the scene again.

Daniel's probe had found nothing as yet, but Kryslie did not expect finding the Ciriot to be easy. They may not have returned to the black land and may not intend to, but then, like she had told Daniel, they did not like to be forced to retreat. She had made them do that. And their prey had escaped after killing some of their number. It was an affront to their belief that they were superior to all other races. Any such lesser being that threatened them, the strong minded ones, they liked to break.

If they saw her there, would they think her a Tymorean? If they did, she would be considered fair prey. To the Ciriot, Tymoreans were verminous enemies and mass murderers.

Kryslie sensed them coming, on foot, and alerted Tymos. He and Konn were ready to take off on an instant and both Tymos and Earthbase would be tracking her through the three devices she had on or in her.

Tymos was lightly in rapport with her mind. Kryslie had warned him that he might have to raise his mind shields fast.

"I know, Kryslie," he had responded soberly. He knew, as well as she did, that they would take their anger out on her first. Yet his sister seemed calm and accepting.

Kryslie first became aware of the pressure of a mind on hers. It was sending her a sense of terror, visions of people dying hideous deaths, of needing to run.

She ignored the mental pressure, and put down the spare radiator hose and picked up a large spanner. She had a lot of potential weapons nearby as well as proper weapons. Though those were not like the ones she had used yesterday – which if used on her would disable her for a perceptible time. She had human style weapons.

"Who is there?" Kryslie called out after starting to look around. "Show yourselves, you cowards."

Nothing answered her, but what might have been the rustling of leaves – if it was not a totally wind free evening. She began to circle the truck, looking all around.

A stone rattled on the ground. Kryslie acted as a human might by turning in that direction and backing away. She felt herself grabbed by something she couldn't see. She struggled, testing the strength of her captor before exerting herself to break free. She waved the spanner around her with deceptive force and felt it connect. The reaction was swift and vicious.

What felt like metal gauntleted hands pummelled her - front, back head and face. She fell to the ground and around her, Ciriot uncloaked.

Six of them and one was purple clad. He strode forward and plucked her from the ground. He put his face close to hers and Kryslie spat blood from her mouth into his face, her eyes blazing with the intent to destroy him.

"Fools! I am not alone," she challenged them, once again twisting and kicking and almost getting free again. Two Ciriot grabbed her from behind and the purple one released her. He deliberately tore the front of her radiation suit as if it were paper, and took a piece of the fabric to wipe his face. Then he spat in her face, a liquid that felt like acid.

"We have what we want, murderer. We are not staying," the mechanical translator said after a series of clicking sounds. He spoke again but those sounds were not translated.

Kryslie felt a solid thump in the middle of her back and lightning fast strands of something snapped around her. The Ciriot dropped her, and within seconds, the tangler net had surrounded her and was drawing her limbs into painful contortions.

Kryslie felt Tymos's mind touch hers – with concern. "I have a tracer on their ship," he told her. "It is not far inside the barrier. The tracks show clearly from it."

His calmness enabled her to begin the mind techniques to push pain aside and her mind to test the vicious restraints and her muscles to flex and snap a few – enough to ease the intentional torment.

In that same moment she was lifted and slung by the tangler's free ends, over the back of an armoured Ciriot. This one strode quickly back to the force barrier and through it as if it was not there.

"Tymos, tell Daniel to program beta resonance on these outer shields," Kryslie thought at her twin. "At the atomic wavelengths of selenium and tungsten, I think."

"Hell, Kryslie, keep your concentration on yourself. Will you be able to get free?"

"Yes," Kryslie assured him. "I have enough slack to free my arm and reach the weak point where the threads come from."

"We have a link to the Jacen Tyr. Reslic is standing by."

Kryslie acknowledged as she was tossed into the Ciriot ship. They supplied no amenities to their prisoner before strapping themselves into blast couches. The odd sounding clicking was probably laughter.

Kryslie slid along the floor when the Ciriot infiltrator took off and turned sharply upwards. She felt the acceleration as they flew up out of Earth's gravity as a pressure trying to flatten her against the wall of the ship. For what seemed like hours, she could hardly manage to breathe.

When she suddenly felt light, she knew they were in space. The ship was moving, for there was a faint vibration in the floor, but they were not in hyperspace, so the tribeship was not far.

When she heard the clang of two ships docking, she knew they had arrived and sent a message to Tymos. A toe prodded her, not gently, but Kryslie remained limp, as if unconscious. The subsequent clicks and muted sounds were not translated, but seemed acrimonious.

She was hefted again, still tangled, and taken from the ship. She stayed limp and concentrated on seeing with her mind, what her eyes could not and was aware that Tymos saw what she did.

Kryslie was taken along a passage way that led deeper into the ship. She was aware of other eyes watching her undignified progress. As they moved, Kryslie sensed with increasing intensity, pain, terror and madness. When they stopped and entered a particular chamber, these emotions hit her at full power. She almost blacked out with the impact, but the Tymorean President had foreseen a time like this and trained her mind to react – now she did, snapping mind shields in place.

She was dumped on the floor, and so she cautiously opened her eyes, but no more than a slit. A flash of crimson next to purple, alerted her to tighten her mind shields further. A Ciriot Prince! They had mind powers that were far greater than those of the purple clad Ciriot.

Kryslie closed her eyes just before a deliberate toe jab reached her face. She heard the clicking speech and the tangling net retracted. Then she began some tiny muscle flexing to uncramp her muscles. At that moment, she could not move fast enough to deal with four Ciriot. Metal clad hands grabbed her wrists and ankles and swung her up onto a table where the hands were replaced by metal clamps. A metal hand grasped her face, felt along her limbs, and tweaked the skin on her face. She kept her body unresponsive, hoping they would move away. They would want her to be awake before they began their fun.

A metal hand held her face and a powerful force battered at her mental shields. When she gave no reaction, the hand released her and she heard the rustling of their robes as they moved away.

Kryslie eased her mind shields and sensed the miasma of emotions around her. It seemed to her that there were twelve other humans that were conscious to some degree, within the chamber.

Then she heard a human voice screaming, "Let me alone you stinking alien bastards."

Kryslie tested her bonds, the metal parted where she applied her strength to it. With legs and arms free, she rolled off the table.

The mechanical voice, some distance away, was emotionless. The words might have been trivia, not the frighteningly intent attempt to break the will of the woman.

"You will keep feeling this pain until you swear to serve me."

"Never, you bastard, I will die first," Jody Basoli was screaming. Kryslie felt for Jody's mind and carefully went into rapport. She was prepared for the pain – the intense mental pain that the Ciriot were expert in inflicting. Slowly, she built up defences and felt Jody relaxing in relief.

Jody sensed her there. "Who are you?" she thought as if to herself.

"Kryslie. I cannot keep this up. Can you understand what I am doing?"

"Yes."

"Start thinking of a wall around you, made of the strongest substance you know of, one that nothing can break."

Kryslie had begun to feel her obeying when she had more trouble of her own. She felt her body being compelled forward, towards the scarlet clad Ciriot Prince. She fought it, but her body was not under her control. The mechanical device translated the Ciriot language into English. "Leave that one. This one is strong and almost free."

Kryslie heard Jody give one piercing shriek before her mind went blank.

"Tymos," Kryslie sent before she began to feel waves of mental pressure that sent all her nerves overloading with pain messages. "Disable this ship..."

Immediately the whole ship was jolted. Kryslie heard a bellow of outrage from the translator.

"Find out what happened," the Ciriot Prince ordered before gripping Kryslie by the throat and trying to squeeze.

The force shield held him off enough for her to keep breathing. Kryslie came to fighting strength and broke free by hitting both side of her captor's face without tempering her full strength. He had not expected that, but a feral light glowed in the hooded eyes of the Ciriot – battle lust, killing lust and worse – arousal.

Kryslie closed her mind to it, needing to defend against its attack, and kill the creature if she had no other option. This Prince knew how to fight, and was strong. Kryslie needed all her concentration to defend herself and try to disable it. It was aroused by her pain, and his arousal escalated when it used a shocker device on her.

Kryslie imaged raising both arms to the Guardians and felt them answer her and new strength filled her, and she had the Ciriot Prince at her mercy. Then Jody betrayed her, slamming a hard object into her head.

Kryslie slumped, stunned. But even as she pushed up again, she felt pressure in that area and a very sharp pain that seemed to go through her skull, down her neck and back. It lasted no more than a microsecond.

"Kryslie!"

She heard her name and saw Tymos, followed by Konn, moving into the area with weapons ready.

Kryslie scrambled up. "I am all right. Jody is there." She looked around for the Ciriot Prince, he had been right with her, but now there was no sign of him.

Konn went to where Kryslie gestured. Jody backed away from him, but there was no time to waste getting away. He grabbed her, but she fought him until he efficiently knocked her out.

"Tymos, there was a Ciriot Prince here, a second ago," Kryslie warned. She moved to go look for the creature.

Tymos grabbed her. "The ship isn't going anywhere. Reslic is coming and we need to get out."

"Why?" Kryslie asked, sensing urgency.

"We detected a self-destruct and two ships blasted away from here as we approached."

Only then did Kryslie notice the flashing orange lights and the regular clicking sounds. For a fleeting instant, she realised that her sense of time was wrong. Then the need to save the other humans took priority.

"There are another eleven or more humans here, and the Ciriot had non-combatants here, children. I sensed them when I came aboard."

"Get to the ship," Tymos told her, moving to look for the humans.

"No, I can help get people there," Kryslie insisted. Tymos didn't waste time arguing.

Kryslie lifted two men and half carried, half dragged them to where Tymos had docked his ship. She took them in, laid them flat and returned for more. Tymos was bringing two and Konn one. They hurried as their mental countdown approached zero.

The light turned red and began flashing more urgently as they reached the ship with the last of the thirteen humans. Tymos slammed the airlock door shut and hit the emergency detach and Konn blasted the ship away. Only then did Kryslie realise they were in one of the smaller Ciriot ships.

"What happened to our ship?"

Tymos explained as he began to move one of the rescued men. "Jonko took off after the fleeing ships. We need to get these people into acceleration couches. Then strap yourself in."

"Where are we heading?" Kryslie asked as she began to move a man against the effects of the g-forces.

"To the Jacen Tyr. These people need help and I don't think their injuries will be easy to explain on Earth. Did they hurt you?"

"Less than they think. The force shield absorbed most and they had no time to start anything more before you arrived. I don't need help. Jody is worse." Kryslie pushed her brother's concern away.

They both felt the hull shudder, and fell against the metal wall. It was like a giant hand had swatted them. The ship began to spiral, and Tymos began to pull himself back to the bridge.

Konn's attention was fully on trying to regain control of the alien ship. Tymos slipped into the couch with the auxiliary helm.

"The tribe ship is firing on us," Konn told Tymos succinctly. "I have lost thruster controls and directional steering. We are still on our last heading and that is straight towards your planet."

Another powerful thump reverberated in the Ciriot ship. The view screens flared brilliantly and went blank. Konn checked other instruments. "Our speed has just increased and shields are down to forty percent."

Tymos raised one arm in supplication to the Guardians he served. Konn gave him an odd sideways glance. Then an exclamation of surprise as the shields came up to full and the steering stabilised. He glanced again at Tymos, and in that moment, the Great One seemed to glow. He shut his gaping mouth and reported. "Shields back at full."

Kryslie pulled herself into the bridge area. "Our passengers are secure, and the tribe ship just blew apart. I don't know how many innocents were still on it."

"We couldn't help them all," Tymos said softly. He shared her sense of helplessness.

"They were Ciriot!" Konn muttered.

"Not all!" Kryslie said in a very hard voice. "But at that, perhaps they are better off now than being enslaved."

Konn gulped, and turned his attention to controlling the ship.

Kryslie spoke in a more natural tone. "I think perhaps I should move the passengers to the escape pods, in case we don't land gently."

The exposed back of Konn's neck reddened. "I have studied this kind of ship, Great One. I know the specs and how they should fly."

Neither Great One chose to comment further. He could only have studied the ships from data they had sent to the archives over a century ago. Tymos merely sent a mental, "OK", to his sister and said, "You stay with Jody. And we'd better seal our armour."

The Jacen Tyr was too far away to help them, and Konn had also discovered that he was unable to slow the ship either. "ETA Earth's atmosphere – twelve hours. Can we cloak this ship?"

The idea had occurred to Tymos, and it was possible.

"Even if we do, we will leave a heat trail through the atmosphere if we cannot reduce speed," Tymos commented. "Did you study that part of the specs?"

Konn kept his face ahead, and scowled.

Tymos considered the knowledge that he had once taken from the mind of a Ciriot pilot. It had been during the war with them on Tymorea. He moved unerringly to the console with the cloaking controls and activated them. He glanced out of the direct viewports, expecting to see a faint shimmer around the craft, but there was none.

"I don't think it is working," Tymos warned. "The shields we have will protect us on re-entry, but we will be visible to the Earth defence systems and the space trackers. Once we are low enough, they will send jets up and they may fire on us."

Konn took an audible deep breath and nodded. "Understood, Great One." He sealed his flight suit.

Tymos began to yank modules from the console. "I will try to modify the comm. system to link into Earth's frequencies." He was working at a speed that Konn envied. He did not seal his suit – he needed to have his hands free of bulky gloves for the delicate task he had set himself.

Kryslie finished transferring the rescued humans to the escape pods. She checked each as she worked. Some were dead. So when she filled the pods she had three living but sedated people in each, and the fourth was dead. They all showed signs of torture, but there were other signs that they were trying something with these people. She thought that they had not succeeded. But she needed to study them and at the moment she did not have the time or energy to do so.

"Is there anything else I can do?" Kryslie asked mentally.

"No. You should wait in the pod with Jody. Your radiation suit is useless and the landing may be rough. I have configured the comm. system to talk to Earth – I hope I can make them believe what I tell them."

Kryslie agreed, and mentally told Tymos so. Then she retreated to the last pod, but did not seal it – in case Tymos and Konn needed to retreat to it as well.

# Chapter 35

"Omicron! Omicron!" Lexina activated the emergency signal when she took in the meaning of the incoming message. "Tymos and Konn have Kryslie and thirteen humans. They are in a Ciriot Infiltrator heading directly to Earth. They have no thruster control, intermittent steering, full shields but they are not cloaked."

"Have the Earth scanners spotted them?" Daniel asked, having run to the scanner room as soon as the alarm began.

"Yes," Anian confirmed. "They have sent alerts to the air force bases nearest the entry vector."

"Where's Jonko," Daniel snapped. "Can he get back?"

Lexina spoke into her communicator, listened and reported. "Not soon enough, since he would need to slow to avoid detection himself."

"Get an ETA and a projected touchdown point. Send messages to any of our people in that area." Daniel went on. "We are not going to be able to cover up this event."

Lexina was listening to another incoming message. "Tymos reports that all but Konn Reslic and himself are in sealed emergency pods. He will jettison them before they try to land. He will also try to jettison the hyperdrive before impact."

"In a sealed pod?" Daniel asked for clarification. "We don't want another radioactive area. Do we have clean-up protocols?"

He trotted off, getting Morin busy organising for a worst case outcome. It kept his mind off the fact that his children were in a dangerous position and his home world was in danger.

He was summoned when Vincent called, and reported all he knew to his second in command.

Vincent was silent for a moment. He then only said, "Trust the Great Ones. The Humans have the ship on their scanners and will treat it as hostile. They have intercepted, but not translated the comms from the ship."

Two ships lay at station keeping off the coast of Florida. Watchers with binoculars were scanning the sky for the first sign of the approaching Genesis 1.

A young navy ensign approached the important guests with a message. He handed it to Joel Adamson, President of the United Earth

Nations. He read it quickly and passed it to his Vice President, Arthur bin Halil.

The Vice President turned pale. "I must notify the police and military in my country. The air force will be on alert."

Vincent sidled closer and whispered so only bin Halil heard. "Kryslie Ward is on that ship."

Bin Halil glanced at Vincent, who was, like everyone else, apparently scanning the skies. He wasted no time leaving the rail of the recovery ship and striding to its comms room where he requested a satellite link to his country. As he waited, he considered everything that would be needed to be done. When he spoke to his Prime Minister, and he told him to record the conversation, he quickly outlined the actions needed. He added the instructions to refrain from firing on the unidentified craft unless fired on first and then only to disable, not to destroy. He also insisted on evacuating the desert area where the craft was likely to land and to take in and isolate anyone in the area after the landing. He also wanted radiation experts on standby, as well as medical personnel.

They had a little over eleven hours.

From that moment, bin Halil lost interest in the 'momentous history making event' and considered requesting transport back to the mainland and a jet to take him back to his country. However, with Genesis due within the hour – all air flights were grounded. He could admit to no one that Kryslie Ward was somehow hurtling Earthward in an unidentified space craft. It sounded impossible and was difficult for him to believe.

He felt the ship begin to make headway, and knew that Genesis 1 had been spotted. Soon the space craft would split into two parts – one the nose cone where the astronauts would be, and the other the section where the landing wings should have extended for a runway landing. The ship accompanying the one he was on was equipped for deep sea recovery of the transformation module.

The first speck was the bridge module and it was designed to be highly buoyant, but even with the three parachutes slowing its descent, it made an enormous water fountain when it hit the water surface, penetrating the water until its momentum was neutralised, before surfacing in a rush.

When it surfaced, an enormous cheer erupted from all observers. Everyone watched as the ship manoeuvred closer and the crane was extended over the side of the ship to lift the bridge pod onto the deck in the barricaded-off stern section. The media contingent rushed to get a better view. The whole event was being recorded for the world media but all that was seen of the astronauts was a brief wave as they exited the capsule and were escorted down to quarantine quarters.

Warning of the incoming object – projected to crash in bin Halil's country, shared the news with the successful return of Genesis 1.

As soon as air restrictions were lifted, bin Halil was flown back to Terra 1 on a navy helicopter and to his private jet which had a priority clearance to take off.

They were still well above Earth's atmosphere when Tymos finished the isolating and sealing of the hyperdrive engine. He found no way to eject it, but as it was now, even if the ship crashed it was protected. He hoped the casing would not crack and leak radiation.

He re-joined Konn at the controls as the outer reaches of the atmosphere caused the alien ship to shudder uncomfortably. They had no way to slow their progress and very little control over their direction.

When they had dropped to the ceiling height for the jet fighters, they became aware of the jets circling them.

"Are they going to shoot us?" Konn asked, too busy holding the controls to remember Tymos's honorific title.

"Not if we don't, I hope," Tymos considered He was trying to work the alien nav controls. He wanted to bring up some kind of radar. In his mind was the knowledge of many kinds of Ciriot ship, but each was different as the Ciriot stole technology from every race they victimised. And even if he knew the right protocols, the sensors on this ship might have been damaged.

"Unidentified craft – you are to slow your speed and follow our directions."

Konn heard the message, but did not understand the language. He said nothing, happy to let Tymos deal with it.

Tymos recognised the language as Arabic but used the communicator and spoke English.

"I'd like to," he said tersely. "But we can barely control this thing. Are we likely to land in a populated area?"

The reply came back in English, but it was a different voice.

"Current trajectory puts your crash point at..," he quoted lat and long figures. "The Arabian Desert."

Tymos breathed a sigh of relief. The Guardians were indeed with him.

"Unidentified craft, what is your designation?" the English voice insisted.

Tymos did not want to say much over the radio, since he did not know who was listening.

"Could you switch to SR protocol 3?" Tymos suggested, but wondered if the pilot knew it.

"Affirmative," came the terse reply.

Tymos reduced the power output of the comm. unit and hoped it was enough.

"Pilot identification?" came the terse question.

"Tymos Ward, Tech 1, Lunar 1."

"Sit rep?"

"Unknown craft, 16 souls, damaged controls, hyperdrive isolated, will try to eject four pods before landing."

"Affirmative."

Tymos switched the comm. controls to stand by and explained things to Konn.

"As soon as we land, I will have Daniel locate a long range beam to us. You need to get away."

Konn nodded stiffly.

"I know you feel you should help, but Earth is not ready to know about us yet. They do have a means to distinguish between aliens and humans."

"What about you, Great One?" Konn asked.

"I was born here and have spent most of my life here and I have ID they will recognise, but you haven't. I can manage the heat."

"Heat, Great One?"

"Questions," Tymos translated. "I can't explain you, until after the Genesis astronauts have been checked, debriefed and have presented the invitation to join the Federation of Peace. And, until this world agrees to join, our help is limited. Us crashing, with humans on board, will wake the humans up to the need to join. I am going to have to convince them that the Ciriot know this world exists and is virtually unprotected."

Konn kept quiet then, except to give status reports.


"Kryslie?" Tymos thought at his sister.

"I heard. We have company. I have the nearest pod still open for you and Konn."

Tymos sent back thanks and turned his attention back to the shuddering controls.


Tymos sent a warning to Kryslie and to the Earth listeners when he jammed the controls into position. He had ejected the first three pods and was sprinting for the last one. Kryslie slammed the hatch closed behind Tymos and Konn, and strapped in before hitting the release control. Nothing happened, even when she hit it again. Before Tymos could stop her, she released her restraint and worked the manual release.

Impact and separation occurred at the same time. The pod bounced and rolled out of the inferno of the fuel from the inertia drive engines. Tymos grabbed and held his sister as they bounced. He held onto the remains of her radiation suit with hands he had not covered with the suit gloves.

"Your force shield isn't on," Tymos told her.

Kryslie released one hand from the rail she had grabbed, to turn it back on.

As soon as the pod stopped rolling, Tymos sent a powerful thought half way around the world to Morin.

"Long range beam, on me, now!"

The tracers on Kryslie and himself were still working. The beam terminus winked into view.

"Go!" Tymos ordered Konn, who freed himself from the pod restraints and used his transmitter to vanish from sight.

"Cut it!" Tymos sent and the terminus vanished.


Tymos opened the pod hatch and stuck his head out. Billows of black smoke were rising into the air and the smell was awful. Although he could not see them, he could hear the circling jets.

"Stay in here, Krys," Tymos told his sister. He climbed out and went to examine the alien wreck.

Kryslie checked on Jody and found her still in the sleep state she had induced. Then she climbed up to view the scene. She felt the heat of the metal around the hatch and immediately removed her hands from it. The force field should have protected her hands. She checked it again and found it was off. She moved the tatters of her radiation suit and examined the activation pad. It looked okay, but with the tumbling and rolling, it might have got damaged or knocked off again. She turned it on and told herself to keep checking it.

She looked out once more, and this time she did not feel the heat. A second explosion from the alien ship shoved her back against the edge of the hatch, and a flare like burning magnesium, blinded her.

She sensed, rather than saw, Tymos coming back and heard him say, "There is not much left of the ship, mostly molten metal and burnt synthetics. I can't tell the state of the hyperdrive pod. The stripes on the suit are black, so something is hot. I will wait out here."

Kryslie eased herself back down inside. With her radiation suit compromised and her force screen unreliable, she may have taken damage. She began a mantra for concentration and turned her mind to sensing if she had taken any radiation damage.

"Some," she decided. "Marginal. Nothing that won't heal in time."

The bruises and cuts from fighting the Ciriot had already begun to heal. From the look of those injuries, her force screen had deactivated during that fight. Now, the main problem was a painful back where she had slammed against the edge of the hatch, and painful eyes. She heard the helicopters and settled to wait.

Tymos watched a helicopter do a high and fast flyover, dangling what he assumed was a radiation detector. A wise move considering his sleeve stripes were so dark a purple as to appear black.

White clad figures dropped from the helo on its next pass, landing between Tymos and the remains of the wreck. Two aimed instruments at the wreck and retreated. Four headed towards him. Of those, two were armed with powerful weapons. Tymos stood quite still.

"Who are you?" came the question over his suit comm. The figures had stopped a short distance away.

"Tymos Ward. There are two more people in this pod."

The nearest white figure pressed a switch on his suit and reported, "Three here."

The helo returned, dropping three 'personal capsules' to be used as shielded stretchers.

One of the white figures drew out a meter and aimed a probe towards Tymos. "Hot!" he stated.

"Please enter the capsule, Mr Ward," Tymos was directed towards a now opened capsule. When he lay on the padded 'bed' the cover closed over him.

The white figures approached the pod and again used the probe. "Hot," was the report. The man moved so he could climb to the hatch opening and dangle the probe inside. "Safe."

He spoke down to Kryslie. "Climb up. We have a shielded stretcher to bring you out, Mam."

"The woman with me is unconscious. I will lift her up first. Is the stretcher close?"

"Right here, Mam."

Kryslie freed Jody and hefted her so the white figure could lift her the rest of the way. Jody was closed in the capsule even before Kryslie could climb up. The third capsule was right next to the hatch, and Kryslie climbed into it and was rapidly sealed in.

The rescue team had her moved quickly to a truck waiting to take the pods to a point outside the established perimeter.

Kryslie let the rescue team do their work. She needed to stay with Jody, so she endured the lack of sensation in the lead surrounded capsule. All she could see was from the small, palm sized view window. That was little enough. She decided not to try to see through it. It was obvious enough when the helo lifted with the capsules.

She was released from her capsule by more white clad figures. One ran a sensor over her and directed her to stand over a section of floor with a drain. She endured the high force shower spray and the sensor scan again.  That must still have been reading something, for the tatters of her clothes were impersonally removed and the shower was repeated. The third sensor scan paused only at her hands. Kryslie looked at them and saw the burns and a faint purple glow. She knew it was her power working to heal her, but she let the person place clear wrappings over them. The person then indicated for her to lift her foot, and this too was wrapped in clear material, as was her second foot. Only then was a warmed blanket wrapped around her. Her sight was improving and she saw Tymos and Jody being treated in a similar manner, except Jody was still unconscious and did not, it seemed, need the hand and foot casings. She was transferred to a second stretcher. Tymos had been divested of his radiation suit, but had been able to keep the ship suit he'd had on under it.

As she was walked along a passage clad with lead sheets, Kryslie decided she had been taken to Terra 5 base.

The next stop was the medical facility, entered through a rear way directly into an isolation room. This one had three beds. Jody was already on one bed, Kryslie was directed onto a second and Tymos followed to the third. Two soldiers with weapons at ready, stood outside the observation window.

Tymos glanced at his sister and thought at her. "I think we outdid ourselves this time."

Kryslie grinned faintly. "It is your turn to talk us out of it. I am tired."

"Fair enough," Tymos agreed mentally. "Since they already know I am involved."

# Chapter 36

Ron Basoli was occupying an office at Terra 1 when he was notified of the UFO crash in the desert near Terra 5. He was torn between needing to be available for the debrief of the Genesis crew and wanting to know how one of his Lunar 1 technicians had ended up on the same UFO. He settled on placing a priority call to Adam Landin, Commander of Lunar 1 and asking the question of him.

"Sir, Ward has not come back from leave yet," Landin was forced to admit. "He sent a request for an extension of his leave. I saw no reason to deny it."

Basoli growled and then an awful thought occurred to him and he ended the call abruptly, to make another. He spoke to UEN President Adamson and requested him to involve the Investigative Committee in the interrogation of the UFO crash survivors – referring to the presence of a known human on it.

One positive aspect of the event was that the media thought it was an experimental jet that had crashed.

Three of the four Investigators were suspicious and hostile. The fourth was Jonko and he gave Tymos the faintest of grins.

In his favour, the Commander of Terra 5 had recognised him. But it did not mean he was released from 'secure' custody. Part of the continued restriction was the fact that his hands had received a high dose of radiation and were now swathed in bandages soaked in a mixture developed to counteract the effects of the exposure. The rest of it was the uncertainty of his involvement in the crash. So far he had not revealed much, citing 'need to know' and 'classified secrets'. He knew, however that the Investigative Committee had the power to demand answers from him.

He had been separated from Kryslie and Jody who both needed treatment for injuries other than the radiation exposure. Kryslie hadn't said anything either, and was now feigning unconsciousness. No one had recognised her yet.

The interrogation, with him in the isolation room and his questioners outside the observation window, had been going on for an hour and Tymos was keeping a firm rein on his anger. He was trying to give a detailed report, but the questioners did not seem to believe him. So far, Jonko had remained silent.

Into a lull in the questions, Jonko suggested. "Let us hear the full story he is prepared to give us, and then find out from experts if it makes sense."

Tymos glanced at Jonko with thanks. He straightened as he recognised the man who entered the outer area. Arthur bin Halil, without his body guards. The questioners acknowledged his presence with slight bows of respect.

This time, Tymos was allowed to speak without interruption. He completed telling them all he intended to say, which was as much as a human would be expected to understand, but he described everything in detail.

"I think a psychiatric assessment might be required here," the lead Investigator suggested.

Tymos ignored the comment and made eye contact with bin Halil.

"Perhaps not," bin Halil said thoughtfully. He knew Tymos would not be lying, and that he was Kryslie's brother, and ...special.

"Arrange for that statement to be transmitted to Terra 1."

The order was acknowledged.

Bin Halil asked then, "Is your sister here also?"

Tymos nodded, and shrugged in the direction of the next isolation room.

"Gentlemen," bin Halil turned to the Investigators. "Thank you for your assistance. It seems that this matter is not as simple as it first looked. I would like you to continue to oversee the investigation into this incident and to maintain your normal confidentiality. This matter is classified at the highest level."

Bin Halil strode out and went to the main section of medical. His presence brought the Chief Medical Officer to his side.

Like the majority of the personnel of Terra 5, Doctor ... was a native of the region. Bin Halil spoke to him in his native tongue before asking to speak to the medical attendant in the isolation room.

The isolation nurse came to the intercom near the window.

"Patient status," bin Halil requested.

"Resting, Eminence," the woman reported. "Both have radiation effects, but are responding well to treatment. The assorted bruises, abrasions and cuts have been treated. Both are still unconscious."

Bin Halil thanked her and returned his attention to the doctor. "What of the other patients?"

The Doctor's expression was hard. "All are still comatose, but have had no radiation exposure. All look to have been tortured to some degree or very crudely operated on."

Bin Halil understood the doctor's look. "Do you have names for any of them?"

"Only for the two women in that room. The one with red hair is Kryslie Ward and the other is Jean De Yves."

"Yes, I did recognise Kryslie Ward," bin Halil confirmed. He turned and found Jonko behind him.

"A word, Sir?" Jonko requested quietly.

Bin Hail nodded and turned to leave medical. His body guards fell into position, two paces behind him, as soon as he left there. He decided to go to the relatively deserted mess hall. He gestured Jonko to sit and the bodyguards to move away.

Jonko got directly to the point. "Kryslie Ward was looking for Miss de Yves on the request of C-I-C Basoli. I believe this incident needs to be brought to his attention and Kryslie Ward needs to be involved in the Genesis debrief."

Bin Halil studied Jonko, he was sure that this man was another like Kryslie Ward.

"You have taken your conclusions further than mine. Have you additional, confidential information?"

Jonko nodded faintly and leant forward. "Only one of four such craft has been found."

Bin Halil hid his alarm. "How can we find more?"

"Tymos gave you all the clues you need. He is a very bright boy," Jonko hinted. "You might consider those others that were on the crashed ship and look for missing people, injured people, and insane people – unusual cases."

"Thank you – I will. I will bring this to the attention of the relevant people."

Bin Halil and Jonko stood at the same time, the latter bowed slightly to the Vice President and left.


Tymos paced the isolation room with increasing frustration. They had told him he was to go to Terra 1 but so far, nothing had come of it. This was the third day since his return to Earth and he felt the need to be doing something.

"Tymos Ward," a woman's voice made him turn to face the big window.

"Dr Long!" he greeted, pleased to see a friendly familiar face. "What are you doing here?"

She entered the room, the first person to do so without the radiation protection.

"I brought your medical records from Lunar 1," she told him.

"I'm perfectly fine and want to get back to work," Tymos insisted.

She smiled and told him, "I am to give you a thorough physical examination and compare it to your last one. The doctor here was concerned about some anomalies he found."

"Like what?" Tymos asked cautiously.

"Eye structure. Bone structure," she suggested, catching a flash of some expression before Tymos controlled his face.

"I don't feel any different and only my hands were exposed to radiation."

"Lie down and be quiet!" Long ordered.

Tymos did, but he was fidgety.

"Would you like something to relax you?" Long asked.

"No. What I need is to do something active before I start bashing holes in walls."

"Well, I don't suggest any more unsanctioned activities," Long advised. "Whatever you have got yourself involved in this time, has stirred up a lot of important people."

"I need to speak to Adamson," Tymos said, trying to sit up. Long pushed him down and put a diagnostic device to his eye.

"Your eye is odd," she told him. "I had noticed that before."

"It is genetic. Kryslie is the same," Tymos said to mislead her.

"I know," Long agreed. "I have already looked at her. What can your eyes do better than other people's eyes?"

"See in the dark," Tymos said at once, but made no mention of the other things his eyes could do. "How is Kryslie?"

"I thought you would know already," Long suggested. "I thought you would be able to tell me why she is pretending to be weaker than she is. Is it to avoid the same questions that you had to answer?"

Tymos let himself grin. "She said it was my turn to smooth things over."

Long returned the smile. "The Chief wants to talk to her, I believe."

"Probably," Tymos agreed amiably. "He had her doing a job for him."

"Did she succeed?" Long asked conversationally.

"Yes."

"He wanted his daughter found," Long said. "Is that the woman with her?"

Tymos nodded.

"I am concerned that she doesn't wake up," Long admitted. "Her symptoms are like the rest of the victims you rescued."

Tymos looked up at the ceiling of the isolation room. "Um, you might try a mild electric shock," he suggested softly. "But they might be unstable, unsettled...when they wake."

Long stopped moving her diagnostic tool over Tymos. "Torture?" she asked in an equally quiet voice.

"I think so - considering what I saw of the other victims. Kryslie copped a bit of it."

"She is well?" Long asked. "I saw marks, but they did not seem recent."

"Kryslie says she is okay, and she should know," Tymos assured the doctor. "I cannot sense anything wrong."

Long continued her examination. Finally, "Well, I can attest to your state of health. Your hands are healing well, but I cannot pass you fit for work yet, or let you out."

Just as she was about to leave, she was paged.

Tymos heard the message. More patients would be coming into the med centre.

"Doc, keep them isolated too."

"Why?" Long asked bluntly.

"If they look like the ones I rescued..."

She nodded, making the connection – even though she didn't know all that had happened. These new patients might be connected to something big.

Kryslie was allowed to move around in a two piece 'doctor suit' with only her hands encased in the gloves full of healing gel. Jody had not yet woken and was currently in a kind of oxygen tent. Kryslie was sitting next to her when Basoli entered the room. He joined her, watched his daughter sleeping peacefully and gestured Kryslie away.

"I have a transcript of a very strange tale told by your brother," Basoli began. "Frankly, I find it very hard to believe. And since there is very little left of the ship he crashed, little evidence to support it. It is well for him that no one who knows him well would believe he would torture people such as those that were brought here."

"No, Sir, and he doesn't lie either," Kryslie told him. "The creatures that took me – were not human."

She looked directly at Basoli and he was shocked enough to let her give a detailed description of the Ciriot. He pulled a chair to him and sat down. He stared, white faced, in the direction of his daughter.

"What ...did they do to you?" Basoli asked, managing to sound calm, even though Kryslie sensed he wasn't.

Kryslie wasn't going to tone it down.

"They barely started on me, but they hit very hard with fists covered in metal gauntlets. And they also used something like a tazer – and that I think was just to make sure they had my attention. At that point they realised that I wasn't alone and put some kind of tangle rope on me. Unpleasant that was. I was carried like a sack of vegetables to their ship. I felt the g-forces as they took off, and I think I blacked out. I knew I was in space because I became aware of the feeling of weightlessness. When we got where they went, I was dumped in a room where others were tied to tables. I was left alone for a bit because Jody was screaming obscenities at them."

As she had intended, Basoli asked, "Jody?"

Kryslie indicated his daughter. "That is what she calls herself."

"Then what?" Basoli asked.

"Tymos came out of hiding. He had found their ship and hidden in it." Kryslie left it at that. She knew what her brother had said from there on.

"He had tremendous hubris to think he could fly an alien ship," Basoli remarked. It was a comment to cover real fear.

"We didn't have a lot of choice, Sir. It sounded like they had set the big ship to self-destruct, to kill us. We only just got away. And that might have been the cause of some of the mechanical trouble."

Basoli was suddenly aware that he had almost lost his daughter for good. Then another fear filled him. "Did this happen because we sent a manned ship into space?"

"What makes you think that, Sir?" Kryslie asked. She wanted to know if the astronauts had spoken of their ordeal yet.

Basoli snapped his mouth shut, but Kryslie had her answer. They had and Basoli had connected the events here, the crash, and the tortured people with the Genesis events.

"It happened, Sir," Kryslie said quietly. "But I would not say it was divine punishment."

"There might be other alien ships?"

"It is possible. Tymos made suggestions to the Vice President to look for certain things."

"Yes. I got that and it is being done. But scanning for tracks only visible in UV light?" Basoli spoke quickly. "You and he have an uncanny habit of knowing things – or making correct guesses and being plain lucky."

Kryslie shrugged.

Basoli wasn't finished. "And it has been very useful, but I think there are things you know that you are not telling and I intend to find out what they are."

Kryslie's face went blank and she said nothing in reply to his implied threat.

Basoli stared at her before saying, "If we find any more alien ships, the air force will bomb them into oblivion."

He waited for a reaction. Kryslie looked at him and said, "That would please me greatly, Sir."

"Hmpf!" Basoli said rising. "You and your brother will be coming back to Terra 1 when I go."

Kryslie nodded meekly, but sensed that Basoli was still determined to find out more about her. He walked out, and went to speak to Dr Long, who was on duty with her Terra 5 counterpart. Both were busy with the influx of odd casualties.

Kryslie considered Jody, and wondered if she should wake the girl to give her a chance to talk to her father before he got too busy again.

She was just rising to walk there when Jody began stirring. So she waited, to see how she was.

At first, Jody was calm, her mind blank and wondering where she was. She sat up, looked around, and moved off the bed. She had to grab the bed to stop her legs collapsing. Then she moved the plastic curtain aside and saw Kryslie.

In that instant, Jody connected Kryslie with the aliens that had taken her. She became a feral thing, she threw herself at Kryslie and tried to bite and scratch and kick and all the while screaming at her. Kryslie was not able to move from the chair she was in and she did not want to hurt the woman, so all she could do was push her away and hold her at arm's reach. She wasn't meant to be putting pressure on her bandaged hands, but she had no choice.

"Jody! It's Kryslie!"

The words did nothing, so Kryslie spoke to her mind. It silenced the screams for a moment, until Jody shook her head and renewed her attack. This time, Kryslie used only one hand to push her, and tried to touch her with her bare arm. Through the brief touch, she sent a surge of power into the woman, enough to jolt her back to herself.

As Dr Long and Dr Shadri ran in, Jody was sobbing. Kryslie wanted to comfort her, but Shadri held her back.

"What happened?" Long demanded.

"She woke," Kryslie said. "But she wasn't really awake. I think she thought she was still back on that ship."

"I will give her a sedative," Long decided.

"NO!" Jody yelled, and then repeated, "No!"

"I can help her, Doc," Kryslie urged. "Let me talk to her."

Dr Shadri disagreed. "I think not. She seems to associate you with the bad memory."

"Well, let her see her father," Kryslie tried.

"Father?" Shadri queried.

"CIC Basoli," Long said quickly.

Shadri agreed to that and went to see if Basoli had left yet.

Long took Jody back to her bed, and told Kryslie to go out to the main infirmary and she would come and tend to the scratches.

# Chapter 37

The official jet took off two days later. Jody sat with her father, Kryslie next to Tymos, and further back were the two bodyguards Basoli had travelled with. Those two burly men kept eyeing the two red headed passengers as if they would cause trouble.

Tymos had muttered to Kryslie, "We aren't prisoners! But it sure feels like it."

The feeling intensified when they reached Terra 1 and were hustled from arrival lounge to guest rooms. Kryslie would have liked to get a change of clothes from her own quarters in the staff section.

They were told they were to remain there so they would be available. Kryslie deliberately tested the limits. "What do we do for meals? Go to the mess?"

The escort shrugged. "You just need to be available at short notice."

"Thanks," Kryslie told him. "I am going to get some food, it was a long flight."

The man shrugged again and left them.

They were not alone in the mess, but it wasn't crowded. Mainly it was off-shift staff having afternoon tea. Kryslie found some recent newspapers, and took them back to the table she and Tymos had chosen.

They could have stayed in their room and watched vid-cast re-runs but they had had enough of small rooms. The papers gave them some idea of what had been happening and the view of Genesis 1's successful, if delayed return. Mechanical problems, was believed to be the reason, ones that the astronauts had successfully fixed. There were pictures of the splash down, one with a far glimpse of the astronauts emerging from the capsule, and the recovery of the transformation module.

The tone of all the articles was positive, but it did not tell them what they wanted to know.

Kryslie had other sources, and she sent a thought to Morin, the telepathic commoner and aid to Daniel.

A short time later, Vincent walked into the mess, fetched a cup of coffee and walked to join them.

He sat and eyed them both critically. "You look well," he said aloud, but his mind added the "Great Ones".

"I am fine, now that they have that stuff off my hands," Tymos confirmed.

"Same," Kryslie added. Her hands showed the pinkness of healing flesh. She held them out. "Though I am not to do much with these yet."

"We do need to know what is happening," Tymos got to the point.

"And I need a new force field generator and we both need replacement transmitters," Kryslie added.

"I can arrange for those," Vincent nodded. "Now, since I have been asked by the CIC to look you both over, perhaps returning to your assigned rooms would be an idea?"

"Finish your coffee," Kryslie advised, seeing Jody Basoli walking towards them.

She was looking awkward and shy. Kryslie smiled at her and pulled out a chair in a tacit invitation to join them.

"I could come back, if you are busy," she said politely.

"Nonsense," Kryslie said at once. "Your father has asked Dr Vincent to check if we are still sane, but for now he is being the concerned friend of our father."

"Oh, my father mentioned you."

Vincent put her at ease at once. "Yes, the CIC asked me to speak to you as well. You have had a traumatic time."

Jody didn't respond.

Kryslie sensed her unease and grinned again. "He is quite friendly in spite of his impressive resume and degrees. We have known him since we were teenage brats. He did help civilise us."

Jody visibly relaxed. Tymos thought at Vincent, "We need to talk to her, find out Nala's prophecy. Can you arrange for us to not be disturbed?"

Vincent nodded faintly. Kryslie added, also mentally, "I need the journal that I took from the gypsy wagon."

"I am not required at the debrief for a time as they are going over the experiments. I will arrange for an office and send for you."


Jody followed Kryslie to her room and Tymos sidled in after her. Kryslie chose to sit cross legged on her bed and offered Jody the chair. Tymos decided to lounge casually on the floor.

Jody seemed to want to speak, but was hesitant. She finally blurted, "How did you find me in that horrible place?"

Kryslie knew she needed to speak carefully. "I let them catch me," she admitted quietly. "I knew what those beings were and how they think."

"They were aliens," Jody breathed, horrified.

"Yes," Kryslie admitted meeting Jody's eyes and keeping the other woman's attention. "And I have fought them before, on another world."

Jody's eyes widened. "You are aliens too!"

"Yes, but we were born on Earth, as Nala was."

Kryslie continued to keep eye contact as she moved to the floor in front of Jody's chair. She took Jody's hands in her own. "I know Nala was your great grandmother. She is distantly related to me too."

"Is she?" Jody answered, almost dreamily, for Kryslie had imposed a light trance on her.

Vincent transmitted in and passed Jody's journal to Tymos, and moved out of the way to observe. He could tell that Kryslie was doing some very delicate mind work and using her Tymorean power as tiny tendrils – searching the human woman's mind for something. He made no move to interrupt, for it was an honour to watch a Great One at work.

Kryslie was asking questions, making statements and sensing the mind under her 'fingers' bringing answers. Jody was no longer aware of what she was saying.

Vincent listened, and learnt how the girl was thinking, deep down, and would use this to help her and her father reconcile – if Kryslie did not do it before him.

Kryslie returned to the subject of Nala and listened to what the ancient Tymorean had told Jody about her mother's family and how Nala had chosen the younger Ron Basoli as a husband for her granddaughter when he had stumbled into the gypsy's camp.

"Why did you come to Hope Valley?" Kryslie asked the tranced Jody.

Jody's mind seemed confused.

"Where the rocket landed. The black lands," Kryslie added, and saw understanding.

"I...promised her...to take her back to her family...they died there."

"I know," Kryslie admitted. "I have been there."

"You have?"

"We, Tymos and I, found them. They will remain there, resting undisturbed. There is a memorial there."

"No one goes there," Jody's mind argued.

"Not now, but we do not forget them. Many were kin to us too. Did Nala mention us?"

Jody was silent for a bit, thinking. "No..."

Kryslie flicked Tymos a message and he passed the journal to her. She released one of Jody's hands and placed the book into it.

"What was the last thing you wrote in that," Kryslie asked.

Jody reviewed memories from when she had spoken to Nala and had been at Hope Valley.

"It was in the morning, after I had been awake all night. I had spooked myself."

Kryslie took the book from Jody's limp hand and opened it at the last, hurried, entry and positioned it in her hands. "Read what you wrote," Kryslie directed the pliant mind.

When the words registered, Jody whispered, "I was waiting for someone...for you...I had a message, but I can't remember."

"Tymos," Kryslie whispered. And her brother moved forward, sat directly behind Jody and gently felt her neck. He stopped his hand and moved her hair aside.

"I see it," Tymos murmured. "A tiny scar."

Vincent sensed Tymos using his power on that small area, healing something. When he nodded to Kryslie, she spoke again. "What did Nala tell you to tell us?"

Whisper like, Jody spoke, "Go to the grave of your mother's people. Wait there. They will come to you – the advocates. The wise ones. Tell them...danger. Already they are amongst us, awakening fears, bringing terror, turning brother against brother, infiltrating our defences, our leaders. Even the royal blood will die; Tymoreans will die, if they land.

"Those already touched must die for they will draw the ships down, will fight to bring all protections down. The touched ones radiate, are beacons for the enemy, will bring the enemy."

Kryslie waited until she was sure there was no more, and carefully withdrew her mind. Tymos moved back again as Kryslie drew Jody out of the trance state and waited.

"Tymorean," Jody breathed, looking at Kryslie. "You are alien and no one else knows?"

"We, Tymos and I, work for peace. We were born here and Earth is our home. If we interfere it is so Earth will become stronger – more able to defend itself."

"Against those others? What were they?" Jody asked.

"Ciriot pirates."

"You saved me," Jody realised. "But why are you telling me this?"

"Because you can greatly help your father to help Earth to defend itself," Kryslie suggested. "Your father has vision. He knows, without knowing why, that to be strong Earth needs allies against the like of the Ciriot. Many disagree and he is one man, and a basically good one. He isn't perfect. I think, should you choose, you could help him safe guard Earth's future. He must be both administrator and visionary – you know there are other races out there in space – good and bad – you have business training, are studying science. You could help him, and advise him."

"Will you tell him who you are?" Jody asked.

Tymos spoke then, "I think, perhaps, we will need to reveal ourselves soon. But it will mean we cannot act as freely."

"If the leaders of Earth don't act soon to accept..." Kryslie began.

"What?" Jody asked.

Vincent spoke then, to cover the fact that Kryslie and Tymos knew things still privy to the Genesis de-brief crew.

"The astronauts encountered those pirates too," he said, startling her. "Tymoreans helped them."

Jody turned to listen to Vincent, guessing he was also a Tymorean. When he had finished, she turned back to Kryslie and Tymos. "You helped them!"

"Yes," both Tymos and Kryslie spoke together. Tymos continued. "It was a pivotal point in Earth's history. The flight had to succeed."

Jody's mouth opened, but she snapped it shut again as she thought on what she had just learnt.

This time, Kryslie did not intrude.

Finally, Jody decided, "I owe you both. I will respect your confidence. After all, I don't think I want to tell my father I am part alien too. If I can help you – I want to."

Kryslie squeezed her hand. "Thank you."


Vincent had made his own evaluation as he listened and watched Kryslie work. He made no objection when Jody left to return to her own room.

Tymos waited for the door to close before he challenged Vincent. "Well, do we pass as sane?"

"By whose definition, Great One," Vincent asked immediately. "The humans cannot hope to comprehend what you are."

"Then you may tell them that I have recovered both mentally and physically from all injuries," Kryslie directed.

Vincent did not disagree. Having seen her working, he had to agree that she was in perfect control of herself.

Tymos said, "I am as sane as the next Tymorean. I want to get back to work. Will you tell them that?"

"As you wish, Great One," Vincent agreed. Then he asked, "Have you considered how revealing yourselves will affect your work?"

"Our work – our true work – is to safeguard Earth," Kryslie reminded him. "We are not doing it alone. If we cannot do it as technicians, we will do it as consultants."

Vincent sensed the unspoken, "We will do what needs to be done."

He backed off asking questions. They were Great Ones. He did not need to advise them, and it was his duty to obey them. His parting words were, "The debrief committee will be convening with the leaders of the Earth regions. Be prepared to talk to them."

# Chapter 38

The summons came the following day, heralded by the delivery of fresh uniforms.

"This must be a mistake," Kryslie commented to the messenger. "I am only a Tech 1."

"The CIC assured me it was correct," the man told her. "You are to be ready ay 1100 hours."

Kryslie took the uniform and changed into it. Tymos warned her he was coming and knocked on her door soon after she had finished dressing.

"Tech Officer, senior class," Tymos commented to her. "I wonder what is going on. This is a huge jump in rank."

"Trust?" Kryslie suggested.

"That he expects more of us?" Tymos countered with a wry smile.

"Hmmm," Kryslie mused. "More responsibility, more authority and more answerability."

"I am sure he has attached some strings."

"He won't be happy until he knows what we are."

"And when he does?" Tymos prodded.

Kryslie gave a shrug. "Don't the senior staff have to sign another confidentiality and ethics statement?"

"Yes, they do," Tymos agreed "And I believe it is a bit more involved than for the lower level appointees. That shouldn't be a problem, but we had still better read it carefully. I recall mention of a case where a breach of ethics was involved. For senior staff they bring in the Investigative Committee, not just deal with it in house. And if the allegation is proved, the committee has the power of sentence or penalty."

"Still, that provides for an impartial hearing," Kryslie considered. "And Basoli's feelings wouldn't influence anything."

"Somehow, that still doesn't reassure me." Tymos decided. "The WSRA motto is truth is paramount. We have not, cannot, tell them everything about us."

"So we...refuse promotion..." Kryslie proposed.

"And confirm in Basoli's eyes that we are hiding things?" Tymos countered.

They both knew they could not refuse the promotion. As Senior Tech officers, people would listen to them and take them seriously. They needed that authority to act now. Both felt a shiver that was not quite a premonition.

A large crowd had gathered within the expanse of the commandeered hangar at Terra 1. The Genesis capsule was on display next to an improvised podium. All the vehicles and shuttles normally housed in the building were parked in precise rows on the tarmac outside.

Kryslie and Tymos stepped inside, announced their presence to the man at the greeting desk and were directed to see the CIC in the hangar office. Without exchanging a glance or thought, they took their security passes and went to find Basoli.

Their Commander in Chief was all business when they reported for duty. He handed them the expected forms to sign, officially notified them of their new position and the expectations thereof, and before either could comment, told them, "Exceptional circumstances have necessitated the WSRA to promote junior staff of exceptional ability to senior positions. The reason for gathering the elite minds will be revealed once the meeting starts. When the meeting adjourns, both of you will be seconded to Lunar 1. All staff will be assigned to specific projects, best suited to their abilities. This has necessitated a major redeployment of staff."

Kryslie and Tymos scan read he forms, noted several possibly ambiguous clauses, considered them for a moment and then signed. Basoli took the forms, glanced at them and then dismissed them.

After leaving the office, they passed several other bemused, recently promoted technicians waiting to see Basoli.

Any intention of seating themselves unobtrusively was quickly prevented when the ushers escorted them to a position just to one side of the podium. An apprehensive Jody was already there. She had a security pass giving her designation as admin assistant to the CIC. She was relieved to see them.

The seats directly in front of the podium filled up with political leaders from all the convocations on Earth. Centre front was Arthur bin Halil and Joel Adamson. The seats further back were filled with scientists, senior WSRA staff, and a select group of media reporters. In the side positions were senior military personnel and the three Genesis astronauts.

Gareth Pitt gave Kryslie an odd look when he saw her sitting near the podium, but followed it with his normal cheeky grin.

Basoli walked up to the microphone and when everyone was seated, immediately calling the meeting to order and welcoming all the invited delegates.

"Ladies and Gentlemen of all ranks and world nations – thank you for attending. Some of you are already aware of the matters to be presented today. We all know of the successful completion of the Genesis Deep Space Mission. The ramifications of this mission are far reaching." Basoli had to pause for applause to die down.

"Part of the mission was to perform tests during travel in hyperspace and to record data from new and distant areas of space. What we have accumulated will keep the scientists busy for years to come. The mission however had an outcome that was not anticipated..."

The audience fell totally silent and were avidly listening. There had been many unanswered questions in the media as to why Genesis 1 returned late. Everyone sensed that the cause was about to be revealed.

Basoli had paused, but now continued.

"Until this meeting concludes, there is a complete media and communications lockdown. No one will be allowed to enter here, or leave. I apologise if these measures inconvenience anyone, but you will understand in due course. What you will be hearing here is highly classified and its release in the media will need to be carefully handled."

The silence grew deeper.

"During its period in space, Genesis 1 encountered two alien space-going races."

Basoli needed to pause again until the initial exclamations died down.

"I will now bring to the podium, the crew of Genesis 1 – Mission Leader, Captain Aaron Casey, First Officer Domenic Tweed and Second Officer Gareth Pitt. Please make them welcome."

The noise was deafening, as this was their first public appearance since their return. The media group photographers were flashing furiously. The WSRA contingent stood and applauded, for by returning alive, the three men had proved to the world, the effectiveness of the work they had done over the past three years.

Basoli slipped off the podium to a seat in the side area. Jody moved to sit next to him, as if providing him with her support.

Casey began speaking, and instantly had the full attention of the audience. Kryslie and Tymos listened just as intently, storing every word in their memory, as well as noting the reactions of the audience.

A range of emotions surged from the political representatives. Excitement initially, to be amongst the first to hear this information, and then fear and apprehension when Casey spoke of the ordeal that he and his team had suffered. Even when told of the rescuers, the fear remained. Many felt that the world would be safe if there were no more missions.

Questions were asked of the astronauts from all sections of the audience, and they answered each as fully and accurately as possible. While they spoke, recordings from the Genesis monitors were being screened on a screen behind them.

When no one had any more questions of the astronauts, Basoli replaced them on the podium.

He was bombarded with questions and comments now – the most vocal were insisting that there be no more missions. The 'pull our head in and hide syndrome'.

Basoli called for silence.

"Ladies and Gentlemen, hiding our heads in the future will do nothing. What has happened, has happened. Facts will not go away. It is to our benefit that when our astronauts encountered the first race, Genesis 1 was in range of the second – those that helped us."

Basoli allowed his detractors to shout their disagreement.

"We don't need either of them. If we did not go into space – they would not know about us!"

"We don't need either of them!"

A more moderate voice, called out, "Nonsense, they might have found us anyway. They might have attacked us without warning!"

That was the opening Basoli wanted.

"The esteemed leader of the European Convocation is, unfortunately, correct," he stated. "Alien activity has been identified here, on Earth, from before Genesis returned."

Shocked silence lasted for half a minute, before everyone wanted to know – how, when, what, where?

A tinkling bell sound called for silence.

"I would like to bring to the podium, three personal witnesses who experienced this alien activity, from within the American Convocation. May I present, Jean de Yves, a student in Astro-sciences at Washington University and Technical Officers Tymos Ward and Kryslie Ward, WSRA Lunar 1."

Kryslie sent a very tight thought to Tymos, "He might have warned us."

The status of all three speakers was enough to impress the audience, and to discourage loud claims of insanity.

Jody whispered softly, "Dad said I had to start."

She took the position in front of the microphone. Tymos and Kryslie stepped back behind her, letting her sense their moral support.

Without preamble, Jody began, "What I have to say occurred at the edge of Hope Valley. For those of you unfamiliar with the name, it is where the rocket crashed forty years ago. The area is still radioactive today and is surrounded by force fields to keep people out.   I had a personal reason for going there, and it was a sudden decision. I told no one of what I was doing, and that was almost a fatal decision for me.

"My great grandmother, Nala de Yves, was a gypsy. She was part of a tribe that was camped at Sliding Springs, the town that was once at the centre of the damaged black lands. She and my mother were away from the tribe when the rocket crashed. When she was dying, she asked me to take her to rejoin her loved ones. I promised to take her ashes there and free them to the winds."

Jody went on to describe her preparations and what she had experienced at the edge of the valley – the sounds and sensations of terror.  In a voice, well controlled, she described what had happened the next day, specifying that is was the day before Genesis 1 splashed down. Behind her, on the screen, were medical photos of her injuries as they had been immediately after her return. The audience inhaled in disbelief.

"I did not expect to ever return here. I would not be here except for my two good friends, Kryslie and Tymos."

Jody stepped back and attention focussed on the others.

Kryslie stepped forward into the focal position. She recalled all she had ever learnt about public speaking, from her Tymorean foster Father, High King Tymoros. Unconsciously, all that knowledge was in her stance, and infused into what she said, so that the audience received the message she intended.

"When Jody went missing, I was lucky enough to learn of Nala and to associate her with Hope Valley. I went there on that chance and found the vehicle Jody had driven there. The wagon and truck had been vandalised, and there were signs of a fight and that someone had been injured."

Kryslie described, with detailed descriptions, her actions and subsequent events. Though she omitted any mention of the Tymorean base, and of searching the black lands.

"While I was there, I too began hearing odd noises – like the swishing of leaves when it was dead calm and sounds like clicking beetles in that area where nothing lives. I was caught by something I could not see..." She ignored the sceptical looks and mutters and stated, "It might have been invisible, but it was not incorporeal. I landed some useful blows and for a short time the creature was visible."

She described the look of the Ciriot, something Jody had been unable to do.

"I had been acting as bait," Kryslie went on. "So you might think that I got what I asked for when they attacked me." She glanced at the screen behind her where more photos were being displayed. They complemented her graphic description of the unprovoked attack. "My brother was close by, but must have been noticed. I was then tangled in a rope-net thing, and carried to their ship. To get to it, they went through the force field into the edges of the black lands."

On the projection behind her was a sketch Tymos had done of the Ciriot ship.

"I was tossed in with nothing to cushion or restrain me as they blasted off. I think I blacked out from the g-forces. When I came to, I felt vibration in the floor and weightlessness, but none of the effects Captain Casey described of being in hyperspace. Not long after that, we docked to another ship – a larger one. At that time, I did not know that Tymos had slipped on board and would be able to help me."

Kryslie ended her report there, and the whole audience was attentive.

Tymos spoke of subsequent events, and there was not one protest when he admitted to killing many black clad Ciriot.

Kryslie sent a mental question, "What about the purple and scarlet ones?"

Tymos paused in his speech to tell her, mentally, "Probably in the ship Jonko tried to catch."

As he went on with his report, Kryslie considered a point in her memory. She recalled the high ranked Ciriot being next to her, and next second, seeing Tymos and they were gone. She must have blacked out, Kryslie thought with misgiving.

Tymos described the inside of the larger alien ship and sneaking along passages to find and free Kryslie. He told how he had learnt of the other captured humans, and of getting them all to the smaller ship and getting away. He mentioned his belief that the large ship had been set to self-destruct, with alien civilians still on board. He continued the story to the point where they crashed and were soon to be rescued.

All three had questions directed at them, and answered them as fully as they could.

Basoli dismissed them from the podium and took over again. "Indications from the timing of events, suggest that the alien ship that destructed was within the solar system. Since the small alien ship crashed into the desert, further indications of suspected alien activity have come from four distinct areas."

Both Tymos and Kryslie looked at the map projected on the screen behind Basoli as he explained the evidence and reasoning that supported his statement. It was based on the very things Tymos had said to look for. "So far we have not located alien ships, and we believe they have some kind of cloaking screen."

He finished by saying, "That, Ladies and Gentlemen are the facts as we know them – all the facts."

The murmuring began, and it had the edge of panic. Basoli spoke again before it got out of hand.

"We must assume that our isolation is no longer a defence. It is to our benefit that we discovered these aliens and so have time to prepare defences. I am not saying that we are currently defenceless. Preliminary plans of action have been tabled and options proposed. This is the reason for this gathering of political and scientific leaders. Any solution decided on, must be a world wide solution and will require resources and manpower from all parts of the world. The relevant documents are on portable document readers placed under each seat. You will have time to read through these before we continue. A break for refreshments and reading time will continue until 1700 hours."

"I wonder if we will be needed to speak again," Kryslie murmured to Tymos, as Basoli departed through a door behind the podium.

"I hope not," Jody commented. "I could not have done as I did was it not for you standing with me."

"You did great," Kryslie assured her. She watched all the rest of the audience finding the readers and moving out for refreshments. "What's this Admin Aide business, are you quitting Uni?"

"Leave of Absence," Jody said. "Until this business is sorted out. Dad assured me they would let me back at Uni whenever I am ready."

Kryslie noted the second use of 'dad' and was pleased.

Adam Landin made his way to them instead of joining the exodus of hungry and thirsty delegates.

"Good to see you both again," Landin said dryly. "I believe I have you back on my staff, Kryslie."

"Seems so, Sir," Kryslie said fingering the collar tabs on her uniform. "R and D."

"Ah, yes. I see the CIC is expecting a lot more from you both."

"I don't expect to disappoint him, Sir," Tymos murmured, keeping a neutral face.

"No, indeed," Landin agreed, also neutrally. "Have you read the proposals?"

"Not yet, Sir. I am planning to eat first."

"Good idea. I will let you do that. I need to speak to some other new staff."

The meeting reconvened at exactly five o'clock with Basoli again in charge of the agenda.

"I expect you have all read the proposed options. They are not mutually exclusive, or fixed in stone. Questions may be asked on each option as it is raised.

"Option 1 is as follows – To agree to the invitation to join a universe wide Federation of Peace. You will recall Captain Casey telling of this. Captain, will you please join me?"

When Casey was seated next to Basoli, he opened the floor to questions.

Adam Landin was in a position to watch Tymos and Kryslie Ward who were seated now amongst the scientific staff. He had recognised the name of the second alien race from private conversations he had had with them. He wondered if they would speak out now, but although they were listening intently, they said nothing. Their expressions betrayed nothing when after a full hour's discussion, the vote by the political leaders was to consider only Earth solutions, who did allow for reconsideration at a later time if it seemed appropriate. They would prefer to deal with off-worlders on a strong footing.

The silver message capsule, still unopened, was slipped back into Basoli's pocket.

Basoli moved onto the next proposal. This involved a massive program to design and build, or modify, vessels to be capable of space and orbital defence, and building defence installations on the moon or orbiting platforms.

The resultant discussion involved both the political and scientific people to decide what was feasible as well as financially beneficial. It went on to consider how the program would be spread out in terms of construction facilities in various convocations.

Before the meeting adjourned for the night and all the delegates had gone to their assigned quarters, agreement for much of that proposal had been reached.

Landin would have liked to ask why neither Kryslie nor Tymos had spoken up in the discussions, but he felt he knew. They preferred to keep a low profile.

The following two days were full on, discussion, argument, compromise and finally decisions. When the meeting finally concluded, the political leaders went back to their convocations to explain all that had been discussed and decided.

The scientists received their final postings and projects and were keen to start work.

Landin called his senior scientists together while they waited for the Lunar 1 shuttle. He gave each a task to start thinking on and reminded them that they would meet regularly to discuss progress and get input from other sections.

# Chapter 39

"Progress?" Landin asked hopefully. He had received a request for a chat from Tymos and Kryslie Ward.

"No, Sir," Tymos growled. "I do not mind the challenge of trying to find a counter to a cloaking shield, but is the CIC trying to make us fail? I mean, if he wanted rid of us why didn't he just tell us to walk?"

"Sit down and let us discuss this," Landin suggested calmly. "I am not about to accuse you of slacking. Our overall progress is on target."

"But we have nothing to show," Kryslie complained. "How can we create something to negate a Ciriot cloaking field when we can't examine and analyse a working one or even an inactive one. Why can't we go looking for another Ciriot ship?"

"How do you know there are more?" Landin asked pointedly.

Tymos glanced at the ceiling, counted the small holes in one of the ceiling tiles, took a deep breath and controlled his frustration. "CIC Basoli showed a map of four places believed to be centres of alien activity. Two of those sites were bombed and they assumed that anything there was vaporised, because no more odd activity is happening there. But no wreckage was found and in my mind there is no proof anything was even there. I propose that if a ship had been destroyed, the generator for a cloaking shield would have stopped working and you would have wreckage and radiation."

Landin tensed. Why had such an obvious conclusion been overlooked?

"So, you believe they have gone somewhere else?" Landin asked.

"Yes," Kryslie said flatly. "Somewhere their activities have not yet been noticed."

"How do you expect to find a cloaked ship?"

"It may be cloaked, but it is still there. You could walk into it." Kryslie noted.

"How would the aliens that leave it, find the way back to it?" Landin proposed the question.

"Easy. A homing signal or something like a GPS," Tymos said at once.

"They might uncloak briefly," Kryslie added. "If we were there then, we would see it."

"What if they don't uncloak?" Landin countered.

"Then they probably have what we need right now," Tymos almost snapped.

"Settle down, Mr Ward," Landin warned. "Do you know that?"

"No," Tymos said less heatedly.

"And do your ...contacts have any suggestions to offer?" Landin asked delicately.

Kryslie grinned faintly at Landin's subtle question. She shook her head. They had already queried the scientists on Tymorea. The best they had was the scrambler field but that was only slightly useful at very close range. Governor Xyron, had people working on the problem too.

"What if a fleet of alien ships came here – would they fly and fight cloaked?" Landin asked to provoke thought.

Tymos answered. "A small group might fly in cloaked, but not a large one, and not once they engaged an enemy."

Landin considered. He could imagine an enemy sneaking in a few ships each night until there was a hidden fleet big enough to do major damage.

"Would you consider a cloaking shield to be generated like other shields?" Landin kept prodding.

Kryslie nodded, and Tymos kept quiet, waiting for Landin to make his point.

"How might you disable a shield generator?"

"Overload it," Tymos said at once.

"EM pulse," Kryslie suggested, but Tymos argued against that.

"Anyone with sense would put an EM transmuting shield amongst the other shields."

"Point," Kryslie agreed. "Okay then, find the shield's signature frequency and disrupt that. It might work if they don't have nested shields." She switched to thought mode to add, "That is why we put the scrambler field outermost on the base shields."

A vague idea occurred to Kryslie as she said that. "If he won't let us go look for an alien ship, would he let us visit Emmanuel's Hut at Hope Valley? Or the Washington Uni archives?"

"I will make the request," Landin promised, but he was sure it would not succeed. At best, Basoli would send someone else to get the information they wanted. It just seemed, that for some reason, Basoli wanted Tymos and Kryslie Ward sequestered up on the moon. "But for now, when are you off shift?"

"We are off now," Kryslie told him. "Why?"

"Then go and relax for a bit – clear your heads," Landin suggested. "You have been working too hard."

They decided to take the advice, and after eating, they went and sat in the garden on a patch of cultivated turf.

"We don't have time to waste," Kryslie said to her twin. "Probably the only reason why the Ciriot haven't started something already is because the fleet is hovering just outside the solar system."

"Possibly, and I know the fleet cannot stay there indefinitely," Tymos agreed. "At least the new space fighters are in production."

"They need to be able to see the enemy," Kryslie said, getting back to their problem.

"Ok, why don't we go back to basics?" Tymos proposed. "How many different kinds of cloaking devices do we know of?"

Into their minds came a list of six types, and variations of each. They compared these to what they knew of Ciriot craft. It was not much help. The Ciriot pirates stole technology from many races rather than inventing it.

"If the Aeronite ship had not been dismantled, we could have looked at that one," Kryslie commented. "We could try using a Tymorean one, except they are so unlike any other kind."

"No, indeed," Tymos mused, thinking on something. "I think we need to go back to Tamir Janzoet's work. What does a cloaking field do?"

Kryslie took the thought. "Effectively bends all radiation, all frequencies around the object as if it wasn't there."

"Radiation," Tymos repeated, an errant thought nudging his mind.

"Yes, I was right! Emmanuel!" Kryslie said with a trace of excitement. "Before we put Janzoet's shield, the scrambler field, around the base as the outer shield, Emmanuel's radiation sensors could see the base through the shields. Once I realised that, I made sure he never pointed them directly at the base."

"An unintended artefact," Tymos said, catching on. "The shield that was outer most then was the cloaking shield. And, it is the only place where that effect was noticed."

"It has to be because of the radiation," Kryslie insisted. "Can we take it from there?"

"We still should check Emmanuel's notes," Tymos thought. "Do you know if all the notes at the hut were transcribed or published?"

"Not without checking," Kryslie told him. "I helped him finish his initial work on the radiation sensors and shields but then I was needed for other things."

They discussed the ideas until they went for their sleep shift, and relaxed more now they had a working plan.

Later that night when Kryslie was on the verge of sleep, she suddenly realised she had held the very thing she needed.

"Tymos?"

"What?"

"It is as well that the Guardians don't swat us for denseness."

"Why?"

"That box Jody had – that she got from Nala. I am willing to bet it is a portable cloaking field generator," Kryslie told him. "She worked for Grainger for a bit. And it isn't a Tymorean design or I would have recognised it."

"No bet, Kryslie. I think you are right. We can have it sent up."

"I would rather fetch it," Kryslie said.

"And how will you convince the little bio-monitors we all have on us that you haven't left?"

"I won't be gone long," Kryslie promised. "And I am tired of Basoli keeping us here."

"So long as I don't get put onto finding the glitch in the bio-monitor program," Tymos warned.

Once they had worked out the theory, Tymos began crafting one potential detector unit which would look like a pair of night vision goggles and intended for close up viewing. Kryslie would work on the other design which was for longer range use and was essentially a modification of a standard sensor probe. They made three of each prototype. One of each, Kryslie took by long range beam to Earth base to be sent on to Tymorea for testing. A second of each was kept in a safe place and the third was ready to be produced at the next progress meeting when Basoli was due to attend. They would ask him to have the units tested.

The proof of their work came with the news that two more Ciriot ships had been found and destroyed. This time, wreckage was found.

An official commendation was forth coming from the WSRA Board, and was added to the collection in the Lunar 1 reception hall.

The overall development program was progressing and the initial production runs turning air fighters to space fighters were almost ready for testing.

# Chapter 40

**12 months later**

After developing the means to locate cloaked ships, Tymos and Kryslie were reassigned to other projects, but they both had the sense of time running out. Earth had been protected for a time by the nearness of the Tymorean Peace fleet, but they had been needed more urgently elsewhere and for the past months were well away from Earth.

Tymos's attention was caught by one of the newsfeeds from Earth. The item made mention of a second assassination attempt on one of the convocation leaders. Tymos heard it through and then used the interactive mode to scan the media archives. When Kryslie joined him, he summarised his findings.

"Two assassination attempts, twelve major robberies, six break-ins at sensitive places," Tymos told her. "That's for a start. But spread over all octants of the globe."

"I don't like the sound of that," Kryslie agreed. "It is not quite what Nala predicted but..."

"But several perpetrators were caught and from what I saw on the news feed, they did not seem to be acting normally and what they were said to have said was odd."

"Were any of those perpetrators ones that had been near areas of Ciriot activity?" Kryslie asked.

"No," Tymos answered. "I had Daniel check into that. But – some of the earlier events were in areas where they destroyed ships."

"So you think these people are victims? Successes for the Ciriot?" Kryslie proposed.

"I will suggest that to Daniel, and ask him to have Jonko look into it," Tymos decided.

"How would Jon tell? Would UV light show contamination? We won't be able to check them."

"If the crimes were recent, that might be a way, but some of the arrests were a year ago. And, come to that, there have not been reports suggesting Ciriot victims for almost as long. Perhaps they have perfected their control technique. I cannot see the bastards stopping," Tymos proposed. "I am assuming they will implant those green motes like Stenn had."

"You and I together could find them," Kryslie said thoughtfully. "But we can't be everywhere and check everyone. We would need a wide area scanner to locate victims with them, and a means to remove or force the motes out."

"Why don't you and I start working on the idea in our spare time? I want to see the newscasts of the arrests on the original uncut film," Tymos said.

"Because?" Kryslie asked, but she had an idea why.

"The prophecy said the touched ones would radiate. We have seen one of those motes, and the entity it split from. I think our eyes might be able to see an indication that human eyes can't. This is just a hunch for now, but if we want to convince Basoli to let us work on the detectors, we will need evidence."

"Fair enough, but how do you plan to get the film if we are not allowed leave to go earth-side?" Kryslie asked, and Tymos grimaced.

"Jon should be able to get it, and I will have him transmit up, or I will sneak down," Tymos said.

"Let me know what you find while I will get started," Kryslie decided, and she went to go to the R and D journal archive computer.


When Tymos found her, some hours later, she knew his idea had been proved.

"Come back to my quarters and see the film," he suggested. She logged off the computer and followed.

Jon was still there, and ready to run the film again. Kryslie greeted him, but studied the film, and at Tymos's suggestion, adjusted her eyes. The person on the film, being held by two police officers, had a distinct green aura, lacking in the police men.

"Three out of every four people arrested for crimes like the ones I pointed out, have that aura," Tymos summarised.

"Can you see it, Jon?" Kryslie asked.

He shook his head. "Tymos thought you might be able to find a filter to bring it out to normal people like me."

"Perhaps," Kryslie agreed. "Can we keep the film?"

"For now," Jonko agreed.

"Good. You can mention what we found to Daniel, but not the committee. We have no way to prove it yet." Kryslie said. "Thanks for getting this."

Jon bowed and transmitted away.


Their off duty occupation went unnoticed for a time, until the long hours Tymos and Kryslie were working was noticed.

"I always worry when the two of you put in very long hours," Landin commented, coming into the R and D lab, very late one evening. "Ericson tells me he has no idea what you are working on. And neither of you have mentioned your idea at the progress meetings."

He wondered if the pair, when they looked around at him, seemed just a little guilty.

"It's just a theoretical idea," Tymos said. "We are not even sure it will be needed."

"Why don't you come through to my office and tell me about it?" Landin made the suggestion sound like an order. If they thought it worth making, he was sure it would be needed.

Tymos was thankful that Landin trusted them, and that he had accepted who they were. They could say things to him, without needing to worry that they would be taken the wrong way.

"My attention was caught by some news feeds," Tymos began, after being told to sit in one of two chairs in front of Landin's desk. He went on to outline his thought processes and what they were working on.

Landin considered what he heard, and understood why they had said nothing. Part of the reason was they would need to reveal they had information not available to humans on Earth. That was a point he had tacitly accepted, and deliberately did not refer to.

"If you convince the chief of the need for this, I don't think he will ask how you made it work," Landin told them. "And most of the senior staff here are used to your leaps of logic, but I can see your problem. The composition of that mote you mentioned – it might be enough to refer to the sensor logs, and trial and error."

"That's just it – we have no way to test it here," Kryslie pointed out.

"The way I see it," Landin proposed. "You figured out how to attract it, and used the method from four years ago to eliminate it."

Tymos thought on that. "That should seem logical enough." He heard Kryslie add mentally, "For humans."

"How soon will your model be finished?" Landin asked, all business.

"A few days," Tymos estimated.

"Fine, as soon as it is working, we will get the chief up here and you can sell it to him," Landin directed.

Basoli arrived for the monthly progress meeting, and for most of it seemed as if his mind was elsewhere. When Landin directed Tymos to present his new device, Basoli became more alert.

He listened intently, and studied the films Tymos showed and when he had heard all Tymos had to say, sat back and considered.

"I can see no such aura, Mr Ward."

Kryslie quietly put a filter in front of the viewing screen. And Tymos ran the film again.

Basoli noticed the green aura around one of the men and asked one of the questions Tymos would have preferred not to answer.

"How did you suspect that aura existed, Mr Ward?"

"I thought I saw something on the news feed, and asked to view the unedited version," Tymos said. "When it was there, I recalled the entity that was here some years ago."

Basoli halted the explanation there. That was a subject that he preferred not to be discussed, even amongst the staff at Lunar 1.

"I will take the idea of this device to the world council. If they decide to take it up, I will be in touch with your commander," Basoli seemed to dismiss the project, but at the end of the session, he asked Tymos and Kryslie to stay behind.

Once the room was empty except for them, and Landin, Basoli spoke again.

"How is it that you seem to know things that others do not?" Basoli asked abruptly.

"We were trained to notice things, Sir," Kryslie said. "And we can put the details together. It is just how we are."

"Hmpf," Basoli grunted. He seemed about to challenge them again, but changed his mind. "Very well, run through your logic again, and fill in the details."

"With the assistance of John Goss, from the Investigative committee, we looked at recordings of a large number of people arrested for some serious crimes. I am talking murder, attempted assassination, major robberies from banks and commodity stores, and so on," Tymos admitted. He knew Basoli had met and was impressed by Jonko (who was using his former name in his work). "Of these, over three quarters of the culprits had this green aura. None of these men were amongst those believed to have been affected by the aliens."

"You are implying what?" Basoli asked.

Kryslie spoke up, "We believe that they were putting controlling motes into people, but the first ones were not really successful. I think they tried in the ones found with odd wounds and abhorrent behaviour, like were at Terra 5 last year. I fear that they have now perfected the technique."

Basoli began tapping the table with his pen. He remembered that time with mixed feelings.

He was also remembering the events that occurred at Lunar 1 four years ago.

"So, how will this device help the people if they have the aura?" Basoli asked. "I can see a use, if we can check all those being detained under suspicion of alien contamination, and empty the detention centres of those that are clean. What else?"

He was still tapping his pen. Kryslie knew her next statement would provoke him.

"I think all important buildings should have this device in a prominent area and all the staff and visitors should walk under it each day."

"Really," Basoli said with thinly veiled scepticism.

"Yes, Sir. We have incorporated what we hope is a means to remove the motes if there is one in a person."

Basoli waited for her to continue.

"Four years ago when we had that alien creature here, I saw one of those energy motes pass out of one of the visitors when he was in a very weak condition and...go into a nearby stronger body."

"You," Basoli guessed correctly. "Is it still there?"

"No!" Kryslie hissed, revulsion clear in her tone.

Tymos took over the explanation. "Sir, at that time we convinced it that Kryslie was nearly dead, and it fled. I was within a shield and all other people were in safe locks. With the base power down to basic levels, it tried to return to the ship it came on. To get there it had to pass through the base shields — or rather the outer one that was powered separate to the main shields — and was dissipated."

It was all truth, just muddled a bit.

Basoli stopped tapping. "You are saying those theoretical energy motes could move from person to person?"

Tymos nodded.

"Would you care to say exactly what you are meaning without skirting the issue?" Basoli demanded.

"Yes, Sir," Tymos agreed, straightening his posture so his attitude changed from a subordinate addressing a superior to one addressing an equal. "I listened to Casey's report - the race that attacked them was referred to as pirates, the ones called Ciriot. In my mind, pirates want wealth and power. Money, valuable assets and to make lesser beings do their will. Those people with the green aura could have been told to find such things, and do other deeds to help with their ultimate goal."

"I will follow that for now," Basoli allowed. He couldn't find a weakness in their logic. "Go on."

"Two assassination attempts, two murders of regional leaders," Tymos said. "Control or kill political leaders, and throw the population into chaos."

Basoli tapped again, more slowly.

"So, when the device detects an infection, and neutralises it...what do we do with the victims? Detain them?"

"There would be no need, sir," Kryslie assured him. "The device has a high potency energy emitter that we believe will attract the mote. It will have to pass the scrambler field to get to it. A meter can measure any increase in energy when a mote hits the field. If a person has an...infection...when he passes under it he should be cleared."

"So, you would like it tested? How?" Basoli asked. "I assume you tested it here? On yourselves?"

"Yes, to both sir, but we had to simulate the mote and that probably wasn't a real test. I would like to try it on the men I saw in the data I watched with John Goss."

"And if the device fixes any infection in these criminals?" Basoli asked. "Do we simply release them?"

"Sir, I don't know the circumstances of each crime," Tymos admitted. "Matters would need to be explained to the authorities and the legal system will have to decide."

"Very well," Basoli agreed. "Mr Ward, I will have you come back with me to try this device."

"Thank you, Sir," Tymos said.

"Show me how a person must approach this," Basoli directed, standing up.

Since the device was not fixed in one position, Tymos held it up and Kryslie walked under it. Basoli walked closer – the device simply looked like an odd design of light. He walked under it as Kryslie had done, expecting to feel – something.  He was not interested in the monitor screen, but Kryslie had been watching it. She saw a blip on the flat line, and flashed a thought at Tymos.

Landin, who had been silent, noted the glance and decided to test the device as well. He watched Kryslie's face, and saw no change as he went past.

Basoli curtly directed Tymos to pack his device for transporting and to be ready to shuttle down within the hour. He went off to take up the offer of a tour through the research labs.

Tymos was about to follow Basoli out but Landin halted him.

"What did you see?" he asked directly.

Kryslie paused, only for a fraction of a second before answering, but Landin sensed it.

"Basoli had one," Kryslie said soberly. "It has been eradicated."

"How did he get it?" Landin asked imperatively.

Kryslie had already thought on that. "My guess is from Jody, his daughter. Or it might have been me. Both of us were in alien hands for a time. But I don't think they could have done it to me during the trip up and they hadn't started on me before Tymos arrived. I was pretending to be unconscious still and they like their victims aware. Anyway, I made Tymos check me first."

Landin nodded accepting her unspoken assurance that she was fine. "Good Work. Where do you think one should be placed here?"

Kryslie said quickly, "Where it will be readily accessible by all staff on a daily basis."

"Where else do you think they should be placed?" Landin asked intently.

"Everywhere," Tymos said at once. "Since we cannot predict which people have them, I would start with all government and military places, all WSRA places..."

He continued his list and Landin made mental notes.

"Kryslie, while Tymos is testing this device, can you get production specs ready for distribution?" Landin directed. "Then, have you another project in mind?"

"Ah..." Kryslie had an intention for her spare time. "I was planning to do some delving into news media archives." She saw Landin looking interested and went on. "I am sure there are still two Ciriot ships we have not found and destroyed."

"Fine, I will let you do that during your shift time. Let me have anything you deem relevant. Off you go!"

Kryslie had not mentioned that the Tymorean missionaries were all looking for clues to the ships and Daniel was needing help to sort through the data being accumulated.

Kryslie suggested to Landin that she should give the coordinates of two possible Ciriot locations to Jonko, or John Goss as he was known, to pass on to the Investigative Committee. The places would need to be checked first, before the air force went in with the new cloak-busters. He confirmed directly to Kryslie when the information proved accurate.

Tymos was soon able to report to Kryslie that the mote detectors had proved themselves, and Basoli was planning to have them rushed into production. He was to train technicians to use and maintain them and those people would be sworn to reveal nothing of what they found during their work. The secrecy was so that respectable people that had unwittingly been "infected" would not have their reputations ruined. If the same person was noted to have needed to be disinfected more than once, an investigator would check their movements and acquaintances to see where the infection was coming from, or if necessary placed in quarantine or protective custody.

Jonko reported privately to Kryslie that Jody was now clean.

# Chapter 41

A squadron of the new space fighters were based at Lunar 1. Tymos had transferred to pilot and was soon promoted to flight leader under Captain Casey. All the trainee space pilots were being trained to the same standard in flight strategy and tactics, as these pilots would be promoted to lead flights as more of the fighters came in-service.

Kryslie was reassigned to be an instructor at Washington University as a temporary fill in for Professor Rostin, who was quite ill. His speciality was shield design. Kryslie was his equal, but could also teach the students how to engineer the generators from plans to working models.

Her tenure stretched longer than originally thought when Rostin was advised to take a sabbatical.

On a day, midway through the current term, the onset of warning alarms startled the whole class. Kryslie quickly interpreted the sound signals.

"Everyone turn off all equipment, collect personal items and proceed to evacuation point delta," she directed calmly.

"What a time for a drill," one student commented sourly.

Kryslie didn't correct him. Her mind was aware of the shields going up. It was definitely not a practice. She ensured that all of her students were out of the lab before securing it. She nodded to the fire wardens, acting as evacuation wardens, and ensured none of her students detoured away from the route to the large underground bunker.

Other groups were also converging there, as well as to the other evacuation points. Kryslie waited outside, and she was watching the faint purple glow of the shields when the explosion of light betrayed that a barrage from an energy weapon had impacted on it. That was enough to make the laggards hurry to the bunker. The shields did not block sound, and she could hear many explosions.

Kryslie tapped her ear and sub-vocalised a message to Daniel at Earthbase. She needed to know what was happening.

Daniel's voice came faint but audible into her ear. "One wave of two hundred Ciriot drone ships appeared just out of the system. Their speed is three times that of the manned ships. The Earth based fighters are launching as are those from Lunar 1."

Kryslie tapped the device off. From within the bunker, an announcement was being broadcast. It added nothing to what she knew. She offered to help the evac wardens do a ground search, but was politely refused. She still intended to search, because something had caused the ships to target the university.

Kryslie kept out of the bunkers, and used her power to hide her from view. She resumed contact with Earthbase and they were able to tell her that so far the damage had been to mainly open areas, and some housing estates. The buildings that reported hits on their shields were, as she and Tymos predicted, official buildings, banks and prosperous shopping precincts. The media considered the damage random, but Kryslie was sure it wasn't. There was nothing she could do personally at the moment, even for the people injured by the attack.

So, she waited for the attack to finish, and considered wryly that she could have been made rich on royalties and patents on the shields she and Tymos had helped design, except that they had done so under the auspices of the WSRA. The shields worked equally well as regular burglar proofing, as well as to protect from attacks from above.

The most positive outcome had been the performance of both air and space fighters. The initial 200 drone ships had been destroyed. When driven off from Washington City, they had turned up and blasted out of the atmosphere, cloaked and travelled to a series of other cities until none of the craft remained.

What wasn't widely reported was that seven cloaked ships that had tried to sneak in under the diversion of the drones were 'seen' and also destroyed. Cloaked Earth made spy planes were now overflying the attack corridor, checking for other cloaked alien ships.

Kryslie spoke to her brother via internet from her Uni quarters after his flight had returned to Lunar 1.

"Basic target practice," Tymos told her. "I think they were testing our defences. The next lot won't be so easy."

"That is what I thought too," Kryslie admitted. "The Uni was a target but I don't know who was attracting them. I have provoked a tightening of entry protocols and I think some people have been getting slack."

"Did the evac work?" Tymos asked.

"Here, yes," Kryslie confirmed. "The media noted that President Adamson was taken to the old war room at the White House. Vice President bin Halil was at Terra 1 and went into the bunker there."

"Good! They are both taking the threat seriously. We had little enough warning of this."

As the general population was preparing for more attacks, Kryslie and her students were discussing how well various shields had worked and ideas to improve them.

The second wave of attackers arrived with less than an hour's warning. Tymos warned Kryslie when the five hundred ships appeared on Lunar 1's enhanced scanners. Earthbase contacted her seconds later when the attack vector had been calculated. The ships were well into the atmosphere before they de-cloaked, no doubt thinking they were, until then, undetected. They were surprised to be attacked from behind by the space fighters from Lunar 1.

This time it was night, and Kryslie slipped out of her quarters and into the dark grounds, automatically checking the shields were up. As she looked, the grid like structure flared into incandescence. In its glare, she saw the streams of hastily dressed people running to the shelters. The evacuation alarms were muted in the grounds.

Then the ground shook and a building beyond a screen of trees exploded into flame. Kryslie glanced up again – the shields were off!

Without thought, she raced at her full speed through the grounds towards the security office where the shield controls were. Security worked from the ground floor of a building near the entrance gates. The door was open and lights were blazing into the grounds, making the building more of a target. Elsewhere the lights were dimmed and shaded from above to betray little useful light to flying craft.

The office had only one visible occupant, wearing a guard uniform, but to Kryslie's adjusted eyes having a green aura around him. He was sending out a signal to the attacking ships.

That ceased as soon as Kryslie reached him. He had no warning of her attack, and she had him disabled and trussed up with a yanked power cable within half a minute.

When she looked around for the shield controls, she saw two men with bleeding wounds, unconscious on the floor. She checked the condition of each, relieved that they were alive. She turned her personal force screen off for a moment – long enough to send them some of her energy and start them healing. She knew she dared not stay unshielded for longer than that. She had kept the shield on continuously since rescuing Jody Basoli.

In the pocket of her black pull-on suit, she had her tech scanner. It was a very useful device that she had improved from her version of twenty years before. She used it now to find out why the shields were off, when all the switches showed they should be on.

The building shook as another bomb or energy blast struck the ground outside.

Kryslie didn't need much time to find the problem. The guard had yanked out a bundle of cables from under the console and cut the lot. It would not just be the shields that were not working. And he obviously did not know the cable colour coding protocol. She did, and so was concentrating on the blue/yellow striped cables, and making use of a basic tool kit that had been in the emergency cupboard and using a torch from there to see what she needed to do while she had her head and upper torso under the console.

The shield failure was noticed and guards were sent to investigate. Kryslie sensed them but kept working.

"Come out of there slowly," a loud voice demanded.

Kryslie still didn't stop. "You can pull me out after I get the shields back up."

"We have technicians coming. It is not a job for an amateur electrician. Come out!"

"I am not an amateur," Kryslie told them, and paused a moment to take her ID from around her neck and toss it out into the view of the new guards. "And you need to take the guard tied with the power cord through the personnel scanner – he was sending some kind of signal when I came in. The other two were unconscious. I checked them, and they need medical attention."

A short time later, one of the guards noted, "The shield grid is back up."

That by itself did nothing, but it was the basis for all the nested shields.

Kryslie was aware, peripherally, that someone was calling for medics, and that the tied up guard was being removed from the room. She had no doubt that the fourth of the newcomers had a weapon trained on her.

"Can you turn everything but the shield grid on the board to off?" Kryslie called up.

"Done," a voice confirmed.

Kryslie mated the severed ends using her hand scanner to match them. After several minutes of fast finger manipulations, she called out again, "You can run diagnostics on shield 1 and 2. If they are in the green, tell me and leave them on."

"Green to both," she was told after a moment.

When all six shields were up and showing green, Kryslie wriggled out of her awkward position and was helped to her feet.

Her helper wore the uniform of Security chief, and he passed her ID back to her.

"Senior Technician Kryslie Ward," he greeted. "I guess you did know what you were doing. Your name is listed in the 'who to call' book. We have never had any trouble with the shields before."

"I helped design them," Kryslie admitted. "That is why I am filling in as teacher right now. Anyway, when your technician arrives – he can fix the rest of the mess. The guy just cut the lot of cables and I don't know what everything is for."

A flare of light lit up the outside and into the room.

"That would have been close," the Security Chief grunted. "I'm Slater."

Kryslie grinned at him. "Glad to meet you."

"Hope you are, because I will need you to give a report to the Chancellor," Slater warned. "And I wouldn't mind knowing how a slip of a lady like you got the better of Harris."

"Firstly, I am no lady and secondly, he didn't see me coming. Have you had a report on him?"

Slater noticeably considered if he would answer before doing so.

"Yup, he was infected. Sloppy fool. He was running late for shift and skipped the log in."

Kryslie nodded. "Have you detected many infections?"

"One or two a week. Can't figure the source," Slater admitted. "Useful gadget though."

Kryslie merely nodded.

There had been no explosions since the failed one on the reinstated shields. They could hear jets flying over though.

"Sounds like the bastards have finished with us since the fly boys have come through. You might as well stay here until the all clear."

That was what Kryslie hoped to do, so she continued the conversation. "I don't think Harris knew what he was doing," Kryslie suggested.

"No matter," Slater told her. "He didn't follow the log in rules and he should have."

Kryslie couldn't argue with that point, although it might have been the effect of the green mote or 'infection' that made him by-pass the scanner. She had no way of knowing.

The need for further conversation ended with the arrival of the repair technician.

Lessons on the following day were cancelled so a damage inspection could be done. The worst damage was to the vehicle garage which was close to the generator building that supplied power to the campus. That building had structural cracks and technicians were testing all the generators and circuits. Power outages were frequent during the day.

The Chancellor, Martin Downey, a recent appointee to the position, was one of the University's earliest students. He had been there, well before Kryslie had been a student here. So far, he had not associated her as a past student.

Kryslie waited for him to be ready for her. He was listening to reports, from all over the campus. The Investigator from the World Council Investigative committee was sitting unobtrusively in a corner, and as seemed to be their policy, did not introduce himself. Kryslie guessed he had been sent by the CIC, Ron Basoli. The man seemed bored by what he was hearing, and she wondered why he was there.

When Downey introduced her and Kryslie began speaking, he suddenly sat up, more alert.

She had no issue to answer for in fixing the shields. She was the listed expert, even if she was normally working on Lunar 1. It was the actions of the infected guard that were being perused. He had assaulted two of his colleagues, damaged university property directly and through his actions in addition to ignoring an important security precaution.

Kryslie was facing Downey across his desk when he suddenly looked at the door and stood up. The investigator merely straightened a little.

Kryslie turned and saw Basoli had entered the room, with President Adamson. She stood quickly and vacated her chair. Several uniformed senior military officers followed the President, as well as four black suited, security men wearing dark eye shades. Downey's office seemed suddenly crowded.

Basoli frowned when he saw Kryslie, but Adamson smiled and greeted her by name as he walked to usurp Downey's chair. Basoli moved the second chair to the side of the desk. He addressed Kryslie.

"How is it, Tech Officer Ward, that you always seem to be around at convenient times?"

Kryslie merely shrugged and said nothing. Adamson added his own remark, "Miss Ward is not one to shirk difficult jobs."

Basoli turned to the investigator and asked for an update. He was given a terse report on the infected guard – his actions and his subsequent treatment."

"Ward, how did you get involved?" Basoli asked.

"When I realised the shields were down, I went to the security office to find out why," Kryslie told him. She gave him a more technical report on the damage, the repairs she had done and assured him that the system check showed green.

"Have you sent through a damage report yet?" Basoli asked of Downey.

"Preliminary only, Sir," Downey confirmed. "I am in the process of getting full details."

"Anything needing priority action?" Basoli asked.

"The generator room," Downey said at once.

"I will keep that in mind," Basoli promised. "I will get back to that later. I have another priority right now."

He drew out of his jacket a silver cylinder. Kryslie recognised it immediately but said nothing.

"We need to open this cylinder without damaging the contents," Basoli advised Downey. "I will need to talk to your experts. However, since Miss Ward is here, perhaps she can tell us if it is shielded?"

Kryslie could have answered that right away, but took out her tech scanner and made a show of checking.

"Yes, Sir. It is," she said after glancing at the screen. She used the moment of silence to send a mental warning to her brother and to have him arrange for the Tymorean President to stand by.

"Can you neutralise it?" Adamson asked her. And all eyes were on her.

"I do recognise this, Mr President," Kryslie admitted. "Has the World Council voted to answer the invitation that is meant to be in it?"

Basoli began to speak, but Adamson waved him to silence.

"Yes, it was a unanimous vote," Adamson told her.

Kryslie did not ask what had changed their minds. The losses of fighter craft and pilots, civilians and property had been heavy after the second raid.

She simply nodded and moved her hand to disengage her personal force shield. The cylinder glowed faintly mauve to her sight. When she took the cylinder from Basoli, she touched it at one end and the cylinder snapped open along its length. She handed it to Adamson, who had begun to rise to his feet with disbelief.

Kryslie stepped back and re-engaged her force shield.

"How...did you do that?" Basoli demanded, as Adamson unrolled the parchment that had been inside.

Kryslie said nothing as Adamson read.

"It is exactly what Casey claimed it would be. Written in English, and with identification protocols consistent with ours," Adamson said stunned. "However, I don't understand the part about contacting them."

The parchment was passed to Basoli to read.

Kryslie sensed the start of disbelief and spoke out – drawing all eyes back to her.

"That is unimportant," she said quietly, but the room was so quiet it seemed loud. "They will come, if I request it."

Her change of stance, her tone of voice, made her seem to be a totally different person.

The guards quietly drew hand weapons. Basoli and Adamson stared at her as if she had turned into a stranger. To the men behind her she said, calmly and quietly, "I have not changed my skin colour to blue or sprouted horny eye ridges. I am the same person you knew yesterday. You will not need your weapons."

Adamson stood again, waved his guards to stand down, and walked around the desk.

"No, you are not the same person you appeared to be moments ago," Adamson challenged her. "Who are you?"

Kryslie's whole bearing could only be described as regal. In the same quiet tone she had been using, she said, "I am Kryslie, daughter and heir designate to High King Governor Tymoros, of Tymorea and acting as Tymorean missionary to Earth."

"That explains the attitude," Basoli muttered. Then he said, much louder, "Do you mean...that we could have had help from them, at any time before this...and not had over a hundred fighters and crew destroyed? You have been lying to us for years! And all this time you have been an illegal alien."

"The last is not strictly true, Chief Commander. Nor was it necessary to claim a position that had no relevance until now. And, yes, you could have had help from the Tymorean fleet before now. However, the leaders of Earth chose not to answer this invitation until now."

Adamson returned to his seat. "Why didn't you speak out when it was being discussed?"

"Mr President, it was not my place or my intention to try to force such a decision on the people of Earth," Kryslie said. "Nor would I have been thanked for interfering."

"When your Tymoreans helped Genesis 1, why did they not destroy all the aliens?" Basoli demanded.

"With respect, Chief Commander," Kryslie maintained an even tone, "The Tymorean Fleet is a Peace keeping fleet. Its mandate is to help defend the worlds in the Federation of Peace. Earth has not yet joined and therefore the fleet will not enter Earth's solar system."

"It didn't stop you sneaking in here," Basoli challenged.

"Just because Earth decided to reject our invitation at that time, did not mean we had to shut you out forever. We are here to keep that option open and help Earth defend itself if that was the people's choice."

"This is all too pat, all too convenient," Basoli said dismissively. "How can I believe what you have said? How can I believe this is not some gigantic scam?"

"You are right to be doubtful," Kryslie allowed, not at all resentful of his attitude. "When the Tymorean delegation arrives, Captain Casey will recognise one of them and from the other, you may take a DNA sample to compare to ours."

"Ours?" Adamson queried.

"Her brother, Tymos Ward, is another," Basoli growled.

"Indeed, Chief Commander. My brother is Tymos, son and heir designate to High King Governor Tymoros, of Tymorea."

"You are technicians!" Basoli stated. His mind went on, "Smart mouthed, smart fingered technicians."

"I have no problem with appointing Kryslie Ward and her brother as Tymorean Ambassadors to Earth," Adamson stated with due gravity. "I think that their past actions speak for their intent."

Basoli scowled and asked the silent military men if they wished to comment.

The Air Force CIC stated, "I agree with President Adamson. Flight Leader Tymos Ward has proved his skill and leadership ability to my satisfaction. He has taught us strategies that we found to be highly effective."

Kryslie moved the attention back to herself. "Mr President, I am at your service to send the reply. I presume you will need to consult with the Council on the wording."

"Indeed, Ambassador Ward," Adamson confirmed. "And I will wish to introduce you to the council."

Kryslie bowed acknowledgement. "I will be available here when needed."

"No!" Basoli snapped.

"I agree, here would not be appropriate," Adamson decided. "You will return with me to the White House as an honoured guest."

The guards still had weapons out, but not aimed at her. She smiled faintly.

"I doubt that I will need a body guard," Kryslie suggested. "I can usually take care of myself."

"Protocol, I am afraid," Adamson apologised. "It is not meant as a slight on your position."

"That is well," Kryslie told him with gentle rebuke but her words were more aimed at Basoli. "It would be a poor message to send – that you do not trust me."

Basoli didn't get the warning. "I expect I will have to get your resignation from WSRA – due to your new position."

"That is not necessary," Kryslie told him. "Once I have facilitated this meeting, I will not be required to be present. I am still willing to serve the WSRA as before. Unless, as I said, you no longer trust me."

Basoli kept silent, but his expression betrayed his thoughts.

Kryslie added, "I think you should accept my past actions as proof of intent."

"I am considering that," Basoli told her. "I also think that there is much that you know that you have not revealed."

"Of course," Kryslie agreed, calm in her assertion. "But much of what I know is not relevant here on Earth. And you cannot deny that I have helped develop many new applications when there was a perceived need for them. As for my private life – that is no business of the WSRA, unless my actions violate the ethics of the organisation."

Basoli smothered a growl. He dearly wanted to argue that point, but the other business was more important. Later – he promised himself.


Joel Adamson escorted Kryslie to his dark limo for the return trip to the White House. The military men followed in two vehicles and his body guards in cars ahead of the limo.

# Chapter 42

Tymos Ward withdrew from a flight briefing after a terse word to Casey, and an equally terse word from the senior pilot for an explanation later.

From his sister's brief mental message, he knew their anonymity would shortly end. Her prediction was that Basoli would waste no time contacting Landin and having him stood down from his position. He activated the chime at Landin's door, just as the Commander disconnected from Basoli.

Landin allowed him to enter and studied the manner of the heretofore technical officer. He noticed the same change in Tymos that Basoli had seen in Kryslie, and approved of it.

"I am to stand you down from duty and keep you incommunicado until further notice," Landin spoke with no preamble. "But I think you already knew that. What is going on?"

"Yes, Sir, Kryslie warned me. I hope the instructions did not require me to be in the brig. That would be totally unsuitable and I would take issue with it."

"Naturally," Landin allowed. "I was told no reason."

Tymos knew Landin deserved an answer. "You are already aware of more about us than the Chief, so I will tell you that Kryslie revealed some of that to the Chief and the President of UEN."

"I...see," Landin said thoughtfully. "Will you tell me the reason?"

"It was necessary. The World Council has voted to answer the invitation delivered by Genesis 1."

"You will be expected to resign your position," Landin warned.

"And I will deny those expectations," Tymos warned him soberly. "It will be a mistake to insist, as there is much I can offer in the defence of Earth."

"I quite agree," Landin admitted.


Kryslie was not invited to sit in on the discussion of the invitation, but that was as she had expected. Instead, she was in a nearby 'waiting room' under the tacit protection of two body guards.

She was aware that rumours of 'an alien' were rife, but only the secret service men who were present when she revealed herself, knew it was her. They were sworn not to disclose it.

Officially, she was the scientific expert who had opened the capsule and knew how to send the message. She would not be summoned until the World Councillors finished deciding on the wording of the reply.

Five hours later, Kryslie was brought in and introduced, but only as the expert. A subgroup of the council accompanied Adamson and Kryslie to the communications room, situated on the lower level of the White House. The ubiquitous guards led and followed.

Kryslie was given access to the equipment and she set to work at once. First she programmed the encryption algorithm to send the message, and which would be needed to decrypt the return message. Then she spoke the message in clear even tones. Once finished, she stood and stepped aside.

"Mr President, the return message will require either you or the Vice President to receive it after a retinal scan identity check."

"When can we expect a reply?" one of the councillors asked.

"That will depend on the location of the Tymorean contact. It may take one to two weeks," Kryslie told the men. There was some murmuring about that. Adamson merely said, "Consider the depth of space."

Kryslie did not comment that it would have been much faster if they had replied immediately.

The question was asked as to whether Kryslie had been sworn to secrecy. Adamson answered for her. "Yes."

Further talk was halted by an incoming message. It was recorded by the regular comms officer. Transcribed and handed to Adamson.

"Vladivostok and Stockholm are under attack," he announced.

Kryslie was arbitrarily escorted out and back upstairs. She was invited to visit and speak with the First Lady, Geraldine Adamson. The well-respected consort of the President soon overcame her fear of talking to an alien, since Kryslie did not look inhuman, and she had associated her name with the person who had saved her husband from a shuttle crash some years before.


Two weeks of hit and run attacks by the Ciriot fleet kept all the world convocations on edge.

When the reply from the Tymoreans was received, Adamson was already in the War Room. He could go directly from there to the Comms Room. Kryslie was hustled there, even though she was not needed to receive the message.

What they did want to know from her was the expected protocol for such a meeting from the Tymorean viewpoint. That was when the currently present World Leaders realised who she was.

Kryslie sighed, purely to herself and behaved as professionally and non-threateningly as she could.

The Tymoreans would arrive in a week's time and it was decided, for security reasons to have the meeting at Lunar 1. She was to send a message giving the location.

Kryslie kept silent except when asked specific questions. It helped people forget she was 'alien'.

Adamson trusted her, but everyone else was wary – and like a prisoner, she was always watched. She tolerated it out of necessity, but didn't like it.

The representatives from the world council that were to attend the momentous meeting were to fly up on the shuttle to Lunar 1. Adamson and Kryslie were already in the reception lounge for the shuttle, for the moment alone except for the bodyguards. Kryslie wasn't in the mood for conversation, but Adamson saw an opportunity to ask a question that had intrigued him.

"You told Chief Basoli that you weren't an illegal alien. You have never explained that statement," Adam stated. "How is that?"

The secret service guards were a discrete distance away. Kryslie noted that in a quick glance before she turned to stare out of the window to the landing pad.

"It's complicated."

"So is world politics – try me?" Adamson invited.

Kryslie breathed a sigh and looked back at the President, "My brother and I were born on Earth and have spent more time here than on Tymorea."

"What is complicated about that? You would have a birth certificate and all that."

"We were born about 1980," Kryslie told him and enjoyed the expression of shock on the President's face. "But I am not over one hundred years old."

"I assume there is a logical answer to that paradox?" Adamson probed.

Kryslie was perfectly serious when she told him, "Only if you can accept that Tymos and I are Advocates of the Guardians of Peace and they act in ways that even we do not understand."

She knew that Adamson had no conception of the beings she had mentioned. He thought it was related to the membership of the Federation of Peace.

"But you are Tymorean...were your parents missionaries, like you are now?"

That was close enough. "You could say that," she agreed.

"Yet you claim kinship to the High King Governor of Tymorea. How is that? More complications?" Adamson probed.

Kryslie smiled faintly. She wasn't prepared to explain things in too much detail.

"Yes. We are genetically closer to his Majesty than we are to either of those we called parents for the first sixteen years of our lives. We are recognised as his true heirs."

"You speak of a high king. Are there other kings?" Adamson was interested to ask.

Kryslie shook her head. "I can't explain the title, but Tymorea has always been ruled by a Triumvirate. Our father is High King Governor – consider him the statesman. Then there is President Governor Reslic, who you will meet. He is the Defender – like the commander of the military. The third Governor is Xyron, and he oversees the scientific and technical things."

"And they are all equal in rank?"

"Yes, and they are the supreme authority on Tymorea." Kryslie had no intention of mentioning the rank of Great One.

"The President Governor – what is he like?" Adamson asked.

"Formidable," Kryslie said with a faint smile. "On Tymorea he is considered to be the Greatest Living Warrior. He trained Tymos and me."

Kryslie spent a few moments describing Reslic in terms Adamson would comprehend.

When the shuttle had landed, and disembarked the downward passengers through another lounge, the other upward passengers were allowed into the lounge where Adamson waited. They would board as soon as the shuttle was refuelled.

Basoli and his daughter entered with guard complement. Jody smiled at Kryslie, but Basoli slid his eyes past her to greet the President. Three senior military officers followed and then Arthur bin Halil entered with his guards. The latter had no difficulty in treating her as a familiar friend.

The flight up to Lunar 1 was uneventful. The shuttle arrived several hours before the alien visitors were expected. The space scanners had the Tymorean ship on an approach vector and two of the new space fighters were due to intercept and escort the ship down.

The welcome committee watched the approach of the Tymorean ship from an observation room on the upper level of Lunar 1.

"I had expected a larger ship," the Air Force CIC remarked.

Kryslie answered him. "This is his personal craft. The Tymorean flagship, Jacen Tyr, is too big to land. It will be standing by just out system. If you wished, you would be welcome to request a tour of it."

The man looked at as if he did not think she had the authority to suggest that. She mentally shrugged when he looked away from her.

The three ships came into direct view and slowed to enter the hangar deck. Kryslie began to walk to the lift to take them down to that level. Lunar 1 security did not try to stop her, they knew her. All the others followed, and arrived after the three ships had settled. The escort pilots were climbing down from their ships to go and greet the newcomers.

Only when Captain Casey and Flight Leader Tymos Ward were in position in front of the hatch, did the visiting ship lower its landing ramp.

"What is Ward doing there, Landin?" Basoli hissed.

"Who is better to greet them than those who already know the guests, and are also our most skilled pilots," Landin said without apology.

Basoli gave no return comment, his attention was drawn to the hooded figure in flowing gold and silver robes that was descending the ramp. Following him was a slightly taller, powerfully built man with blond hair and a uniform indicating high rank – complete with braids and trimming. At first, no one noticed the oddity of a sword strapped to the man's back.

Casey saluted, Tymos bowed his head slightly to the tall man, and both bowed slightly to the hooded man. Then they escorted the men to the waiting humans.

Tymos made the introductions, and Reslic quietly acknowledged each by repeating the name. He did not need to introduce Kryslie but Reslic greeted her as Great One, but tactfully in Tymorean not English.

"Welcome to Lunar 1, your Excellency," Kryslie said clearly, and spoke Tymorean to greet her brother, Llaimos.

She stood back then to let Reslic be escorted by Adamson and bin Halil. Tymos took a position on the other side of their brother. He had been introduced as Great One Llaimos, but again in Tymorean.

"Playing mysterious alien, little brother," Tymos teased, speaking in Tymorean. He, like Kryslie was feeling renewed, just by having the three of them together.

"No more than either of you did," Llaimos remarked. "Your astronauts saw one like I, and so here I am."

They switched to thinking at each other, and during the walk to the reception area, Llaimos quickly updated them on his work in the vaults of Aerdna and heard in turn of the prophecy of Nala and how it appeared to be unfolding.

"How long will you stay?" Kryslie asked.

"As long as needed," Llaimos assured them.

"How is Pyr?" Tymos asked. "He must have grown."

"He has. He is nearly as tall as I am, and he sends his regards. He wanted to come, but he is taking my place as Father's right hand whilst I am engaged elsewhere."


The meeting room was carefully prepared with security in mind, but also to keep the guests at ease.

Security guards flanked the doors, but the military members of the welcome group passed their weapons to them. The visitors were not asked to remove theirs, and did not. Tymos glanced at Kryslie with a faint grin. He would bet that the humans could not guess how many hidden weapons Reslic carried.

A table was set for the meeting. Tymos and Kryslie stood behind Reslic and Llaimos. When everyone else of the group was seated, Adamson stood again to give his speech of welcome. Reslic responded with a speech of his own.

Then, as if casually, Llaimos removed his hood and proved, firstly that he did not look like some kind of monster and secondly that his resemblance to Tymos and Kryslie was unmistakable.

Reslic pretended not to notice the intense interest, nor how subtly the Great Ones had changed from politely servile to demanding of respect.

Even though Kryslie and Tymos kept their comments to explaining concepts unfamiliar to one party or the other, frequent glances were directed at them and Llaimos. Jono Reslic dealt with the discussions and negotiations with skilful ease.

Landin and Basoli were present as representatives of the WSRA. They listened silently, and also studied the three red heads more than the blond they took to be the leader. During a break, they went directly to Tymos, Kryslie and the richly dressed visitor.

Kryslie greeted them correctly, and asked of Basoli, "Do you still wish to prove our relationship to the visitors with a DNA test, Chief Commander?" Her serious tone hid her intention of slight disrespect.

"That will not be necessary, Ambassador Kryslie," Basoli said stiffly.

Landin eased the tension by suggesting, "As our meeting will undoubtedly take time. We have prepared guest quarters."

"Thank you Commander Landin, that will be welcome indeed," Llaimos acknowledged.

"It is obvious to me that you are related. Am I correct?" Landin went on.

"Yes, commander. Llaimos is our little brother," Kryslie said quietly and with a faint grin. Llaimos was slightly taller than both Tymos and herself.

Basoli proved to have been listening. "I did not understand the title he gave you, Sir," he looked at Llaimos. "I heard him use the same term when greeting Ambassador Ward."

Kryslie moved her head in a slight gesture of negation. In her mind, she told Llaimos "Don't mention Great Ones."

"We are all children of High King Tymoros, Sir. It is how we are normally greeted," Llaimos said politely.

He was being deliberately misleading, but Basoli accepted it with only a faint tightening of the muscles in his face. He had hoped to discover something more about Tymos and Kryslie.

Basoli looked like he was keen to leave, so Kryslie made it easier for him.

"I wish to introduce Llaimos to the leaders here, and the Vice President is coming over."

Basoli and Landin quickly moved aside. Kryslie greeted Arthur bin Halil with polite correctness as he studied the stranger. He bowed slightly in greeting. "I am extremely pleased to meet another brother of Kryslie Ward."

In Llaimos's mind, Kryslie added, "Believe it or not, this man is my son."

With great effort, Llaimos controlled a start of surprise and some embarrassment. "I believe the delight is mutual. Kryslie has spoken of you."

To Kryslie's mind he asked, "The father?"

She responded in kind, "Not a subject for polite conversation. Stick to business."

They talked until the meeting resumed.


Once general agreement was reached on several important points the meeting was adjourned for the day. In the prepared quarters, Kryslie explained to Reslic that the other leaders, the leaders of the individual convocations on Earth who comprised the World Council, would meet by vid-link to hear the recommendations of the group at the meeting.

"This I surmise may take time," Reslic noted.

"It might, your Excellency," Kryslie agreed.

Reslic followed that remark with, "I sense they distrust you."

Kryslie smiled faintly, "It is simply that the word 'alien' has too many terrifying connotations in Earth literature and mythology. They think I am now something quite different. However, President Adamson does trust me, and Vice President bin Halil is my son and Commander Landin has faith in our integrity and respects our intelligence. So we have support. Chief Basoli finds us irritating – no doubt a personality clash."

Reslic did not hide his surprise at her admission of kinship to the Vice President, but made no comment on that. Instead he chose to tease Kryslie and the listening Tymos by saying, "I can understand why you might be found to be irritating, Great Ones." He inserted a memory of how they had been when they first went to Tymorea. He found it amusing that the Great Ones still blushed and still did not feel entitled to rebuke him for such subtle disrespect. Llaimos, however, openly grinned at his discomforted siblings.

Reslic quickly went on, "The Chief Commander has no conception of the nature of Great Ones and that it does not imply great age. How has Earth handled the constant nuisance raids of the Ciriot?"

Tymos had that information ready in his mind, courtesy of Earthbase. Reslic listened intently. Then he reported in turn. "There are indications that several tribeships are joining. When they feel they know Earth's strength, they will come with an overwhelming force. It makes me wonder what we might have learnt had they not destructed the other ship. Tell me your observations on how Earth will deal with them."

Kryslie and Tymos proved that they had learnt their lessons well, providing Reslic with intuitive details on many related matters. It all provided background details that the leaders might not reveal but were vital to the ultimate defeat of the Ciriot attempt to subvert Earth.

The evening meal was to be a formal affair. Kryslie advised Reslic that the 'uniform' would not be required, but formal attire would be. She admitted that she had designed the protocol. For Reslic, she suggested the traditional formal robes of the President Governor.

Llaimos took the opportunity to comment, "Isn't it fortunate then, that I brought you and Tymos your Robes of State? Perhaps that will convince them that you are important people - though I doubt that they can tell the difference between the robes of a President Governor and those of Great Ones. On this occasion, you do not need to appear merely human."

Since she and Tymos were more than a little tired of being restricted from doing what they needed to do – they agreed.

They had reasons though, for appearing politely reasonable, politely cooperative and emphasising their 'humanity', but soon enough they would need to act freely.

The pre-dinner reception enabled the senior base staff to meet and learn about the visitors and become at ease with them.

Kryslie found Jody Basoli looking out of place and guided her to meet Llaimos first. Tymos was with him when she approached, and Jody noticeably compared them all.

"Jody is CIC Basoli's daughter, and a great granddaughter of Nala," Kryslie told Llaimos.

"A delight indeed to meet a distant relative," Llaimos assured her. And he asked her questions about herself, and soon had her thoroughly charmed and no longer fearful of the strangers. When she was presented to the more formidable Reslic, she was able to talk to him with perfect aplomb.

It did indeed seem that the formal Tymorean robes brought them greater respect, and Kryslie noted this to her brother when they were briefly alone.

"Landin has been okay about this," Tymos admitted. "But then he has known what we are for years. His idea of incommunicado was to transfer me from staff quarters to guest quarters, and ground me from flying training drills. He has kept me instructing flight and ground crews and he conveniently forgot to lock out the guest room computer. You?"

"A high class prison," Kryslie commented. "That is if you can call the President's residence that. Have you noticed that the military types are having no trouble talking to Llaimos and Reslic, but don't know what to say to us?"

"Uh huh," Tymos agreed. "Though I suppose if they consider us inferior to them, they may tend to overlook us too?"

"Mmm," Kryslie mused. She was watching waiters moving amongst the guests. "So long as they don't forget to invite us to eat."

The vid-conference took up most of the second day, and during that time, when Reslic wasn't directly required, he toured Lunar 1 and watched the pilots in training.

In a reasonably short time, though, a "Declaration of Intent" had been drawn up and agreed to. It was the first step in joining the Federation of Peace, and an important document. It stated the planet's intention to treat peacefully with other races. It now only needed to be formally signed by all members of the World Council on the behalf of all the people in their convocation.

President Adamson and his entourage were to travel to each convocation not already represented, to have the document formally signed. Kryslie was to travel with him as the Tymorean representative.

During their tour, the military men returned to their duty stations and left Basoli to represent them to the Tymorean visitors.

Tymos openly defied Basoli, and continued to train the pilots. He had been officially made an Ambassador by Adamson and therefore no longer directly answerable to the WSRA. Nothing further was said after Reslic commented critically on the high standard of expertise of the new pilots.

# Chapter 43

The shuttle flight back to Earth was not uneventful. The space fighters escorted the shuttle to the upper reaches of the atmosphere, and the air force rose to meet them. In the short distance between the two levels, a missile was fired from a cloaked Ciriot ship. The shuttle was rocked by the explosion against its shields.

The shields held, but the rest of the trip was tense with apprehension that another attack might come. As they were preparing to land, the passengers were advised that the attacker had been located and destroyed.

Kryslie followed Adamson off the shuttle and into the reception lounge at Terra 1. Outside on the tarmac, the President's plane, still called 'Airforce One', was being worked on by an army of technicians. Adamson told her that it was being outfitted with the latest shields, and extra safety and emergency features. He also added they would have a full escort of fighters when they took off.

Hardly discreet, Kryslie thought to herself. It would be like telling the enemy that they were a juicy, fat target.

The itinerary and fuelling stops were already planned; Kryslie had no need to be involved in that. She was back to being a 'stranger' to Earth and the subject of wary scrutiny. As a result, she reverted to wearing her 'Robes of State' in public, and kept her plainer garments for private times.

They were three days into their tour when they landed at Terra 2 in Russia. Kryslie noticed Gareth Pitt amongst the welcoming committee, but at first he did not recognise her. She sent a gentle mental probe in his direction and was relieved to sense confidence and self-assurance. She identified the uniform he was wearing as Flight Leader. Behind him in precise rows were the space pilots in training.

Kryslie had no intention of re-kindling the intimate relationship they had enjoyed before the Genesis Mission. Now – it would be too complicated.

Pitt found her. He knocked at the door of her assigned quarters, and she decided to let him in. The guards outside had not challenged him.

"Nice clothes," he said by way of greeting. "What is this I hear about you being an alien? What kind of scam are you pulling?"

His tone was sceptical and accusatory.

"I am what I am," Kryslie told him. She was sensing changes in him. He was not the same friendly person she had been involved with. By comparison he was arrogant and domineering.

"You are no more alien than I am and I intend to prove it."

He reached to grab her, but she held him off with a strength that surprised him.

"This is not the time, or place," Kryslie warned him.

For an instant, Pitt tensed. Then he tried a different tack.

"God, I missed you. You were all I could think of when…when those bastards were messing with me."

That sounded like the old Gareth, but even so, it was not the time to re-start anything.

"I am glad you are alright," Kryslie said gently. "I am glad my kin found you and helped you."

She pulled him close for a moment, kissed him and gently pushed him to the door. He looked forlorn, but she needed to stay focussed.

Pitt took himself out, straightening and composing his face before the guards saw him. He nodded at the guards and stalked off.

Kryslie was known at Terra 2, and not considered dangerous. The security on her was general, not as intense as that around the President. She took advantage of that to have a degree of freedom and to get outside to where she could feel Earth's aura and renew herself. She found a quiet secluded area, and sat on the grass. There were guards patrolling within calling distance but they did not come near her. She relaxed in the solitude.

A sound roused her from the light meditative trance. She twisted around as a weight landed on her. Her senses recognised Gareth Pitt, but she could not touch his mind. She did not want to hurt him, so she withheld her full strength and used only enough to roll free. The guards should have heard the scuffle, and she suddenly realised she could not sense them.

Pitt struggled back onto her and she felt the tingle of her personal force shield as it neutralised a powerful jolt.

"Damn you! You have a force screen on!" Pitt hissed in an unfamiliar voice.

The tingling increased to a painful level as Kryslie tried to grapple the weapon out of his hand. Her body was glowing with the energy being dissipated by the shield. Pitt was on her again, pushing her onto the ground and holding her there with his body as he felt over her with one hand. The weapon in the other was still emitting a killing voltage. Kryslie rolled again, needing to get free before the force screen overloaded.  She was more than alarmed at Pitt's behaviour. She could not help him while shielded and she dared not un-shield. The thought of calling out occurred to her, but if Pitt was somehow controlled, she did not think it right to publically humiliate him.

Come to that, he had been through the scanner, she'd seen him. What was the reason for this?"

Kryslie stood to run, but Pitt caught her ankle.

"Kryslie, please...help me."

Just for a moment, she felt his mind. The old Gareth...and then nothing. The hesitation was enough. Something jabbed at her ankle, sharp with a severe jolt of energy. Her mind registered shock and the need to ground the energy fast. Then she instantly analysed a local point overload, and a knife jab.

Her mind went into instinctive fighting mode. She did not remember who her antagonist was, only that he wanted her dead.


Kryslie woke in the morning with the Terra 2 shift change tones. Almost immediately, she heard the visitor signal at her door. She slipped out of bed and put on an ankle length robe. As she did, she noticed the bandage on her ankle. A brief memory of scraping it on a rock ledge in the garden crossed her mind as she activated the door to open.

The young security guard stepped in and stood at attention. "Mam, Commander Vasilov requests your presence."

He spoke in heavily accented English. Kryslie replied politely in Russian.

"I will be ready in a few minutes."

The guard nodded, turned abruptly and went out. Kryslie closed the door.


A scrape was nothing. Kryslie removed the bandage; saw only a small amount of blood and no sign of a wound. She healed quickly and wasn't surprised. The bandage went into the disposal chute and she quickly dressed. Her mind was more concerned by the unexpected summons than the fact that she did not remember bandaging herself.

In the promised few minutes, she had dressed and packed her travel bag. The guard was waiting in the passage to escort her. They did not head in the direction of the base commander's office and since all the Terra bases had similar floor plans, she deduced they were heading to the infirmary.

"Has something happened to the Commander?" she asked with concern.

"No, Mam," the guard replied tersely in Russian, but he volunteered no information.

She saw both Commander Vasilov and President Adamson in the main infirmary, talking to the Chief medical Officer.

"Ambassador Ward," Vasilov greeted her. "I understand you know Flight Leader Pitt."

His tone was neutral. His mind betrayed 'know' to mean more than just being an acquaintance.

"Yes, Commander," Kryslie admitted. "Has something happened to him?"

"He was attacked last night. The guards found him outside the boundary this morning. He is conscious and asking for you," Vasilov told her.

The CMO moved to the door of a private room and gestured. Kryslie had a moment's warning of how bad Pitt was. A quick glance told her a great deal. She unshielded and took his unbandaged hand, and sent power into him to help him start healing.

"What happened?" she asked with concern.

"No idea," Pitt told her in a whisper.

His neck was also bandaged so his throat had been injured. "Was going to do a night inspection..."

"Is there something you wanted of me?" Kryslie asked him.

"Find out... who... did this?"

"I will need to leave it to Commander Vasilov, Gareth. I fly out with the President this morning."

She felt a gentle pressure from Pitt as the CMO suggested letting him rest.

Commander Vasilov was less formal when she emerged. Kryslie was thoughtful. She hadn't seen Pitt since his brief visit to her room and she hadn't heard anything unusual while in the garden. She volunteered that information to Vasilov without being asked.

"Two guards on the south side were found unconscious," Vasilov told her.

"I saw them when I went outside," Kryslie said, thinking back. "I don't recall if they were there later. I had put them out of my mind."

Vasilov seemed to want to challenge her statement.

"I have known Kryslie Ward for a number of years," Adamson spoke up. "She acted to save my life. I think she is not the sort to injure anyone deliberately and violently."

Kryslie realised that 'the alien' had been suspect, even though the staff at Terra 2 knew her.

"Mr President, thank you. However, I know Commander Vasilov must investigate all people. I suspect that also means you."

"Except I cannot move without a squad of guards," Adamson said wryly.

For a fleeting instant, Kryslie had a sense of something she had forgotten. The sensation vanished as quickly.

"Our flight will leave at 1000 hrs," Adamson advised Kryslie. "I will see you at breakfast."

Kryslie nodded. "Yes, Mr President."

# Chapter 44

The President's personal guards had become used to Kryslie and subconsciously relegated her to the 'safe' category. However, the guards on the other leaders were not as ready to trust the 'alien female'.

Kryslie ignored the aura of suspicion and remained courteous and polite when called on to explain aspects of the Declaration of Intent and the expectations of belonging to the Federation of Peace.

The concept was far beyond the experience of the political leaders and demanded of them a high degree of faith. Kryslie did not try to influence their minds directly, but only by using words and her own belief to inspire them. They would believe in time, she knew, when they saw the Tymorean fleet in action. But that could not happen yet. The only other thing she could do was be an example of openness and integrity.

Her mind heard, and then forgot, the reports of sabotage from the places she had been to. Minor things picked up by routine maintenance and the increased awareness of peril due to the President's presence, she had decided.

So far, their tour had been relatively uneventful. The Ciriot hit and run raids, although random, were keeping away from them. Their luck changed when they were approaching the airport at the Yugoslavian capital of the Eastern European Convocation. Seven Ciriot attack ships uncloaked and attacked the aircraft, getting in several damaging hits to the left wing, tail and underbelly. The plane began to fall.

Kryslie went to the cockpit before the shaken cabin crew regained their feet. The pilot was trying to hold the shuddering jet. The co-pilot was slumped over his controls. Kryslie moved him back in his seat and added her strength to the controls. The pilot was aware of someone, and felt the difference, but was too busy sending out a mayday message and preparing for an emergency landing.

In the confusion of hastily evacuating the aircraft after it had slid to a halt on its collapsed undercarriage, the pilot lost track of his unasked for helper. He found himself sliding down the emergency ramp beside his unconscious co-pilot. All passengers and crew were accounted for when the plane's fuel tank exploded.

The President was whisked away in the darkened limo as soon as it was driven close to the evacuees. Adamson insisted that Kryslie travel with him. He knew she had helped get them down and get everyone out.

Andrija Petrovic, the Serbian born convocation leader had medical experts waiting at the UEN building. Adamson claimed to be uninjured but it was apparent he was experiencing a bit of post-emergency shock. Kryslie assured them that she was fine, but allowed them to check her over.

Adamson was convinced to rest, but Kryslie had reasons that precluded her from doing the same. During the confusion on arrival, and the hustle through the media contingent, she had spotted a tall figure that had a red aura. She had not seen the face of the man, but he had entered the UEN precinct. She needed to find the man, as all her instincts were warning of danger.

Instead of resting, she requested a tour of the building and for a time, no one recalled that she was the alien. The first impression, that she was human, was holding. She did not see the figure she sought during her tour, but did get a mental picture of the building. When she returned to her assigned room near the President's suite, she thought to request replacement necessities, and this was acted on immediately, as they realised that the President would require similar things. Fortunately, the official document was safe, in the case that had been secured to the President's wrist.

Kryslie gave every indication of resting when her requests were delivered. The servant who delivered the clean clothing apologised for only having a blank uniform for her to change into. She thanked the man anyway, and accepted his offer of having her official robes washed.

Some of the privileges of travelling with the President included being able to request privacy and not be disturbed. She did this after eating the light meal they provided for her.

Kryslie locked the door after the last servant and put her tech scanner and transmitter into the uniform pocket. In a gesture that had become instinctive, she checked her personal force screen and ensured it was still on. Then she was ready to scout the building and find the man with the red aura. Her senses were telling her it was a Ciriot controlled victim and it was no use telling the guards here that, as they would not be able to see the red aura.

Kryslie transmitted to the far end of the building to a point she had seen, and searched first in the area that housed the servants. When she encountered people, she became immobile and used her power to remain unseen, and to subtly deflect people around her. She could sense which rooms were occupied and flicked in and out of those that were.

Her search took her to all the places she had been shown, but there might be levels they had not taken her. She was considering how to find those possible levels when she heard the explosion and felt the building shake and loose items rattle. At intervals along the passage, lights began flashing, bathing everything with red.

Instant awareness of the Ciriot attacking came as alarms began to ring throughout the building. She allowed herself to be seen near her room and have her 'presidential party ID' visible, and was immediately hustled through a doorway that had been hidden by a force screen.

Not far behind her, the President was being hurried by his guards through the same door. They walked together down a ramp to a bunker like doorway that was opened by the guards using a card in the electronic lock. Beyond the door was a passage with doors leading off either side. A door was opened, and two of Adamson's secret service guards entered, checked it and reported it clear. The other two of Adamson's guards followed them into the room.

Andrija Petrovic looked in and requested the President to remain there. He hurried off. The room was comfortably appointed, with reclining chairs, a table, computer console and basic cooking facilities. There were no windows of course as the room had to be below ground level. Two rooms led off it. One was a sleeping room and one was a bathroom.

Adamson went to the chair and reclined it until it was almost a bed. Kryslie looked at him and noted that his colour was poor. She went to him and asked how he was. He took her hand and patted it. "I am fine. Too much excitement, that is all."

That was not what Kryslie sensed. She smiled though and moved to the nearest secret service guard and voiced her concern. The man looked over at his charge and quickly activated his ear-throat radio to request a doctor.

The medic arrived promptly, and requested privacy for his patient. Kryslie was escorted to a room nearby and requested to stay there.

Concern for Adamson was foremost in her mind, but she also needed to find the man with the red aura. The attack was still ongoing – the shields on the building had to be down.

With deliberate intent, Kryslie went out into the passage. She had a reasoned argument ready if anyone tried to stop her, but there were no guards in sight. And there should have been two outside the room with Adamson, but they might be inside.

Her instinct told her where the auxiliary shield controls should be and that was her target. The lack of guards was making her uneasy. She reached a room where four men sat at consoles around the room and entered quietly. She moved to the nearest, but was grabbed from behind in a move that was meant to disable her.

Meant to. Kryslie reacted instinctively, surprising her captor into dropping her. She spun and attacked, noting peripherally that the four other men were not reacting to the noise of the scuffle.

"Dead," Kryslie realised, as she flung her attacker against a wall with the force of her kick boxing move.

He did not lose consciousness, and came back at her with a silent snarl of rage. Kryslie saw the red aura now, steady in spite of the pulsing of the danger lights. She sensed his insane intent and defended herself.

The man's neck broke as he slammed against the wall. She drew out her scanner and moved it over him. Yes, he was dead, but the danger from him was not over. The device registered a very high pitched squeal. The neck of the guard exploded, sending gore over her. Kryslie went over to the body and knelt down, and felt where the explosion had originated. She had seen deaths as bad as this on Tymorea, during the war there.

Her fingers encountered a metal lump, made of an alloy the scanner did not recognise. She tried to pull it out. It moved but did not pull free — there were threads coming from it and disappearing into what remained of the torso and spine. The red aura continued to glow around the dead body until the last of the threads pulled free.

Kryslie saw her hand start to glow and dropped the object. She took a weapon from one of the guards, an energy weapon, and turned it to maximum. At such short range, the metal melted and the threads burnt.

An intensely strong premonition sent Kryslie running back to Adamson's refuge. At first she thought the room was empty, that the President had been moved again. There was no light, no movement, and no sound. She found the light switch and nothing happened.

She entered cautiously, adjusting her eyes to see in the darkness. The fading body heat of the first guard showed where one body lay and she stepped over it. The second guard was a few feet away, also dead and his body showed where a high energy beam had hit him.

Kryslie sensed someone in the room and moved silently. Behind the reclined chair she saw another body, outlined with the glow of the red aura.

"No!" she said softly, as she knelt next to Adamson and further scanned the room.

He had fallen on the floor, as if he had been struck down going to help his guards.

Kryslie felt for a pulse and sighed when she felt it, weak and ragged, and his skin was cold and clammy. She unshielded, and sent energy into him and concentrated on the steady rhythm his heart needed. Under her hand, Adamson's heartbeat returned to normal and his pulse steadied.

When she felt he would stay alive, she moved her hand over his body feeling and looking for injuries. She found blood on his neck and scanned the area with her tech scanner. It found a match of the unknown alloy from the man she had killed.

"Damn!" she swore, before bellowing for a medic. What had happened to the doctor who had come to help him? She answered that question by looking beyond Adamson. There was another body, and she did not have to go closer to see his throat was cut. No one had answered her call. Under her hand, the red glow was strengthening.

Kryslie knew what was needed, and time was short. She moved to where the doctor's bag sat on the table and searched through it. She found a set of sterile surgical instruments, sterile sheets and gloves.

Adamson was unconscious, and she did not want to give him drugs. With quick deft movements, Kryslie prepared to remove the alien devices she knew were in Adamson, before they could get a strong hold on him. Her mind gave her details of what to do. It was not that she had done anything like this before, but she had the memories of Professor Governor Xyron of Tymorea and he knew surgery.

She placed the sterile sheets around Adamson's neck, and began. Even though it was dark, she could see clearly with her adjusted eyes. She made a neat incision over the first lump, moved neck muscle aside and grabbed the metal with tweezers. It began flashing red as soon as it was out of contact with Adamson's flesh. She held it in her gloved hand, the flashing continued but more slowly. It needed body heat, she realised, but she could not keep holding it. Thinking quickly, she stood and moved to the dead guard with the still glowing wound and pushed the bead in there.

She returned quickly to Adamson and used a touch of power to stop the blood oozing from her incision. She felt with her fingers for the other metal lump. Speed was essential. When she felt the lump, she pulled firmly, but already it was gripping to the spine. Kryslie aimed a touch of power at it, felt rather than heard a metallic squeal as it came free. Kryslie tossed the alien thing away from her and heard it hit a wall. The closing of the wound would be tricky in the dark as she could not see clearly enough to sew severed veins and muscle, but her ability to start wounds healing would do as well, since it worked to return wounds tissues to their original state. She wasted no time on regrets that she could not speed heal like Tymos. Instead she concentrated, dropping into an almost trancelike state, keeping her hand over the site of the wound.

A sharp intense shock and an agonisingly sharp pain in her wrist distracted her. She thought it only lasted a second...

Lights came on and the air began to circulate, shouts, loud and immediate. Orders, imperative, impatient – Kryslie finally took in the sense of them.

"Move away – NOW!"

Kryslie recalled her task, and her hand moved back to it.

"Hands behind you now, or we shoot."

She hesitated, seeing a scene of carnage in front of her, and the scalpel on the floor beside her.

"Adamson needs help," she said. "He had..."

A powerful stun hit her in the back, pushing her onto the President. She did not completely black out, as others would have, and though she could not move, she was aware of rough hands dragging her away. Voices began yelling for a doctor.

Kryslie felt her arms being forced behind her, secured tightly with high sec restraints. Her legs were secured with energy binders. She was in no condition to fight it, or to protest.

The vision of Adamson looking slashed and bleeding shocked her. How had that happened? She sent a mental plea to the Guardians. "Don't let him die. If I did this, kill me, spare him."

But she did not die, and the pain from the stun hit her in waves of blinding agony that overwhelmed the mere discomfort of wrenched shoulder muscles from the restraints.

As she was dragged out, she heard someone calling for a stasis chamber for the President. For now, Kryslie knew, Adamson was still alive.

"Bomb in guard by wall," Kryslie forced out, hoping they would heed her.

A vehicle took her elsewhere and Kryslie did not care. The pain was finally easing as she controlled it as she had been taught, but it was not the pain that tortured her now, but the gloating sense of triumph in her mind. She could not block it; it seemed to be coming from within her. Then the vision of the man she had killed, after the bead exploded, alternated with Adamson's slashed body and an orgiastic delight. She felt the arousal that she knew was not her own, for the mind sending the sensation to her was also enjoying her pain, her condition and her position.

She felt dirty and diseased.

The pain had gone but she was weak – unable to replace her reserve of energy. Nor was food offered to her in the secure prison cell which she guessed was in the domain of the Investigative Committee.

They – the Investigators – had already dissected off her outer garments and taken swabs from her skin and scrapings from under her nails, samples of hair, fingerprints and a DNA sample. They had yet to begin asking questions.

Her transmitter and scanner were gone and they had released her, under guard, for long enough to force a one piece suit on her.

# Chapter 45

Tymos felt a surge of pain in his mind and knew it was Kryslie. Then he felt nothing, like she had blocked him out. It had only been an instant, so for a time he continued teaching the newest space pilots the basics of astronavigation.

An hour later, he felt a mind touch from Llaimos. "Come," was all it said.

Tymos dismissed his students and walked to the Tymorean suite. He walked into the centre of a ring of weapons. Reslic was standing calmly, Llaimos rigidly unmoving.

"What is the meaning of this?" Tymos demanded, neglecting the courtesy of using Basoli's title.

"Orders from the World Council," Basoli said expressionless.

"Why?" Tymos demanded.

Landin looked strained and pale. He handed Tymos a print out of the orders and reasoning.

Tymos scan read it. "No! This is not true."

"Great One," Reslic warned in Tymorean.

Tymos turned on him, speaking Tymorean. "Kryslie is no mass killer and she would not harm Adamson. She is an Advocate of the Guardians of Peace..."

"Use English," Reslic said interrupting him.

Tymos repeated his opening and went on, "...We pledged them our obedience. If she did this, they would already have dealt with her. Would have disempowered her! She would be dead!"

"You will remain in this suite, quietly, Mr Ward," Basoli told him, returning the discourtesy of omitting his title of Ambassador.

Tymos turned on him, eyes blazing with an intense anger. Landin had never seen Tymos get angry, certainly he had not expected this.

"You are impinging on diplomatic truce with this action. You are endangering the very treaty that Earth needs badly. I do not believe these claims and I demand that Kryslie is returned here for judgement."

Tymos used 'command tone' on Basoli. Landin sensed the force behind the demand, even though it had not been directed at him.

"On what grounds do you demand that," Landin asked as Basoli seemed unable to speak.

Tymos's anger hadn't cooled and he almost seemed to be glowing. Reslic was not moving, nor prepared to rebuke the Great One. If the humans thought that strange, it was because they did not know what a Great One was.

Llaimos did move to his brother and held him by one arm, as if restraining him. His face showed no sign of the power surge as Tymos's building power grounded through him.

Landin noticed the blazing anger subsiding. Llaimos answered the question.

"Kryslie, Tymos and I are Advocates of the Guardians of Peace. We serve them directly." His voice was soft and calm. "President Reslic is the bearer of the Sword of Judgement. It is an artefact of the Guardians and a conduit to them. The Guardians entrusted the Tymorean people with a duty – to preserve peace in the universe. Those that fail in this duty are judged by the sword. If Kryslie is guilty of betraying that trust..."

The watchers could see Llaimos's hand tighten on Tymos's arm, though Tymos betrayed nothing.

"If she believes she has betrayed this trust, she would willingly offer herself to their judgement – for better or worse."

The sense of his words penetrated the minds of the two humans. Basoli looked almost shocked, and Landin looked ill.

Llaimos went on, "We came here in good faith. We will remain in these rooms as directed. In return, I ask that all information possible about this matter is presented to us. Kryslie is to be returned to us, for we will judge our own."

Basoli stalked out, but Landin hesitated. "Do you understand why this action was taken?"

"Yes," Llaimos confirmed.

"Paranoia!" Tymos snarled.

"I'm sorry," Landin finished, before following Basoli out. The armed guards followed, but would remain outside the door.

Basoli had waited for Landin. "I expected the Tymorean President to say something," he said once the door to the suite was closed. "To take charge."

Landin was thoughtful. "If you consider what Llaimos said, I think he and Tymos outrank the President."

"Children? I hope not," Basoli snorted.

"Not children," Landin disagreed. "Definitely not children. He called them Advocates of the Guardians. I think that implies they are a great deal more than we have thought."

"Hmpf!" was Basoli's only reaction.

Inside the suite, Tymos controlled himself.

"When you are calmer," Llaimos said quietly. "Would you try to reach Kryslie's mind? If there is any truth in the allegations, there is also a reason. It is this we must know. We know that there is Ciriot involvement on Earth. We know how they will work, from the prophecies. We are not invulnerable to their methods."

Reslic spoke now. "And if the Ciriot have compromised your sister, we also need to know. We have pledged to protect the humans from the Ciriot. The humans have only to finalise the treaty. That must not be jeopardised."

"I know," Tymos agreed, subsiding completely. "But Kryslie is my sister!"

"And mine, brother," Llaimos reminded him. "You are not alone in your grief."

"She is not dead!" Tymos insisted.

"Then there is hope," Llaimos told him.


Kryslie could not sleep. As she lay awake for endless hours, her memory of events slowly returned, but only up to the point where she was about to help Adamson. And no further, and that bothered her.

Finally she was moved to an interrogation room, still in restraints, but the leg shackles were eased enough to let her walk. She barely had the strength to do that. Before the questions began, a doctor was called to see her. He insisted on the arm restraints being eased, and after noting the sunken, blackened eyes, insisted that an energy drink be provided. The guards had confirmed that she had neither wanted to eat or drink.

Kryslie drank almost a litre of the drink with the one hand they had freed, before the doctor was satisfied. He nodded abruptly and left the room. She did not deem it worth mentioning that her guards had not made it possible for her to eat or drink.


She was allowed to sit, and for hours, she answered their questions as fully as she believed she could. The man appointed to be her legal rep said nothing. Kryslie did not care. She admitted truthfully and she believed completely, her actions on that day from when she had arrived at the UEN Precinct. They cared nothing for prior events, such as when she had helped land Air Force One.

Nor did they consider her reasons for doing what she had done. Instead, they asked her about all the other deaths, many she knew nothing of, and asked about the knife attack on Adamson.

She had killed one man, the one with the red aura, whose mind was totally insane. The explosion had not been her doing. She had killed no others, only tried to help. Adamson had been verging on a heart attack, she had helped with that. Then she knew that she needed to remove the implants that made him glow red, before the device exploded in him.

They thought that she was raving, for no one else had seen this 'glow'. They accused her of causing the other knife wounds on him, since if she had been capable of cutting out devices, she was capable of the other.

She was told of the forensic findings, how traces from some of the other bodies were found on her. They mentioned the doctor, the secret service guards and the vice-consul Bojan Ivanovic. She had Ivanovic's blood all over her.

Kryslie kept to her belief and did not spare herself. She spoke the truth as she knew it and never asked for them to stop, to give her a rest. When she seemed to be too woozy to answer, the doctor stopped them and made her drink again. When she collapsed, the doctor insisted that she be allowed to rest, and she was carried back to her secure cell. There, once she roused again, she had only her thoughts and the gloating of that other mind to occupy her.

Arthur bin Halil received word of the President's precarious hold on life with a real shock. He had known that when Adamson stepped down, he would take over as President, as he had known that one day he would succeed his father. Then, as now, he had not expected it to be so suddenly.

He read the confidential report with growing horror. That any person could do all that, kill so many in cold blood, and even attack the President when he was working to achieve protection for the Earth and help to repel the alien Ciriot – it was obscene. The report told of a suspect, who had admitted to some of the crimes, including part of the attack on Adamson. Anger and a killing lust rose in him, like it never had before. He recalled the Investigator who had delivered the report.

"How is President Adamson?" he demanded.

"Clinging to life, Your Eminence," the man said, keeping his tone even.

"He was placed in stasis and transported back to the best hospital in New York. They have repaired all his wounds and are watching his heart carefully. He was on the verge of an attack when he went into stasis."

Arthur bin Halil prayed to the souls of his distant ancestors to preserve Adamson's life.

"The suspect?" Arthur snapped.

"In custody. The case is to be tried in three days' time. The World Council has insisted that you preside."

"Of course," Arthur agreed. "Tell me about the accused."

The man said, "It is a female member of the President's party."

Arthur went cold inside. Kryslie! It couldn't be!

It was. The man named her, but no more. He would not mention any of the evidence against her, for that would not be proper.

"Kryslie Ward is a member of the visiting Tymorean delegation. Have you requested a representative from them?" Arthur asked.

"The World Council has requested that they be sequestered, and they have agreed."

"Why was I not advised?" Arthur asked pointedly. "They are under diplomatic truce and the actions taken contravene that."

"A precaution, your Eminence," the man insisted. "And the required quorum was achieved in approving it."

Arthur reined in his anger. While the President could contravene an order of the council on some issues, the Vice-President could not. But now, he was Acting President..."

"If the council will not allow representation from the Tymorean delegation, I insist that all evidence and data on the incident be made available to them. They have pledged to honour our traditions and to respect our laws. If one of theirs has broken that pledge, it is their right to judge them. Kryslie Ward is Ambassador from the Tymorean Delegation and so has full diplomatic immunity."

The Investigator's face went hard. He clearly did not wish that to be invoked.

"The crimes were committed in a UEN Precinct," he protested.

"Irrelevant!" Arthur snapped. "The Tymoreans have the right to invoke immunity. I will insist on a trial so all the evidence can be aired, and if they agree to a trial, our verdict will be presented to the Tymorean delegation to act on."

Arthur watched the investigator leave, his posture rigid with annoyance. Then he made a few calls of his own and had his assistants organise the transport to the Eastern European capital.

He wanted to talk to Tymos Ward, but if he was to preside at a trial he could not be seen to be involved with either side.

He was though and he could not admit it. He could not talk to Kryslie Ward and ask her what happened, or ask to see the evidence. He had to have an open mind.

But his mind knew and his soul knew that Kryslie Ward was honourable. All he could do for her was to scrutinise the evidence presented, question it, and probe it for weaknesses.

# Chapter 46

The court convened. In the chamber were representatives from the World Council, the investigators and the Attorney for the World Council on one side, the defending Attorney and accused on the other. A jury consisted of important people from all convocations, and they sat in a row of benches at the rear. Armed guards stood at intervals around the chamber. The observatory, a glass fronted room set at an upper level above the jury, was crowded with media representatives.

Arthur bin Halil, acting as presiding judge, entered last. He took a look around the chamber before sitting and allowing everyone else to sit. He glanced at the observatory and considered having it cleared, but it would not be wise. This case had created a great deal of emotion all around the world.

And then, he spotted a dark haired man sitting at one edge of the observatory. He knew that man as John Goss, an investigator for the council. It reminded him of another man, Vincent, the doctor he knew was also Tymorean. If only he would be here.

When silence fell, he tapped the gavel in the traditional way and announced, "This court is in session,"

His eyes briefly met those of Kryslie Ward, but she looked away. He saw the confident face of the Council attorney. He began the proceedings.

Within a very short time, Arthur was convinced that the appointed defence lawyer was biased. He did nothing at all to question the evidence or defend his client. He called a halt to proceedings and drew the lawyers to the bench. He asked questions of the defence lawyer to determine bias, and as a result, arbitrarily dismissed him. A murmur of comment went around the court when the man left.

The committee attorney protested, but backed down under Arthur's accurate and scathing comments.

To the open court, Arthur announced, "This is a politically sensitive case. The accused is part of an important diplomatic mission. They have agreed to have this case against their Ambassador tried in our court as a testament of their good faith and integrity. We must do no less than to have an absolutely fair trial. This case is adjourned until a suitable defence lawyer is appointed."

The court was cleared and the accused returned to a secure cell.

Arthur bin Halil returned to the judge's chamber, followed by the other World Council members. Though they knew they must not discuss the case, there was no sense of disagreement to his action.

The Councillors began to discuss who might act as defence for the accused. Arthur sat in silence, wishing for an answer to getting one of Kryslie's kin here.

In that moment, a court usher knocked on the door. Permission was given to enter. Arthur's heart lifted when he saw John Goss and Dr Vincent.

The former, with his Investigative Committee ID, was listened to as he presented Vincent, and quoted his credentials.

"He has offered to act in the role of defender to the accused – in the interests of a fair and just trial," Jonko told the Committee members.

Since everyone knew the trial would be a long one, they agreed so that it could resume at once.

Arthur nodded, confirming the offer. "Very well, Doctor, your offer is accepted. How much time do you need to prepare?"

"If I could ask for an adjournment until tomorrow? I need to view the evidence and talk to my client."

"Granted," Arthur agreed, hiding his relief. "Advise me if you need more time."


Kryslie looked up as the cell door opened, but did not move from the wall where she was standing. The weapons of the guards warned her of the outcome if she tried. Vincent sent them out and gestured for Kryslie to sit at the table opposite him.

Her posture was upright, her expression neutral. She seemed to be in control of herself, but her eyes betrayed her. There was fear there, but Vincent knew it was not for herself, but for the Tymorean cause. She had agreed to be tried in the human court, and to waive the immunity that would have meant she could leave Earth. That, she well knew, would cast doubt on the Tymorean mission.

Vincent reached out to touch her hand, to get a sense of how she was. Kryslie pulled it away.

"Don't touch me, Vincent," Kryslie said in a firm voice, and with a hint of warning.

He moved back and asked, "Did you do all they claim of you, Great One?"

"I do not want to think so," Kryslie told him. "If I did, I am not worthy to be venerated as a Great One."

It was not the answer to his question.

He watched her and considered the statement she had made.

"Did you use a scalpel on President Adamson?" he asked the most vital question.

"Yes."

Vincent studied her, and suggested, "Tell me what you did."

Kryslie met his eyes and spoke very quietly. "I remember finding the doctor who had come to help Adamson dead with his throat cut. Two guards were in the room, dead, one with an energy wound. I remember calling for assistance and when no one came, knowing I had to act. I remember getting out the instruments from the doctors bag, and cutting him..."

"Where?" Vincent asked as Kryslie stopped speaking.

"I cut the side of his neck," she said. "I ...remember looking down and seeing slashes all over him as the guards arrived."

Vincent's face betrayed nothing. "Why did you cut him?" he asked quietly.

Kryslie spoke slowly. "I don't know."

"Do you remember a red aura?" he asked next.

"No," Kryslie said at once.

"Do you remember killing a man – breaking his neck?" Vincent asked.

"Yes, he was trying to kill me and I threw him against the wall."

"Do you remember an explosion?"

"The building was being bombed. The shields were down."

Vincent patiently questioned Kryslie, working from the statement she had made. What she said now convinced him that something was very wrong. She had mentioned a red aura in her statement and now she did not remember. He did not believe she was lying. He knew her too well.

In fact, her statement made voluntarily right after her arrest, was what he must take as truth. Something had muddled her mind since then, and Kryslie was unaware of it.

He knew that the Ciriot had caused some humans to have a green aura. Tymos and Kryslie could see them, but humans could not – unaided. The red aura had to be related, but different in some way. The prosecution considered that a sign of delusion, he did not. Yet he had no proof – or did he?

"What happened to your scanner, Kryslie? Did you have that with you?" Vincent asked imperatively.

"Yes, but I think they took it from me."

"Who?"

Kryslie shook her head.

Vincent did not betray his frustration, or his fear. Kryslie had killed a man who had a red aura. She had seen such an aura around Adamson – there might be more people like that. He could not see them.

"Have you been sleeping, Kryslie?"

"No," she admitted.

"I shall give you something," Vincent decided.

"No. I don't want anything. When I sleep, all the dead, all the ones I didn't save, parade in front of me."

Vincent's concern grew deeper. "Are you eating?"

"They offer me little enough," Kryslie said. "But I cannot eat."

"What about drinking?" he persisted.

"Some."

"Do you realise you are not helping yourself?" Vincent warned her.

"Vincent, if I had the energy, I could leave this place even without my transmitter. You know I could, but I will not. If I was strong enough, the temptation would be over whelming."

"Why is that?" Vincent asked gently.

"Because, I am still very, very human and part of my mind is telling me to get out and run far, far away. And I know what is at stake here."

"What good will it do us if they find you guilty?" Vincent asked.

"It will do us no good if I run away," Kryslie said, revealing that her mind was still functioning. "I cannot prove that I am not guilty. I know what I remember and that is enough to condemn me."

Vincent had to agree. He was startled from his thought when Kryslie asked a question. It was not, "Can you get me out of this mess?" but "How is Joel Adamson?"

"Hanging on," Vincent told her, and he did not understand the emotion her eyes betrayed.

"I asked the Guardians to spare him. That if I was guilty, to take my life instead of his."

Did that mean she had doubts of her innocence?

"You are still alive," Vincent said, feeling the first shiver of hope. "Surely that is a good sign."

"Don't try to give me hope, Vincent," Kryslie ordered. "I think perhaps they have been busy elsewhere and do not know of this...or that it must be that my kin repudiate me to prove to the humans that Tymoreans can be trusted, share the same sense of honour as humans."

"No! I do not believe either," Vincent vowed.

"I do not know what to believe," Kryslie said finally. "All I can do is trust in the Guardians. I will let them judge me. I am their pledged advocate – it is their right. And if I am deemed unworthy – I will abide their punishment."

"Have you asked them for help?" Vincent suggested.

"They have not answered me. I think perhaps they do not interfere directly."

She did not tell Vincent that she had not asked help for herself, but for the people of Earth.

# Chapter 47

Vincent met Daniel's eyes and could give him no hope.

"I want to see her," Daniel insisted.

"She said she would see no one but me," Vincent told him. "She will not even let me examine her."

"Stubborn, like her mother," Daniel said, a quaver in his voice as he was fighting for control. "And it is all Llaimos can do to keep Tymos from coming here."

Vincent tried to banish some of the older man's despair.

"Much of the evidence is circumstantial, or could be interpreted in several ways. If I can believe her first statement, she went to see if she could fix the shields and found four men dead and the fifth controlled by a Ciriot device. But even that can be viewed as she could have gone and killed the men to bring the shields down."

"That is not proof," Daniel said fiercely.

"No, but she said then it was self-defence, that the vice consul attacked her and had a red aura around him. When he died, his neck exploded. When she saw Adamson with the same aura, she acted to save him."

"Then why don't they listen?" Daniel exploded.

"We have no way to prove the existence of such an aura, or its cause," Vincent said helplessly. "If I had her scanner, I might have a chance, but it cannot be found. And now, Kryslie herself does not remember. I will do everything I can to cast doubt, but I am praying to the Guardians for help."


"Don't you see!" Tymos demanded. "Nala's prophecy – the touched ones will radiate – draw the ships down. The shield was down before she went there and found the man with the aura. That one was attracting them."

Llaimos did not utter the line that came to his mind, "Tymoreans will die."

Instead he said, "And do you think the dying words of an old gypsy woman would hold weight with the World Council?" Tymos slumped back in the chair. He was close to breaking down.

"We believe in her," Llaimos said, moving to stand behind his brother and starting to gently knead his shoulders. "Vincent is doing all he can. He has cast doubt on much of the evidence and many of the charges. We cannot interfere or we will risk all that is at stake. We, of all, must trust in the Guardians. Can we do less than our sister?"

Tymos had no answer. They were waiting for the verdict of the court. Reslic was with Basoli and Landin watching the direct feed from the court. Neither Llaimos, nor Tymos needed to be there. Kryslie was a part of them. They would know, when she knew.

Arthur bin Halil had the sealed envelope in his hands. He knew what the decision had to be, and he did not want to pronounce it. To delay, he directed the accused to stand.

Kryslie looked at him, met his eyes. There was no fear there, only acceptance.

"Is there anything you wish to say," he asked her, hoping desperately now, for a miracle.

Kryslie spoke clearly into the hushed silence. "You must act in the interests of truth and peace," she advised her son. She felt his torment. He had had to pronounce the death sentence on his father, and soon he must do the same on his mother. All she could do for him was to be strong and let him know she would forgive him.

Unable to delay further, Arthur read the verdict of the jury. It was wrong, his mind screamed, wrong!

"Guilty of the death of Vice Consul, Bojan Ivanovic and guilty of inflicting grievous harm to the President of the UEN."

He could ask for a recess to consider the verdict, but for this crime there was only one sentence. Except, he could pass the responsibility on...he felt like a coward.

He waited until the satisfied murmur died down, then he spoke into the silence.

"The accused, Kryslie Ward, has been tried in accordance with the rules and laws of the UEN. She has been found guilty on two charges. The penalty for both is death. However, Kryslie Ward is a member of the Tymorean delegation to Earth and as such subject to diplomatic considerations."

He had to ring the tones for silence before he could continue. Shouts accusing the Tymoreans of all sorts of things continued.

"The spectators will be silent, or they will be cleared from the court," Arthur threatened.

Silence fell.

He continued. "In respect of our customs and laws, they waived the right to protect their own and allowed the trial. They reserved the right, if the accused was found guilty, to carry out the sentence. The World Council agreed to this. I, as presiding judge, as well as members of the council, will oversee the sentence. This court is ended."

He dropped the gavel, and retreated quickly from the court as the babble broke out again, and before he had to see the black hood of the condemned placed over Kryslie's head. He went to the judge's chamber and locked the door. He wanted no one to see him just then.

A voice spoke gently from behind him. "Kryslie trusts her fate to the Guardians of Peace. We all do, and so should you."

He spun around and recognised John Goss, but he could not speak. So, he was Tymorean too.

"This is my father's death curse coming true," Arthur said finally.

Jonko shook his head and said, with deliberate emphasis, "Your father's curse was merely piss in the wind compared to the power of the Guardians."

"And what if they find her guilty? I could not find fault with the evidence."

"In your heart, do you believe she is guilty?" Jonko asked gently.

"No."

"Neither do those of us who know her best," Jonko confirmed. "That is why we trust in the Guardians."

Arthur nodded.

"And you know her, and know she would not shirk her duty, even if that duty was to die."

Jonko finished, and they were both remembering how Kryslie had attended his father's execution. How she had held to his father's hands until the end.

Arthur nodded again, unable to speak.

"If you must speak of this – speak of the positives. The hope that humans and Tymoreans will be friends – are still friends – in honour, in truth, in vision," Jonko advised. "The treaty must go ahead or the Earth might be lost."

Arthur studied the man speaking to him. "You really believe that."

"Yes. I know what the Ciriot can do. Did do, on Tymorea. I know what Kryslie and her brothers did to save our people and restore the planet to life. On our world, they are Great Ones, and I do not believe Kryslie has become anything less."

"Thank you," Arthur said with true humility. "I needed to hear that."

"You are most welcome, You're Eminence," Jonko bowed and in the next moment was gone.

# Chapter 48

Reslic could see that Tymos had himself under tight control. He knew the verdict already. The link between him and his twin was still as strong as it had been.

"Kryslie has blocked us out," Llaimos told Reslic.

"Wise of her," Reslic said deliberately.

Tymos glared at him.

"Great One, I will not apologise for saying this. As I taught you as students – that bond you have is both your greatest strength and greatest weakness. Kryslie knows she must not weaken you. Your work here is not yet done."

"I know that, damn you!"

"Then I offer this advice, Great One," Reslic continued without remorse. "Right now, the most powerful thing you can do for Kryslie is to believe in her. Believe, that in spite of the evidence – she did not deliberately intend to kill."

"How can you say that, be so calm, when it is you who will bear the Sword and judge her?" Tymos accused.

Llaimos spoke then, "It is his duty as President Governor and he will do it, as we must do ours."

Tymos pulled himself free of Llaimos and walked to a wall with a viewport out over the lunar surface. He stayed there, like a statue, until Llaimos urged him to bed.


Kryslie felt the black hood come down over her face and welcomed the darkness. She kept herself erect, through willpower alone. She would not betray weakness. When the guards moved her, she sensed Vincent with her, and Jonko and Daniel and a silent ring of Tymorean missionaries.

She felt their belief in her and it strengthened her. It was as well they could not share her memories.


For an instant, she felt Tymos's mind touching hers as the sense of hateful satiation swelled in her. She blocked Tymos out, but could not block that other – the one that revelled in the verdict. She wanted to be sick, but she could not.

Vincent was allowed to remain for a time when Kryslie was taken to the cell of the condemned.

"You will be transported back to Terra 1, and from there to Lunar 1. Council representatives will be present."

"Thank you," Kryslie said, voice muffled by the black cloth. Then after an uncomfortable silence, she spoke with morbid deliberation. "In this country they prefer to use a firing squad. In Arthur's country they prefer poison, or to bury the guilty in the hot sand of the desert."

Vincent kept silent, but Kryslie divined his abhorrence of all methods.

"Is it more barbaric than a surge of burning power? That is the effect of the Sword of Judgement. At least, if I must die that way – I will. It would be hard to explain why twenty bullets didn't kill me."

"Is there anything I can do for you," Vincent asked.

"No, Vincent. I wish solitude and for you to keep Daniel away. I cannot...."

Kryslie didn't finish. She couldn't. Vincent departed, wishing he dared offer comfort.

He joined her again when they came to take her to the official jet that would take her to Terra 1. He was allowed to take her arm and direct her steps. He sensed her tight mental control and her physical weakness. He knew she had not eaten since the day of the bombing, and still refused to eat. She was becoming insubstantial. Nor had she slept, and if the hood would be removed, he knew she would be looking like death. Yet she kept herself erect, even with the restraints keeping her arms behind her as they had since she had been arrested.

He could see within her, a magnificence of spirit and that she was still, truly, a Great One.

The Lunar 1 personnel were given leave, en-masse, for the period when Kryslie was taken there. Those that really knew her, refused to leave. They showed their support to her, to Tymos, in the only way they could.

The observers from the World Council were uncomfortable now, in the presence of the Tymoreans. The unflinching gaze of the Tymorean President seemed to be judging each of them. He stood, with the magnificent jewelled sword, unsheathed and his hands resting on the hilt and the point touching the floor.

Reslic watched impassively as the two hooded, gold and silver caped figures walked Kryslie to face him. He had ignored Kryslie's insistence that she would walk alone. Her brothers had been equally determined to be with her.

They were in a screened off section of the hangar deck, and for the time, the monitors overlooking the area were turned off. The humans watched, and Reslic felt the impact of their emotions as they realised that those who walked with the condemned were her closest kin. It made them uneasy, not because they feared treachery, but because it showed how strong their belief was in their sister.

"It is the custom of our people," Reslic spoke in a carrying voice. "For those of high rank to be judged by the Guardians of Peace. It is my duty as President Governor to wield their power through the Sword of Judgement."

He let the words sink into the minds of the observers.

"It is also our custom, that those who have been judged face their sentence without hiding behind any artifice. Please remove the hood."

Tymos pulled off the black hood and flung it as far away as he could.

Kryslie blinked in the light and turned her face up to Reslic.

"I am ready," she whispered, shrugging off the hands of her brothers.

The restraints had been moved to the front, and she lifted her arms up together and out towards Reslic.

At a quiet word from Reslic, she dropped to her knees. Reslic spoke an invocation in a very ancient dialect of Tymorean, and picked up the sword and rested it on her hands.

The observers saw her body jolt, as if by lightning, or electricity. She remained upright for a moment, and then collapsed onto herself and didn't move.

Reslic waited a long moment before kneeling to recover the Sword. He felt Kryslie's neck, and his own heart leapt in joy, but his face betrayed nothing.

He gestured to the hooded figures, and turned away from the observers as he carefully re-sheathed the sword.

The observers filed out as Kryslie was covered by a cloth of gold and silver.

Kryslie felt so weak, but she was alive. In her mind, clear once more of the hateful images and obscene sensations, she heard instead the gentle voices of the Guardians.

"Foolish child, did you think we would forsake you? Did we not help the man you cared for? Did we not hear that you would give your life for his? You have served us well, you did no wrong."

"I felt so unclean, so unworthy," Kryslie told them.

"And now?"

"I want to serve you," Kryslie said in her mind.

"No matter the cost?" they asked.

"No matter," Kryslie echoed.

"Rest now, child, the battle you fight is not yet over. You may, if you feel you must, prove yourself."

"I will," Kryslie promised. "I will never let you down."


Frances Long entered with a trolley once the observers were gone. This was far from a pleasant duty, but she would not delegate it to anyone else. She saw the Tymoreans, and it took all her will power to approach the covered figure and the two robed figures, standing as if guarding it.

Tymos and Llaimos uncovered their faces, and Tymos gestured for Long to bring the trolley closer.

Seeing his calm face eased the tension in her whole body. He uncovered Kryslie's face, peaceful but so pale. Then he lifted her gently to the trolley.

Long began the formalities, and reached for Kryslie's wrist. She jerked in atavistic fear when she felt a pulse, strong and steady. She stared in shock at Reslic, and back at Kryslie. And in an irrelevant aside noted that the restraints had not just fallen off, but vanished completely and the brown coverall was flecked with silver and gold.

She looked at Reslic again and his face was no longer hard and expressionless.

"We never claimed that the judgement of the Guardians would mirror that of men. Men are fallible."

"They," Long gestured out the door, "All think she is dead."

Reslic did not glance that way. "That of which she was charged and sentenced is over," Reslic told her. "The Guardians still wish her to serve them. They have healed her enough to live. The rest must be up to her. There is to be no medical intervention."

"As you wish," Long agreed, uncertainly. "Is she to stay with you?"

Reslic nodded. "We will take her back to our suite. You might however, recommend a dietary regimen that she should adhere to."

"Isn't that intervention?" Long asked with surprise.

"You will not be the one to enforce it," Reslic said with a faint smile. "That will be the task of the Great Ones." He used the Tymorean words for the title. "Then, when the observers have gone with the message that justice was seen to be done, you may quietly spread the word to all that cared for Kryslie, that she was granted a second chance."

Tymos escorted the doctor from the screened off area. "I will come with you to speak to Commander Landin."

Behind him, Llaimos and Reslic would transmit Kryslie and the trolley to their suite.

Tymos did not announce his arrival by activating the door chimes; he simply walked in to where Basoli, Landin and Arthur bin Halil were quietly talking.

Basoli saw him, and for once did not protest his high handed entry. Knowing what had been carried out, here on WSRA premises, had made him feel ill. Seeing Tymos intensified it.

"I came to speak to you," Tymos said, glancing at the three men. Something about his unexpected serenity made them lean towards him.

"As his Eminence can attest, the justice of men has been seen to be done. What I will tell you now will not be widely spread. The judgement of the Guardians of Peace is not that of men. Kryslie has been granted a second chance. She will still serve them, as I will continue to do and until there is a need for her to act, she will remain in our suite. I hope you will believe, that we will both, always, act for the cause of peace."

Arthur bin Halil, stood and came to Tymos and took his hand, "Your words are a great gift, and what I needed to hear. I have been appointed to act as President until Joel Adamson has recovered fully. I will be completing what he started, and I will return here with the fully signed Declaration of Intent."

He gave Tymos the bow of equals, even though he knew from Jonko, what Tymos was to his own people.

"Thank you," Tymos said quietly, sincerely.

The acting-President left the room, heading for the shuttle that was due to leave within the hour.

Landin was less restrained than the acting-President, in coming up and taking Tymos's hand to shake it gently. "I am relieved by your news, and I hope I may be allowed to discuss certain matters with you at a later time?"

Tymos understood what he wasn't saying directly. "Sir, you would be welcome, I think. However, a period of solitude will be needed."

"Indeed, even to one as strong as your sister, this will have been a severe shock to her spirit," Landin said quietly. Tymos nodded once, keeping tight control of his own reactions. Landin sensed that he was not as calm as he was projecting. "Take as much time as you need – for both of you."

Tymos nodded again, and was about to leave when Basoli spoke up.

"I find I have under- appreciated you, Ward, and your sister. It is an honour to have you as members of the WSRA staff."

"Thank you, Sir," Tymos bowed slightly to him and quietly left the room.

Francis Long remained. "I was told that her recovery was to be her doing, and I was not to intervene. However, her pulse was surprisingly strong, in spite of the depleted state she is in."

"I do not think it would be intervention to keep a friendly eye on her, Doctor," Basoli suggested.

"I agree," Landin said. "I would like to be sure all is well, and her spirits are improving. Please include Tymos in that concern."

Long finally smiled as well. "His Excellency gave me permission to let those who cared for her know of her second chance."

Basoli was aware of the ramifications if it were known off the base, and in the media.

"I think, we should let it be known in a more meta-physical way," Basoli suggested. "Not a blatant – she is still alive. Those that respected her and stayed here to support her brother, I do not think are the sort to reveal the truth widely. Those that stayed are more truly friends. Others that hear of it will be assuming that a second chance is more of a mystical belief."

"I understand," Long acknowledged.

Another was listening to the meeting that Tymos had interrupted.

Jody Basoli had learnt of the verdict of the trial of Kryslie and had needed to seek a calmative from the doctor to deal with it. The media had made a deal of it that the sentence was to be carried out at Lunar 1, and she had made her father bring her in spite of his belief it was no place for her. But it was something she really had to do. To be here. And she had come to listen to the meeting, with the same impelling need.

She slipped out of her covert listening place and followed Tymos as he went towards the Tymorean suite.

"Tymos?" she called softly, but he heard her and turned, waiting for her to catch up to him. "Is it true?"

He heard the pleading in her voice, and asked, "Is what true?"

"That Kryslie is alive – that she has a second chance?" Jody said so quickly, that her words tumbled together.

Tymos reached an arm around her as he said, "Yes."

When Jody burst into near hysterical tears of relief and elation, Tymos transmitted them both to the arboretum, and walked to a secluded place before his own control slipped. When it changed from him giving her comfort to her returning comfort to him, there was no one around to notice. And some hours later, when he returned to the suite, his serenity was real, and not the illusion he had felt he needed to show.

# Chapter 49

The shuttle arrived at Lunar 1 with the knowledge that acting President bin Halil was bringing up the fully signed and notarised Declaration of Intent.

His arrival was recorded by the selected media group, who had disembarked first. If Arthur was disappointed that only Landin and Basoli met the shuttle, he did not betray it. He simply reminded the media people that there would be a formal reception that evening, lunar time, when the exchange of treaties would take place.

Landin, directed staff to assist the media recording technicians in setting up, and kept the journalistic contingent happy by providing refreshments and food.

A second shuttle brought up those of the world council who were able to free up time to attend, and who did not find travel by shuttle unsettling. The Genesis astronauts were attending as honoured guests.

Since the trial of one of the 'aliens', interest in seeing what they looked like was intense. Those who had actually met them were in high demand on talk shows and for interviews.

In spite of being told, "They look a lot like us," many people still did not believe it possible.

The reception was considered a success by all. The formal exchange of treaties was recorded for posterity and to be screened worldwide over the news feeds. The Declaration of Intent was read aloud in its entirety, so the population of Earth knew the promises being made on behalf of all people of Earth. Then, President Reslic presented the formal reply from the Federation of Peace. This too was read in full, so the people of Earth knew the promises made to them by the Federation of Peace.

Most of the attention during this time was on the impressive figure of the Tymorean President. Reporters, ensured that they obtained close up views of the Sword of Judgement. Reslic had, in honour of the occasion, worn the Sword in a ceremonial sheath that enabled its full splendour to be seen. He politely refused to allow anyone to touch it, or to remove it from its traditional position at his back.

Attention was also directed at the two hooded and caped figures. The richness of the gold and silver fabric made them seem exotic indeed, and there was an aura of inapproachability about them. Earlier interviews with Casey, Pitt and Tweed, had mentioned these robed aliens, and there was curiosity to see their faces, but Tymos and Llaimos did not oblige them.

Some of the more forward reporters did approach with questions, and their recording technicians tried to see more than the brilliant blue-green of their eyes, but without success.

The questions were answered politely, and it was made clear that questions relating to the recent legal proceedings would not be answered – since polite silence met such questions, as if no question had been asked.

Mainly Llaimos and Tymos would answer questions relating to the treaties, but Tymos did hide amusement when asked how he had learnt to speak English so well.

"We of the Federation of Peace are trained to learn new languages and cultures quickly. Understanding a culture is an essential skill in promoting peace."

The reception was only scheduled to last two hours, and wound down quickly after the Tymorean delegation had quietly retired from the gathering. The media group were keen to get their recordings back to their studios, and the leaders were equally anxious to return to their responsibilities. The two shuttles departed within an hour of the reception ending. No one seemed to realise that the Acting President had remained behind.

One flight of space fighters escorted the shuttles down, providing yet more interesting pictures for the news feeds.

Arthur bin Halil had questions, and he had not known how to ask them. Yet as Llaimos moved out of the reception, he had said quietly to the acting president, "I have a wish for some less formal talks. Will you walk with me?"

Arthur had nodded, and gestured for his guards to keep back and keep any wandering media away.

The station security detail had orders for the Tymoreans to move unhindered and for the other guests to be allowed in only the areas Landin had approved.

So there was no one to observe that two of the important guests were having a quiet discussion. Llaimos still had his hood obscuring his face, but some of the station security smiled a greeting to him as he passed. They all knew what he looked like.

Arthur, being familiar with Lunar 1, soon realised they were heading for the arboretum. He told his guards to stay by the door, and he walked along the path towards the centre of the garden. Llaimos halted him by an open patch of grass. At first, bin Halil did not notice the figure wearing a plain brown work suit, sitting there and resting chin on knees. His attention was on the brilliantly lush vegetation growing around him.

He was more than a little startled when he heard a familiar voice.

"What you wish to ask about is sitting beside you," Kryslie said softly.

Arthur turned, surprised to see her there. "You are looking much better," he said with practiced poise. Kryslie stood, gracefully.

"What you really mean is – since I am meant to be dead!" Kryslie said bluntly.

"When they covered you..."Arthur said, confused.

"A symbol that judgement was made and the matter is closed," Llaimos explained.

Kryslie then went on, "The Guardians still have a use for me."

She sensed a desperate need in her son and drew him off the path and out of line of sight of his guards. Llaimos remained in sight of them, but turned his face away as Kryslie embraced her son.

"I told you some years ago that I am proud of you for doing what was right. That has not changed. Please do not regret that, and accept that I will act as is needed. You do not need to protect me."

Kryslie released him.

Llaimos turned back and casually noted, "I am not so sure about not needing protection. I see you have not yet taken his Excellency to a draw in your recent training sessions."

Arthur felt that Llaimos was teasing Kryslie and it was on old joke between them. He was sure when Kryslie returned, "Perhaps I should imply to him that you are out of shape, hmm?"

He relaxed, feeling assured that Kryslie was well and honoured to be allowed to witness this private moment between his Tymorean kin.

"He hasn't let me," Llaimos gave a wry grin. "Tymos now...? Perhaps you will let Arthur watch your next training session. It might reassure him that you are not completely feeble..."

Since she sensed her son's interest, she agreed without sounding reluctant. It would be incentive to try harder to avoid being swatted by Reslic as if she were still a student. She watched Llaimos escort him away before she transmitted back to the suite.


When the idea was proposed to Reslic, he suggested using it as a demonstration of skills and allow a general audience from Lunar 1. He met Kryslie's eyes, but she said nothing.

Since her return to Lunar 1, Kryslie had not been seen by any of the Lunar 1 personnel. When she took part in the demonstration, she would not be identifiable. They would all be dressed head to foot in black, with only eye slits. She and Tymos would alternate, so only three figures would be in sight at any time.

Interest in the demonstration was intense. The recreation gymnasium was crowded and those unable to watch directly would be able to view the event on the internal vid. The duty crew knew they would be able to watch later and did not decrease their vigilance.

The display was impressive. Individually, one on one, or two on one with swords, staves or unarmed, the audience was silent and awed. Then the lights were dimmed and simulated lasers criss-crossed the display area and three figures did a gymnastic display of great skill. The suits they wore for this were demonstrated to glow if touched by one of the light beams. Then, throughout the five minute display, none of the twisting tumbling figures were touched by the light.

Kryslie had been part of this, but when the lights from the beams stopped and before the station lights came up, she transmitted out and Reslic returned, so that when the lights did come on, and the revealed their faces she was not seen.

The applause was deafening, but instantly silenced with the abrupt start of the red alert sequence.

Tymos followed the off duty pilots as they raced to their alert stations. Reslic strode out of sight and transmitted to his personal craft and requested permission to depart. He left the landing bay and blasted off in the direction of the flagship. In minutes, he had reached the long range beam terminus he had requested and was abruptly off the scanners.

The Ciriot force had arrived, and the brief lull was over.

# Chapter 50

Jody approached the Tymorean guest suite when the guards were distracted. People were moving purposefully around the base performing red alert duties. She had been sent to her quarters – for as a visitor, even one working as a student in the labs, she had no official duties here. But she acted as if she had a message from her father to the Tymoreans and was allowed to approach the door and activate the chimes.

She knew that Tymos Ward had gone with the pilots, and heard that the Tymorean President had left abruptly. She expected only a single occupant in the suite, but hoped for two and was rewarded.

Llaimos moved forward to greet her, and smiled. He had his face exposed, but the second figure did not. Both had changed out of the black practice suits but unlike Llaimos, Kryslie was not wearing the gold and silver robes.

"Kryslie?" Jody asked quietly, looking at the brown caped and hooded figure.

The shorter figure turned, and uncovered her head. "Hello, Jody. Was there something you wanted?"

"To see you?" she whispered.

Kryslie gestured to a seat, and invited Jody to sit. She did, tentatively.

"I'm here," Kryslie said neutrally.

"Are you all right? Really? They wanted you to die!"

Kryslie nodded. There were things she did not want to talk about. That was one, and what they said she had done was another.

"Was this a result of something the aliens did to you when you came to get me?" Jody asked with accurate insight.

"I was not there long enough," Kryslie told her, believing it.

"Then why?" Jody insisted, needing to know. "Why did you do all those things they claimed you did?"

"Whatever I did do would have been for an imperative reason," Kryslie said, knowing her true self. "But I cannot remember it all."

Llaimos chose to sit with them, and followed up on the question and answer. "Perhaps you need to remember," he suggested.

"Llaimos, I don't..."she began. But he was right. She needed to remember.

"Dad had the transcript of the trial. I read it," Jody admitted.

"So did I," Llaimos told her. "And I also read the statement you made. Why don't you tell us what you remember?"

Kryslie forced her suddenly tense limbs to relax.

Jody was looking ill when Kryslie finished talking. Llaimos, like Kryslie had seen much worse.

"The red aura is mentioned in your statement, and removing the implants was your reason for operating on Adamson – why would you forget that?" Llaimos asked.

Kryslie shuddered. "It has to be important."

"The Ciriot would want you to forget," Llaimos suggested.

The memory of satiated laughter haunted her mind. Kryslie just nodded.

"What happened between the time you were about to heal Adamson and the arrival of the guards?" Llaimos asked.

"Nothing," Kryslie said, but she began idly rubbing her left wrist.

Llaimos leant closer and took that hand and studied the wrist. He saw the faintest trace of a scar. He rubbed the spot but felt nothing there. "Something did happen," Llaimos stated quietly. Kryslie looked and met his eyes, and allowed his continued gentle rubbing on her wrist to relax her into a light trance. Jody just watched, and let Llaimos do what he was doing.

Kryslie seemed dissociated from her body, and allowed herself to examine her memory as if her mind belonged to someone else. She felt Llaimos link to her mind to see what she remembered. He whispered in her mind to go back to the beginning.

Kryslie went back to when she had gone to Jody's van to look for her. The experience of the alien's treatment was at a remove and she did not feel it so intensely. They had taken her to their ship, and left her loose when they were strapped into cushioned seats. On the tribe ship they had tested her awareness and thought her unconscious and left her. She had started to go to Jody, after freeing herself from the table...the Ciriot Prince had somehow forced her body to him, she had fought him...something had hit her, distracted her...a fleeing instant of further pain...then Tymos was there.

She had been unconscious for a time, she realised, so they would not have done anything...surely.

Her mind moved forward to the tour with Adamson. The matter of Gareth Pitt. He had come to her in the garden – savage, insane – and she had to fight him. He had said something about her force screen – he could not have known of such a thing. He was trying to kill her – had jabbed something through her force screen. He had been dangerous, not himself, and she...she had been the one to seriously injure him. She saw it now, more as a remembered nightmare. She had forgotten that. Had mentally blacked out for a time – or her mind had been stopped for a time.

With a sense of unreality, she moved forward to the Eastern European Precinct. Remembered seeing a man with a red aura, looking for him, finding him with the four dead security men. He had tried to kill her too, and killing him had been an accident; she had used too much strength. His neck had blown out and she had removed something from the body, and the aura had died. Her scanner did not recognise it, but she had made an analysis, could have compared things to it later.

Then Adamson – he had the aura when she went back to him – had the dead man infected him? Or someone else? Must have been another – her scanner was gone, and the investigators did not have them, or Jonko would have found out. She remembered knowing of the need to remove the bead things, doing that, and then the sharp pain in her wrist...and that mental blanking out again. Her body remembered what she had done...she had been unshielded then...and she had slashed at him. It had been her!

Kryslie jerked her mind from the trance and hid her face in her hands.

"What's wrong," Jody asked. She had stayed a silent witness to Kryslie seeming to stare across the room.

"Things we need to consider," Llaimos said carefully.

Kryslie whispered in Tymorean. "I did those things to Pitt and Adamson."

Llaimos spoke back to her in the same language. "The Guardians know it was not done with your will. They cleared you of that control. Now you are fully aware, pre-warned."

Kryslie took a deep breath and nodded.

Llaimos went on, "There are things we must do. I think we must carefully re-examine the three space travellers."

"Yes," Kryslie agreed. "And Jody – at least get her a personal force shield. I think I was fine until it was off."

"Not exactly," Llaimos disagreed. "Pitt did something to you when your shield was on. I think a very localised overload. Whatever he did, you blanked out and went into instinctive survival mode. We need to check you too."

"Bro, I scanned the implants, but my scanner could not identify it. If I had the data, I could use it to look for similar things. How can you scan me for things that it doesn't even see?"

"Kryslie, think! You read the screen, do you remember what was there?"

"I...yes. I can work with that. It will give me something to do."

"Hmmm," Jody made a sound, and Kryslie looked at her.

"Sorry," Kryslie apologised for speaking in front of her. "There is something I want you to do...wear...I mean."

Jody decided Kryslie was looking less haunted and more like she used to. "What?"

Kryslie explained what a personal force shield was and how it would protect her. Llaimos fetched one and Kryslie took Jody to her sleeping room and helped her put it on and showed her how to operate it.

"Keep it on constantly. I am not saying you will be a target and need it, but ... it's a precaution. I have had one on since...I came back here."

"Is dad allowed to know of this?" Jody asked.

"There is no need. I will tell him if it is appropriate," Kryslie told her.

Jody's pocket beeped. "Dad. He is looking for me. I'd better go. I am glad I could talk to you and you are okay."

Kryslie smiled. "I am fine," she assured Jody, and walked her to the door. But when the door closed, the smile vanished.

"It isn't just the astronauts," Kryslie said soberly. "Vice Consul Ivanovic had one, and I can't be sure he was the one that infected Adamson. But he had to have taken the shields down for them to bomb there. And when he died, a device in him self-destructed, but he did not stop glowing until the other one was removed. We have no way of knowing who has the red aura until it is activated. There could be thousands of unwitting carriers."

"We will have to find a way to deal with these carriers that does not need us at each one," Llaimos added. "If we can find them."

"Stasis," Kryslie suggested. "We have to keep them alive, but static."

"Where?" Llaimos asked the obvious question.

"Earthbase. There are still unused chambers. We can set up a portable stasis field in one. The missionaries will have to look out for them, and when one is found, go in and abduct them – under full shields – and take them there. A perfect job for Konn Reslic."

"That leaves the problem of the astronauts," Llaimos pointed out.

"Casey is here," Kryslie said. "Tymos can check him. Last I heard, Pitt was at Terra 2 – recovering. Tweed was at Terra 5."

"I will tell Tymos what we need to do," Llaimos offered.

"And I will talk to Daniel and Konn," Kryslie decided. "I haven't been to Earthbase or spoken to him since..."

Llaimos touched her hand. "He knows you were given a second chance. And I think you should go to him."

# Chapter 51

Arthur bin Halil had gone directly to main mission, and there he could see on the screens, the waves of fighters flowing past the moon, heading for Earth. He was mentally praying to the gods of his ancestors. He was in contact with the military commanders, but he needed to be there to oversee the battle plans.

"I need to be in the War Room," he said to Landin and Basoli.

"We can launch the space fighters," Basoli proposed. He had kept them grounded to be available to protect the Acting President.

"Summon Casey," Landin instructed a technician.

Casey came at a run, followed closely by Tymos Ward, both were in flight uniform.

Landin stated what was needed. "Acting President bin Halil needs to be in Washington. Ideas?"

"We have five flights of twenty, ready to launch, Sir," Casey reported. "Just give the word. I would advise waiting for a gap, then we can do a transverse orbit to get down."

Basoli questioned Casey, not at all comfortable with that plan. He looked at Tymos and overcome his personal feelings and asked. "How close are your Tymoreans?"

"They are coming at maximum, Sir. ETA seven hours."

"Should we wait?" Basoli asked.

"If I may offer a suggestion," Tymos requested. Basoli and bin Halil nodded.

"I think I can adjust the shields on one of the fighters to simulate a cloaking field. It won't be a perfect cloak, but the Ciriot will have deduced that we do not have that technology."

"What will that do, Ward?" Basoli demanded.

"We could travel away from the main fighter group and they won't expect us to be there. His Eminence will need to be in the rear cockpit." Tymos explained.

"You think that will work?" Basoli scrutinised him.

Tymos stood in that 'regal' pose that made his next statement believable.

"I know I can get his Eminence down safely. And I will be able to land on the back lawn of the White House."

Casey merely nodded his agreement.

"Then that is what will be done," bin Halil stated, ending the discussion. "I will need a flight suit."

"I will see to it, Sir. This way," Tymos directed.

Tymos sent one of the new cadet technicians off with instructions to bring the flight gear to the Tymorean suite.

Arthur was not completely surprised by the destination, but he was when he saw Tymos collect something from the again hooded Kryslie and gesture for him to go into one of the side rooms.

"There is one other thing you need to put on, before the flight suit." Tymos explained what the personal force shield was for.

Kryslie had followed to the door. "Keep it on, all day, every day," she emphasised. "It should protect you from becoming infected."

"You imply no one is safe," bin Halil realised.

Kryslie spoke soberly. "No one in a position to give orders and lower shields. Please wear this, it is important. We do not know how the 'infection' is spreading."

"Thank you," bin Halil said, accepting the protection. Kryslie backed away, closing the door so Tymos could help him put it on in private. When the flight suit and the internal jumpsuit arrived, she passed them in too, and Tymos helped the Acting President into them and checked the seals.

As Tymos escorted his important passenger to the flight deck, he was instructing him in the important flight drills and emergency drills.

Tymos took off in the middle of the flight, but did not follow the formations aiming at a flank attack on the enemy. He flew to one side and activated a portable cloaking device that he had asked Kryslie to bring from Earthbase. Once it was on, the view through the cockpit window took on a faint mauve aura.

Arthur bin Halil had been warned about the g-forces on blast off, but the flight suit buffered most of it. And if the situation was not so serious, he would have revelled in this experience of space flight. And the sheer speed.

"Why did you delay the counter strike," bin Halil took the opportunity to ask.

"Partly to ensure your safety, Sir," Tymos admitted. "Secondly, the first waves are drones – unmanned and predictable. They are still deadly, but not as much so as the manned ships."

Tymos had his mind on the area of space around him and in front of him. The Lunar 1 flight had engaged the enemy, well to their portside, but that would not mean trouble he needed to avoid. It was up to him to avoid other ships, since those others could not see him. A drone ship broke off from the main group due to a hit on its steering controls. A beam of energy lanced out from an Earth fighter, and it exploded right in front of them. Tymos rolled in a tight turn to avoid it, and then straightened back onto course. A damaged, out of control ship reeled in front of them, again Tymos reacted. He was so fast he was almost ahead of the action.

Bin Hall fell silent, this was the most terrifying experience of his life, but he trusted Tymos, completely.

As they moved away from the fighting, in an orbit to bring them down in Washington, they were aware of aerial battles between aliens and defenders. To bin Halil, they seemed random and he commented on it.

"The drones are targeted," Tymos told him over the suit comm. "Somewhere down there is a Ciriot toy with a red aura. That person is attracting them."

"Can't anything be done?" bin Halil asked.

Tymos didn't tone down his answer. "If they are activated, they are vicious and dangerous and will let nothing stop them doing what the aliens want of them, nor will they surrender. Most will die. The bombs and weapons are targeted to them. If we find them soon enough it might be possible to help them."

"Like Kryslie was doing for Adamson?" bin Halil realised. None of the jury had believed her reason.

"Yes," Tymos said tersely. "That way takes too long and there are only two of us that can do it safely. We have another plan that we hope will save those people - before the self-destruct sets in. Kryslie is working on modifying the detectors to find the latent targets and as soon as possible we will have the technicians adjusting the fixed units to do the same. With those, if an infected person is detected, we can pick them up before they are activated. Otherwise, we will need to get to the beacons as soon as we can."

Bin Halil took 'we' to mean Tymoreans, and did not ask for confirmation.

"We won't be able to save them all," Tymos warned, with regret.

"Whatever you do, will be a blessing," bin Halil said sincerely. "Does the White House know to expect us?"

"A message was sent to give them your ETA," Tymos assured him.

The look of a tornado in the garden, brought all the guards to full alert position – weapons aimed at the disturbance. Once on the ground, Tymos uncloaked the ship, and opened the hatch.

"Wait, Sir," Tymos said over the suit comm. He spoke to flight control and told them he was down, with the Acting President. Then he instructed bin Halil, "Keep the helmet on. I saw blips on my screen as we came in, I think they are Earth fighters, but I want to be sure."

Tymos slowly raised the hatch, and took off his head unit and listened. He heard two different engine sounds, still a distance away, but coming quickly.

"Climb out quickly," Tymos ordered, watching the sky.

For a moment, they were both exposed on the roof of the fighter, then Tymos transmitted them both down, next to the armoured car that had drawn to a halt near the fighter.

It had been a risk, doing it in front of all the guards and soldiers, but they needed to hurry.

Bin Halil removed his helmet and allowed the guards to do a retina check. He was hustled into the armoured car, just as a bomb fell between the car and the building. The car revved away, and Tymos transmitted back to the roof of the fighter and climbed in. His helmet went on next, and once it was sealed and he was strapped in, Tymos lifted vertically until above roof level and took off firing as three drone ships came in on a strafing run.

He notified flight control of his position and intention to re-join the space fleet. He then sent a message to Earthbase on a separate frequency.

"There is a beacon in the body guard of the Acting President. Get Konn on it fast."

Tymos might consider Konn unpleasantly arrogant, but he was a son of the Tymorean President. None of Reslic's sons were less than highly trained. Konn was skilled at stealth, infiltration and fighting. He had the added distinction of being too dense for the alien's crude mind control devices to affect.

And Earthbase had coordinates for the White House, a position inside the layered shield defences, and as formidable as the defences were on such an important building, they were not impervious to Tymorean transmitters.

Tymos pushed that problem to the back of his mind as he listened on the battle frequencies, and rocketed straight up into the far reaches of the atmosphere and beyond. The sheer number of the drone ships was frightening when you considered that two dozen cities were being attacked simultaneously by thousands of ships.

When he neared the next incoming wave, he cloaked and shot past them, and rolled fast to come up behind them. He moved with them, so the scanners on his ship could study them. These were manned, but as he checked several, he realised that they had many different species piloting them. He grew angry. Slaves, and so tied to the ships they would die if taken from them. He sent an encrypted message to the Jacen Tyr, which was speeding Earthward, escorting the Tymorean fleet.

By the time Tymos reached the edge of the atmosphere, Daniel had reported, "Konn has returned with two victims, White House shields are intact and the vessels are veering off."

Tymos released an inner breath and sent a commendation to Konn. He turned his mind to the battle, and accelerated off to join the Lunar 1 squadron. He chose not to take over a flight, but to remain as a roving interceptor.

The Terra 2 squadron, led by Gareth Pitt, cut a swathe through the incoming drones on their way up, turned and attacked from the rear, until turning again to fire on the van of the next wave.

The Lunar 1 squadron regrouped and headed for the refuelling shuttle. Tymos flew a defensive watch for any cloaked ships that might decide the squadron was easy prey.

"Defensive octahedron," Tymos instructed, via Casey. "Watch for cloaked infiltrators."

The flights obeyed, and Casey added further orders for the deployment of refuelled and waiting units. So far there had been no losses from the Lunar 1 squadron. They wanted that record to stand as long as possible.

# Chapter 52

Kryslie followed the progress of the fighting through Daniel at Earthbase and main mission of the Lunar Base. The latter received direct feeds from the other WSRA bases. There was nothing more she could do at the moment. Reconfiguring the specs for the 'infection' detectors had not taken long, and the process of updating them was in progress. That it was effective was obvious from the trickling intake of static guests at Earthbase.

Llaimos was keeping in touch with the Tymorean fleet.

The signal chimes at the door of the suite heralded a visitor. Kryslie covered her head and Llaimos gave permission to enter. It was Landin, and he looked grim.

"Come in, Commander," Llaimos greeted. "How may we assist you?"

Landin looked at Kryslie, but she did not look at him until the suite door closed behind him.

Without uncovering her face, she asked, "How can I help you?"

"I have a problem," he told Kryslie bluntly. "I am totally out of line telling you this, but I think you need to know and I hope you can help. The Chief's daughter is under guard. She was caught trying to sabotage vital equipment."

Kryslie tensed and straightened. "When did this happen?"

"Monitors caught her in engineering half an hour ago, but odd damage has been occurring in other places over the past two days. I haven't told the Chief yet."

"Jody has been working in various departments?" Kryslie requested confirmation. Landin nodded and Kryslie was thoughtful. She had believed the personal force shield she had given Jody would block commands from the Ciriot, if she was infected.

"Check each place carefully and call a security drill at once," Kryslie said with authority reminiscent of her old self.

"We are on priority red alert," Landin reminded her, but was not about to object to her suggestions.

"This needs to be done before it escalates further," Kryslie told him. "Have the security screen linked to the on-station roster. When the pilots return, send them through too."

Landin nodded, not questioning it. Kryslie knew more than he did about the current situation.

Kryslie went on, "I will need to be able to move about freely."

"I have not cancelled your station ID," Landin told her. "I will have a uniform sent here. Will that do?"

"Thank you Commander," Kryslie said, sincerely grateful for his continued trust. "Where is Jody? I will go and see her as soon as I have dressed in the uniform."

"Detention room," Landin said tersely. "I will tell them to let you in."

Llaimos intuited what Kryslie would need. "I will go and request an update from the Commander-in-Chief."

Kryslie hoped he could keep Basoli busy for long enough.

It felt strange to be back in the WSRA uniform, but Kryslie put that feeling aside. As she emerged from the Tymorean suite for the first time when she might be recognised, she was concentrating on projecting an aura of, "I belong here, and nothing has changed."

Those that knew her, simply smiled in recognition and continued purposefully about their red alert duties. Others seemed not to see her at all.

Landin was in the detention room, asking questions of Jody, who was insisting on her innocence. She saw Kryslie and her eyes begged for help. That she truly believed what she said, was clear to Kryslie. But Jody did not know as much about the Ciriot devices as Kryslie did. In spite of going through the detector grid each day, Kryslie knew it was likely that she had been infected by the Ciriot. Until today, mere hours ago, the detector would not have picked the newer Ciriot devices up.

Without comment, Kryslie drew out the scanner she had modified to replace the one that had been taken from her. This she moved over Jody's body as Jody grew more and more alarmed. This was a Kryslie she had never seen before, distant and almost cold – totally controlled.

Finally, Kryslie gestured Landin aside and spoke to him with her back to Jody and the detaining guards.

"She is infected," Kryslie confirmed, using the euphemism for Ciriot controlled. "But, you won't be able to remove this by going through the scanner."

Landin quickly deduced her meaning. "Like Adamson."

Kryslie nodded. She knew what she needed to do, but it would be provocative. She needed to be blunt.

"She was probably infected before I went after her. I have to remove it."

Landin's face hardened, but he nodded. "Other options?"

"Possibly stasis," Kryslie said.

"Negatives to that?" Landin probed.

Kryslie did not mention the ramifications that would affect her, personally.

"It might not work. The devices have had a long time to set in. If there are other infected ones here, and they are activated, they might sabotage the stasis and leave her open to being activated."

"The security scan you ordered?" Landin questioned.

"Should detect potentials and actual," Kryslie assured him. "Any others found to be infected need to be detained in stasis."

"What is the difference?" Landin asked.

"If they are activated, they will be attracting ships here. I think, too, that the Ciriot can 'see' where the people are and selectively activate them. There was one in the Acting President's retinue when he arrived back."

"Was," Landin noted, realising he had gone pale.

Kryslie went on, "They are usually ordered to bring down the shields."

"Why hasn't that happened here yet?"

Kryslie met Landin's eyes and said, "I put a personal force shield on her. It seems to block some of the communication – possibly feedback to the Ciriot. I only put it on her at the start of the alert. She might have been acting on latent commands."

"More secrets?" Landin accused, but mildly. He meant the personal shields.

Kryslie shrugged slightly. "A precaution."

"What is involved in removing the infection?" Landin asked, but he felt he knew.

"Either I or Tymos will need to do it," Kryslie told him. "It cannot be done under anaesthetic or the device will believe the host is dying and self-destruct. If it is not removed and the host begins to radiate, that person is on a countdown to death either from a direct weapon impact or the self-destruct. "

Landin murmured an unprofessional curse.

"Why you? Why Tymos?" he asked the question Kryslie had preferred he hadn't.

"Because of what we are," Kryslie admitted. "Tymos can heal the damage the device causes as it is removed. I can begin that healing. We can both block the pain sensation in the victim as we do it."

"There's more than that," Landin sensed.

"Yes. It will sense our power...life force if you like...and crave it."

"That will be dangerous for you," Landin said, thinking that she was revealing more of herself than she had allowed before. What power did she and Tymos have?

"I know what to do. I can keep the thing static for a short time," Kryslie told him, infused her voice with assurance.

Landin saw through it. "We will go with stasis for now and check everyone else," he gave his decision.

A deep part of Kryslie was relieved. She did know what she was doing, and the risk. To operate, she and Jody would need to be unshielded. When she removed the device, she had very little time to control it, remove the self-destruct mote and heal Jody. All of this had to be done unshielded.

"We will go up to medical," Landin said in a normal tone. He looked at Jody, "There are some tests we need to make."

The guards escorted the currently docile Jody out the door. Kryslie walked beside her friend, no longer seeming remote.

"What is wrong?" Jody felt she could ask.

"Do you remember how Nala told you things that you couldn't remember?"

Jody nodded.

"Something like that," Kryslie wasn't exactly lying. "I have convinced the Commander I can help."

"I am infected – aren't I?"

Kryslie nodded. "I can help. Trust me."

"I do," Jody said, but she was very afraid.


Llaimos found Kryslie back at the suite. "Landin had to tell Basoli he put his daughter in stasis. He flatly refuses to believe that she was sabotaging equipment, or that she is infected. He says they both went through the scanner this morning."

"Not since I changed things," Kryslie said. "He needs to go through again, Jody may have infected him."

"Landin issued the drill, but he is resisting the order," Llaimos said. "I think he knew the command came from you."

"Stubborn oaf," Kryslie said uncharitably. "He may have changed his mind about Tymos and me, but he didn't want to. And I think he only tolerates me because I have stayed out of sight. Still, he will have to go through it – or be in breach of WSRA protocol himself! This is a safety issue."

Llaimos sensed Kryslie was avoiding another issue.

"Why did you not insist on removing the device?" Llaimos asked directly. "Is it because if you do, people will no longer be able to tacitly pretend you are not here?"

He had put his mind right on part of her reason.

"That is what my cowardly inner self thinks," Kryslie admitted. "But the rest of me needs to prepare. I need to have everything I need ready in medical. I need something to contain the self-destruct and control devices. When I do it, I need to be unshielded and so does Jody. So, ideally I would like a very tight local area shield around us. I don't dare let others get too close. And I will need to be fully charged with power."

Kryslie hid her fears more deeply than Llaimos could sense. She would need that power to subdue the controller when it touched her.

"All that should be possible," Llaimos considered. "I think you have all points covered."

# Chapter 53

It had been a very long seven hours.

When the Tymorean fleet were close enough to see through the direct view ports, cheers erupted in main mission. The Tymoreans requested permission to join the fight, and as the flights from the Terra and Lunar bases withdrew, began to show their skill.

Basoli and Landin received the human flight leaders in Landin's office. The fighters were coming under the base shields to refuel and for the pilots to have a break.

Only five of the six flight leaders came in. Casualties had occurred as the pilots tired. Sixty fighters had been lost from the original three hundred, but the losses to the air fighters near the surface were proportionally higher.

"Reports?" Basoli requested. He looked at Casey, but the senior flight commander deferred to Tymos.

"The first lot were drones," Tymos stated bluntly. "Unmanned, programmed with limited manoeuvres, but predictable. The next waves were manned, but the pilots were slaved to the ship. This meant they were able to anticipate and had limited ability to act outside of the ships programming. How much better they were than the drones would depend on their degree of motivation - if they preferred to live for the promised rewards or die."

Basoli looked shocked, but the pilots all had seen the difference.

"We haven't seen the Ciriot squadrons yet, and for that you can be thankful. We have only encountered the few trying to do sneak raids under cover of the drones."

After Tymos finished, the flight leaders reported on the performance of their pilots, and made suggestions to help reduce future casualties. Tymos was asked, by Basoli, to advise on strategies for fighting the Ciriot manned ships, he withheld the, "since you know so much about them" remark he was thinking.

At the end of the debriefing, Basoli ordered that all the pilots go through the scanner in the reception area and that it was going to be a mandatory routine. He also insisted Pitt went to medical to get his arm checked. He shouldn't have been flying at all, but everyone present knew why he had.

The men nodded and departed. They were exhausted, hungry and smelling of body sweat.

Tymos had no sooner reached the Tymorean suite when the red alert escalated to a 'total shield failure'. An almost unheard echo requested, "Security to medical".

He raced out, finding extra energy from within himself. Kryslie told Llaimos to, "Check Casey, Tweed, Pitt and Basoli" before she transmitted to medical.

In her mind, Tymos warned her that Pitt had been ordered there. Kryslie felt cold dread.

Jody was no longer in stasis, and she was radiating. Her mind was a mixture of determination and madness, and there was nothing of her will directing it. She had grabbed sharp scissors and a scalpel, the only weapons she could have found – and several staff were unconscious and oozing blood from deep slashes. She was eyeing off the security guards who had just arrived, and had weapons aimed at her.

"Hold fire!" Kryslie ordered with 'command' voice. The weapons stayed steady, and Jody spun around to see her and sprang to attack. Kryslie reacted faster, and had Jody disabled and disarmed before the guards could move a step closer. Jody struggled furiously as the command in her mind to get free and go to main mission and destroy the scanners pounded her mind.

Kryslie held her easily, telling the guards to 'keep back'. She pushed Jody to the floor, holding her with one hand, and ignoring the flailing limbs as she checked to see if Jody's force shield was still on. It wasn't, so Kryslie reactivated it. Jody's struggles eased, and a hint of Jody's inner self was showing in her eyes.

"Fight it!" Kryslie told Jody fiercely. "You don't want to do what those bastards want!"

"I can't." The voice was little more than a sigh.

Kryslie looked at Doctor Long and snapped, "I need sterile instruments and a blast bin, now!"

She held Jody while she waited, aware of the 'imminent attack' warning and non-essential people withdrawing to their quarters. That meant fewer people in danger here.

The instruments arrived fast and Kryslie wasted no time in starting. She had Long spread things out, and told her to keep back. She met Jody's eyes, and imposed her mind on the other woman, blocking the controlling compulsions. She felt something recognise her – want her – and ignored it. Then she took a deep, calmimg breath, dropped her personal shield and drew on the ambient energy in the room. The emergency lights dimmed right down, but no one associated that with her. Long grabbed a torch and gave her more light, but Kryslie could see well enough. A quick slash over the place where the device was, a surge of power to stop the bleeding, her fingers feeling for the bead device, gripping it before it could burrow away, more power to keep it docile. The bin arrived; the guard held the lid open. She put the metal bead into it. Jody still radiated red.

"Close the lid, don't stay close!" she warned, as she felt for the controller bead.

This one was harder; she found and gripped the second bead and gently pulled, tugging against the resistance of the tendrils, attracting the bead to her with a trickle of power, healing the damage done by the tendrils.

The base shook, blast doors slammed shut and the warning alarms escalated to critical – the base had been breached. No time to think of that...

The bead pulled free, she threw it into the bin as the first bead exploded. She moved her body to protect Jody and snapped her shields up but she wasn't fast enough. Long saw her jerk and go rigid for an instant.

Kryslie stopped herself making a sound as she felt something go into her like a bullet. When she could speak, she forced her voice to sound calm. "Doctor, you will need to close the wound."

The emergency lights had gradually come back up to their normal low level, as Long knelt next to Jody and ordered a guard to hold the torch. She knew Kryslie was still doing something, by the look of concentration on her face.

"Neat job," Long said to Kryslie as she began to stitch up the incision. "There's not much bleeding." Then Long realised that Jody was conscious. "She is awake," Long said calmly to Kryslie.

"She needed to be," Kryslie explained. "I am blocking the pain for her, but she will need something when I stop."

"Are you all right?" Long asked Kryslie as she saw another spasm contort her face.

"Yes, I'm fine," Kryslie lied.

Long stopped speaking and Kryslie was grateful. What effort she had to spare from Jody was trying to block the hissing, "Yes!" her mind was hearing and the sickening knowledge that this time she was on borrowed time too. She hadn't been fast enough, and the control bead had shot back at her and was even now insinuating itself around her lower spine.

Kryslie stood up after Long had finished closing the wound, and had administered a sedative to Jody. She stood back to let two guards lift her patient onto a bed and turned her full concentration to overcoming the mind trying to control her. She had just succeeded when an insane bellow warned of the next attack. Basoli's solid weight shoved at her, catching her before she was ready and pushing her hard to the floor.

"Hey, Sir!" a guard shouted at him. "You can't do that!"

Kryslie twisted and moved Basoli's weight off her, enough to roll free, twist and control him. He was still trying to pummel her, as Jody had done.

The emergency lights dimmed to nothing as Kryslie drew more power in. She was going to have to operate on Basoli. He was radiating, so brightly even the humans must be able to see it. He also seemed to have only one desire – to kill or hurt her. He began to yell threats, insisting on being freed, promising to reveal what she had just done, telling her the world council would see she died this time, calling her vile things.

"Be quiet!" Kryslie ordered him and his face turned darker with fury. "Jody is fine now! And unless you want to die horribly in less than twenty minutes, you will let me help you too."

It was as well the others around her could not hear Basoli thoughts, or rather the thoughts of the mind controlling him.

Kryslie heard, "Shields are back up," in her mind from Tymos as the pitch of the emergency alarms lowered.

"I am going to have to do what I just did, again," Kryslie told Long, who heard the weary resignation in her voice.

"Tell me what to do," Long offered.

"No, keep away until I am finished," Kryslie insisted. In her mind, Llaimos told her, "Casey and Tweed are infected. I cannot find Pitt."

"Bring them here," Kryslie mentally told Llaimos. To the doctor she said, "Casey and Tweed are coming here. Put them in stasis."

"You can't do that," Basoli's mind yelled at her, and his struggles increased to frantic.

"Be still!" Kryslie commanded this time, and he stopped, but was twitching and trembling.

Long received the new pack of instruments and began laying them out as before. The blast bin was put within her reach, open and waiting. Kryslie waited for Long to stand up and move back before beginning. On the edge of her mind, she knew Llaimos had transmitted in with Tweed and Casey, both were unconscious, and he was directing Long to open two more stasis chambers.

She also knew Tymos was hunting Pitt.

Kryslie moved her scanner over Basoli, now he was not thrashing around. The devices she sought were not in the neck as in Jody, but in the upper chest, and deeper.

Basoli's eyes blazed at her, full of hate. It matched the hateful 'yes' in her mind. Yet she met those eyes, searched for the level where there was pain, and where Basoli was trapped, and promised him help. She touched the real Basoli and blocked the pain.

Kryslie felt Llaimos rest his hand on her shoulder, and feed power to her.

"Stay clear, Bro – please," she asked him.

"I will shield you while you work," Llaimos told her.

Kryslie nodded, and shielded her mind from his. It was too late for such shields now. Once again, she drew on the ambient energy, making the lights dim.

She ignored the thoughts of horror and incipient nausea from the guards, from Basoli, as she first cut the clothes away from Basoli's shoulder, and then cut deeply into his flesh. She needed to concentrate on the task.

The bead under her fingers resisted more strongly, the self-destruct bead, tried to slither from her grip, but she caught it and threw it in the bin Llaimos held open. The tendrils on the other bead, held on tenaciously, and she needed to use power to bring the bead out. It took longer, but she persisted, pulling at the bead and winning against the tendrils, millimetres at a time. It came loose suddenly and the tendrils sprang around her fingers. She moved her hand towards the bin as the other bead exploded. She gripped the bead tightly, not wanting it to find another host. Everyone had glanced at the bin, even Llaimos, for that vital instant when the bead ejected, and powered into her.

Her own pain, overcame her for a moment, and Basoli began to moan. Once again, she couldn't move, and the pain threatened to make her black out, but she fought to stay conscious, and stubbornly won. Inside her, the bead squirmed around in her private woman's place. As the pain turned to unblockable obscene pleasure, Llaimos touched her shoulder and the sensations receded.

She forced her concentration back to Basoli, bearing her own pain, and using her energy to block his and sending power into him to start the incision and tendril damage healing.

She felt Llaimos lean over her and reactivate her personal shield, and half lift her away so Long could take over.

He stood her up and unwound the sickening bead and tendrils. Her mind knew it was only the husk but Llaimos didn't. He drew a heat beam on it and destroyed it.

When Kryslie seemed to teeter, he lifted her and moved people aside to get her to a chair.

"That is enough for now," he told her.

"I am not finished. There is Casey and Tweed."

"They will hold in stasis. We will guard them."

"Where is Pitt? He must have freed Jody," Kryslie asked

She did not open her mind to her brother, but his face betrayed ill news.

"I am sorry, Kryslie..." he began. Kryslie dared to brush his mind.

"Dead? How?" she demanded weakly.

Then she saw it, as Tymos had. The blast of the falling bomb had taken him. Then he told her mind, "There is a patrol of fleet ships above. The blast came from a shielded ship."

Kryslie shivered. Llaimos mistook it for an emotional reaction, and took a blanket from the nearest bed and wrapped it around her. But it wasn't just shock at Pitt's death. It was because she knew they, the Ciriot, knew where she was, and they wanted her!

"No!" Kryslie told the muted voices in her mind. "Not until I get you. Not until you pay for attacking Earth and corrupting honest upright people for your perverted pleasures and making slaves of sentient beings and turning them into helpless targets. I might die – but you will be destroyed first."

# Chapter 54

Landin began to sort out all the emergency messages. The computer was still working, which was merciful. The compromised sections had been sealed off. He reopened doors in safe sections to allow the damage control teams to start work. Life support was still on line.

"Casualty report," he queried the computer. This would only be an estimate at this time.

He listened to the list. Seventeen pilots in landing bay two, including Gareth Pitt. Seven more casualties in adjoining sections as the air decompressed.

Half the remaining space fighters...the shields had gone out first...

"Shield status," he demanded of the computer.

"Powering up," was the reply.

"Who is working on the shields?"

"Ward, T. Technical Officer."

Landin stopped worrying about the shields.

"Where is Kryslie Ward?"

"Medical."

He paged medical and got no reply.

"Condition report, Medical?"

"Two contained explosions, no damage."

Landin wondered what was happening there, but he didn't have time to go and see. He would trust that all was well if Kryslie was there. But the Chief was going there before the bomb hit.

"Where is CIC Basoli?"

"Medical."

"Condition of CIC Basoli?"

"Stable."

"How many patients in medical?"

"Two in stasis, two injured."

"Name of injured?"

"Jody de Yves, Ron Basoli."

"Nature of injuries?"

"Unknown."

Landin knew why Kryslie had gone there and what the emergency had been when the shields failed.

Whatever was happening there seemed under control, and surely medical was about to be swamped.

Landin moved onto the next of the thousand and one details of the disaster and tried to forget one.

Had the bomb fallen one inch closer to main mission, he would not be juggling emergencies now.

Tymos joined the emergency teams recovering what was left of the bodies of the dead.  Better that he be the one, as he had seen such horrors before.

The remaining flight leaders, excluding Tymos, reorganised the remaining space fighters, and pilots and launched the refuelled fighters.

The base personnel continued with the tasks to deal with the aftermath. It would be a very long job.

Finally, Landin had time to visit medical. He had the time to note that the Doctor looked exhausted, and all the medical staff were busy with patients, before Basoli saw him and demanded attention.

Kryslie allowed Llaimos to take her back to the suite, and tried not to feel like a coward for delaying the help to Casey and Tweed. She allowed Llaimos to make her herbal tea. It was the only hot drink they had the makings for there. He pressed the cup into her hands and though she took it, it seemed she was staring off somewhere far distant.
Llaimos made a tentative mind touch and encountered a solid mental block. He let her alone with her thoughts and queried reports from within Lunar 1, from Earthbase and the Jacen Tyr.
Surely, he thought, there was something he could be doing. Then he glanced at Kryslie and felt he needed to be here, with her. He waited, and watched.

Kryslie held the drink and let her mind begin one of the earliest meditative chants she had learnt. It freed her mind from her body and allowed her to think clearly. It seemed she could look at herself from within. Her body, riddled, diseased. Five of the dreadful beads, insinuating tendrils to control her limbs, feeding on her power and replicating quickly.
The Guardians had not removed the first three – simply made them dormant and given her time to act. Now they were active again. It had taken three to control her then when one would overcome the strongest human. She was stronger now – five of the beads were not enough.
But there would be seven...

She, not Tymos, must free the two astronauts. She faced the knowledge that this was what the Guardians had meant when they had asked, "Whatever the cost?"

The cost would be her death. She had promised. But it would not be in vain. She would take the Ciriot Princes with her. She would go to them...

Kryslie thought then, with the wisdom taught to her by the Elders of Tymorea, with the wisdom given to her by the Guardians, until she had a plan. One that would end the war on Earth, destroy the evil Ciriot Princes, and free those they had enslaved.

She envisioned raising both arms to the Guardians, in obedience to them, in supplication, and prayed, "Give me the strength to do this."

She felt, perhaps, a faint breeze in her mind. Then she prayed again, a prayer of strength for those she would leave behind. In her mind, she lowered her arms and strengthened her determination. She would not be weak.

And so, when Tymos returned, exhausted, mind weary, and depleted from helping to save the badly injured who were still alive – she and Llaimos embraced him, supported him, eased his mind, and helped him to bed.

Kryslie was ready when word came that Casey and Tweed had begun to radiate, even in stasis.

"I will do it," Tymos offered.

"No," Kryslie insisted. "I have the knack. I will remove the things and then you can heal them."

Tymos agreed, but told her that while she was unshielded, he and Llaimos would shield her. She agreed gratefully. They would keep the powerful pull of four Ciriot minds at bay for a while longer - long enough to finish her job here.

To distract herself, Kryslie asked, "If they can overcome the stasis field here – what of the ones they have at Earthbase?"

Llaimos had already considered that. "The shields there were already stronger there than here, but Daniel had them made even stronger. The stasis field will hold. The people will be safe. Once the Ciriot are gone, there will be time to help them."

"Once the Ciriot are gone," Kryslie kept repeating in her mind.

They went this time, not to medical (which was full of the victims of the attack), but to a storage area that had been cleared out to hold the two stasis units. Even humans were able to see the red aura now.

Doctor Long had anticipated what Kryslie would need. Two waist high examination tables, two trolleys of sterilised equipment and sterilising hand wash, were close to the stasis units and two blast bins.

To one side was a clear screen of toughened Perspex, and it was obvious that this procedure was going to be watched, and recorded.

She did not mind Landin being there, but she wished Basoli had not come. Still, it made no difference – the astronauts would die, if she did not help them.


Tymos and Llaimos stood behind her – too close, but at least they were protected.

Llaimos had seen what she did to Basoli, now Kryslie explained to Tymos what she would be doing, and stressed that he must not unshield until she said it was safe.

She glanced around and checked everything. This time she did not need to draw on the ambient power, her brothers had shared their energy with her until she held so much power that anyone who touched her would have been zapped. It would not change the outcome, but it would ensure her control of her body and mind.

Kryslie forgot those around her and concentrated on her task. Casey first. She turned off the stasis field, lifted Casey from there to the nearest table, oblivious of the stares of amazement that she, so slight and short, had the strength to lift a solid man. He began to stir, and Kryslie found the restraints and used them to hold Casey in place. He was waking from the stasis effect, but not yet struggling.

Kryslie scanned him to find the devices. They were at the back of the neck, where Jody's had been, and where there was one in her. She eased the restraints and rolled Casey over, and held him in place again. She cut the clothing around the area where she needed to cut, and then sterilised her hands before placing sterile sheets around the site. Then she made the incision, and Tymos snapped off her force shield. She felt their widened shields snap around her.

Kryslie sent power to stop the bleeding and to damp the pain and felt around until she found the self-destruct bead pulsing under her fingers and gripped it. Tymos opened the blast bin, exactly when she needed it. Kryslie returned to her task and found the control bead clinging to the spine. She gripped it, but this one felt different, released easily. Then she realised that Casey had some sort of prosthesis on his spine and the tendrils had not been able to insinuate into it. She sent a brief thought to her brothers about it. With gentle movements, she drew the bead out. The whole process was being recorded by a remote camera.

She was ready for it this time – the movement too fast even for the camera to record. The instant when the bead shed its husk and shot into her chest stopping abruptly just short of her heart. She strengthened her pain blocking to cover her own too and she did not betray the action by more than a slight hesitation.

Casey was conscious now, and he had no idea why he was being treated in such a barbaric way. The observers saw the red aura die out once the bead was removed. Kryslie laid the husk on the tray, for the observing camera, and then, like before, Llaimos burned it to slag and ash. The bead in the bin exploded.

Llaimos moved Kryslie away and felt him activate her shield again, as Tymos unshielded.

The camera hovered. Watching as Tymos placed his hand over the odd wound that had not bled much. Perhaps the faint mauve glow might have been noticed, had the light been less bright. But the camera saw, the wound closing and healing until there was no more than a faint scar and traces of blood on the sterile sheet.

Kryslie steeled herself to repeat the procedure once more as Tymos ignored Basoli's demands to know how he had done what he had. Instead, Tymos released the restraints, and helped Casey to turn over and sit up.

"What were you doing, Ward," Casey hissed.

"I'll explain later." Tymos promised. "Let the doc check you over."

Kryslie waited until Casey was safely away, behind the protective wall. Then she went to Tweed.

This time, Tymos helped her move Tweed from the stasis unit to the table, and then moved back and joined shields with Llaimos and around her.

The devices in Tweed were also in his neck, but in him, the self-destruct bead was pulsing more rapidly. Kryslie had not even removed her hand from the bin when it exploded.

Tymos saw her face, and moved to take her hand. "Let me heal it. You have work to do."

As soon as the pain eased, Kryslie drew her hand away, and returned to Tweed. She found the controller, solidly entrenched. Kryslie tempted it with a trickle of power. It would have been starving with its host in stasis. It seemed to wriggle towards her fingers, craving the rich life energy it sensed, and behaving in a deceptively docile way. Kryslie drew it out, slowly, healing the tendril damage. She clenched it in her fist, waited for it to act.

"Another bin," she requested, as the bead ejected into her right wrist, and seemed to shoot up her arm.

When Tymos opened the bin, a few minutes later, Kryslie dropped the husk within, and he slammed it shut.

She moved back on her own, and snapped her shield back on. The glow around Tweed had gone.

Tymos took over the pain control as he healed Tweed.

Llaimos drew Kryslie close to him. She allowed herself the brief luxury of his concern. When Tymos had finished with the dazed Tweed, and Long was checking him over, Basoli came over to Kryslie. His face was pale, as if with shock.

She hid her face, on the front of Llaimos's robes, and did not seem to hear Basoli's questions. Tymos exchanged a glance with his brother and Llaimos requested for them a period of privacy. After which they would answer questions.

The three Great Ones retreated to the Tymorean suite, hearing Basoli saying, "I want to know how they did that!"


"Are you okay," Tymos asked of Kryslie once they were away from public scrutiny.

Kryslie looked as pale as she had when the Guardians had judged her. She knew she had to hide the truth from them, and drew a steadying breath.

"They are...particularly nasty devices." Her brothers knew that was an understatement. "I truly hope...there are no more here."

They both looked concerned, so she asked, "Did they try to attack while we were removing the devices."

Distracted, Tymos turned to the computer to find out. "Yes, at least three cloaked ships tried. Two were destroyed and one fled."

"Any line on the direction that coward took?" Kryslie managed to sound normal.

"It was followed by one of the Tymorean ships but they lost it," Tymos said.

"What needs doing now," Llaimos asked.

"I need sleep," Kryslie told her brothers. "Can you two handle the questions? I do not want to freak Landin, Basoli and the doctor any further."

"I think you are misreading the Chief Commander," Llaimos proposed. "He is not a fool, and he has had time to think on what you have saved him from."

"Maybe he has," Kryslie allowed. "But I can see that I make him very uncomfortable. I will be sending Landin my resignation from the WSRA before I rest."

Tymos stared at her. "Why? Surely we have proved that we have only worked for Earth's benefit."

"Think about it, Tymos," Kryslie said gently. "I have become too high profile, and I think you will find some of it will rub off on you."

Tymos shook his head, not wanting to agree.

"And ... everyone below thinks I am dead, or should be. Up here, there might be tacit silence about the fact I am still alive, but if...when...those below find out I am not, there will be unpleasantness. And I cannot do the work of a missionary if I must remain in this suite of rooms."

"Landin has not said you must..."

"He has always known we were more than we seemed, and has never said anything," Kryslie agreed. "And I do not want to jeopardise his career, but my main concern is Basoli."

Tymos began to understand. "He was rather agitated just now..."

"Yes, more than just rather," Kryslie agreed. "He is a very good man, and the WSRA reflects his reverence to truth and integrity and right now I seem to be challenging everything he is. Starting with I am alive when I should have died. Now that might be able to be talked around, but if it gets known it might reflect badly on the WSRA."

Llaimos added his comment, "And if you had not stayed alive, he and Jody would not be alive now."

"Exactly. I think, to him, I have become like one God-touched. Certainly I have proven, in lots of unspoken ways that I am more than merely human. So, assuming he can rationalise my continued existence, there is no way he will let me be merely a technician – he will keep expecting miracles from me."

There was reluctant agreement in Tymos's eyes, as he thought things through.

Llaimos put the full truth into words. "He has seen you as what you are – a Great One."

"And humans will want to treat me as some kind of saint – which I am not! Nor do I want to be treated as a celebrity of some kind," Kryslie said bluntly. "But having said that, I don't plan on leaving yet - our mission here is not finished."

"What will you do - after we finish this business?" Tymos had finally accepted her decision and reasoning.

Kryslie managed a casual shrug. "I will decide then."

She turned then and retreated into her sleeping room before she betrayed to her closest kin that she did not see a time after...or they figured out that resigning was her way of tying up loose ends...putting her affairs in order.

# Chapter 55

Kryslie remained in self-imposed seclusion. Only her brothers saw her and they made sure she ate and drank.

Llaimos made occasional tentative overtures to her mind, but continued to encounter solid mind shields. He asked her why.

"It is not personal, Bro. A precaution. The Ciriot controlled me before. Handling their devices made me feel dirty again. I dare not risk they can get at me again. There is still work to be done."

"I do not feel I am doing much," Llaimos admitted.

Kryslie reached out for his hand. "Believe me, Llaimos, just having you here is giving me strength. I cannot express how much you are doing for me."

He squeezed her hand gently and let her distract him with questions on the progress of the fight against the Ciriot. If it took her mind off her fears, he would do what he could. Even Great Ones had fears.


As the days and nights of on and off fighting all over the Earth continued, the Tymorean fighters fought alongside their human counterparts. Out in space, the Tymoreans were working to locate the tribeships of the Ciriot, and where all their ships were coming from.

Cloaked Ciriot ships had begun sneaking in through the diminishing numbers of slave and drone ships. Some had landed, loaded up the caches of metals, jewellery, technological goods and things their unwitting collection agents thought valuable.

These though, were overloaded, slow and of reduced manoeuvrability but - thinking no one could see them when cloaked – were easy targets. They were disabled, taken in tow and their stolen goods confiscated to be returned to the planet below. The Ciriot crew were questioned without mercy but none would reveal the location of the tribeships.

The Ciriot infiltrators kept coming – not in fleets, but in sneak and hide strikes, on random vectors. They aimed for maximum damage, maximum terror.

As many as were detected still in space; an equal number made it to the atmosphere. They were harder to bring down, more agile than the drone ships and crewed by creatures that were personally motivated. Earth's defenders suffered a rising number of casualties from their hit and run tactics.

One place they were really pounding, to the confusion of the humans, was the radioactive zone in the middle of America.

Llaimos noted this to Kryslie, as she was intently monitoring reports from all over Earth and space.

She replied absently, "Convinced no doubt that within that area are riches beyond their dreams since so many beacons are radiating from there."

"So, they are still radiating, even in stasis?" Llaimos asked.

"Yes, but none have died. I think the destruct signals are blocked. And if the creatures are concentrating on there, we know where to look for them. And it might amuse you to know that Daniel had an extra shield added, that is about six feet above the surface. So when, the bombs or energy weapons impact it, the released energy is transmuted to electrical and it is been fed into the humans power grid at a very steady rate and some of that energy is being used to maintain shields in important places."

Llaimos saw the irony. "It seems that fewer beacons are appearing. Have you noticed that the fighting seems to be more random, less focussed?"

"The beacons attract the drone ships; the ones with Ciriot pilots have more freedom," Kryslie commented tersely. "But I am glad that fewer are becoming beacons – too many have died and there were more than we even imagined. Even with Jonko, Keleb and young Byron helping Konn, we only got a fraction."

Kryslie squashed the memory of Gareth Pitt and felt the renewed pull on – not her mind – but her body. The tendrils inside her were spreading, taking over. Resisting that pull was becoming harder.

The Ciriot had made no profit, or too little to appease them. They blamed her. They wanted her. They wanted to take their anger out on her.

Kryslie left the main room of her suite and returned to her sleeping room. Soon, she promised herself, soon the time would be right to go after them. She had to hold on...

There was an uneasy lull, when the Ciriot ships withdrew abruptly from their worldwide targets. Some chose to mass over the blackened radioactive waste – determined to crack its secrets. There were shields down there – strong shields – that must be hiding a vast treasure.

Joel Adamson had resigned as President of the UEN, stating that he did not have the strength to lead in the current emergency. The new

President, Arthur bin Halil, as his first official act, requested a flight of Tymorean atmosphere fighters to take out the massed Ciriot fleet.

Tymos led the flight – it was short and vicious. The Tymoreans were victorious but they lost a quarter of their number in destroying all of the Ciriot. The other Ciriot, still in the atmosphere suddenly aborted their sneak raids and headed directly up into the atmosphere and scattered in as many different directions.

Of the victorious Tymorean flight, only Tymos returned to Lunar 1. He brushed off the congratulations from Basoli with, "It's not over yet."

And it wouldn't be until they had found and destroyed the Ciriot tribe ships and the Ciriot Princes. So no more humans or Tymoreans would die.

Tymos went directly to the suite, and demanded of Llaimos, "Where is Kryslie? We need to find the tribe ships and end this obscenity of a war."

"I think she knows that. She went into her room to prepare," Llaimos told him.

Tymos tried to reach his sister's mind and felt nothing. Alarmed, he ignored politeness and courtesy and slammed open her door. She wasn't there. Like a dervish, he checked all the rooms of the suite.

"She is not here," Tymos said, as he thought where she might have gone and why.


When the attack alarms sounded – he knew. She would be going for the shields. She knew them as well as he did – but where. She wouldn't go to main mission – there would be too many to stop her – no, she might as no one would expect her to do that. He transmitted into main mission, glanced around. Landin moved to him.

"What is up?" Landin demanded, seeing Tymos agitated for the first time ever.

"If Kryslie comes here, don't let her near the shields," Tymos told him tersely, before turning to leave.

He transmitted from Landin's startled view, and went to the computer hub.

He saw a silhouette in front of the banks of flashing lights, "Kryslie! Don't!"

The figure disappeared. He realised the shields were already down, moments before the computer tones warned the base. She would need the shields down if she wanted to leave.

Tymos was racing to the launch area even as the launch order came over the comm. system.

A similar instinct drove Llaimos out of the suite, ignoring dignity and running through the human base following a trail of injured personnel, wrenched open doors and broken objects.

He saw Kryslie first, wrestling with a sealed hatch and transmitted to catch her. She turned a face to him that was feral, with no trace of Kryslie in the expression. She attacked him, and he needed everything he had to match her, but was losing ground. He could not hold her.

"Tymos, to me!" he yelled mentally. In the instant she threw him and raced down the passage. He scrambled up and raced after her, hoping that whatever was controlling her did not realise she could transmit.

Tymos saw in his brother's mind where he was and where Kryslie was going. She was coming to him, to try to get away on his ship. He stood between the entry to the bay and his ship, standing still, using his power to be invisible. If she sensed him, she would know what he was doing. She raced in, not sensing him, not seeing him and Tymos caught her, struggled to hold her, and then Llaimos was with him and the wild creature still fought to get to the ship.

"Morin!" Tymos sent the thought to Earthbase and put the strength of his power behind it. He felt the startled mind of the telepathic aide, down in Earthbase. "Long range beam, on me, now! Then set it to the Jacen Tyr!"

The terminus appeared in front of them in the next instant. Tymos transmitted the three of them to Earthbase. As soon as they were out of the beam it blinked off and on again.

In front of the startled Daniel, and an unusually agitated Vincent, the three Great Ones transmitted again.

Vincent stepped forward to follow and Daniel gripped his arm. "Take me with you!" he demanded. Morin moved forward too, and then hesitated. It wasn't his place, but he had had an odd message from Kryslie, only moments before Great One Tymos had yelled at him.

Vincent gestured to him, and told Lexina to cut the beam after they had gone. In the next instant, Morin found himself on the Tymorean flagship.


Jono Reslic sensed the terminus form and the hair on his neck seemed to stand on end.

"Clear the deck," he snapped. As the crew raced out, he instinctively drew the Sword of Judgement instead of a conventional weapon.

The last of the duty crew passed the hatches as Tymos and Llaimos dragged Kryslie through the terminus. She was silent, but struggling with all the power of a rogue Great One.

The Sword was just a hairsbreadth off the skin of her neck when Tymos and Llaimos wrestled her still. She met the eyes of the President with a look of steely intention and muscles that were still twitching as if trying to move her.

Reslic analysed what he saw, and sensed. He saw Kryslie exert a powerful effort to control her body and to continue to meet his eyes. There was no fear there.

Few could meet the eyes of the President when the power of the Guardians surged in him, demanding justice.

"What have you to say before I end the obscenity you have become?" he demanded of Kryslie.

With calm out of all proportion to the uncontrollable twitching, the sense of wrong – she spoke.

"I swore to serve the Guardians to my last breath and beyond. No matter the cost. And this I will do. Let me go! This I command you, as their Advocate. The Ciriot Princes want me and I cannot hold them off for much longer. When I turn off my personal shield my last protection will be gone and I will go to them, they will make me come to them. I will radiate, but I will draw the remaining drones to me and thus to the colony ship. Place tracers on me – in me – and follow me.

"Destroy them, all of them. The Ciriot don't deserve life, and death will set the slaves free. You will not try to save me. I am, as you can see, corrupted, polluted, beyond redemption. Death will free me from what I have become. I willingly embrace death, if it serves the Guardians, if it removes this evil, if Earth is safe."


"You are no longer a Great One," Reslic pronounced, but Kryslie still met his gaze, without fear.

His mind, and through him the Guardians of Peace, considered her words.

Reslic gave a head gesture to Vincent, who knew with grim certainty what he wanted, and transmitted away, and back in an instant.

"Tracer!" he commanded.  He saw Daniel's waxlike face, and Morin supporting him but he had nothing to spare for compassion.

Kryslie still did not look away from him, but her control over her body was failing.

"Send Daniel away, please," Kryslie entreated, softly. Reslic made no such command.

Her body was trying to fight free as the pressure of four Ciriot minds increased.  Vincent pressed tracer to the back of her neck and another at the base of her spine.

"Internal," Reslic commanded. "Quickly."

Vincent fitted a small object to an air injector, and applied it to Kryslie's chest and squeezed. He had no time for pity as her body jerked. Her face showed her controlling the pain, but still she did not look away.

Vincent, trembling, stepped back.

Kryslie felt the command in her mind, direct from the Guardians. "Step forward!"

The sudden move surprised her brothers. Without the slightest trace of fear, Kryslie stepped forward.

The Sword of Judgement was not a normal weapon, but it drove, as of itself into Kryslie's neck severing spine and spinal column and the few tendrils that had ventured upwards.

The concussion of power transmuted into light, blinding those that watched.

Kryslie felt the power being drawn from her and a white hot searing of energy piercing her mind.

Beside her, Tymos and Llaimos could not see. They felt her collapsing, but their own power almost gone too and they could not hold her. They released her, and she fell in a heap. They stumbled backwards and felt their power returning. As their sight returned, they saw Kryslie jerkily pulling herself up – more like a puppet than a living being.

Tymos's moment of hope died. There was nothing of his twin in that parody of a body. The eyes were blank and unseeing, like it was an animated corpse. Yet deep within him, he knew Kryslie still lived.

Beside him, Reslic was issuing orders - to clear the flight deck, to launch all but one ship, to make formation and cloak.

The clumsy figure tried to look at Reslic, but if Kryslie's mind still existed there it was still in shock from being disempowered.

"Go!" Reslic commanded.

A pause, and suddenly the body of Kryslie became more animated and able to move more freely.

Tymos fought nausea and needed Llaimos to hold him as he realised that Kryslie's shield was off and it was the distant Ciriot that controlled her fully. He tried to jerk free of Llaimos, to go after her, to help her. He felt he had betrayed her...

Jono Reslic felt the Guardians power abate and he sheathed the Sword. It didn't even show traces of blood. He made no attempt to do more than that. The after-reaction to invoking the Guardians took time to overcome, and he needed time to control his own powerful reactions to what he had needed to do. He wanted solitude, but he had duties.

Great One Tymos was being restrained by Great One Llaimos. Daniel and Vincent watched, unable to move, and Morin was wide eyed and looking terrified.

Reslic heard the report of the fighters launching, and going to stealth mode. He heard the computer report an unauthorised launch. He recalled his duty and summoned the duty crew back.

Finally, he turned to meet Vincent's gaze, and sensed the message, "I will tend to these."

He nodded and turned away again, to watch the last ship blasting away from the planet and out into space.


Vincent moved to one side of Daniel and put his arm around the older man and led him to a private chamber and away from the returning crew.

"Morin," he spoke quietly to the younger man. He gestured with his head to a small dispenser unit nearby. "Request five glasses of restorative drink from the dispenser. It works like the one at Earthbase."

Thoroughly cowed and overawed, Morin was glad of something to do. He added to the order five servings of his favourite horribly sweet chocolate dessert.

Vincent smiled at Morin when he saw the addition. "That might help," he praised him, although he doubted that Great One Tymos would touch it. "Help Daniel, will you?"

Vincent handed the drinks around and quickly swallowed his own. Llaimos copied him and they both urged Tymos to drink. In the end he obeyed, but without really knowing what he was doing. Colour and awareness came back into his face.

"Damn you both," Tymos said as his stomach settled and his mind cleared. "I don't want to feel better. You both know what those bastards will do to her. How can we sit here and let them?"

"She will not feel anything they do to her below her neck," Vincent said with clinical detachment.

Tymos turned on him. "We can handle mere pain, Vincent! They will torture her soul!"

"It was her choice," Llaimos told his brother gently. "She will lead us to them and we will end this and avenge her."

"Avenge!" Tymos snarled. "It will not be enough!"

He pulled free of his brother and went to where Daniel sat looking pale, shocked and old - refusing to drink or eat - and seemingly not to be aware of Morin's fussing.

Tymos slumped down beside the man who was his birth father. "Daniel, take the drink. It will help. I need you. We need each other."

It was not the command of a Great One, but the need of a son that made him obey.


"That's better," Morin said with satisfaction. "Great One Kryslie told me to make sure you ate and drank and looked after yourself. She knows you too well, Boss."

"Don't you realise what just happened, you wet eared whelp!" Tymos demanded.

"Yes, you acted just like she said you would. Only I decided to let Great One Llaimos deal with you. You are too grouchy!" Morin said, standing his ground.

"What else did she say?" Tymos asked, modifying his tone.

"That she had things she had to do, and it meant she had to go away. I guess that meant to do things only a Great One can do."

"She isn't a Great One anymore," Llaimos said gently.

Morin stood straighter and stared back at the Great Ones. "Yes she is! I looked at her. She knew exactly what she was doing, and if what you said is true – I would have run and hid. She never flinched, never! You all believed in her before – why not now!"

"Out of the mouth of babes," Daniel said, sitting straighter. "He is right."

Daniel tightened his arm about his son.

# Chapter 56

Slowly, Kryslie felt her mind waking – enough to know she was in a ship flying in space. She could not feel her body, but her hands in front of her were flying the craft. Her mind couldn't recall how to do it. It was being overwhelmed by the nauseating, sickening, satiated glee. "You're ours! Your own people could not kill you and now you are ours."

The voices spoke of what they would do to her, and her courage fled. If she could have turned the ship away, she would have.

She saw the red aura around her hands, and recalled her plan. The last of the drone ships had left Earth; there were no more beacons there. They would come after her, and the Ciriot would be making her come to them.

All she could do now was remember her plan. She could do nothing else.

After what seemed like a long time, the ship was drawn into a vast cavern and surrounded by armed Ciriot. They swarmed over the ship, wrenched open the hatch, dragged her out when she did not move herself. Dragged her to the feet of four scarlet clad Ciriot when she became like the bone thrown in amongst four starving dogs.

None of them hid their thoughts. They had her, a Tymorean, totally theirs and weak, helpless, easy prey...

They gloated at her state, competed to outdo each other, strove to get a reaction from her. Their delight turned to anger when they realised that none of their tortures, either inflicted directly or caused by the controlling tendrils was being felt. They finally noticed the healing wound and realised her neck was severed.

With their metal gauntleted hands they slapped her face until some sense came into it. A translator box changed their clicking speech into Tymorean. "Who did this?"

"Kill me...couldn't," Kryslie forced out through swollen and bleeding lips.

Her words excited them. If she could not be killed....and these human like bipeds could be so weak...

They tried first to make her talk, to reveal where the Earth hid all its treasures. She could hardly make a sound, her mouth was so dry. A slave brought water, and the Ciriot made the controllers make her drink.

To distract her mind, she told them non-sense. When they left her to send messages to their dwindling number of agents, Kryslie used the time to try meditation, but the peace she sought would not come.

They returned, hours later or days later, and punished her with electric shocks to her brain until they realised she could not function after them. They dumped her in a heap on a metal floor, in a cubicle where the walls displayed moving pictures of beings suffering torture. This was why they had not yet damaged her eyes or ears. This was torture moving to a new level.

But the shocks had wakened her mind, and she had fooled them into leaving her alone. While they planned the next series of humiliating, abasing, degrading punishments – she built shields around her essential self and prepared to endure.

Even if she couldn't feel her body, she could watch them doing obscene things to it, and see them shown over and over on the screens around her. When that garnered them no reaction, they tossed her into a cage of their slaves and let her be used by them. Again, the expected reaction did not come, so they made the controlling tendrils have her hands grab the nearest slave, and start tearing limbs from him. The man screamed and finally passed out from the pain and blood loss. They kept her at this because they could see the horror of the deed on her face.

Finally the other slaves crowded together and sat on her to make it impossible for the tendrils to make her move.

A purple Ciriot came to retrieve her, swinging a short whip indiscriminately. And for a time she was kept alone in a completely dark room.

The dark did not bother her. At least she was not seeing over and over the torture of sentient beings, and being unable to help any of them. For herself, she cared not. She would not survive this, did not deserve to. Her body had tortured innocents, even if her mind did not want to. She was no more than a tool of evil.

She tried to add up the time she had been on the ship. Surely her kin had time to find her, and surely this would end soon.

The Ciriot told her that they would never release her, laughed in a higher pitched clicking tone and told her that her friends would never find her. She tried not to let that affect her. After all, she had expected that to be the case, even with the tracers on her. However, it was as she had thought, the Ciriot Princes were becoming over confident, thinking her helpless. But she was beginning to feel tingling in her limbs, and soon she would be able to act. And then, she would have the oblivion her tortured soul craved.

They had figured how to hurt her, and delighted in her mental pain. It was worse, because her pain came from them hurting others and both kinds of pain excited them in an orgiastic way, and she felt that too.

When her mind grew inured to her body hurting the slaves, they dreamed of another torture. At least most of the slaves had been insane, and death was a release, but the children were innocents, and she had to watch them being brutally whipped, and endure them being forced to hit her, or be whipped more. The Ciriot did not realise that she was now feeling that pain, since they knew she could not abide watching the children being hurt.

Then they made her rend them too, and her mind called out for the Guardians to end this — but they did not answer her.

But slowly, as she had hoped and believed it would, her body healed - even the severed spine and spinal column. Soon she would be able to work her lower body. Her legs would be weak, but she was nothing but thin flesh over bone, almost insubstantial.

When they tired of or were sated with their torment of her, they now left her tied by her wrists and dangling in their sight. They never tired of gloating at her state.

Arrogant and over confident, Kryslie thought to herself in the shielded part of her mind. They did not realise that she was learning their clicking speech, observing their activities, analysing their ship.

Then the day came when she could scratch her nose, and it was time for her to act.

They chose to make her torture children again, and she did, lest they realise her rejuvenation. And she could not help the children, for she no longer had the special Tymorean power. Her soul was wounded to the point where she could not act.

But the miserable whimpers of the captive children reached through her own soul sickness and she said to them, "This will be over soon. For all of us."

And they looked up at her with undisguised hope.

"Can anyone of you untie me?" she asked of them, and most stared numbly at her. One struggled to his feet, used her body as a tree to climb, reached her shoulders and knelt there to fiddle with the knots. They fell together.

"What you do," he asked. She did not know what language he spoke, only that he was not human. She felt the meaning in her mind.

"Bring help," she whispered.

"Come, me, you?" he asked to help her.

She nodded, and they went through the sleeping ship to the bridge of this ship, unguarded except with the overconfidence of the Ciriot.

She knew what to do, from her hours of study. First she would recall all the Ciriot ships from Earth – the ones manned by Ciriot that were still hunting for treasure. But her fingers were broken and swollen.  She felt the first stirring of hope when the boy proved able enough to follow her directions. She had him open the comm. channel, and she spoke in the clicking tongue, with the inflection used by the arrogant Princes. Then, she had him press the buttons to remove all but one basic shield. He was her hands when she ensured that the joined ships would never fly again and could not report her meddling. Then she sent the boy off and waited to see the results of her work.

She had not seen all of the ships, and she had no wish to. The Princes had private quarters in their individual tribe ships, now all docked together. They emerged like angry ants when the alarms told of incoming ships. They smelt of their own pleasure and of tortured partners.

Their faces became grimaces of anger when they saw her, walking around free, became insane masks when they found they were helpless, trapped.

As the first lances of energy began picking out and destroying the lesser ships, the anger of the Princes turned to bloodlust. They destroyed her eyes, punctured her ears, began beating her to a bloody pulp, and when they finally ceased, began laughing insanely as they realised that she was still alive, in agony and helpless.

It gave them more amusement thinking their ships were impervious to the attacks. The lesser ships did not matter. They held their own return fire, thinking to trick this enemy, and let the englobing force move in closer – to destroy them all at once.

Then they fired every weapon from every turret...and nothing happened.

They checked their instruments and fear... terror...finally overcame them. They lost control of their bodily functions and turned into gibbering worms and in their minds they heard an insane but satisfied laugh.

"Even you could not kill me – but I have destroyed you."

A concentrated, coordinated burst of energy surrounded the joined tribeships. The virtually unprotected hulls blazed into incandescence and all within became atoms.

Even without sight, Kryslie felt the heat, saw the brightness and embraced death with relief.

But it seemed that she stood up, straight and whole and walked into the light.

# Chapter 57

The Tymorean interceptors lost signal from the tracers that Kryslie had on her several hours of following it in a random zigzag of directions. In all that time, they saw no sign of the tribeships, but they knew those would be well shielded and cloaked. When the signal had vanished, they began a search pattern but they feared the ships had fled from that sector of space.

There was no doubt that Kryslie had been taken onto one of the tribeships, and was behind the cloaking screen. They could not know if the tracers had been found or neutralised.

After two days of fruitless hunting, Vincent insisted on taking Daniel back to Earthbase. He had work to do there, things to distract him. Morin had instructions to watch out for him and proved to be the only one of them that stayed positive and optimistic.

Tymos refused to leave the flagship's bridge and he oversaw the hunt for the tribeship and his sister. Llaimos stayed with him except for when he went to bring him food to make him eat and drink.

Five more days passed, and during that time Tymos had sensed nothing from Kryslie except a sense of disquiet from the deep twin bond. He could only imagine what they might be doing to her, and the truth was probably much, much worse.

By then, Tymos's mind was attuned to every function on the bridge. He jerked, moments before a comm. officer reported to Reslic.

"The Ciriot ships are leaving Earth. We are tracking them ..." he gave the heading.

Reslic gave the order for an intercept course.

Then came a second report. "We have the tribeships, Sir, they are uncloaked."

Fierce exultation welled in Tymos. Kryslie had done it. She had beaten them. She was still alive.

The Flagship and the remaining interceptors went into stealth mode. The cloaked ships flew slowly closer, on carefully calculated courses, to form a globe around the colony ship formed by the joining of the tribeships. Only when all were in position did they uncloak and begin picking off the slaveships and infiltrators docked alongside the larger vessel.

The Tymoreans wondered why the colonyship had not fired a defensive shot. When all the smaller craft were destroyed, Reslic ordered all the Tymorean ships to close in until their shields overlapped. Still the Ciriot colonyship did not fire weapons.

Tymos sensed Kryslie then, as did Llaimos. The mental laugh sounded insane, but satisfied.

"You could not kill me, but I have destroyed you!"

"Fire," Reslic ordered, and every Tymorean ship aimed energy weapons at the Ciriot tribe-ships.

Tymos felt the deep twin-link finally break and a cry of purest agony came from his lips. "Kryslie!"

Llaimos gripped Tymos harder, supported him as he seemed about to collapse. Reslic stared at the view screen as the brilliance faded.

The flagship's shields were pummelled by flying debris. He did not watch as Llaimos half carried Tymos off the bridge. Instead he ordered the fleet ships to expand the globe and analyse the debris.

Jono Reslic watched the Great One systematically examining every piece of wreckage bigger than a man's hand. He did not know what he hoped to find. At least he was doing something and not still sitting in a state of shock.

The comm. system chimed, and the face of his youngest son Ennis appeared.

"Commander, there is a priority call from Homebase."

Reslic had it sent through to his private chamber.

"Ty," he greeted as the face of High King Governor Tymoros appeared. Reslic saw the signs of controlled grief in the expression of his friend and fellow Governor.

"How is my son," Tymoros came to the point.

"Grieving," Reslic said. "The initial shock is lifting but he is still in denial. I will stay here as long as he needs. I can do little else."

"At least we will not lose two Great Ones, as we once feared," Tymoros said gently. "Do you think he would come home for a while?"

"Not yet," Reslic said. "The shock of Kryslie's going was intense. I think it was only Llaimos who kept him sane."

Tymoros's face paled. "And the Guardian's, I think."

"Yes, they had a hand in this, though they did not enlighten me. I acted, as they directed. Kryslie...her death was not without gain. The Ciriot Princes – four of them – are dead. The thousands they enslaved

...died too, but their spirits are free. We have yet to check, but I believe there are no more Ciriot on Earth."

"Then there is a reason to be glad," Tymoros drew comfort from that.

"There is more reason than that," Reslic said. His own emotions were powerful enough to come close to cracking his own control. "The Guardians disempowered her, denounced her, but she still served them. She said she had promised to do that...to her death and beyond. She embraced the loss of her power, knowing her body was corrupted and knowing she was no longer fit to be a Great One.

"It took seven of their vile controllers and the combined effort of four Ciriot Princes to control her body – but they did not – ever –fully control her mind. Her courage awes me. The Guardians did not kill her when they took her power. They severed body from mind and I think that was the only way she could hope to beat them. She knew that and she trusted that they would heal her enough to let her defeat them. They did and she did. She had to have been the one to remove their defences."

"And there is nothing left?" Tymoros asked, without hope.

"Better death than to live with what she had become," Reslic said. "Though Great One Tymos searches..."

They talked of other things then, including the need to send ships to another situation.

"Send Perrin," Reslic directed. His brother was the second in command of the fleet. "I will redeploy all but a squadron from here."

"I have had a communication from your son, Stenn," Tymoros went on. "He reports that the situation of the people in the vaults on Aerdna is deteriorating. It is his hope that Great One Llaimos will return soon."

"The Great Ones will go where they feel the need is greatest," Reslic commented, without saying where Llaimos felt most needed now.

Before ending the conference, Tymoros returned briefly to the original topic. "You did as you had to, Jono. And although it is difficult at times like these – I learnt long ago, not to give up hope."

Reslic nodded, Tymoros had read him correctly.

Even with his close link to the Guardians, sometimes hope was hard to find.

# Chapter 58

Reslic's state of reflection was broken when Vincent requested entrance. The Tymorean doctor had already discussed the Great One with him, so this had to be something else.

"Your Excellency," Vincent greeted.

Reslic gestured for Vincent to sit. "What brings you back again?"

"We have received an official invitation from the President of the United Earth Nations - to a formal reception to thank us for our assistance. You and the Great Ones are specifically invited."

Reslic glanced at the view screen where the picture showed the ship Tymos had commandeered.

"Is there a need for us to be down on the planet now?" Reslic asked.

"Several, I think," Vincent considered. "The men and women we have in stasis in our Earthbase constitute one matter. Our medics would know more of the devices than the humans. And to hunt out any remaining Ciriot or their artefacts or puppets, would perhaps require our technology."

"Anything else?" Reslic asked.

"I had the thought that Great One Tymos might teach the humans how to deal with these new radioactive areas where Ciriot ships were destroyed. And, of course, he would be the best one to deal with the removal of the Ciriot controllers. He has a healing gift that has to be from the Guardians themselves."

"It would give him some purpose," Reslic suggested.

Vincent nodded. That had been his thought too.

"What do the humans know of what happened here?" Reslic asked.

"Nothing, as yet. When the three Great Ones departed abruptly from Lunar 1, I arranged for a message to go to the Commander that we had a lead on the Ciriot leaders and were seeking the tribeships."

Reslic considered the invitation and the current situation. "Then reply that we would be pleased to accept the invitation but must remain on station here for a short while longer. I expect that the cessation of attacks may let them feel we succeeded. Tell them that we will advise them of our intended return and will report then."

Vincent nodded, agreeing with the decision.

"Do you think that Great One Tymos is ready to return to Earth?" Reslic asked then.

"If he were needed there, he would go, and would not do less than his best. Whether he goes there or somewhere else, I think he needs to be away from here. There is nothing here."

"Those were my thoughts also," Reslic sighed quietly. "Will you talk to him and remind him of what needs to be done. I will be ready to move the flagship back to station just out of Earth's system. I have activated all but one squadron to be deployed to assist my brother. One squadron will stay available here to search for Ciriot contamination."

Reslic seemed thoughtful.

"Was there something else, your Excellency?" Vincent suggested.

"Stenn has suggested that Llaimos might need to return to Aerdna. If he goes, I will recall Stenn – have him come here and be on hand. He is a friend of the Great One."

"A very good suggestion, Excellency," Vincent agreed, with a genuine smile. "Stenn seems to have regained his sense of humour, and his sense of irreverence toward Great Ones. Perhaps he can make Tymos realise that he can still smile."

Reslic smiled then. "As well as his irreverence to President Governor's. As his father, I find it refreshing."


"I thought my suite was private," Tymos stated when he found Vincent there.

"And that is why I am here, waiting for you," Vincent said smoothly. He did not stand up from the chair as he normally would in greeting the Great Ones. He was there in his role as physician, and in that role, he had authority even over a Great One. "Great One, if I may have a few moments of your time, there are things I need to bring to your attention."

Tymos looked on the verge of anger, but he maintained his control and sat in a second chair and stared towards the far bulkhead.

Vincent spoke first of the invitation and wondered, as he spoke, if Tymos was listening.

But courtesy had been well trained into him as had respecting those who were older than him. Outranking all Tymoreans had not changed that yet.

"It was not just me and Kryslie," Tymos said. He had trouble saying his sister's name. "It was the fleet pilots too. It would be fitting that they be recognised as well. I would say the same of all our missionaries, but the humans do not know of them."

"I agree, Great One. I think the human pilots deserve recognition too. Will I make that point in my reply?"

Tymos considered, and nodded. "They will be expecting Kryslie."

Vincent remained silent, wondering if Tymos was ready to talk of her.

"How can I face them, and admit that I did not try to save her? That I didn't know..." Pain was evident in Tymos's voice. It was the opening Vincent wanted.

"I don't think you could have helped her," he said gently. "Don't you think that if it were possible – the Guardians would have done so? Perhaps they could not –not without damaging her essential self?"

"But they are the Guardians," Tymos protested.

"Guardians, yes," Vincent said quietly. "Perhaps a race of beings far beyond us – but not, I think, Gods."

"Kryslie must have known," Tymos blurted then.

"I believe she did," Vincent agreed. "And she kept it from all of us because there were important things to be done. And, perhaps, her way was the only way to find those evil creatures and get us close enough to act against them."

"She did not deserve what they did to her!" Tymos said, now betraying his anger with a violent shudder. "Surely the Guardians saw it was not her fault? Could have helped her?"

"One of us, who can no longer control what we do, is an agent of evil – even if unwilling. They could not let her – powerful as she was – be loose in the universe. Deep within you – you know that."

"But I could have removed those things – like she did for the others."

"For mere humans, when the devices were not so well entrenched," Vincent said. "I think you are missing something very important."

Tymos stared at him.

"The devices feed on the host's life energy. Hers, so strong – let them proliferate as they did not in any other."

Vincent held Tymos's gaze, and went on, "It took three devices to overpower her at first. She overcame them! This time it took seven devices and the combined will of four Ciriot Princes to do it."

Tymos's face lost all colour.

"I think you need to stop thinking of what they did to her – in favour of what she did. She knew her body was...unclean...but she kept doing what she believed was right. She did not flee from the human's prison, or their trial for murder. She could have, and we could have protected her. But to prove her integrity, she did not. We could not have proved to them that what they called murder was necessary. She knew that. And not once, did she disgrace us, or herself. She accepted the judgement of the Guardians with absolute faith. She showed that same magnificence of spirit here on this ship."

"But the President..." Tymos began to protest.

"Not the President!" Vincent interrupted. "When he draws the Sword of Judgement, he embodies the Guardians, they are present. And I do not think Kryslie realised that when she spoke to the President – but the Guardians heard her, heard how she hoped to serve them and they agreed. She proved her promise to them when she stepped forward."

"But she is dead!"

"And her spirit has been freed! It is not fettered to a diseased and polluted body."

Tymos turned his head away as tears fell unheeded down his cheeks.

Vincent waited a while, and then took himself out.


Llaimos pressed a flask of drink into his brother's hand.

"Drink it, Tymos," he directed firmly. "I need to talk to you."

He waited patiently as his brother finished sipping the restorative drink.

Tymos spoke before he did. "I have probably indulged myself long enough." He had tried to sound resolute, but from the pity on Llaimos's face he knew he had failed. "You have to go."

"Yes," Llaimos admitted. "The situation on Aerdna is deteriorating, but I need to know that you will be all right. I ...miss Kryslie too."

"I have been selfish, and of course you miss her. But you seemed so strong..."

Llaimos smiled wryly. "Neither of us has been thinking clearly. Vincent told me what he just told you, some days ago. He told me that the President admitted to him that there was a point on which he felt he had failed when training you."

That got Tymos's attention.

"The President said that he would have preferred that the bond between you and Kryslie did not exist. He feared such as this – that he might lose both of you at once."

"He tried hard enough," Tymos recalled. "He did succeed in teaching us to block each other out. Kryslie learnt that well, even though she did not wish to. Back then we were stubborn little..."

"Brats?" Llaimos supplied with a faint grin.

"Close enough," Tymos admitted. "When do you need to go?"

"As soon as I can," Llaimos told him. "I should have gone already. Are you all right? Will you be able to face all those who respected Kryslie and tell them...?"

Tymos stood and pulled his brother up, and embraced him.

"I will remind myself that I am a Great One, and not a bowl of mush," Tymos tried to project assurance. "Thank you for being here, bro."

Llaimos returned the embrace, saying tacitly that thanks were not needed.

"And," Tymos went on, releasing his brother. "I may not have practiced being a diplomat or statesman, but I have all of Father's memories and experience in my mind. I will not disgrace the Tymorean Trust."

# Chapter 59

Tymos transmitted from the Jacen Tyr to Earthbase at a time when the base seemed deserted.  Keleb, met him and greeted him almost warily.

"I am sorry for your loss, Great One," Keleb said quietly.

"Our loss, Kel," Tymos recognised his friend's grief. "How is Daniel?"

Keleb spoke bluntly. "He looks like he has aged ten years, but apart from that, I think he is okay. Morin bullies him and has been good for him. They have gone into the town to get a formal suit. I believe you insisted they be part of the Tymorean delegation to the White House Reception?"

"I think he deserves that honour, don't you?" Tymos challenged.

"Completely so, Great One, but if I may be so bold...I am not sure that applies to Konn Reslic."

"Do you wish I had insisted that you come?" Tymos thought to ask.

"Hell no!" Keleb exclaimed. "And Jon agrees with me. We still need to be taken for what we are – human."

"Half –human," Tymos countered with a faint grin. "I had thought you would think that, and not to belittle your contribution – Konn did save a lot of otherwise doomed Ciriot 'toys'. And if they ask us for a formal Embassy delegation – I intend to have Konn as Ambassador."

"You would do that better!" Keleb retorted.

"Not really," Tymos admitted seriously. "It is a job for a bureaucrat, not a Great One."

"Probably," Kel agreed reluctantly. "Will I spread the word you are here?"

Tymos shook his head. "Not yet. People can find out later. I want to be alone for a bit. In the garden."

"As you wish, Great One."

"Kel, cut out the Great One bit. I don't need that from you," Tymos said, sounding irritated.

"As you wish," Keleb echoed and waved himself off.


Tymos's quiet period of reflection was disturbed by muttering that was getting clearer, as if the speaker was getting closer.

"Who does he think he is anyway? Lord High and Mighty son of the President? Lord Muckety if you ask me!"

"You have picked up some quaint Earth expressions, Morin," Tymos commented, amused in spite of himself.

Morin almost leapt in the air with startlement. He spun around. "Ah...Great One...I...um...sorry, I mean no disrespect, Sir."

"May I ask the topic of your discourse?" Tymos asked. He would have accepted a 'no' but Morin took it as a command.

"Ah...Great One...it was Lord Reslic, Sir. Mr Konn," Morin flushed with embarrassment.

"I see," Tymos murmured. "He is back to being his fully self-important self is he?"

"Great One, I didn't..."

"So what has he done to upset you?"

"Me, sir, nothing. It is him and that brother of his. Don't take me wrong, I like the brother, he knows how to have fun, but Lord Konn is so intense, so full of importance..."

Tymos began to hear the edges of the cause of Morin's discomfort.

"Morin, which other of the President's sons is here?"

"Lord Stenn, Great One," Morin offered.

"Scoot," Tymos told Morin, who left at once.

Morin intended to hover, just in earshot, but he very quickly changed his mind as soon as Tymos began to speak.


Tymos waited for the two quarrelling brothers to come into view. Oh, they were not being loud, but Tymos had acute hearing and half a minute of their totally petty disagreement, had spoilt the peace he had achieved in the garden and made him angry.

"I had thought that all of the President's sons were adult!"

Tymos's voice whipped both into silence and immobility. He stood from the rock ledge and walked closer to them.

Stenn was torn between wanting to greet his friend and respect for the Great One. The latter desire won. He fell to one knee and bent his head. "I beg your pardon, Great One."

Konn was simply rigid and white faced. "My apologies, Great One. I was out of order!"

"Way out!" Tymos agreed. "I do not want to hear the subject of that conversation again!"

"No, Great One," Konn promised.

"Get away," Tymos told Konn and the subdued Fleet Officer retreated at once.

"Get up, Stenn," Tymos said, moderating his tone. "And you don't have to Great One me."

Stenn rose fluidly. "Oh, I do! I have never seen you so angry. When I hear that tone, I have a very fine sense of humility."

"How long have you been here?" Tymos asked.

"I arrived just as Daniel and Morin were to go 'shopping' I think they called it. I decided to go along and see what this planet of yours was like. I like it. As to actually here, about ten minutes. Where is Kryslie?"

Tymos went tense. He found he could not come out and say, "She's dead."

"Not here at the moment," was all he could force out. He didn't quite sound casual, he still sounded angry. To cover it he went on, "So why are you here? I thought you were on Aerdna."

"When Great One Llaimos returned there, I was recalled. His Excellency implied I might be useful here – helpful."

Stenn suddenly wondered just why he was there.

Tymos gave him a friendly thump on the shoulder that rocked him back a few steps. "I am glad you are here but please, don't rile Konn too much. I am hoping to make him Ambassador after I leave."

A glance at Tymos stilled the, "Are you joking" retort.

"Kel and Jon are around, they will be glad to see you," Tymos went on. Stenn accepted that idea as a reason to withdraw.


Morin proved to be Stenn's best source of information. The young man did not really understand what he had seen and heard, but Stenn could fill in the details.

"Dead? Disempowered? Rogue?" he thought, stunned. His instinctive reaction was, "Never!"

But Morin had mentioned Ciriot devices – seven of them – and that made the emotional pall around this Earthbase make sense. Everyone here knew. Well, maybe except Konn, who only had time for himself. No one here was talking about it.

He hadn't heard any mention of it when he was briefly back on the Jacen Tyr. He had learnt how many pilots had died defending Earth...well, having a Great One die wasn't good for morale. Having one go rogue was too horrible to contemplate...but not Kryslie. Never!

It also explained the cold emotionless distance he had sensed about his father and maybe how he was meant to be helpful. Tymos needed friends around him right now to distract him from that deep anger he had sensed just before.

Well, he was the right Reslic for the job!


Stenn found himself in a borrowed formal fleet uniform at an event called a 'reception', acting as personal aide to his father. The President of course, was talking to important looking natives with his usual aplomb. He saw Morin doing a similar service to Daniel and winked at him.

Tymos was moving from group to group, most containing Tymorean pilots and he guessed, native ones. Those mixed groups seemed to understand each other quite well.

Stenn briefly wished he had made time for a crash course in the local dialect. Konn, of course, was off impressing the natives, male and female, as the son of the Tymorean President!

That made Stenn feel glad he was merely an aide. He could watch and observe without being distracted with babble. Like, seeing how Tymos went tense talking to many of the people. Like he had done when he was asked about Kryslie. Somehow, he didn't think that word of her death was being spread. Perhaps she was just busy elsewhere ...now that was a better way to think of things.

An unobtrusive nudge from his father recalled his attention.

His father explained, in Tymorean, that the man with him was the President of the United Earth Nations. Stenn smiled, bowed and studied the man more closely.

"Bring fresh drinks, would you?" Reslic asked of him.

Stenn bowed and went off at once.

Konn timed his move to the drinks table to coincide with Stenn's arrival.

"What is a deaf mute doing at this reception?" Konn teased quietly. "You did nothing here!"

Stenn ignored him. His brother was a master of the snide, sly verbal jab and timed them for when the recipient dared not retaliate.

The Great One was approaching, so Stenn returned with the tray to his father.

"I see you are mixing well with these people," Tymos noted.

"Yes, Great One," Konn agreed. "They all seem to find me interesting."

"Well, make sure the interest stays in plain view. Just be aware that most of the women here are married and a candidate for the role of Ambassador needs to above reproach."

Konn coloured to a rosy flush. "Yes, Great One," he muttered before bowing and departing.

Tymos turned and saw Landin and Basoli approaching. He did not feel like smiling.

"We haven't heard from you for a while," Landin said by way of a greeting. "I received your resignation, but you gave no reason."

Tymos glanced at his 'robes of state' and said, "I have other duties now."

"A role you will fill well, I am sure," Basoli offered. "I haven't seen Kryslie this evening. Is she here? And your brother, was it?"

"My brother, Llaimos, was required elsewhere, and Kryslie wasn't able to be here. All things considered, it would not have been a good idea."

Neither man missed the tenseness of the answer, nor the less than polite tone.

To change the subject, Landin asked, "So it is likely that there will be an official embassy here?"

"Likely, yes," Tymos agreed. "But it won't be decided tonight."

"Perhaps we can suggest a cultural and scientific exchange," Basoli suggested.

"A thought for the future," Tymos managed to sound polite.

"In the meantime, you will need to schedule a discharge briefing, for your resignation to have effect," Basoli stated. "As will your sister."

Tymos seemed to stand taller, and his tone was rigidly polite. "I will arrange a time when my new duties allow. And if I cannot stand proxy for my sister, you will have a very long wait to finalise her resignation."

"It's WSRA protocol," Basoli pointed out neutrally. "Without it, moving to other scientific positions may incur legal intervention."

"I don't think you need to worry about her selling WSRA secrets to anyone, so if you really want to take legal action, go for it. She will not care."

Tymos knew he should not get angry – they didn't know – but he spoke out anyway.

"Kryslie is dead!" he said, before turning to walk away.

He stood staring at the wall beyond the buffet table. A few minutes later, he heard a polite cough behind him. Tymos wasn't sure he wanted to talk further to Basoli, but the needs of his new position were important.

"I apologise, Ambassador Ward. I did not know, and I too have grief of my own. My brother...killed himself...and I blame myself for not helping him enough."

He did know how he felt, Tymos realised, finally sensing true empathy from Basoli.

"I must apologise too," Tymos admitted. "And I accept your apology."

Basoli nodded and moved away. Landin moved up.

"You have my condolences, Tymos. May I ask what happened?"

Landin had always been a true friend; he deserved to know – at least some of it.

"She put an end to the Ciriot Princes, the ones that started the worthless invasion. That is what matters," Tymos told him.

"Then we have a lot to be grateful to her for. I believe this is not common knowledge," Landin asked gently.

"No, and it won't be. There are reasons for that – I am sure you can think of some others," Tymos told him.

Landin could, beginning with Kryslie being believed dead before that.

"Will you be telling the President? I have noted that he has had a special concern for her," Landin suggested.

"I...will tell him, but not tonight. This is meant to be a celebration," Tymos murmured.

"Perhaps a change of duties is best," Landin suggested.

"It is only until I train a bureaucrat to take over," Tymos admitted, wanting to get away from Landin's sympathy before his control cracked. "In the meantime, I need to introduce two people."

Landin watched as Tymos moved to the side of an aging man, and directed him towards President bin Halil.

"Ambassador..." bin Halil began.

"Tymos. Just Tymos, your Eminence."

"Only if I am to be Arthur," bin Halil insisted as forcibly.

"Arthur," Tymos emphasised. "I would like you to meet my father, Daniel Ward."

The President's face betrayed surprise, but he covered it well.

"I am extremely pleased to meet the father of Tymos and Kryslie Ward."

In Tymorean, Tymos spoke to Daniel as Jono Reslic approached. "Arthur is Kryslie's son."

Tymos felt a lightening of Daniel's spirit and had the satisfaction of startling the Tymorean President, even if it did nothing for his own mood.

Daniel stared at the UEN President for a moment before replying, "My son has just given me some interesting information, of a legacy," Daniel began. "Perhaps we might be able to make time to talk?"

"Legacy?" bin Halil looked at Tymos, who had suddenly become distant.

"Tomorrow, Arthur. I will tell you tomorrow," Tymos said tersely.

"I will hold you to that, Tymos. Eight O'clock. Before the first of the meetings I have arranged with your President Reslic."

Tymos forced a smile and withdrew abruptly. Jono Reslic murmured to Stenn and sent him after Tymos.

Search as he did, Stenn didn't find him, nor did Tymos return to the reception. He reported the lack of success to his father, who made no comment. Unfortunately, Konn was near enough to overhear and used the subject as a basis of more unsubtle needling.

At the end of the reception, Reslic returned to the flagship, taking Konn with him, and told Stenn to go back to Earthbase.

# Chapter 60

With an instinct for trouble, Jono Reslic woke from sleep, dressed casually. It was only a few hours since he had left the reception on the planet. He followed his instincts to the food serving area of the flagship. Even then, he was preceded.

"I said..." Great One Tymos spoke with deliberate intent. "That I...did not...want to hear more of this type of...discussion."

Reslic was unsettled by the edge of anger in the Great One's voice. More so, since two of his sons were fixed in place like rigid statues, by the cuttingly accurate observations the Great One went on to make.

If there was any colour paler than white, Konn and Stenn would have gone that shade.

Reslic walked closer, and if anything, the two of them seemed to see him as some sort of saviour or protector.

"Your Excellency," Tymos greeted without looking around.

Reslic noted that Tymos's hands were glowing faintly. "I believe these are your responsibility."

"Indeed, Great One. With your agreement, we will take this discussion to a more appropriate setting."

Tymos merely nodded, but his hands were beginning to flex.

As if conjured, a hastily dressed ensign appeared beside Reslic. The young man had the look of the Reslic line; he flushed as Reslic gave him quiet instructions and trotted off.

Tymos strode ahead, heading for the training deck. Reslic waited for Konn and Stenn to move stiffly after the Great One before following. They knew, then, that help from their father would need to be earned.

On the training deck, the ensign had prepared practice squares, by lighting up areas of the floor. There were two metal staves in each.

Reslic directed Konn and Stenn to one. He may not have been dressed as befitting his rank, but he was at that moment both His Excellency and Konn's Supreme Commander. And all of his sons knew the distinction between those beings and simply their father.

"It seems I cannot allow the two of you within a solar system's width of each other," Reslic told them in controlled tones. "This friction is going to end here...now. Whatever it is between you – you will settle now. Begin!"

The traditional bow between opponents was sketchy at best. Konn came at Stenn first, venting his anger at being caught. Stenn was ready. Reslic eyed the bout, missing nothing.

The ensign approached Tymos, a little nervously.

"Great One?"

Tymos glanced briefly at him before turning his eyes back on the bout between the brothers.

"The Commander suggested that you might like to warm up. I am available if you wish."

The ensign, Tymos guessed to be one of Reslic's many sons, was young, earnest, honest and still mostly innocent. A refreshing presence.

"I haven't met you before, have I?" Tymos asked, still watching the bout.

"I am Ennis, Great One. Ennis Reslic."

Tymos knew in his mind that his Excellency seldom made idle 'suggestions'. He had a reason, probably several excellent ones, for proposing this. He didn't try to reason them out. He held his hand out for one of the staves and turned his attention to the young man.

Ennis bowed to the Great One in exactly the correct degree. Tymos returned the bow, also in the correct degree for acknowledging an opponent of lower rank.

Tymos had no thoughts that this opponent would be inexperienced. No son of Jono Reslic would be a weak opponent. Ennis had probably been learning to fight since he learnt to walk.

The bout required concentration, but his mind was capable of more than most Tymoreans. He was still aware of, and angry with, the other opposing pair. Yet he knew he had no quarrel with Ennis, nor was he an enemy. Instinctively, he withheld killing blows, but that was all. And the bout would continue until one or other of them disarmed his opponent.

Tymos had been trained by his Excellency, and he recognised the same training in his younger opponent and was easily anticipating his moves. His mind began to wander, and a solid blow from Ennis's stave brought it back to where it was meant to be. He returned several solid blows to his opponent as the bout continued.

Tymos sensed Konn and Stenn losing their anger with each other, and that they would each have painful bruises.

He felt his own legs tripped and he landed on his back on the deck, but still with his stave in his hands.

Ennis stepped back, apologetic, and about to offer his opponent a hand up. Tymos used the hesitation to launch an attack of his own from the deck. He attacked and rose in the same move. He had Ennis down in seconds.

"You are too trusting," Tymos told him critically. "Get up."

Ennis flushed, obeyed, and was ready when Tymos came at him; stave twirling in a fully controlled but mesmerising attack. Ennis parried it, stopping the spin with a solid block that would have broken or dislocated bones in a weaker opponent. He launched an attack of his own.

Jono Reslic spared a glance of disgust for the two fighters lying flat on the deck – who were probably feeling totally exhausted. He turned his attention to the other fighters, face expressionless. He picked the moment when the Great One's mind wandered again, and saw his son attack. The stave being used by the Great One flew across the deck. He maintained his position, observing. Ennis dropped his stave and went to the Great One.

"I'm sorry, Great One, I..."he held out his hand, and Tymos pulled enough to make him stumble forward, but not actually fall over. A subtle reminder of his previous criticism.

"Never drop your weapon," Tymos told him as Reslic delivered a 'reminder' to the ensign.

Tymos let Ennis help him up. The young man was flushing noticeably red. "An excellent bout, Ensign Ennis," he commended, flustering the ensign even further. "There is no need to apologise for your skill and for successfully delivering a needed lesson."

Tymos didn't look at Reslic, but saw Konn glowering at his youngest brother, and Stenn giving him a 'thumbs up' and a faint grin.

Jono Reslic briefly met Tymos's gaze. He didn't need to ask if Tymos had got the point of the exercise. He had – anger was counter-productive. No matter how skilled the Ensign was, Tymos as Great One and Reslic's equal, should have won.

Tymos wasn't angry at Konn and Stenn anymore and would have left things there. Reslic had other ideas.

"Up," he told his elder sons. He gestured for Ennis to retrieve the dropped staves.

"Stenn, with me," he ordered.

Tymos knew what Reslic intended and agreed with the unspoken intent. "Konn."

He sensed the still simmering anger in the sweating, red faced fleet captain. Konn knew better than to betray anger or reluctance to agree.

Tymos wasn't gentle on him and made no allowance for exhaustion. And even as he pressed attacks mercilessly on Konn, he was instructing him on what would be expected of him if he became Ambassador to Earth.

"I was born on Earth," Tymos told Konn, who had not known that. "I have an extremely personal interest in seeing it protected and seeing it has the best possible representation."

Konn felt a solid blow connect, winced and forced his mind to consider defence and the Great One's words.

"You have yet to prove to me that you are the best person for the job. Right now, I'd sooner appoint young Ennis, or even Stenn to the job."

Anger gave Konn renewed strength, but Tymos met his attack with deceptive ease.

Tymos spoke of the role of Ambassador, impressing his words with the force of a command.

He ruthlessly examined Konn's inner personality and held his faults in front of him, but just as bluntly praised his virtues.

When Konn had reached the absolute dregs of his reserves of energy, he said, "I yield, Great One," as he slumped to the deck.

Tymos stepped back immediately and passed his weapon to Ennis.

Stenn was already slumped on the deck.

"Ensign, see the deck here is cleared," Reslic directed, and then spoke to the thoroughly lessoned men and said, "We will be ready to transmit down to the planet in two hours."

As Reslic began to turn to leave, he said, "Great One, my quarters are at your disposal to freshen up."

Stenn and Konn emitted identical groans as soon as the President and Great One departed the training deck. Each then gave a weak laugh.

Reslic had a skill at phrasing requests as suggestions, Tymos recalled. So he answered the unasked questions. "I recall that anger can be counterproductive in a fight and realise that great anger in a Great One is a dreadful concept. I have grounded my excess energy."

Reslic smiled faintly. "Do you feel up to discussing the agenda for today's meetings?"

"It will be more fruitful than sleep right now," Tymos decided.

Back at his suite, he offered Tymos the chance to freshen up and used the time to order restorative drinks and two substantial breakfasts.

Tymos had a private audience with Arthur bin Halil first thing, but he was calm and in full command of himself. He would not tell the President the full ramifications of Kryslie's death, but as her son, he deserved to know details. And perhaps this private time would be a good opportunity to tell Arthur more about his Tymorean connections.

The White House security was surprised when he presented himself on foot at the outer gate. They ordered up a car to take him the last distance.

For this meeting, Tymos was dressed quietly in an Earth style suit and not the silver and gold robes. He did not wish to be blatantly noticeable. This was a personal visit. He could change into his robes later.

Exactly at eight o'clock, a White House aide announced him at a private sitting room. Arthur bin Halil was waiting.

"Mr President," Tymos greeted him formally, for the sake of the listeners.

"Ambassador, thank you for coming this early. Please have a seat."

The door closed.

Tymos waited for Arthur to sit before he did.

"You promised me an explanation of your father's cryptic words. I don't think I am going to enjoy hearing it."

Tymos paused before speaking. "There isn't an easy way to say this – Kryslie is dead."

He saw bin Halil go pale, but he must have suspected something like this.

"We will be presenting an official report later," Tymos told him. "But the gist of it is that the Ciriot leaders are no more. In her final moments, Kryslie succeeded in defeating them more thoroughly than thought they had done to her. It took seven of their insidious control devices and four of those mind ghouls to turn her body into our enemy, but they did not control her mind. So she overcame them and allowed their death. She chose the release of death, to the continuance of life as our enemy."

Bin Halil did not speak for a long time. "She truly humbles me," he finally said. "I can only strive to live up to her example."

Tymos realised the human President was right and part of the anger that Reslic had helped him release had been due to that.

"Yet, you gave me the gift of a Grandfather," Arthur went on. "I never expected that. Did he know of me?"

Tymos shook his head. "Not until then, but I felt he needed to know you."

"You are a wise man, Tymos Ward. It is always better to have the continuance of life than only the pain of death."

"Well, I can't see me having children," Tymos muttered, unexpectedly feeling embarrassed. "You might be the only grandchild he gets to meet."

"Surely there is time..."Arthur suggested.

Tymos shook his head. "When I am finished here, I will not be staying."

"Because of memories?" Arthur truly wanted to understand this Tymorean.

"No. They will travel with me. It is...well...surely you have realised that we have not aged since you were born...."

"I had, but I decided it was not of sufficient importance to take issue with."

"Soon enough it will attract attention and cause unease," Tymos said. "Nor will I go back to Tymorea that often, for the same reason. My role in the scheme of things is to go where I am needed. Llaimos will succeed the High King, breed sons to succeed him, and pass the Governorship on to the best of them. And then, he will become like me."

"I could wish it were otherwise," Arthur spoke from his heart. "So, Tymoreans will remain here, working unthanked, as I believe they have done for many years."

"Yes, for now, Daniel will coordinate them," Tymos admitted. "Openly, we will have an official embassy. I am training my successor."

"He will have a high standard to emulate," Arthur commented.

Tymos smiled, "He will be up to it when both I and President Reslic finish with him."

"What still holds you here?" Arthur changed the subject.'

"Unfinished business," Tymos said. "I have requested a medical group from Tymorea to help us with those we abducted from prominent places."

Arthur knew who he referred to. "Most are believed to be dead."

"We could not save all of them. Those we did, we have kept in stasis and now it will be safe to treat them. Their return will be...a sensation."

"If we release the information on how the aliens used them, and that we were able to keep these safe and that they are free from any further taint after a period of seclusion, treatment and so on...it will be an occasion for joy. Will they remember any of what happened?"

"Probably nothing from when the controllers were activated," Tymos considered.

"Do you have a list of names of the people?" Arthur asked. "It would be tactful to give the news to their families first."

"You will have it," Tymos promised.


Throughout the rest of the day of formal meetings and the drawing up of agreements – a great deal was achieved. Tymos endured the formality by imagining Kryslie's voice teasing him for being a petty bureaucrat.

The humans assumed that Reslic was the superior, and Tymos preferred that. Reslic had a great deal more personal experience in these things and he only had second hand experience.

Everything that needed Reslic to sign as Tymorean Representative was completed that day with impressive smoothness and little or no argument or dissent. It was known that the Tymorean President needed to return to his own world. It was also made clear that Ambassador Tymos had equal rank with the Tymorean Governors and could make binding decisions on their behalf.

Tymos was also to be in command of the remaining flight of Tymorean air-space fighters and the medical team that was en-route.

The humans were looking forward to a beneficial alliance, and facing the daunting task of rebuilding with hope not despair.

# Chapter 61

The Tymorean Ambassador was very difficult to find in the ensuing weeks. The media had heard of the 'secluded ones' and wanted to know a great deal more. They most particularly wanted to know where the people had been held.

Once the first few had been treated, by having the controllers removed and self-destruct beads removed, and there was no indication that they were still able to attract alien attention, Tymos agreed to having the remaining patients transported to an exclusive clinic in a rural area of the United States.

The Tymorean staff was augmented by local and international doctors and nurses. When the location was 'leaked' to the media, none of the investigative journalists found evidence that they had only arrived recently. The medical staff were openly forthcoming about how the patients had been cared for since they had been taken ill.

Family members of the patients were flown in and housed at Government expense when their loved ones were almost ready to be released.

Tymos worked himself to exhaustion each day. And the rotating medical teams were beginning to venerate him as some kind of saint. They no longer felt belittled that he would not let any of them physically remove the alien beads, only to close his incisions once he had deemed it safe.

The tendrils infecting the patients were flaccid but still well entrenched in the muscle tissue. They came out without a struggle, but without his healing gift, the damaged tissue would have been irreversibly compromised. The healing took energy, and he could only help ten people each day before he needed to retreat to the private garden to renew himself using Earth's aura.

He was protected from the media attention, and not one of the doctors mentioned their belief that he was using some kind of healing gift.

Over five hundred people had been kept in stasis, and the first of these would soon be well enough, physically, mentally and emotionally to go home. Tymos left the rehabilitation to the specialists and the counselling to Vincent, and their duties rarely overlapped.

So, Tymos was surprised one evening to see Vincent and two visitors enter his 'private' garden.

"You look like the bottom of a well," Stenn Reslic commented, irreverently. "Not a particularly Great image."

Tymos didn't feel like smiling. "I am resting, okay!" he anticipated Vincent's intended lecture, and ignored Stenn's attempt at humour and the other visitor all together.

"Since you do not stop between dawn and dusk," Vincent noted, omitting his title verbally, but Tymos sensed it in his mind. "This is the only time I can talk to you."

"Get on with it, Vincent!" Tymos said, dully. He just wanted them to leave.

"Very well. I am pulling rank as your physician," Vincent told him. "Every single doctor in there, Tymorean and human, can see you are overworking. Every single one of them realise you are using some kind of healing gift on those people  and can see you are burning yourself out. And they realise that what you are doing cannot be done to any comparable standard by any other means. They have unanimously insisted on restricting you to three patients each morning and afternoon and that you break for a substantial meal at lunch and tea."

"Tyrant," Tymos accused, but he had too little energy to dispute the direction. "Are you making yourself my keeper?"

"No, I am," Stenn told him. "Since I know all of your tricky ways, and acting Ambassador Konn has a new and truly efficient assistant in Teresa. You know her I think – a full blooded second generation missionary. And as my final official act, I am to introduce you to the new liaison between the WSRA and our scientists. I believe you have met."

Jody Basoli stepped forward. "I won't get in your way."

"Is this your father's way of trying to keep me available? I have had his official debrief!"

"No," Jody told him. "It was my idea."

Tymos sat up and showed a bit more interest. "It is a good idea. I didn't intend to cut myself off from my friends."

Stenn laughed. "Really? So what have you been doing for the past two weeks?"

Tymos didn't try to justify himself, and was glad when Jody went on.

"Dad thought it was a good idea too. He's got a lot less...well, pompous...lately. I think he is embarrassed by being called a visionary."

"Rather him than me," Tymos said, lightening up a bit. "I assume that my efficient acting Ambassador approved it?"

"With due consideration of course," Stenn grinned. "I have decided you were right about him. He does have what it takes for that job. A thick hide helps of course. He has encountered a few objections, and the expected paranoia about us aliens."

Vincent stood back up and prepared to depart. "I will leave your guests to explain their duties to you," he said. He was satisfied by seeing Tymos beginning to smile again.


"So, where is his Greatness?" Morin demanded when Stenn returned to Earthbase alone. "Isn't he supposed to be finished with our former guests now? He said he would be here for dinner."

"Ah...he accepted another invitation," Stenn said carefully, and then he winked at Morin.

"Well, well...that gypsy girl?" Morin guessed.

Stenn nodded. "She has been doing an excellent job of keeping on his blind side. A stealth attack worthy of a Reslic."

Morin snorted. "You ain't done so well with Lexina!"

"Give her time. She will come around," Stenn insisted.

Then Morin asked, considering, "Do you think his Greatness and the gypsy will get connected?"

"What?" Stenn understood what Morin had said, but making no sense of it.

Morin snickered and explained. Stenn merely winked back at him.


Tymos moved on to organise and attend a multi-nation summit to discuss the new radiation zones caused by crashed Ciriot ships. Jody had helped with the organisation, and attended as WSRA liaison.

When he gave the keynote address, he outlined what he believed could be done about the areas. The concept he proposed was totally new to Earth's scientists, and there was much scepticism. However, those people that knew Tymos personally, tempered the response – they believed that if Tymos said it was possible – his idea would work.

There were Tymorean scientists attending, to whom Tymos's ideas were still theoretical, and they would help Tymos teach the basic theory to the humans, but the putting it into practice was going to be a largely human endeavour.

The proposal put to the summit was that he, Tymos, would train Earth scientists and technicians in transmutational shield theory and design and help build the installations that would transmute the radiation in those areas into electrical energy to be fed into the various power grids at a nominal cost. And that nominal cost was to be used to maintain the facilities, and to teach and upgrade the workers involved.

President bin Halil, who was in attendance, received the authorisation of the World Council to pay the initial outlay for the work.

The intended heckling by environmental groups was silenced. Their anger at the existence of the lethal areas vanished at the proposed elegant solution that would provide cheap electricity for over two centuries.

The solution was unanimously accepted, and any remaining detractors were convinced when Tymos was able to demonstrate his theory on a small scale, within the agreed time frame. That had not been difficult. There had already been a working transmutational shield at Earthbase, and all Tymos had to do was build a second generator and design the small scale demonstration.

Once the initial theory sessions were over, Tymos travelled to each of the radiation zones, to study the geography and to design and locate the power plants.

It would be several years before all the plants were up and running, but his detailed program was progressing with very few problems.

When Tymos's schedule indicated that he would be on American soil, Daniel insisted that he stay at their Embassy in Washington. As naturally as if they were married, Jody came with him and was greeted by Daniel as family. Stenn followed, being the near invisible aide.

On one such occasion, about a year after the end of the Ciriot invasion, Tymos was there for a formal reception.

Morin found Stenn as he was setting out Tymos's formal robes.

"Do you think his Greatness started something?" Morin asked Stenn, in a confidential whisper. "That gypsy is glowing like a neon sign."

Stenn now knew what 'started something' meant. "I think the only one that doesn't know is the one who fired the gun," Stenn told him. He then had to explain. "Sorry, that is fleet speak for... you know... paternity."

"Hmmm. I think his Greatness will look like he had a cream pie hit him in the face when she tells him," Morin claimed.

Stenn could picture Tymos as a cat licking cream off his face. "You pick up some really odd notions." He laughed. "But in this case, appropriate."

Tymos, Great One, Prince of Tymorea and Ambassador to Earth, finally really looked at Jody and embraced her in front of all the important guests at the reception. He didn't care that everyone stopped talking and stared at him. Her whispered words had given him the first totally joyful feeling for months, and when he made an announcement of his own, the applause was thunderous, and the congratulations sincere.

Daniel was especially thrilled. He had met his first grandchild as a grown man. The next one he could see grow up. He did spare a thought to warn Jody, "You know it is probable that Tymos will not...cannot...stay here to help you raise the child?"

Jody was not upset. "I know that, Daniel, but I wanted this – for me, for you, for Dad – for a lot of reasons and I expect he or she will have a lot of godparents."

Vincent overheard that and assured her, "If the child takes after the father – plenty of advice!"

# Chapter 62

He had been with Kryslie when Arthur was born, and thought then that he would never put a woman he cared for through that agony. But Jody had chosen to give him a child, and eagerly looked forward to the moment of birth. As he had so many years ago, Tymos shared the moment, and the joy as the child was born. It was so much more intense, since the child was his. He eased Jody's pain, and held his child until Jody was ready for her.

"What will you name her?" Tymos asked in awe.

"Serenity," Jody said at once.

And that, Tymos decided, was what he felt. All that would make the moment better would be if Kryslie were there to share it.


Tymos imaged his arms rising high into the air. To the Guardians of Peace, he sent the thought, "Whoever allowed this miracle – I give thanks."

He felt a gentle touch on his mind.

"She, who you think of, knows. She has chosen to live again, to serve again, though without power. If her will is strong enough she may once again become Great."


Jody reached out and brushed at the tears on Tymos's face, but she saw the peace there.

"I am happy," he told her.

# Epilogue

The light flowed around her. The gentle voices of the Guardians of peace welcomed her.

"Why do you welcome me when I am nothing? I am corrupted, unclean," Kryslie whispered.

"That which was corrupt is no more," a voice told her, and she felt something like an arm around her.

"Your spirit is pure, a shining beacon. Will you still serve us, as you promised?"

"How? I am dead."

"What is death?" the gentle voice asked.

Kryslie did not know that answer.

"Could you live without everyone you ever knew?" another voice asked.

Kryslie thought on that. "If I knew that those I loved were well."

A view opened in the walls of bright light. She saw her brother with a child in his arms - a child with bright red hair. She saw Daniel's delighted face and the true pleasure of her friends.

Then she saw a globe lit tunnel, and Llaimos seemed to look up and he smiled as if he could see her.

"Yes, I will continue to serve you," Kryslie promised. "Wherever, however you will let me."

She felt a gentle hand on hers, and felt herself moving as if through time and space, but not into true death. Not yet.

## The End

# Another time, another place

by

Margaret Gregory

Tym slipped out into the moonlit garden of the Embassy. Jody was asleep. The baby…his daughter, was asleep and the last of the adoring friends had finally gone.

The little girl had a lot to live up to. As odd as it seemed, she was half-sister to the leader of the United Earth Nations, granddaughter to both the Coordinator of the Tymorean Missionaries, and the Director of the World Science Research Authority. His own position as a hero of the war against the invaders seemed to pale into insignificance, but then, the humans of Earth did not know of his title of Great One.

The garden was quiet, and he could be alone with his thoughts. The emotions of the past day, so totally overpowering, were suddenly gone. He felt flat, lifeless - or was he simply too tired to feel them?

In some ways, that was a relief.

He did not want to hate his daughter for being alive when his sister was dead. Her conception and birth had nothing to do with Krys's death. In fact, learning of her advent, and the subsequent months of anticipation, had purged the anger from his mind. Waiting for her had given him something positive to think on, to block the searing mental pain where once the twin bond had been.

When he first held his daughter, the emotion had been so intense…no word could really describe it. He had helped to create a life!

He raised both arms high and wide, speaking to the air and invoking thoughts of the Guardians of Peace, the powerful beings that he served. "I cannot thank you enough for this miracle of life."

The soft night breeze seemed to swirl closer to him, to caress him. It seemed to bring peace to his soul.

"If only Krys could have been here to see her…"

When he first held his daughter, he had recalled thinking that. Though at the time, Jody had been his main concern, and he had pushed his regret aside, along with the memory of his sister being blown into an expanding cloud of atoms.

Somehow, that thought no longer brought the pain, or anger. It was odd…

It was almost as if…

No. Krys was dead! She had ensured that those creatures that had tried to devastate the Earth - not only failed, but were finished.

Yet there had been a moment, just after he set eyes on his daughter, when it had almost felt like she was there…at the other end of the twin bond…that she knew of his daughter and was glad for him.

Surely not…surely he wanted it so much to be true…

The soft breeze strengthened and seemed to whisper into his mind, "She still serves us."
 For the first time in months, he dared to explore the gaping blankness in is mind where he had always been able to sense his twin.
"She still serves us," the soft mental voice had said.
That had been the voice of the Guardians speaking to him. Was Krys miraculously alive? Might he see her again?

In another time and another place…

✼✼✼✼✼


**OTHER NOVELS by MARGARET GREGORY**

## THE WILD ONE

Sixteen year old Jai Cassidy thought she was finally free of her family until she is discovered by her other relatives…the ones that aren't human. Jai uses her natural perversity and cunning to escape their control, but catapults herself into the middle of a deadly feud between two alien races.

## ATAPI SORCERESS

### The sequel to The Wild One

Jai Cassidy is beginning her mission of reversing the decline of the non-humanoid Atapi. As a sorceress and an Atapi-Human hybrid, she is vehemently disliked by the male Atapi sorcerers and the humanoid rulers of Korvu. Her task is complicated by the treachery of a group of alien engineers, who are inciting insurrection and harsh reprisals.

## KORVU – THE BEGINNING

### A Prequel to The Wild One

Jai Ansuni was the first female Atapi sorcerer for thousands of years, but she dare not reveal it. However, when tribal sorcerer, Stacion Ansuni escalates the enmity between Atapi and Kumatan to an ominous level. Jai and her womb mate, Con, try to mitigate his atrocities but can two young Atapi, not even a score of years old, win against the powerful sorcerer?

### The Tymorean Trust Book 1 - POWER RISING

When peace rules Tymorea - Peace reigns in the universe.
Chosen to be the Advocates of the mystical and incorporeal Guardians of Peace, twins Tymos and Kryslie must first learn to control and use the power rising in them - or it will destroy them. On Tymorea, only the ruling Triumvirate Governors are powerful enough to guide the strong-willed alien-bred twins until they have mastered their power.

### The Tymorean Trust Book 2 - GREAT ONES

The peace of the Guardian Planet, Tymorea, is in deadly peril. War there will create ripples of unrest and destruction throughout the settled universe. Tymos and Kryslie, still adolescents, have barely mastered their power and Llaimos is still less than a year old, but they are the three chosen to be Advocates of the mystical Guardians of Peace, to safeguard the Tymorean Trust.

The Tymorean Trust Book 3 - THE RETURN TO EARTH

Even before the war on Tymorea, the Elders foresaw that Great Ones Tymos and Kryslie would have an imperative mission on Earth.
But as the Tymoreans prepare to build an Earthbase to support them, they discover that specifications for two vital protective shields are missing.
Now, nearly a century later, Tymos and Kryslie must find his work and build the generator before the base is found.

The Tymorean Trust Book 4 - EARTH MISSION

Just before their graduation from the prestigious WSRA Washington University, Tymos and Kryslie Ward deliberately disappear.
The Great Ones have foreseen the capture and death of the new Tymorean missionaries and discovered that the leader of the Eastern Imperium plans to undermine the United World Nations.
Tymos and Kryslie must protect their kin and prevent a potentially devastating world war.

The Tymorean Trust Book 5 – ALIEN CONTACT

Tymos and Kryslie Ward, hide their Tymorean intelligence and abilities while working as low ranked technicians at the WSRA's lunar base. When an alien ship arrives at Lunar One, pursued by a powerful enemy who will stop at nothing to get what he wants, only the two Tymorean Great Ones have the knowledge and abilities to overcome him, but to do so they must risk their sanity, and their souls.

WANDA: FROM BAD TO WORSE

If she was going to die young, like her mother, Gwen Willard was determined to die rich and she had very few years to do it. Her first step was to leave home. She met Hooch, who taught her some exciting and illegal skills. She was the Dracos lucky mascot until she came to the attention of the police. Then her uncanny knack for predicting trouble, warned her to flee to the city and change her name.
Life wasn't easy. She was 15, had little money and no regular job, but her new skills came in handy. Then she crossed the path of an evil and unscrupulous man and she didn't want him to have his way.

## WANDA: CHOOSING CRIME

Wanda was free. She was never going back to jail. But she was homeless, almost penniless and Harrison Franklin had a long and vengeful memory. Jim Phillips had a long memory too, and Wanda had saved his life. Could he save her from Franklin?

## WANDA: RISKING LIFE TO LIVE

The euphoria of successful heists were what kept Wanda Dean alive. At 23, she was crime boss Harrison Franklin's top agent – well paid for absolute obedience. That's all that mattered. Until she met Mike Johnston and her boss ordered him killed. For that, the Franklins were going to pay. In Risking Life to Live, justice conflicts with loyalty and the penalty for betrayal is death.

**SHORT STORIES:**

GRAFFITI GIRL

Valerie has become known as "The Graffiti Girl" but she is more than
just a street artist.
She sees and paints life her way.

In Valkyrie, the second story, Valerie, blinded by an explosion,
must learn to paint and see again.

GHOST WRITER

Edwina is a ghost with a mission - to find out why she died.
Only to do so, she must first help another girl.


**Connect to Margaret Gregory**

My Smashwords author profile:
https://www.smashwords.com/profile/view/msgdragon
Connect with me on LinkedIn:
http://au.linkedin.com/pub/margaret-gregory/72/a36/186/
Friend me on Facebook:
http://www.facebook.com/margaret.gregory.399